THE FORTUNES OF OLIVIA RICHMOND

LOUISE DAVIDSON

MOONFLOWER

Published by Moonflower Publishing Ltd.
www.MoonflowerBooks.co.uk

1 2 3 4 5 6 7 8 9 10

Copyright © Louise Davidson 2023

ISBN: 978-1919618784

Cover design by Jasmine Aurora

Printed and bound by Jellyfish Ltd., Curdridge, Hampshire

Louise Davidson has asserted her right to be identified as the author of this work. This is a work of fiction. All rights reserved. No part of this publication may be reproduced, stored in any retrieval system, or transmitted, in any form or by any means, electronic, mechanical, photocopying, recording or otherwise, without the prior written permission of the publishers.

Moonflower Publishing Registered Office: 303 The Pillbox, 115 Coventry Road, London E2 6GG, United Kingdom

MOONFLOWER

For Andi, who is my Alice
And Dean, who is my Tabby

DEATH

The oar made a sickening crack as it connected with the boy's head. He staggered, sending ripples across the black surface of the pond as the boat pitched in the water. Then he was reeling, hands waving. He reached out, eyes wide, a silent scream on his lips. For a moment her own hands twitched, as if thinking of snatching him back – but then he crashed against the side and was gone. The black water swallowed him whole.

She waited.

All around her there was the buzz and hum of insects in the heat. Bubbles burst on the pond's surface: three, two, one… then none.

When she was sure it was safe, she began to scream.

Thursday 14th August 1890
Tragic Godstone Drowning Inquest Concludes
CORONER RULES

The inquiry into the death of twelve-year-old Christopher Kemp has reached its conclusion after three days of questioning.

The body of Master Kemp was retrieved from Wakeley's Pond at Astor House, the family home, last Wednesday afternoon.

After a deliberation of two hours at the Old Assembly Rooms, Mr Reames, coroner for the western division of the county of Kent, addressed the room.

'It is my duty to remind you all that this was an inquiry to verify the facts of this tragedy, and to either rule death by mishap or to pass our findings along to the appropriate legal authorities. While there are many who could be blamed for this tragedy, as coroner I am more concerned with intent than guilt. Based on the evidence submitted and the testimony of those involved, it is the ruling of this inquiry that Christopher Kemp died by misadventure. We commend his soul to God and pray for his deliverance.'

ONE

Six of Pentacles Reversed

WANTED. Young ladies of education and experience for a variety of respectable situations. Must be flexible, industrious, and willing to travel. For further details as to positions available, please contact Mrs Erma Spencer at 23c Milton Road, Finsbury Park. Discretion and support provided.

I saw the advertisement the day after Mother's funeral. I wanted to answer it immediately but Anthony would not hear of it.

'We need you here, Julia,' he said. 'At least at the moment. People keep calling and the doctor says Jocelyn must have bed-rest. It has all been too much for her and you are so good at being practical about these things.'

'Practical' meant not crying. I had been careful not to let him see me do it. Not even when the policeman, who had come to deliver the news with his helmet tucked under his arm at a respectful angle, described to us how Mother had collapsed in the greengrocers and died lying on the floor, waiting for the doctor.

Instead, I threw myself into planning the funeral. With Anthony at the office every day and his wife Jocelyn close to the time of her lying in, there was no one else. Grief, especially when it was as dry and complicated as mine, had no place here. I freshened my shabby mourning dress every evening and wore it to sit in the parlour, waiting for Mother's friends to arrive to give their condolences.

The staff took my instructions with barely concealed disdain. Who was I to be giving orders? I was the dependent; a spinster sister who had already outstayed her welcome. My place in my brother's house relied entirely on my usefulness and they all knew it. I pretended not to notice their contempt.

'I suppose if I wait that means I can be here when Mr Harris calls,' I said. 'It will give a better view of things.'

For a moment Anthony looked like he wanted to argue, but he said nothing. We had tea brought in and settled down to wait for the lawyer, careful not to speculate between ourselves about our mother's will.

'You should say more about yourself,' said Anthony, as I sat at the small stationery desk by the window, sorting through calling cards. 'One of Mother's friends might show you kindness.'

'I would be surprised if any of them even knew I needed a position,' I said, affecting a light tone as I made a note of a name. 'Mother was hardly going to tell her friends about my being in service.'

Anthony's face creased in disapproval. 'You make it sound as if you're a maid-of-all-work. Besides, that is not what I meant. There are other things. Many women of your age make a decent living as companions.'

I couldn't help but laugh at his pompous tone. 'What do you mean "women of your age"? I am only twenty-seven. I may yet meet some tall, dark stranger who has made his money somewhere exotic and now wishes for a wife with some life experience.'

I was trying to sound as though I was teasing but Anthony gave me such a pained, pitying look that I turned back to the letters and cards, my rigid smile still fixed in place. We both knew how unlikely the idea was.

'I appreciate that it has been difficult for you both, having me here,' I said, after a moment.

'It is a strain on Jocelyn.'

I pictured my sister-in-law, swollen with pregnancy and irritation, hissing when she thought I couldn't hear, 'What if someone recognises her? What if the McArthurs hear of it? You know what it means to be in their circle. We will never be able to show our faces again.'

That morning, she had made a rare appearance at breakfast and suggested that possibly I should go and stay with Aunt Beatrice. Aunt Beatrice, who was staying for the funeral, had looked at me, horrified, and muttered something about a young lady's need for independence and her own lack of space. Not, she had added gracelessly, that I was that young anymore.

I selected a new card to reply to, not trusting myself to meet my brother's gaze.

'As soon as I can, I will find myself a new position,' I promised. 'And then all will be back to normal.'

'I hope you understand, it's not a question of you staying here, of course.' Anthony adjusted his collar. The skin on his neck was pink where the starch irritated it. 'More the sudden and… prolonged nature of it. Next time we will have to make alternative arrangements.'

The clock ticked on the mantelpiece. Outside a hansom cab went past, the heavy, hollow sound of horse shoes echoing down the quiet street. The pen nib made a harsh scratch as I underlined a name on an envelope.

'There will not be a next time,' I said.

'Of course,' said Anthony, with a nervous smile. 'Life would have to be really unkind for that to happen.'

I looked at my brother in his fashionable waistcoat and gold watch chain and felt the fraying cuffs of my worn dress with my fingertips.

'Yes,' I said.

There was a knock at the door.

'Come!' called Anthony, relieved, I suspected, for an end to our conversation.

'Mr Harris, sir.' It was the maid's voice.

I rose, smoothing my skirts as Anthony greeted the lawyer.

Mr Harris was a small man with thinning hair yet lustrous eyebrows. He bustled in, mumbling greetings, and set his briefcase down on the desk before absent-mindedly taking the seat behind it. This relegated Anthony and I to sitting opposite him, like school children in front of the headmaster. I tried to catch Anthony's eye, to be children in conspiracy together again, but he kept his gaze averted, as though trying to suggest he was nothing to do with me.

The lawyer launched quickly into his report. 'Of course, your father's unlucky business ventures mean the family resources are somewhat depleted,' he said. 'And there is the complication of other dependents…'

I kept my face a careful blank although it didn't matter as Mr Harris directed all his comments to Anthony.

'But your mother was able to keep some back,' Mr Harris continued. 'It is not much. Around one hundred pounds, give or take.'

Anthony gave a loud exhale, his face showing the same shock and confusion as my own. Mother had always made it clear that her finances were meagre, that she lived with Aunt Beatrice out of necessity and kept only one servant because her income would not allow more. And yet it seemed she had been hoarding a small fortune. It was more than I had earned in the past three years. My hopes rose. Possibly my situation was not as dire as we had thought.

'This, along with all her worldly goods, has been bequeathed to yourself,' said Mr Harris, indicating Anthony. 'With some small remembrances to go to her daughter – some pieces of jewellery, a china tea set, and books, to be distributed by yourself, Mr Pearlie, at your convenience.'

I looked from my brother to Mr Harris. Anthony was nodding, as though this was just as he had expected. I suddenly felt cold.

'Is that it?' I asked, trying and failing to disguise my dismay.

'That is what the paperwork says,' Harris confirmed. He sat back, his fingers laced together over his stomach. 'There is, of course, no stipulation as to what your brother may do with the inheritance once it is in his possession.'

I turned to Anthony, a flutter of relief in my chest. I expected him nod, to squeeze my hand and look as glad as I was that I could be in some small way independent. But my brother said nothing. His ears and neck seemed to be turning a deep shade of pink in a way that had nothing to do with starch. He cleared his throat.

'I admit, Jocelyn and I have discussed buying a larger property,' he said. 'We do want a big family and this particular area does not necessarily reflect our station. Jocelyn has mentioned Muswell Hill and that is not inexpensive.'

'You could also buy into a partnership,' nodded the lawyer. 'There are ways of investing. We will make sure you make the right decision.'

I looked from one to the other but their focus was only on each other. It was as though I were a ghost, silent and forgotten, watching the living.

'Anthony?' I said.

He blinked, as though just realising I was there. His face had the vacant, faraway look that I recognised from our childhood, when Mother would lose her temper with one of us. He hated her scenes and her rages; I would have to proceed carefully.

'A new house sounds wonderful,' I said, forcing a smile. 'I just wonder where that leaves me?'

'Oh well, we can do something, I'm sure.' He gave me a weak smile. 'We can arrange for some new clothes and, once you have a placement, we will have a better idea of what you need.'

'Oh, come now.' I turned fully in my seat to face Anthony but he stared at a point past my ear.

I noticed his hands were clenched into fists and, suddenly, I felt frightened.

'Anthony, it need not be that much. Not to be indelicate, but this is more than three times my annual salary. Less than half of this sum could change everything for me.'

'Julia, please.' Anthony cut me off, glancing at Harris, who appeared absorbed in paperwork. 'Mother has hardly forgotten you.'

It was Father's death all over again, the house emptied and everything sold to pay for the impressive school for my brother, with nothing left for me.

I gave a cold laugh. 'Really, Anthony… Books? China? What am I meant to do with them? I can't take them with me wherever I go next. No, I'll have to leave them here. Surely you see how ridiculous this is?'

He had to know it. Of course he wouldn't see me turned out with nothing but a tea set.

When the silence continued, I felt a burning at the back of my throat and a painful tightness in my chest. Behind us, the fire spat something out onto the hearth. It sat on the cold stone, glowing white hot and then fizzled and died.

'It is still early in the discussion,' Mr Harris interjected soothingly. 'We could put a little aside for… extraneous expenses.' His eyes flickered to me for the first time. 'But a full budget would have to be done before we decide.'

Anthony nodded, as if this made perfect sense.

'Anthony, please, think about what you're saying. Our mother has died and I'm to get nothing while you're to buy a new house?' I bit my lip, willing myself not to cry.

'Please remember, I have been helping to support Mother for many years.' Anthony lifted his head, suddenly defiant. 'Clearly she felt this was the most fitting arrangement in light of that.'

'It is commendable that she should want to repay your attentions.' Mr Harris shot me an admonishing look from under wild eyebrows. 'It shows appropriate maternal gratitude and is very much a credit to her memory.'

'It is indeed a true sign of her nature.' Anthony agreed.

His pompous tone, a mimicry of the lawyer, sent me over the edge.

'Yes, it was certainly like Mother to look after Anthony,' I agreed, my voice taut. 'It is unfortunate that her maternal instinct did not extend to her daughter. As I recall, I received nothing after Father died, either. You were left everything then also.'

Anthony's cheeks flushed. 'I do not appreciate your tone.'

I was embarrassing myself and yet I could not stop.

'Including his books, which I don't believe you ever read,' I snapped.

'I do not need to defend myself for things that happened when I was a child,' my brother continued. 'Things for which I had no responsibility.'

'But what about your responsibility now?' I demanded. 'I need your help and you're too busy peacocking for the elites of Muswell Hill.'

Anthony nearly leapt from his seat, face red with fury and embarrassment. 'I have always accepted any responsibility I have towards you, but my family must come first.'

'I am family!' I cried. 'Am I not?'

He didn't reply.

My eyes suddenly burned with the sting of tears. My heart beat with such ferocity I thought it would burst from my chest. My breath felt shallow and useless.

'I can see there is some discussion needed,' Mr Harris said, beginning to gather up papers. 'Anthony, why don't you drop by the office next week and we will see what is to be done.'

'No, please.' I stood, nearly upsetting my chair. My face felt hot. 'You clearly have much to discuss and I have somewhere else to be.'

'Wait, Julia,' Anthony began. But I did not turn back.

'Good day to you, Mr Harris.'

The office door cracked and swung on its hinges as I slammed it behind me.

From the desk of Mrs Erma Spencer
October 19th 1890
To Miss Julia Pearlie

My dear Miss Pearlie,

I do hope you are fully recovered following our brief meeting yesterday afternoon. I know you expressed some concern over your current situation but do not fret. Having heard your story, I appreciate your strength of feeling and fears, but I have put all my efforts towards your case and I can confirm that I have, indeed, found a placement for you.

It is somewhat out of the way – a little village called Fellwick in Norfolk – but I am sure you will not find it too disagreeable.

Dr George Richmond of Mistcoate House is looking for a companion and etiquette coach for his daughter, Miss Olivia Richmond. His letter states that she has just turned seventeen and can be somewhat spirited, but I am sure none of this will deter you, given the circumstances.

As for your lack of reference – most regrettable though it is – I am certain it will not be necessary due to your experience and training. However, if one is requested, I am sure something can be arranged.

I have taken the liberty of telegraphing your details to Fellwick this afternoon. If all goes well, you should hear from Dr Richmond's staff within the week and, this having been settled, there will only be the matter of my payment for this introduction.

October 23rd 1890

Dear Miss Pearlie,

I am writing on behalf of Dr George Richmond to offer you the post of companion to Miss Olivia Richmond. Please confirm your arrival in Fellwick on November 4th at the soonest opportunity. We will arrange for you to be met in Fellwick and brought to Mistcoate House.

Please note that Dr Richmond has expressly stated that you must arrive <u>no later</u> than three o'clock in the afternoon. We shall expect you to be punctual.

Yours faithfully,
Mrs Eda Hayes
Housekeeper
Mistcoate House
Fellwick

November 4th 1890

Anthony,
  I
  ~~Please just~~
  Goodbye.
  Julia

TWO

The Fool

The fourth of November dawned, wet and grey. I left London on the first train to Ely, squashed into a crowded third-class carriage with my bags perched on my lap.

I had waited until the letter from Mrs Hayes had arrived to tell Anthony of my departure. It was the first time we had spoken since the meeting with Mr Harris. Anthony had listened like a father being regaled with a child's nonsense story, saying little aside from offering to cover the cost of my tickets, as though it would spirit me away faster. I refused and used what was left of my savings.

During those last cold, silent days at Anthony's, packing had been straightforward. After all, I had still not unpacked my things after my flight from Kent.

I had paused only once in my preparations and that was when packing a small, colourful biscuit tin that Mother had sent with me on my first placement. It held all my secret things: photographs, an encouraging note from Father, dance cards from London and, most importantly, my diary from my previous position at Astor House. It was foolish to keep it, I knew. Really, it was a mercy that the police had not thought to search for it when they came to question us all, although I had carefully stowed the box away at the bottom of my trunk. I could not have anyone finding my diary or John's letters.

John...

Crushed inside that cold, shaking carriage, I squeezed my eyes shut and clutched my bag to me. For a moment, I imagined that I could smell the warm wool of his coat and the spice of his beard oil, feel the pressure of his hands against the small of my back and the warmth of his body pressed against mine.

In my mind, his voice murmured in my ear: 'Tonight at ten?'

As I sat, rocked by the train carriage, I remembered how I had turned to the meagre fire in my room at Anthony's, ready to throw the diary into the flames but then, instead, packed it with the rest of my things. Someday I would destroy it, but only when the time was right. I couldn't do it yet.

Anthony had always said I was too much of a romantic. Too concerned with others and what they were thinking or feeling.

Perhaps he was right. Perhaps it was time to be more concerned with myself.

The train was even more crowded when we finally pulled into Ely, with several passengers standing in the aisles obscuring my view of the station clock. Mrs Hayes' letter had been very clear that I must arrive before three, and with the slow train journey and my need to secure a coach for the last leg of the journey, I felt a queasy anxiety about my arrival time.

I readied myself to exit as soon as the train stopped. However, when the conductor called that coaches could be found at the inn opposite the station, there was a surge forwards, leaving me scrambling for my bags and hobbling on numbed legs behind the crowd streaming across the platform, through the iron archway, and across the road to the coaching inn opposite.

By the time I arrived, four of the waiting coaches had already been secured. Another was being loaded with too many passengers and, besides, the driver said they were not going in the direction of Fellwick.

'Please,' I begged, adjusting my bags, a bead of sweat rolling down my back. 'I must be in Fellwick by three o'clock and everyone seems to be full.'

'You'll not have much luck here. Try the postal coach,' he suggested. 'Around by the side of the inn.'

In fact, when I eventually found it, it was parked some streets away, the driver leaning against the front wheels, smoking a damp-looking roll-up.

He watched me with a bored expression as I explained my need.

'We'm not leaving 'til two,' he said.

A cold wind shook the trees, bringing a smell of grass and horse dung, and sprinkling us with icy droplets. It had been raining all day and everything felt soaked. I shivered and pulled my coat tighter around me with my free hand.

'May I wait inside the coach at least?'

'We'm be loadin' 'round you,' he advised.

I took this to mean yes.

The inside was not richly furnished. My seat was a large, wooden box, made more comfortable by an old blanket, covered in horsehair, folded over the top. But I didn't mind. I sat on it, leaning my head against the side of the coach as the rain intensified, beating against the window. Lulled by these noises, I closed my eyes and tucked my hands into my armpits, drawing my knees up, making myself small and snug.

I must have slept because suddenly my head was bouncing with the movement of the horses. Outside the small window, the inn was gone. Fields of reddened grass now stretched around me, studded with dark, distant copses, clustered together like witches on a windswept moor. Sunlight caught on flat pools of still water, streaking through the earth like rivulets of silver, and birds leapt in the air, their wings beating against the tall reeds that waved in the wind.

The rain had stopped and above us the sky was a pale, flat sheet of white, lit by a band of gold along the horizon where the sun dipped behind the trees, which stood naked and ragged. To think that I had thought that Norfolk would look like Kent! Now I saw that the two were as different as rich golden butter and sharp, dark bramble jam.

As the coach trundled through a forest, I thought I spied something moving through the trees in the distance, a lumbering figure striding with a heavy, irregular gait from trunk to trunk. At the sound of the approaching coach, it seemed to turn and stare at the road but then, just as suddenly, I blinked and it was gone. The driver cracked the whip and the horses picked up speed.

I heard the river before I saw it, coursing to the right of us. The icy grey water frothed and churned as it tumbled over sharp, angular rocks. Then came the mill with its massive waterwheel, lazily scooping out handfuls of river water, before dumping it back with a spray that glittered in the weak sunlight.

The dirt road became stone and the coach rattled as we crossed a bridge that led us past a painted sign that read FELLWICK.

We had clearly arrived at the end of the market. Tables were being carried back towards the hall and school-house; grubby, faded fabric bunting hung between lampposts; debris from cabbages, lettuce and straw-packed boxes littered the streets.

A small queue of farmers stood outside the town's red brick bank. They turned to watch as the coach rattled past, their hands raised to the driver. Rounding the corner by the butcher's shop, we passed through a wooden archway and finally stopped in the middle of a large courtyard next to a handsome, Tudor-style building with a hanging sign above the door reading: The Hive and Honey.

I unfolded myself from my seat, my joints clicking as I climbed down. The driver disembarked and fixed me with an expectant look, hand outstretched.

'That'll be five bob.'

I winced.

That's the last of it, I thought, handing over the money.

'Do you know the way to Mistcoate House at all?' I said. 'I am under the employ of Dr Richmond at Mistcoate House and need to—'

'I only deliver to the town.' The driver cut me off. 'Don't know the houses.'

Seizing a heavy bag, he stamped off in the direction of the post office.

I stood, clutching my bags and peering around me. Already, long shadows grew as the sun dipped and the town seemed to be shutting down for the day. Surely it wasn't three o'clock yet? Back in Kent nowhere had been so quick to turn away business, even in the winter. And yet, here, women hurried past, baskets full, heads down. A man was busy fitting shutters to the tea room windows. There was no sign of someone looking for a passenger to ferry to Mistcoate.

Possibly, I wasn't in the right place.

I looked around for a better location to stand and wait. As I turned, I met the eyes of an old man, bundled up against the cold and moving at speed.

'You'm best get inside, miss,' said the man, hobbling past. 'Gettin' dark.'

'Could you tell me where Mistcoate House might be?' I asked.

The man stopped short and stared for a moment before shaking his head and starting to hurry away.

'At least tell me the time?' I called after him.

'Just after three,' he replied, without looking back.

That did it. Seeing that everywhere else seemed to be closing, I gripped my things and strode towards the door of the public house, the glass of which glowed a warm amber.

I stepped through into a wide, low-ceilinged room. Lanterns dangled above scrubbed wooden tables and a log fire crackled in one corner, filling the room with the smell of dried turf, blackening the beams above it. At the end of the bar, two men eyed me with surprise and not a little curiosity.

A door creaked and a dumpy, curly-haired woman stamped into the room, carrying a wooden case, her thick, freckled forearms straining against the weight.

'Good evening,' I said.

She stopped short at the sight of me and then glanced over to the two men, as if expecting an explanation for my presence. Both of them had paused their mumbled conversation to watch me.

'Hello, miss,' she said slowly, setting the crate down. 'Can I help?'

'My name is Julia Pearlie. I am expected at Mistcoate House,' I explained, almost breathless with desperation. 'I have been delayed and possibly missed my guide. Please, I need directions.'

'Is that so?' The woman was now staring at me in open interest. 'Well, you're very welcome, Miss Pearlie. I'm Sally Daly. Me'n my brother run this place. I didn't realise they had someone new comin' to the house. Just what'll you be doing at Mistcoate?'

'Fumbling around in the dark, I'd say,' sniggered one of the men.

'I'm sorry?' I said, glaring.

'Oh, don't mind Bert,' the woman said. 'He's Fellwick's answer to the music hall. 'Ent you, Bert?'

Bert leaned forward over his half-empty pint glass, leering.

'The lass asked a question,' he said. 'Be rude not to oblige. She'll learn soon enough when she wakes up and has that ghost hanging over her.' He laughed unpleasantly. 'Olivia Richmond would frighten anyone.'

'Stop that,' snapped Sally. 'Plenty enough to give people the creeps without you adding to it.'

'Could you possibly give me directions to the house?' I gripped my bags tighter, my voice too loud. 'Please. I should like to be on my way before the sun sets.'

'I'd say so,' said Bert. 'No one wants to be about here at night.'

'That's why we're in here,' muttered his companion. 'Nice and safe.'

I gave the thinnest, most polite smile my tense jaw would allow.

'Of course we can tell you the way, miss.' Sally narrowed her eyes at the men and lifted a hinged door in the bar. 'Come with me.'

As she ushered me out, Bert's voice followed me. 'Watch yourself now, miss,' he called, as the man next to him chortled into his glass. 'Terrible one for the ladies, is the Shambler.'

Confused, I turned to Sally. 'What is…?'

'Ignore him,' Sally said, briskly. 'Old fool. Now look, here.'

She drew me out into the middle of the cobbled square. It was getting colder, and our breath formed clouds in the air as she pointed through the second archway towards a large stone church.

'Normally you'd turn right at the bandstand and take the forest path,' she explained. 'But if you're looking to make quick time, I would cut through the church yard.'

Even from this poor vantage point, I could see that the church yard was an overgrown, muddled affair with grave markers raised on mossy hills by growing tree roots.

'But if you would like to wait, we could always—'

'Thank you very much, Miss Daly,' I interrupted, squaring my shoulders. 'I shall remember you to Mrs Hayes for helping me.'

To my surprise, she flinched.

'Please don't,' she said, and disappeared back into the inn.

The church loomed over the village, its main doors reached by a series of stone steps. The graveyard next to it was crowded and erratic, with large stone slabs rising out of the earth and the bent, crumbling forms of weeping angels casting contorted shadows.

As I let myself through the creaking gate, I became aware of voices off to my left and, making my way down the stone-strewn dirt path, I began to make them out.

'I understand, Mrs Lewes,' a woman was saying, in a hushed voice with a hint of Yorkshire in the accent. 'But Mrs Dewbury is adamant.'

'Sarah has not been to lessons in three days.' This voice was higher, and tense as piano wire. 'She needs to be in the school room.'

I followed the path, passing an overgrown bush which gave way to reveal a small side door set into the wall of the church. A tall, slim woman stood in the open doorway, gripping the handles of a bicycle. Oil lamps glowed behind her, lighting her face, which was flushed, either from exertion or with the damp chill of the autumn air. A neat little hat trimmed with feathers perched on top of her ash-blonde hair, the plumes fluttering in the breeze. She wore a cycling outfit in a mix of charcoal grey and mustard wool. This, complete with a high-collared, tight-waisted cycling coat and thick black stockings, made her look very much like a tall wasp. She must have just finished cycling, for when she spoke, her voice was breathless and halting.

'If Mr Lewes could only make amends—'

Mrs Lewes' fiery red hair flared out against the shadowy gloom of the graveyard. She was nearly a head shorter than the cyclist but this did not cow her. She took a step forward and the sharpness in her voice made me pause.

'There are no amends to be made,' she said. 'Certainly not on *our* part.'

'Mrs Lewes,' the blonde cyclist murmured, her voice low and reproachful. 'Charlie Dewbury was carried home. Your husband broke a cane over him.'

'Nonsense,' said Mrs Lewes. 'It's the prattling of boys. My Thomas would never—'

A twig snapped under my foot. Both women turned to stare at me, the red-haired Mrs Lewes's expression flickering from fear to a guilt-ridden look of loathing.

'I beg your pardon. My name is Julia Pearlie and I am due at Mistcoate House. Am I on the correct path?' I said.

The two women glanced at each other.

'It is getting dark,' said the cyclist. 'Have you—?'

'Is this the way?' I cut her off, my frayed nerves unravelling.

'Yes,' she conceded, after a moment's hesitation. 'Straight ahead. But if you can wait, I can fetch my brother to accompany you through the forest.'

'Thank you but I am already late,' I said, turning away from her kind expression. I strode off. Behind me I could hear the two women whispering.

'What about Sarah Dewbury?' Mrs Lewes said.

'I will speak to my brother.' The cyclist's voice. 'But I doubt he will say anything different.'

Then I heard no more as their voices fell away behind me.

I walked until the trees began to close in overhead and the world became a shrouded green cave. Birds roosting overhead made soft cooing noises, rustling in the branches and shaking droplets of cold rain onto the pathway. I busied myself practising my apologies for once I arrived at Mistcoate.

Were it not for this, I might have noticed sooner, but I was distracted and so it wasn't until I stopped to take stock of where I was that I realised what was missing.

The birds had stopped. Everything was silent and still.

Hairs rose on the back of my neck.

Grave markers loomed on all sides and beyond those, there was nothing but the thickness of the woods. Were the shadows to my left somehow darker than they should have been? As though there was someone standing in the gloom...

I fought to quiet myself, to make sense of this creeping sensation across my skin, until the thought arrived, quite unbidden, in my head.

Something was here with me.

Possibly, it was just an animal, I told myself. If confronted, it would flee. The trees rustled. There was darkness to my left, where the undergrowth of the graveyard merged with the forest. It was there. I could feel it watching me.

A memory flared in my mind like a flame.

A Soho street. My distracted governess asking a man for directions. My gaze drawn to a pale girl in the doorway, her lank curls against a grubby lace collar, staring at me from the shadows...

A branch snapped, and I cried out, my heart in my throat, 'Who is there?'

A young man stepped out from the trees, pushing a bicycle.

'My apologies,' he said. 'I was calling but I am not sure you heard. My name is Ed Byres. How do you do?'

THREE

Strength

'I believe you met my sister Alice at the Rectory? She thought you would welcome a guide.' He stepped forward, reaching for my bags. 'Let me take those for you. I'm sure you're quite done with carrying them. You're clearly an accomplished walker, you're nearly at the gate already.'

The Reverend Ed Byres, dressed in a high white collar and long sweeping coat, did not look at me as he tied my valise onto the bicycle. Instead, he kept up a breezy one-sided conversation in a soft Yorkshire accent that left me to stare at him.

He was a tall man, not much older than myself, but stood with a slight stoop, as though embarrassed by his stature, his face set in an apologetic expression. A few rebellious strands of hair had escaped the pomade and hung over his forehead as he fastened and pulled at the buckles on the leather straps with hands that were roughened and red. A working man's hands. Not what I expected from a curate.

'My apologies again,' he said. 'It wasn't my intention to startle you.'

'No, no. I don't know what came over me.' I reddened at his sudden, direct gaze.

'It is an eerie time of day,' he observed, amiably. 'And I imagine it is unnerving travelling alone. I can help with that at least.'

He wheeled the bicycle past me and inclined his head in the direction of the path.

'Follow me. I am sure they will be wondering what has kept you.'

I let him pass before peering into the undergrowth where I had sensed the dark presence.

Nothing.

When I looked back, his long stride had already taken him a distance ahead, and I hurried to catch up with him, my satchel bumping against my thigh.

'I am not normally late,' I said, as I drew closer. 'And the worst thing is I am at a loss as to how to explain myself.'

I noticed my voice had taken on an anxious, breathy pitch, and tried a tentative smile. 'My apologies, I know I am already prevailing on your time and here I am, complaining.'

'Not at all,' said Reverend Byres. 'If anything, I am sorry I cannot be of more assistance. I would come inside and speak on your behalf but I am not certain it would help matters.'

'Oh?'

He hesitated. 'Dr Richmond holds certain beliefs that make me somewhat unwelcome at Mistcoate,' he said.

It was an unusual thing to say and I tried to think of an appropriate reply. 'I suppose there may not be much room for the spiritual in the home of a medical man,' I said, and then suddenly I thought of the two sneering men in the public house. 'I am sure I would keep my distance if I knew I was being spoken of the way I heard people in the village speak of Miss Olivia.'

Byres gave me a curious look, so I relayed my encounter with the two men in the inn. As he listened, he shook his head.

'My apologies for Bert Sutton,' he said, propping open a large iron gate. 'I shall have a word with him.'

I was impressed that he knew precisely who I was talking about by description alone. But then, a pastor must know his town.

He gestured for me to go first, and I hurried through the gate and found myself under a canopy of trees leading onto a wide dirt road. The sound of the river was clearer here. It made a faint, constant roar as it raced towards the south, a great watery pathway to the ocean.

Byres and I fell into step.

'It does make one wonder what type of man would be so malicious as to spread gossip about a child,' I said.

There was a long silence, and then Byres said, 'Miss Pearlie, I would be remiss if I did not inform you that Miss Olivia is a source of some speculation and concern in the village.' He sounded as though he was choosing his words carefully. 'She is a singular person and sometimes does things that are difficult to understand.'

'What do you mean?' I asked.

'For one thing, there is her habit of going for midnight walks alone,' he said. 'There is a rumour that she haunts the woods.'

'Haunts?' I frowned. 'That's a very strange way to put it.'

Reverend Byres cleared his throat, clearly uncomfortable. 'Well, there is the matter of her appearance.'

I stopped. 'What about it?'

Byres turned, still gripping the handlebars of the bicycle.

'Has Dr Richmond not appraised you of Miss Olivia's condition?'

'Obviously not,' I said, trying to disguise my confusion. 'What exactly is her condition?'

Byres shook his head. 'I am making it sound worse than it is. You will see for yourself but she is exceedingly pale...' He paused, searching for the words. 'The local children tell stories about her, I understand. There used to be a craze for sneaking up to touch the front door of Mistcoate, although of late that has not been a concern.'

We had stopped walking without realising it.

I narrowed my eyes, searching his face. I wondered if he was somehow joking, but his gaze was direct and his tone earnest. No, he was not trying to fool me. In fact, I realised, he was trying very hard not to scare me. This made it worse.

'Why would they do that?' I asked.

He looked about us, hesitating.

'Reverend Byres?' I pressed.

Somewhere a bird took off from a tree in a panic of fluttering wings and muffled squawking. Byres took a convulsive step back, his hand thrown out as if to try and shield me.

The darkness was thick now around us.

'Honestly Reverend,' I said, 'I am surprised that a clergyman would indulge in this kind of nonsense about a child.'

'It is not my intention to gossip.' Byres shook his head. 'Merely to inform. The Richmonds are reclusive. Miss Olivia has been without society for quite some time and has developed odd habits that you should be aware of. I agree that, being so sheltered, she is still just a child. Hopefully, she will grow out of her interest in frightening others.'

'So far, it is not Miss Olivia doing any of the frightening, as far as I can determine.' My tone was disapproving.

Byres flushed. 'I am sorry if I have disquieted you,' he said. 'I am certain that you have nothing to worry about. Still, it has been noticed that those who stay at Mistcoate House tend to lose their nerve before long. The village has reason to suspect this is due to Miss Olivia.'

'And what reasons are those?' I demanded. 'A lonely child's odd habits?'

Again, Byres hesitated. Then he turned and began to wheel the bike onward. I followed and he inclined his head towards me as I matched his step. When he next spoke, his voice was so low I could barely hear it over the rush of the river.

'Four years ago, a solicitor called Oliver Towers moved into the area. His wife and infant son had died from complications with her lying-in, and Towers decided a more secluded way of life would suit himself and his daughter, Emily. Emily was a quiet, solitary child. She struggled to make friends with the local children and soon it became clear to Towers that his daughter was, if possible, more miserable in Fellwick than she would have been in London. He appealed to Reverend Smythe, my superior, who suggested a visit to Mistcoate, as Emily and Olivia were the same age, and both were isolated children. Soon a friendship formed between the two girls. For months they were inseparable friends. Then Emily began having nightmares, even suffering from bouts of nocturnal incontinence. Towers was so troubled he considered sending her to a hospital. He appealed to the Richmonds for intelligence and even had the housekeeper, Mrs Hayes, question Miss Olivia. But the girl pleaded ignorance.

'One night, Emily ran away. Towers was beside himself and searched her rooms. He found letters, all written in various hands, but all signed with his dead wife's name. At first the messages were comforting, but as he read on they became… unsettling. Spiteful. Threatening, even.'

Byres glanced at me to check that I was still listening. 'I wouldn't like to repeat them to you. It was no wonder the poor girl was terrified. Thankfully, Emily was found in the very graveyard we just left; filthy, hungry and nearly frozen. When questioned, she would only say that she would return home if her father promised her that she would never need to see Olivia Richmond again. According to Emily, Olivia had given her all those letters. Needless to say, Mr Towers was furious and accused Miss Olivia of spying on the family.'

'Spying?' I said, so surprised I nearly stopped.

'The letters quoted private conversations that took place in the Towers' home,' he explained. 'The last letter, in fact, referenced Towers' fears for Emily's health and his plan to send her away. Nobody could understand how Olivia could have known about that.'

'Oh, honestly,' I said, 'girls talk to each other, you know.'

Byres gave me a look. 'Emily swore she had told Olivia nothing. And I must say, I am inclined to believe her.'

This didn't make any sense to me.

'Then how on earth did she do it?'

'That,' said Byres, 'is something Olivia refuses to answer. The Towers family left the area soon after this occurred.'

When I didn't speak, Byres smiled ruefully and adjusted his grip on the bicycle handles. 'My apologies, Miss Pearlie. You are about to start a new position and I am not helping. Please believe me when I say that I take no pleasure in telling you these things. I merely feel it would be remiss of me to keep you in the dark when this is just one of a series of odd incidents surrounding Olivia Richmond and I doubt anyone at Mistcoate will be forthcoming. Hopefully this goes some way to helping you understand why the townspeople are frightened of her – even if they will not admit it.'

'I assure you I do understand.' I spoke calmly, but my skin prickled and the hairs on the back of my neck were raised. This was not the arrival I had envisioned at my new position. Everything about this made me anxious.

Byres pointed ahead. 'Well. There it is, then. Mistcoate House.'

FOUR

The Emperor

In the dying light, Mistcoate House's red-bricked facade blazed through the dark bodies of the trees. The road widened and became gravelled as we approached a driveway wide enough for a coach. I had expected to see a large set of gates, but Mistcoate House had no need for such things since the woods encircled it on all sides.

The structure was a sprawling, two-storey affair, squatting close to the ground with an ornate wrap-around porch that fitted like a collar, while cracked and peeling shutters framed its tall, dark windows. The expanse of lawn was overgrown, and the grass stood above ankle height. As we approached, a breeze shook the blades, causing a secretive whispering. *Turn back... turn back...turn back...*

But I can't, I thought. *Even if I wanted to.*

As we approached, the door opened and a figure appeared on the porch.

'Here you are,' murmured Byres. 'I shall do my best for you here.' His voice rose. 'Good evening, Mrs Hayes.'

'It is after three.' Mrs Hayes was stern-faced as she descended the stone steps to meet us. She looked in apparent surprise at Byres before turning to glare at me.

'Did you not see Toby? I gave instructions that he was to fetch you and he said you were not there.'

'It is not his fault,' said Byres, in a jovial voice that rang out across the lawns. 'The postal coach arrived later than expected. At any rate, as you can see, here she is, safely in your hands. Miss Julia Pearlie, this is Mrs Hayes. The housekeeper at

Mistcoate.'

Mrs Hayes must have been in her early forties, tall, straight-backed, and wearing a simple blue dress, in a style which had gone out of fashion years ago. Her thick, silver-streaked hair was pulled back from her face and her nose had a strange crick in it, as though it had been broken and not set properly, making it somewhat off-centre. Possibly she had been in an accident, as she also had a scar across the left side of her mouth, forming a puckered line along her lips. Still, she was a handsome woman, for all that.

She glanced at the bicycle with my bag strapped to it.

'Is this everything?'

Byres was already unbuckling the straps. He did not seem to have noticed that Mrs Hayes had neither thanked him nor offered him any hospitality.

'I will leave you here then, Miss Pearlie,' he told me, quietly. 'Good luck.'

He set my bags down, and turned the bicycle back up the path, giving a little wave as he did so.

Mrs Hayes made a strange snorting noise and gave my sleeve a sharp tug, which brought me straight back to the schoolroom.

'Inside,' she ordered.

I lifted my luggage and followed her, bags swinging as I climbed the stone steps, into a long, tiled entrance hall where a few pale lamps flickered. Ahead of us, I saw the end of a grand, oak staircase through a framed aperture in the wall.

'Dr Richmond has been waiting.' Mrs Hayes' voice echoed as we stepped inside. 'Leave your bags here and I'll have the boy bring them up to your room.'

'You are from London?' I said, slipping the smaller bag off my shoulder. 'I recognise your accent.'

'Bermondsey. But that was years ago.' Her grey eyes raked over me. The scrutiny felt like a candle flame held too close to the skin.

She pursed her lips. 'You may wish to tidy yourself up.'

Flushing, I turned away and smoothed my hair and straightening my rumpled clothing, glancing at myself in the glass of the grandfather clock. Above us, oil lamps flickered, but their light was so low, it was hard to see my own reflection.

As I turned back, a sound reached me, just on the edge of hearing. A soft, echoing wail that seemed to come both from inside and outside the house. Mrs Hayes did not seem to have heard it.

'Is that it?' she said, glancing at my hair with disapproval. 'I suppose it will have to do. Come.'

She walked through into a large hall, beckoning for me to follow. I looked up, and saw that the centre of the house was hollow. The first floor landing was a mezzanine gallery that overlooked the entrance hall. High above it, the ceiling held a painted fresco of a blue and golden sunrise, although it was now smudged with smoke from the lamps and the grime of age.

Unlike the Kemps' home, which had been as stately and contained as a palace, Mistcoate House felt more like a tower of rooms that had been knocked over and scattered on the ground. Corridors jutted out from the central hall like the legs of a spider and seemed to go on forever, room after room after room, all with forbidding-looking wooden doors with iron handles carved with what looked in the dimness like leering, grinning faces.

'Your rooms are on the first floor on the servants' side of the house,' Mrs Hayes informed me, stopping at the foot of the staircase. 'They are reached from the kitchen stairs through that hallway.'

She gestured with a flick of the hand to another dark open doorway, which faced the one we had just walked through.

'I am not to sleep next to the school room?' I said.

'That is on the second floor, and we are currently using it for storage. You will find it quite unsuitable,' said Mrs Hayes. 'Your room will be on the same floor as Miss Olivia and Captain Richmond. Dr Richmond felt that would make things simpler.'

Captain Richmond, Mrs Spencer had said, was Dr Richmond's father. He was elderly, she had informed me, and his health was failing.

I heard voices from the kitchen corridor and turned to see a lean girl in a maid's cap stood shaking a spoon at a surly-looking boy dressed in ill-fitting workman's clothes. His hands were thrust deep into the pockets and he had averted his gaze at the sight of me.

'That's Marian and her brother Toby,' explained Mrs Hayes. 'Toby is still at home but Marian's room is on the second floor.'

'And the other staff?' I asked, looking around the hallway at the series of doors.

'There are no other staff. Most of the house is shut up with only the three Richmonds here.' Mrs Hayes gave a smile that didn't quite reach her eyes. 'You'll learn which rooms are open as we go. The rules here are simple. Curtains and shutters are closed in the middle of the day. The front and back doors are locked at all times. Miss Olivia goes nowhere without either me or Dr Richmond knowing.' Seeing my expression she added, 'This is all for Miss Olivia's safety. You stick to that and we'll get on well. Now, come along.'

With that, she swept past me and disappeared back through the aperture and around a corner in a rustle of skirts. I plunged after her into the shadows, passing a series of unlit oil lamps mounted on the dusty oak-panelled walls.

Why not light them? I wondered.

In the gloom, I nearly crashed into the back of Mrs Hayes when she stopped abruptly in front of a mahogany door.

'This is Dr Richmond's study,' she told me. 'Please don't bore him with pointless waffling. He must leave soon to catch the last train to London.'

Before I could respond, she knocked.

'Come in,' said a man.

Mrs Hayes stepped inside, but for a moment I stayed where I was. My stomach twisted painfully as I listened to the voices on the other side of the door. Mistcoate wasn't at all as I'd expected. Everything was dark and so very strange. But it was too late to turn back.

I stepped inside.

The study might once have been plush and comfortable but was now worn from neglect and overuse. The scratched, varnished desk was covered in papers, half-empty ink bottles, and broken pen nibs, while the high mahogany shelves that lined the room threatened to burst with papers, folders, ledgers, and reference manuals. Heavy velvet curtains screened the window, and the oil lamps created an uneasy light. Despite the chill, the fireplace sat blackened and empty, with two sagging wingback chairs pulled close to it. There was also, I noticed with distaste, a small table, piled with dirty dishes. Although Mrs Hayes made no move to clear them, I noted how her eyes flickered to it and the way she laced her fingers together in front of her, as if resisting the urge to tidy.

Dr Richmond sat behind his desk without a jacket or necktie, dressed in an old, embroidered waistcoat that hung unbuttoned off his wide frame. I was shocked to see his shirt sleeves were rolled up, displaying muscled forearms as he peered at me through the smoky gloom. He looked, I thought, like a pugilist in an expensive shirt.

'Miss Pearlie?' he said, in a deep husky voice. 'Good. You have arrived safely. Mrs Hayes, will you let my daughter know Miss Pearlie is here?'

Mrs Hayes gave a stiff nod and left. The door made a soft sound as it closed, sealing us in.

'Please take a seat.' Dr Richmond indicated the chairs by the fireplace.

I tried to ease one around to face the desk but they were made with heavy, solid frames and their feet stuck to the carpet. Eventually Dr Richmond got up and moved it for me, his arms barely straining as he lifted it off the rug.

'There. Sit,' he said, when it was in place.

The chair was so deep it felt as if I was falling back into it, my feet lifting off the floor like a child's.

Dr Richmond resumed his place at the desk and began rolling down his shirt sleeves. Like Mrs Hayes, he kept his gaze on me constantly, as if appraising me. He seemed, I thought, to find me more pleasing than the housekeeper had.

'I apologise for my lateness,' I said.

'No matter.' He fixed his cuffs in place with quick fingers. 'Now you are here, we can begin. First, how much did they tell you in London?'

'That I am to act as an etiquette coach.' As I spoke, I tried to sit straight in the sagging chair. 'I understand you intend for Miss Olivia to take part in the London season next year?'

'This year, in fact,' he corrected me. Rising, he moved over to a sideboard where a silver tray sat, laden with bottles, and reached for an empty cut-glass tumbler on the tray. 'I am currently involved in a series of studies at the Royal College in London. It is my intention that, should they go well, we will move to London permanently. Ideally, I would like us to be settled by the summer, and for Olivia to have come out in society in time for our arrival.'

'I see.' My stomach sank as I considered the task ahead of me. This year's season started in February; Olivia would need to begin attending events from April at the latest. Six months was hardly any time at all to prepare.

Dr Richmond selected a whiskey bottle and poured a neat measure into his glass. 'I have not shared these plans with anyone in the house as I would not wish to raise their hopes,' he explained. 'My father is not in good health. His military career weakened him and there have been other... disappointments that have aged him considerably. Should you encounter him, you will find him much frailer than a man his age should be. It is my belief that he would receive better care in London.' He took a long sip before continuing. 'As for Olivia, she is getting to an age where she will want more than I can offer her here. I wish to ensure London holds some promise for her and as her mother is no longer with us, it seems the correct thing to do.'

'And you would like me to ensure that she fits in,' I said.

Dr Richmond turned to face me. 'More than that. I would like her to be married.'

I stared at him. 'I understood Miss Olivia to be just seventeen.'

Dr Richmond shook his head. 'I do not mean right away, of course. A year or two in London first but ultimately, yes. She is healthy, intelligent, and pretty in her way. There are worse specimens married off every day. Some downright horrors if my colleagues' stories are to be believed. Surely it would not be so difficult for us to make some suitable introductions that may, eventually, lead to a match?'

He held my gaze, searching my face as he awaited an answer.

'With time, perhaps,' I conceded, a note of caution in my voice.

Dr Richmond leaned back against the sideboard in a soft tinkle of glassware. 'You cannot do it?' he said. 'Many young girls receive less time.'

But they were brought up in that world, I thought.

Aloud, I said, 'No sir, I am confident I can fulfil my role. I just wonder what could be achieved if we had more time?'

'Time is something we do not have, Miss Pearlie.' His voice was firm. 'Olivia's education has suffered since my sister Florence left us. She raised Olivia after my wife's death and, without her, I am sorry to say that Olivia has become somewhat indulged. I fear, unless you can guide her, we shall arrive in London and Olivia will have no means to navigate that her new society.'

It made sense, although it would not be easy. But the money from the work would sustain me, and that was what mattered now.

Clearing my throat, I said, 'I hesitate to bring it up sir, but there is the matter of my pay.'

Dr Richmond raised his eyebrows. 'Mrs Spencer did not give you those details? We had discussed…' He mentioned an amount, and a pit formed in my stomach.

It was a much smaller number than I had prepared myself for. But, as I looked around at the empty grate, the threadbare rug, and the low oil lamps a thought occurred to me, spoken in an icy voice that was not my own but felt like cold water down the back of my neck.

He cannot afford more.

Was it a trick of the light or was his collar dirty? It would be an excellent trick, I realised, to hide frayed sleeves by rolling them as he had done. Good God, who was this man? A country doctor with a crumbling old house and aspirations. How long had he been out of polite society? Who would he even recommend me to once my work was finished here?

But it was pointless to think this. I needed a situation, and a reference. I was trapped.

I thought of Anthony's face, at once defiant and wretched in the face of my poverty, and felt what a deep and heavy burden supporting myself was going to be.

'It is a very economical sum,' I said, after a moment.

His face tightened. 'I am no fool, Miss Pearlie. The season is expensive and we would need to retain your services for at least a month on arrival in London in order to make correct introductions. It all adds up.'

'Indeed sir, you are quite right,' I said, thinking quickly. 'But, if I may begin to be of use right away, you might consider how it will reflect. Most of the London set know each other already. Your family, while utterly respectable…' This drew a strange look from the doctor, a slight movement of the head, '…will be relatively novel. Prospective husbands and mothers-in-law will look for signs of poor value in unknown persons, like how much one is willing to pay for clothes, housing… and servants.'

I paused for a moment, watching Dr Richmond as this information sank in. The light of the lamp caught the lines in his otherwise handsome face, making him seem drawn and tired.

'And just how would they know?' His voice was low.

I hung my head in a show of penitence and regret. 'Surely sir, if you are only able to engage me for less than a year, when I move on to find a new situation, one of us will have to disclose my previous payment.'

There was a moment of uncomfortable silence.

'You think it could become gossip?' asked Dr Richmond.

'Possibly, sir. However, I do have a solution. To pay an economical amount for an unknown quantity is common sense. But once the value of that quantity is known, it also makes sense to secure it, does it not? Then you would appear quite shrewd. No one could criticise you. My suggestion is that we have a meeting once a month. You meet with Mrs Hayes, do you not? Well, this would be very similar. You and I meet, I take you through Miss Olivia's progress and possibly there is some sort of test, where you can assess her. Once you are convinced that she is moving in the right direction, we can discuss a small increase.'

'By how much?'

My suggestion made him pause but he did not dismiss it outright. He drummed his fingers on the glass and drained the last of the whiskey.

'I can accept that,' he said. 'However, Miss Pearlie, this may work against you. We have no time to lose. I will be looking closely and, should Olivia show no signs of improvement, I will be forced to find a suitable replacement at the nearest possible opportunity. Do you understand?'

'Perfectly,' I said. 'May I ask one more thing, sir?'

His eyebrows rose. 'More?'

'I know it is highly irregular, but, if you are satisfied with my work, I should be grateful to have the reference written once I have been here three months, stipulating the nature of the engagement.'

'And how do I know that, once you have it, you will not abscond early?' asked Dr Richmond.

'If I abscond early, it will be without my pay and, I confess, I shall not get very far without it,' I said.

'No?' He studied me with interest. 'And why would you trust me so little as to want an early reference?'

'In my experience, my need is not necessarily an employer's priority,' I told him, frankly. 'Especially once they have decided that I am no longer useful to them.'

Dr Richmond regarded me, the sharpness of his eyes belying the effects of the whiskey.

'I see.' His voice had grown soft. Almost warm.

Afraid I had revealed too much, I turned to look at the family photographs lining a shelf, hoping to disguise the sudden burning I could feel in my eyes. How hateful that, no matter how familiar humiliation was, it never ceased to sting.

'Well, if we have struck a bargain, I will take you at your word. We shall have our first test this evening.' He strode over to a series of silk cords by the door and pulled on a thin black bell pull.

'But Mrs Hayes said that you would be leaving for London tonight?'

'I would like to leave for London knowing that my trust is well-placed. For that to happen, I must observe you with Olivia. We meet in the parlour at six.'

A dull thump reverberated through the ceiling as something hit the floor upstairs.

Dr Richmond and I looked at each other and then the doctor wrenched open the door, stepping out into the corridor. Silence and then, after a moment, a loud shriek.

'Father?' Dr Richmond's voice echoed off the high ceilings. 'Mrs Hayes!'

I followed him back down the dim corridor into the large, entrance hall, and stood at the foot of the stairs, looking up at the gallery level above. Portraits hung in between the mahogany doors. One was of a soft-faced woman of around forty, smiling at something outside the canvas, her hair arranged in curls. Dr Richmond's mother, perhaps? Then another of a man in regimental uniform with medals across his chest. The captain, I was sure. Then one of Dr Richmond, younger and looking uncomfortable at the painter's scrutiny.

Next to that, there was only a darker patch of wall, as though one painting had been removed. The only missing person was Florence Richmond, and I wondered why it was not hanging with the others.

One of the doors on the first floor opened and Mrs Hayes appeared, flustered. A furious voice followed her into the hallway.

'I'm not going!'

When she spotted us, the housekeeper stopped.

'Is everything well, Mrs Hayes?' called Dr Richmond.

'Miss Olivia is…' began Mrs Hayes, but she didn't complete the thought. 'My dove, please,' she said, turning back to the room.

The door slammed as she disappeared back inside. I turned to find Dr Richmond watching me, the faintest ironic smile on his face.

'I would get started now if I were you,' he said. 'Remember, the parlour at six.'

He turned and was gone, leaving nothing but the sound of the stately grandfather clock in the corner and the uncertain ticking of my heart.

I thought of that shrill, rebellious shout from inside the room.

'It's like Christopher all over again,' I thought, with cold fear.

Yes, hissed an icy voice from the back of my mind. *Look at how that turned out.*

Something hit the other side of Olivia's bedroom door, as if a shoe had been hurled.

I squared my shoulders and climbed the stairs.

FIVE

The Magician

Mrs Hayes answered my knock at Olivia's door, her cheeks flushed and eyes over-bright.

'Finished?' she said. 'I'll show you to your room.'

'Dr Richmond would like me to prepare Miss Olivia for dinner.' I tried to step inside but Mrs Hayes moved to block the door.

'I do not think that is wise,' she said, firmly. 'Olivia needs some time. I will see she is ready.' She began to retreat back inside.

Part of me wanted to let her, but I knew I could not. At my first placement, the sour-faced nurse had been retained for the younger children while I was put in charge of the two eldest. This meant that any crime on my part was immediately brought to 'Nanny', who either complained to the mistress or found her own subtle ways to make life unpleasant. I had often told myself that, if I had the opportunity again, I would stand my ground so that she never dared question me. Now the time was here and if I failed, I could only expect more trouble down the line.

I wedged my boot into the doorway, the soft, cheap leather doing nothing to prevent my foot being crushed between the heavy wood of the door and the frame.

'Mrs Hayes, I am sorry but it really must be me.' I kept my voice low. 'I appreciate your help but this is what I am here for. No time like the present to start.'

For a moment, I thought Mrs Hayes was going to argue, but then she stepped aside with a grimace.

In the large bedroom, the heavy cream curtains had been pulled against the oncoming night but here, the lamps were turned up, making this room the brightest I had encountered in Mistcoate so far.

I would be the first to admit that I was ignorant about the living arrangements of well-to-do young ladies. Recently, the only rooms I had known were the nursery, the school room and my own meagre cell. I did not own enough to cause a mess in my own quarters and spent my life cleaning up after the children. Now, I stood amazed at the luxurious squalor in front of me.

The polished wood floor was littered with shoes, piles of books and lumps of pale, hardened candle wax. A tangle of dirty clothes lay strewn across a small chaise longue at the end of the bed, while every surface seemed covered with used candles and dusty boxes full of glass jewels and curios. A discarded tray protruded from under the unmade bed, the edges of the embroidered quilt made greasy with butter from the plate. As in the other rooms I'd visited, the fireplace was cold and full of ash, which spilled over the grate and onto the hearth. Smoke had smudged the walls, which were wallpapered with a cream, floral design, and the thick rugs had burn marks in them.

There was no sign of Olivia. Mrs Hayes shut the door and stood behind me, hands folded in front of her, her face impassive and still. I was on my own, it seemed.

I spoke in my firmest voice. 'Good evening, Miss Richmond. I am Miss Pearlie. Please come out.'

The curtains twitched and shadows moved across the floor behind them.

'I shall not come over and drag you out,' I continued. 'You are, I'm sure, far too old for such things. But I am very happy to wait and shall do all evening until, possibly, Dr Richmond comes. Best to get it over with now.'

There was a furious pause. Then the curtain slid back. I felt myself make a small sound in the back of my throat that I hoped was not audible.

Olivia Richmond was the colour of frozen milk, her skin so immensely pale that it seemed to glow. Ice-blonde hair hung about her shoulders like the tattered edges of a flag. Her pale blue eyes had an unfocused and other-worldly appearance. Despite my shock, something about her seemed somehow familiar. It took a moment before I realised where I thought I had seen her before.

I had been ten. My governess had taken a wrong turn during a trip to Oxford Street, leading us to the dark, crowded streets of Soho. As we hurried from corner to corner, desperately seeking directions, I realised that we were truly lost, and was beginning to feel a fluttering panic. That was when I saw the girl watching me from the shadows.

She was standing at the end of an alley through an arched entryway that might once have been a coaching inn. As pale and insubstantial as a ghost, she looked close to my age but she was much smaller, as if a strong breeze would blow her away. Her hair hung loose in limp white curls, framing her grimy forehead and pointed ears. She wore an oversized, old jacket and no shoes.

It would have been easy to miss her but it was her eyes that drew me. They stared out from over the chapped red hands clasped over her mouth, and bore into mine.

I could feel the cold, clammy touch of fear on my face as she uncurled a finger, eyes never leaving mine, and pressed it to her cracked lips, an indication for silence.

As she did this, the door next to her opened and a woman appeared with the shadow of a man looming behind her. The sudden movement made me gasp, drawing the woman's attention.

The ghost-girl pressed back against the wall but the woman, seeing my expression, put her head around the door. The man stepped out and stood over the child, saying something I did not hear, running a finger down her cheek. All the while, her reproachful eyes did not leave mine. I knew that I had betrayed her somehow. I had failed in a way that I couldn't quite understand, and I would be punished for my failure. I believed that I was now cursed.

At that moment, my governess, finally having clear directions from a delivery man, pulled on my hand and we were gone, striding up the street to Golden Square and out onto Bond Street.

Strange. I had forgotten all about it. Even when the memory rose to haunt me during my final days in Kent, when Christopher Kemp was dead, his sister Lucy was spirited away and the childhood certainty of my impending punishment came back, I told myself I was being fanciful. That I had imagined the whole thing. Now, it seemed as if the girl had found me again.

I shook my head.

But it's not her, I reminded myself.

I cleared my throat. 'There you are, Miss Richmond.'

She pulled a face. 'Not Miss Richmond,' she said. 'Miss Richmond is what people call Florence and I am not as old as her.'

'Your aunt?' I said. 'I should say so. Is she older or younger than your father?'

'Dr Richmond's older sister,' said Mrs Hayes from her post by the door. 'She was thirty-seven when she left. But remember, my dove, *you* are Miss Richmond now that Miss Florence is no longer here.'

'Did Papa tell you?' asked Olivia. 'He says I'm not to talk about her.'

'He told me she cared for you until… recently,' I said, trying to keep up with her.

'Hardly recently,' sniffed Mrs Hayes. 'Five years. I've been doing what I can in that time.'

So that is it, I thought. *She resents the competition.*

'What would you like me to call you?' I asked Olivia, smiling encouragingly.

'Miss Olivia. Like all the servants do,' said Olivia. 'And I shall not be coming down to dinner. I am unwell. It is my nerves. I have a sensitive temperament.'

Her pale eyelashes fluttered, as thick and silken as cobwebs. Her gaze never seemed to settle on me; more on the air around me.

'Nor will I be well tomorrow. Or any day,' Olivia continued. 'I have no need of arithmetic or sewing or whatever tiresome thing you are here to teach, so you may as well return to wherever you came from. Otherwise I shall lock myself in this room and not move an inch until you are gone. I have had it with governesses.'

'I am not a governess,' I said.

'And soon I will be eighteen and on my own—'

'I would not be so keen to wish for that,' I interrupted. 'It is difficult being a woman on your own.'

'Only if you are poor or unremarkable,' said Olivia. 'I am neither.'

Raising my eyebrows I turned to Mrs Hayes, who gave me a grim, thin-lipped smile.

'Well, you seem quite resolved.' I returned my attention to my new charge. 'It is a shame. I had hoped to discuss your new wardrobe as, from what I can see, none of this will be fit for London now that it's all spent so much time on the floor.'

Olivia's brow creased. 'London? What about London? Mrs Hayes, is he taking me to London?'

Mrs Hayes looked from Olivia to myself and back.

'I am sure I don't know,' she said, her voice tinged with uncertainty. 'You will have to ask Miss Pearlie.'

'Tell me now,' Olivia demanded, almost stamping her foot.

'I do not think you will be much interested,' I said. 'You have made yourself perfectly clear. Mrs Hayes, would you be so kind as to tell Dr Richmond that I am leaving? I shall go collect my things.'

'Please,' said Olivia, through gritted teeth. 'Tell me.'

I smiled. 'Dr Richmond has engaged me to prepare you for the London Season.'

There was a pause.

'What is that?' Olivia asked, turning to Mrs Hayes.

'It is something for the gentry,' said Mrs Hayes. 'Well-born ladies are presented to the Queen.'

'Some, yes.' I was surprised that Olivia didn't know this. There was clearly much work to be done. 'Mostly it is a series of events and parties. Balls, horse races, the opera. It is an opportunity to meet the right people. To see and be seen. Making the right impression is important. That is why I am here. He will explain it to you tonight.'

Olivia turned to Mrs Hayes. 'You said Papa was going to London.'

Again, Mrs Hayes looked wrong-footed. 'He…'

'…has delayed his departure until the morning,' I jumped in. 'He wishes to discuss your preparation over dinner.'

Mrs Hayes' mouth formed a perfect 'O' of shock.

'And just when was this news going to reach the staff?' Patches of red appeared high on her cheeks. 'I take it that he is also expecting a full dinner?'

Olivia strode out from the bay window. Though she moved with certainty, she walked with her fingers splayed, either at her sides or just in front of her, as if to feel her direction.

'It cannot be helped,' she said. 'Toby is still downstairs. He can help Marian with dinner.'

'The maid is cooking?' I asked, surprised.

Mrs Hayes gave me a fierce look. 'Not all of us can afford a range of staff. Sacrifices must be made in order to pay for fancy etiquette coaches from the city.'

Olivia turned to me suddenly. 'Miss Pearlie, go tell Papa that I am coming. Mrs Hayes will help me dress.'

She was squinting at the things scattered on the floor, holding them close to her face to make out their details, before discarding them.

Good lord, I thought, my breath catching. *She can barely see.*

'I'm sure Mrs Hayes will be needed downstairs,' I said, disguising my shock. 'Dinners don't organise themselves. I will help you get ready. I need to appraise your wardrobe as soon as possible.'

'Do you think this will do?' Olivia held up a wrinkled cotton dress, dyed a terracotta hue, with a high neckline and loose waist. It was the sort of thing I would have dressed Lucy in to run around in the garden and looked, I thought, too small for Olivia.

'Do you not have any afternoon dresses?' I asked.

'What is an afternoon dress?' said Olivia. 'Mrs Hayes?'

I turned to Mrs Hayes. She looked from me to her charge and snapped, 'A dress for the afternoon.'

Feeling the beginnings of triumph, I seized a garment off the floor and pressed it into Olivia's hands.

'Never mind,' I said. 'We will find you something and I will dress your hair. But first we must create a little order.'

I began to pick up the other things on the floor.

'I can see that I am not needed,' sniffed Mrs Hayes. 'And there is now so much to do. Excuse me.'

The door gave a curt click as she left.

Olivia turned at the sound of it. 'I should—'

'No, Mrs Hayes is quite right. She is better off with – Marian, was it?' I said, collecting more garments. 'Now, here are some stockings and I will give these boots a polish. Go and get changed.'

Olivia disappeared behind a wooden screen, leaving me to collect clothing, move shoes and deposit the dirty dishes out into the hallway. In all, it took three outfit changes before we agreed. At first, she emerged dressed more like a child ready to go cycling than a young lady going to dinner, and was sent back with a linen dress that she said was only for summer.

By the time I had the room in almost liveable condition, I had located a white smock dress; however, a search of the drawers revealed only unsuitable stays and many laddered stockings.

'Try this wrapper on with it,' I suggested. It was a pale grey silk, printed with orchids at the hem. Once tied, it was a little too big on Olivia's small, slim frame, but at least it made her look fit for dinner.

'Very smart,' I said, pleased. 'The colour suits you. Come and sit. We'll have you looking ready for Ascot in moments.'

Olivia slid into the dressing table chair in front of the mirror. Something about her wild hair suggested thin, slicing bits of wire that could cut the pads of one's fingers easily but as I brushed it out, it became soft and pliable, shining as the boar hair bristles smoothed it. Olivia waited until a complicated moment to lean forward, dragging me with her, and take a chocolate nestled in sugar paper from a drawer in her dresser. She bit into it, the smell of cherry liqueur rising.

'I'm sure your father would not want you to spoil your appetite for dinner.' I wrinkled my nose. 'I am also certain it is unhygienic to eat out of a drawer. We must start with manners, I think.'

'I know how to eat,' she retorted, sulkily.

'But you do not know how to *dine*. There's a difference.'

'You wish me to use a fish knife?'

'Well, at least you know what a fish knife is,' I said. 'That is something.'

'I know what it all is. We have all the silver put away. When Flor – I mean, Aunt Florence – was here, she'd have the table set and we would have dinners with Papa and Grandfather. She told me to start at the outside and work my way in.'

'That is correct.' I twisted a length of her hair to pin it. 'What else?'

'Napkin folded in half, the point facing outward,' she recited. 'No elbows on the table. I cannot remember which service is *à la Russe* and which is *à la Francaise* but she used to talk of that too.'

'It is a shame Miss Richmond is not here,' I said. 'She might have enjoyed this process. Possibly we could visit her? Where is she now?'

There was a pause.

'Your hair looks like it is dark,' Olivia said, studying me. 'I shouldn't like to have hair so dark.'

'True,' I said, careful to appear unaware of this sudden redirection. 'Your own colour suits you better.'

'Yours is fine. I just shouldn't like it.' She began picking at her fingers. 'Funny. Flor had dark hair like yours. I'm sure that when I see you up close, you will look quite like her.'

'I shall take that as a compliment,' I said, reaching for the box of hairpins. 'I will have to look out for pictures of her.'

'There aren't any,' said Olivia, and I thought of the missing portrait in the hall.

A great wail began from a far corner of the house. It started off low, growing in intensity and duration until the very corridors seemed to echo with it. There was the sound of running feet on the parquet and, just as that died down, the wail began again. Olivia stiffened in her chair as the cries reverberated around the house. Then, just as suddenly as they had begun, the sounds subsided.

I risked a glance at her face in the mirror. Her hair was pinned up in a simple chignon that emphasised the elfin delicacy of her face, with its pointed chin and high, rounded cheeks. Now that I was over the shock of them, I could see how large her eyes were, how her nose turned up a little. She looked less like a small child and more like a young lady.

Perhaps, I thought, hope beating its wings against my heart, Dr Richmond was right. A little of the new mascara to darken her lashes, a light touch of rouge about the cheeks to make her look lively, and Miss Olivia Richmond could be a genuine beauty.

She did not seem to have noticed her own transformation. She had a miserable, far-away look.

'There now,' I said, giving her a squeeze on the shoulder that caused her to flinch. 'Dr Richmond will be so impressed.'

I followed her down the stairs into the main hall and then through a set of double doors on our right, into the parlour. It had the same creamy wallpaper as Olivia's room. The damask curtains were drawn, the lamps were lit and a fire was beginning to burn in the grate. Aside from us, the room was empty.

'We shall have to work on being fashionably late,' I told Olivia. 'There is nothing sadder than being the first guest to arrive.'

She made no reply but collapsed into a chair, legs sprawling like a colt.

'We will also need to practise sitting,' I observed.

Olivia rolled her eyes. I wandered to the far end of the room, where a pianoforte stood in the corner. The lacquered exterior shone in the lamp light and when I lifted the lid, the ivory keys were rich and still as the surface of a jug of cream. I had not played the piano in so long. Of course, I had been allowed to use the one at the Kemps, but it had been in great need of tuning, and then John had arrived and there had been so much to distract me.

I placed the flats of my fingers gently against the keys and felt their soothing coolness. Our music teacher at school had always taught us to use a gentle touch – 'No bashing at the keys, ladies. We are not *Liszt*.'

'That belonged to Florence,' said Olivia.

'Do you play?' I asked.

'No. I imagine you do though. All the others did.'

'We will need to ensure you do,' I said, ignoring her tone. I sat on the stool and began to pick out the beginning of *Für Elise*. 'It will not do to have you outranked by the other young ladies.'

'Does that matter?' she asked.

'Oh yes,' I said, beginning to play in earnest.

'It will be a waste of your time.' Olivia straightened in her seat. 'I'm useless at these things.'

'You are too hard on yourself,' I said, continuing to play. 'We do not have to turn you into a virtuoso. A few decent songs are enough. Come look.'

With a sigh, Olivia lifted herself out of the chair. I kept my head down, lost in the joy of the music flying from my hands. I only knew Olivia had reached me when I saw her shadow fall across the keys. She leaned in close to watch me.

'You're not even looking at the keys.'

'I don't need to,' I said. 'Neither will you if you practise. Place your hands on top of mine.' I felt her hesitation and nudged her with my elbow. 'Go on.'

With some hesitation, she agreed, laughing a little as my fingers moved quickly across the keys.

'It is like standing on your father's feet to dance,' I said. 'Have you ever done that?'

It was the wrong thing to say. Olivia snatched back her hands.

'No,' she said. 'Papa never had time for it.'

'Mine neither,' I lied and allowed the music to fade away.

The parlour door opened and Dr Richmond entered.

'Ah, ladies,' he said, as though surprised to find us there. 'Excellent. Olivia, was that you playing?'

'It was Miss Pearlie,' said Olivia.

'Remarkable.' Dr Richmond moved to the sideboard that housed the parlour's alcohol. His steps were steady but his movements were quick and his eyes gleamed. 'You must have studied music for quite some time.'

'Since I was young,' I said. 'But it has been at least a year since I tried an instrument as beautiful as this one.'

'Please feel free to help yourself to it,' he told me. 'That is what the thing is there for. It's not as though Olivia gets much use out of it.'

'Are we going to have champagne?' asked Olivia. 'To celebrate Miss Pearlie's arrival? We haven't had any since my birthday and it has been weeks since then.'

'Miss Olivia drinks?' I asked.

Dr Richmond turned, clutching the neck of a decanter.

'Should she not? I believe that a passing acquaintance with it will prevent her becoming overly enamoured with it.'

'I suppose I agree,' I said, doubtfully. 'Provided it is not too much.'

'Have *you* ever had champagne, Miss Pearlie?' said Olivia.

'I am distantly acquainted with it,' I said.

Dr Richmond's smile broadened, although whether this was in mockery of me or delight at his own sudden largesse was hard to tell as he opened a cupboard above the sideboard to reveal a series of speaking tubes. He chose one, blew into it and said, 'Marian, open a bottle of champagne and bring it through for us.'

Olivia clapped her hands, beaming.

'Enjoy it. It's the last one,' Dr Richmond told her. 'Will you have a seat, Miss Pearlie?'

I made a show of folding my hands and sinking into a seat, perching on the edge of it.

'I would like to see Miss Olivia arrange herself, if possible.' I turned to my charge. 'Will you please take your seat, miss?'

Olivia copied my movements precisely, with a glance at her father to see if he had noticed.

She saw that, though, I thought. *What a curious girl.*

The champagne arrived, carried in by Marian, the lean, mousy-haired girl from the kitchen. She backed into the room with her shoulders raised and her head down, as though trying to fold herself up small enough to disappear.

Mrs Hayes followed, her face set in a sort of strained repose that any servant could recognise in a housekeeper as blind fury. I almost wanted to follow Marian's example and shrink back in on myself, especially when Mrs Hayes spotted me sitting on the pale damask chair, still in my travelling clothes.

'Yes, Mrs Hayes?' enquired Dr Richmond.

'I'm afraid, sir, that the captain will not be joining you for dinner.'

'Does he need me to check in?' Dr Richmond did not take his eyes off the champagne bottle as he spoke. Marian set it down on the sideboard table and began to unpack the glasses from the tray.

'Possibly, sir, but it can wait. I can see your refreshment is ready.'

'Mrs Hayes,' said Olivia, 'do you think Miss Pearlie looks like my Aunt Florence?'

'I'm afraid I don't see it, my dove,' said Mrs Hayes. 'But perhaps. You know Miss Florence's face better than I do–'

'Florence! Florence!'

The cry came from above, long and dire.

There was a rustle as Mrs Hayes fled the room without a word. Hurriedly, the maid abandoned the glasses and followed.

'Should you go?' Olivia turned to her father.

Dr Richmond did not reply, but sat with his head cocked, listening.

'No,' he said, after some moments. 'It seems to have stopped for now. Eda will deal with it.' Then, 'Have you been bothering him again? He gets like this when you've been filling his head with nonsense.'

Olivia's mouth pinched.

'I must talk about her with someone,' she said. 'You won't.'

'Shall I pour?' I asked, rising and reaching for the bottle. Families rarely forgave you for witnessing private arguments, and I could not let them forget I was there. 'It sounds like tea, doesn't it? Except this fizzes more than tea.'

I spoke to ease the tension and cover the sound of feet running on the parquet above us.

'Olivia asked me about London, Doctor,' I said, bringing the filled glasses to the chairs. 'Have you ever taken her to...'

I listed places I had heard of but never visited. As it happened, my knowledge of London's nightlife was somewhat out of date and Dr Richmond made gentle corrections in such a way as to disguise any ignorance on my part.

'I am afraid my work means I am not out at shows much,' I said, smiling at

Olivia, who had quickly finished her glass and was already a little excitable.

'I should love to go to a theatre,' Olivia announced. 'Epidemius St. Joseph appears every Thursday at The Alhambra, and they say people have to be carried out, they are so overcome.'

'Who is Epidemius St. Joseph?' I glanced at Dr Richmond.

'Please,' he said, wearily, 'do not ask.'

'He is a master,' breathed Olivia and her colour deepened. 'He is a mentalist.'

'He is a swindler,' corrected Dr Richmond.

'He's a spiritualist,' said Olivia, as though her father had not spoken. 'Many people have said he was able to tell them their deepest secrets. I should give anything to meet him.'

Dr Richmond snorted and emptied his glass.

'Fascinating,' I said. 'How does he know their secrets, do you think? Can he tell from their faces?'

Olivia shook her head. 'I imagine he just looks at the ghosts around them. That should tell him everything – or, at least, give him clues.'

'You believe he can really see ghosts?'

I had to control my smile. I turned to Dr Richmond, expecting to share a look of amused indulgence at Olivia's belief in a Music Hall act, but he shifted in his chair, staring into his glass.

'Enough, Olivia.' His voice was low and dangerous.

'Of course,' said Olivia, ignoring him. 'I can. And he is much, much more accomplished than me.'

'*Olivia.*' Dr Richmond set his glass down so hard that I thought the stem would break.

Olivia shrank back in her seat.

'He does not like me to talk about it,' she whispered to me. 'But that is because he does not understand.'

'I understand that you are taking this delusion to an extreme.' Her father glared at her. 'Please do not embarrass yourself further. It is the champagne. I should have known better. Look, it is nearly a quarter past seven. We must ring for dinner.'

He rose and walked to the speaking tube.

'Marian? Mrs Hayes? Hello? Damn it.'

It gave a sharp ring as he replaced it too hard. He left the room, the door banging closed behind him.

'He is drunk,' announced Olivia.

'He is not happy with your teasing,' I said. 'It was wrong of me to encourage you. You should not go telling ghost stories.'

'You do not believe me,' she said.

'That you can see ghosts? No. I do not, Miss Olivia. No one can see ghosts.'

There was a rustle as she moved to sit next to me. Her pale eyes bore into me, her face fervent. 'I could show you, if you like. Only we can't tell Papa. I could read your cards,' she said. 'I know things.'

I thought of Reverend Byres' story about Olivia delivering the mysterious letters to Emily Towers from her dead mother, and suddenly I felt cold.

'If Dr Richmond does not like it then we shouldn't,' I told her.

There were footsteps in the hallway. Olivia leaned in and whispered, 'But don't you want to know about the boy?'

I stared at her. 'I'm sorry?'

Olivia tapped her forehead, her face strained and earnest. 'The boy with the cut on his head. The one who's always wet.'

'Wet?'

Her eyes seemed to fill up the whole world. It felt like I was falling into them.

'He is always standing close to you.' Her voice was almost hypnotic. 'He has been following you all evening.'

I froze, my thoughts filling with the smell of pondweed and the sound of children screaming. Were my hands shaking? Olivia did not notice.

'Papa doesn't understand,' she whispered. 'But he can't see what I see.'

'Ladies?'

Dr Richmond stood in the doorway. There was a scrape of wood and the maid backed into the room again, this time dragging a folding table, which she set up between the armchairs. Olivia gave me a quick, frightened look.

'Apologies, Miss Pearlie,' Dr Richmond said, apparently oblivious to the tension in the room. 'As we were expecting my father, we had arranged to eat in the parlour. I hope it is not too inconvenient to ask you to assist Marian? Mrs Hayes is busy at the moment.'

'Of course.' I rose from my seat.

As I moved, I heard it. The delicate *plip* sound of a water droplet hitting the floor.

Something moved just at the edge of my vision. A small, shadowy figure in the corner. I stood, frozen, aware of the way water dripped from long tendrils of hair.

Plip...

'Miss Pearlie?'

I blinked and it was gone. There was nobody but Dr Richmond and Olivia, watching me.

'I'm sorry,' I said. 'I'm sorry.'

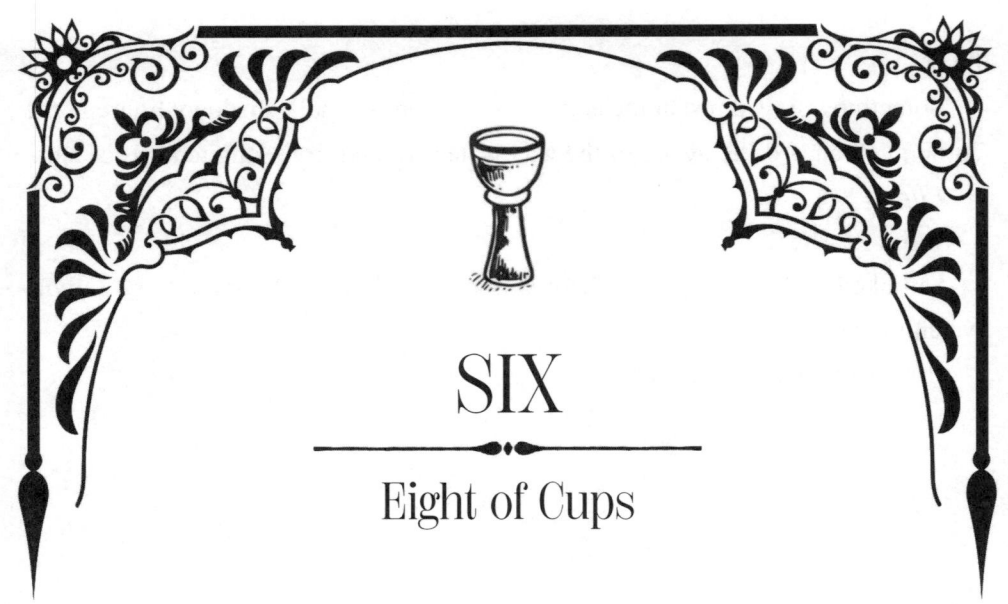

SIX

Eight of Cups

I woke in the darkness with a start, as though from a dream.

Thirsty. I'm so thirsty, I thought. *Where am I?*

I reached out, blind and groping for the water jug and glass on the chair next to the bed. My hands closed around something but this was porcelain and the wrong shape. All the same, it was a cup and it was full. The water was tepid and tasted like dust but I gulped at it, rivulets running down my neck, soaking the collar of my nightgown.

At last, I lay back, gasping, in the strange bed, the cup cradled on my stomach. I had not braided my hair and it rustled against my pillow, moved by the breeze from the open window.

Did I open that? I couldn't remember.

The night air brought the earthy smell of rain. As I lay there, breathing it in, memories of last night filtered back like dust motes whirling in a sunbeam.

The evening had continued in an unfamiliar haze of wine. Marian set the table in the parlour, which, with the fire and the champagne, felt overly hot. Then the dishes arrived: boiled potatoes, garden peas, roast beef, and steaming carrots. Dr Richmond asked for a bottle of red, which he poured into both our glasses before sending it back to the sideboard.

If Olivia noticed this slight, she didn't say anything. Instead she chattered about London. I sat, rigid and watchful, terrified to turn my head too quickly in case I saw that small, dark figure behind me. I drank the wine to calm my nerves, giving Olivia occasional instructions and sounding, I thought, too much like my mother.

'Now sit up, straight back, hands on lap. No, of course you can lift them to eat. No, never rest your arms on the table. Nothing below the wrists. Smaller bites please, Miss Olivia. It is vulgar to insult your host by appearing hungry.'

Mother would be so proud of you, said the icy little voice in my head.

I tried not to listen and ignored the persistent feeling of someone watching me from the corner of the room.

Dr Richmond continued to drink, mollified by the sight of Olivia endeavouring to play the blushing debutante. The novelty would wear off by the morning, I knew, but it was enough. Once the dessert had been cleared by a furious-looking Mrs Hayes, Dr Richmond nodded and said that he thought I should do very well.

'You're to do as Miss Pearlie tells you. Understood?' He cut a sly look at his daughter, a smile playing at the corner of his mouth. 'I will not have you shaming me when I take you to London.'

Olivia's eyes grew wide. 'You *will* take me?'

'That depends on your lessons with Miss Pearlie. If you can put on a good show then I see no reason why not.'

I nodded, although I was not so certain that Olivia Richmond would have a much better reception in the fashionable salons of London.

Then again, a cynical part of me thought, the dashing, tragic doctor, head of the family now his father was ill, would make a marvellous dinner guest, especially if he came with his pale, precocious daughter. I imagined them sitting at a table, resplendent in dinner dress. Dr Richmond would make tender, intelligent comments about Olivia, who would nod, smile and know how to use all the cutlery. It would be its own form of entertainment and, I was sure, guarantee them invitations into some of the more hedonistic parts of Kensington.

I wondered if he knew. No wonder he wanted me to prepare her.

'I shall escort you to bed,' I said, when the meal was over. 'Follow my example for leaving the table. First the gentlemen will rise.'

Dr Richmond played along, standing and nodding to Olivia in a pantomime of manners. Olivia made a great show of sweeping grandly out of the room, collapsing into giggles as she climbed the stairs. She began undressing before I had even closed her bedroom door and made it very clear that I would not be needed.

'I'm a lady, not an invalid,' she said.

I did not argue. The stress of the day, two helpings of dinner and more wine than I had ever drunk had left me aching for bed. I closed the door with a sharp click behind me.

It was only then that I realised I had no idea where my room was. Lamps glowed in the hallway, casting the ground floor below in deep, rich shadow. Straight ahead, on the other side of the mezzanine, there was an opening leading to a small corridor from which light glowed, like a light in a distant bedroom. To my left, the landing ran down to a smaller, darker entryway into a shadowed hall. I suspected, with a sinking feeling, that was where my rooms lay.

I considered knocking on Olivia's door and asking for a candle, but I decided against it. I would be fine in the dark. I had often walked through Astor House in Kent in the dead of night without fear or trepidation. I turned to my right, ready to slip through the doorway into the servants' corridor.

That was when I heard it. A shuffling step on the other side of the landing and a voice. I stopped, listening. My heart pounded as I turned towards the sound.

A plaintive voice was whispering, 'Anna… Anna?'

A man emerged from the corridor, illuminated by the lamps. His dressing gown hung open, the belt trailing on the floor to reveal rumpled pyjamas and bare feet. He wrung his frail hands as he shuffled this way and that, lost in his own house.

'Captain Richmond?'

My voice echoed. The man gave a small, startled cry and leaned on the railing of the mezzanine.

'Who are you?' he demanded, cowering.

'I'm Miss Pearlie, sir,' I said, edging closer to him. 'Your son engaged my services.'

'I'll bet he did.' The old man spoke with such venom that I paused.

'Sir?'

His expression of contempt crumpled into confusion. He looked about again and then spotted me, as if for the first time and gave a gasp, drawing closer.

'Florence! Florence, thank God. Where is your mother? I cannot find her anywhere.'

He looked so lost and frightened I didn't have the heart to correct him. I hurried forward and took one of his frail, gnarled hands in mine. It had the smooth, cold feel of paper. I fancied that if I doubled my grip, I might break his fingers. He looked up at me, watery blue eyes wide and imploring. I realised, with a shock, what Dr Richmond had meant down in the study. Captain Richmond must have been in his mid-sixties yet seemed much older.

'She is just downstairs,' I said. 'She sent me to return you to bed. It is too cold for you to be wandering and with no slippers too.'

'Good girl,' murmured Captain Richmond. I could see light through an open doorway down the corridor he had emerged from. Reasoning this would lead to his rooms, I led him back the way he had come. 'Downstairs? Checking on the maid? I told her not to, you know. Wrong, wrong… wrong time of year,' he mumbled, hazy and confused.

'So right,' I agreed, in the same calm voice I'd often used for Lucy Kemp when she woke in the night.

I found Captain Richmond's room at the end of the corridor. The bed was a large, curtained affair with a great many pillows. I eased him into it, trying not to grunt with effort. Despite his infirmity, he clung like a baby that refused to be put down and almost dragged me into the bed with him.

'Why did you do it?' he whispered. 'What were you thinking? Running away. You have ruined us, Florence. Do you understand? *Ruined us.*'

'Nonsense,' I murmured, but my mind filled with questions.

Run away? Why would Dr Richmond's sister run away? She was a grown woman, in her thirties. What could she have been running from? Was this why Olivia was not meant to speak of her?

Captain Richmond had begun to sob, mumbling through his hands like a child. He did not even seem to notice as I tucked the bedding around him, murmuring soothing words.

I stayed until the tears turned to quiet snuffling and then slipped from the room.

The house was still. Downstairs somewhere, Dr Richmond laughed. I couldn't think what he could be laughing at all alone, but I was too weary by then to concern myself with it.

I retraced my steps around the mezzanine, past the staircase and through a narrow doorway leading into a dark corridor. A dim light flickered through a partially open door at the end of the hall. I eased the door open on creaking hinges to reveal a small, L-shaped room with whitewashed walls and a double iron bed tucked into a snug nook that could only be seen if you peered around the corner of the door frame. At least the fire had been lit in here, and it was warm. I wondered who had lit it for me.

I slipped inside, shutting the door quickly to keep the heat in. My bags had been placed at the foot of the bed, and small attempts had been made to make the room cosy. There was a colourful rag rug on the floor and a small watercolour painting of violets and snow drops above the cast iron fireplace. Someone had placed a slightly worn cushion on the wooden chair in the corner, and the mirror above the chest of drawers had been polished. A clean ewer and basin waited beneath my sink stand.

I turned down the tiny lamp and undressed without it, my fingers thick and clumsy with wine and exhaustion, before falling into the cold bed sheets, made thin and soft from many days wind-whipped on the line. I had time to notice that the bed had smelled of strange soap, but I was asleep before the fire died out.

Now I lay in the dark, listening to the sound of my own breathing and the steady thump of my heart. I needed rest, but my thoughts turned to Olivia. I had hoped an older charge would mean fewer tantrums and less difficulty, but this was clearly not the case. How long had she been alone, indulged by the housekeeper? What had Mrs Hayes called her? My Dove. So familiar and odd. But it was right, wasn't it? With her beautiful pale exterior and sharp, watchful eyes, Olivia was very much like a dove.

Clearly, I reasoned, to gain Mrs Hayes' favour, I would need to gain Olivia's approval and I fancied, with a sinking feeling, that I would not get very far with anything without Mrs Hayes' help.

If I hadn't been so still in that moment, I might not have heard the sound that came then.

A soft noise outside my door, like a light footfall.

Could it be Mrs Hayes? But it was so late. There was no clock in my room, but it must have been three in the morning. I rose, my movements made silent and careful by years of tiptoeing around sleeping children, and moved to the foot of the bed to check the door.

Another footstep came from the hall. Then a sound like a sigh.

Hairs stood up on my neck.

Someone was in the corridor outside my door and I realised with sudden certainty that, whoever it was, I did not want them to come in.

Had I locked myself in? I couldn't remember. Were there keys to this room?

I froze, my eyes fixed on the door in the thick shadows. A creak of the floorboards. The sound of a breath. Time slowed. The door handle began to turn.

I stared, the sound of my own heart pounding in my ears.

The door eased open, a sliver of deeper shadow widening. From the dark recess, I felt the intent gaze of something, unseen, peering into the room.

'Who's there?' I demanded, trying to sound fierce.

The door slammed shut.

I gave a cry of fright and sagged back.

My mind raced as I thought of what to do. Had I startled an intruder? Should I raise the alarm?

A quick scrabble around at the vanity produced matches and I was able to light a candle stuck into a saucer that stood on the windowsill. I seized a vase as a makeshift weapon, pitching its contents out of the open window. With this tucked under my arm, the candle-saucer held in my free hand, I wrenched open the door and stepped out into the hall to find... nothing.

Had it been an illusion? The residue of a dream?

It's all in your mind, I thought. *Go back to bed while the sheets are still warm.*

But I couldn't. Something felt wrong. Around me, the house seemed to sigh, its walls expanding and retracting, shadows deepening and moving. I edged forward, the candlelight trembling due to my shaking hand, and tried to look for figures hiding in dark corners. But there was nothing untoward.

That is, until I reached the doorway leading to the main hallway. Then I spotted it. A sliver of flickering light playing underneath Olivia's door, dancing on the hallway carpet.

Maybe that was it. Perhaps Olivia had come looking for me.

My naked feet made no sound as I hurried up the hallway. There were voices behind the door. Olivia was speaking to someone.

'And she says that I must go to London so I hope you will—'

I reached for the handle. 'Miss Olivia?'

The door opened with no resistance. I stared.

The room was ablaze with light. Candles burned on every surface. A slight breeze through the window made the flames gutter and snap on their wicks. Olivia was on the floor at the foot of her bed, legs crossed, a set of tarot cards spread out, some face up and some face down. In front of her, leaning against a chair was a large canvas depicting a dark haired, amber-eyed woman with a small, pale child tucked on her lap. She had Dr Richmond's penetrating stare, but the way her lips curled at the corner of her mouth made me think of her mother's portrait out on the landing.

This had to be Florence Richmond's missing canvas. Had it been taken away to the top floor to be locked away after her departure from the house? How had Olivia found it?

As I fumbled for something to say, Olivia turned to look at me. Her eyes were a dark, ruby red in the light of the candles. She stared at me and then past me. I heard an odd, scuffling sound and then, as if pushed by a hidden hand, the bedroom door swung shut, plunging me into darkness.

I seized the door handle but it would not move. I had a mind to call out, to demand that she open the door but then I remembered why I had ventured out in the first place. Someone had opened *my* door. I looked down into the shadows below the mezzanine and imagined a dark figure hiding under the stairs, lying in wait as I crept down to investigate.

Suddenly, from somewhere below, came the soft sound of a giggle.

Plip...

With a gasp, I fled back to my room and wedged a chair against the door. I spent a fitful hour listening to the creaks and groans of the house around me before drifting into a confused, restless sleep.

SEVEN

Six of Cups

The sound of horses woke me just after dawn. A biting chill filled the room as I rose to close the window, a wave of nausea almost knocking me back into bed. There was a fine film of sweat on my skin and I shivered as I reached for the handle.

'Casters, hurry. I cannot miss the train.'

In the pale morning light, I saw Dr Richmond below me, bundled up against the morning cold with his collar pulled up and a thick scarf around his neck, sitting in an open dog cart.

'Right you are, sir.'

The driver, who had just finished loading his case into the back, scrambled into the driving seat. There was a jangle of metal as the horse tossed its head. A whip cracked and, moments later, the echoing crunch of hoof beats on gravel as the cart rattled off.

I pulled the window closed and turned back to the room, hands cupping my elbows.

Ridiculous really, I told myself, *to suddenly feel unsafe.*

A wail began in one of the distant rooms, an anguished, pain-filled howl. It rolled from room to room, making the hairs of my arms and neck rise. There was a shuddering pause, as of one drawing breath, and then it began again.

The chair was still against the door.

Look at this, I thought. *All this nonsense over a bad dream.*

I lifted it back to its place and stepped through the doorway onto the main corridor in time to see Olivia's door open and the housekeeper emerge, her hair undone, her eyes bleary.

'Mrs Hayes?'

She jumped as though she had been shot, her hand lifting to her chest. 'Is that the captain?' I said, before she could speak. 'I could assist you. I have helped care for dying relatives before.'

'Captain Richmond is not dying,' Mrs Hayes snapped, glancing towards the source of the noise. 'Not any time soon and probably not of what ails him, so I'm afraid you would find yourself quite useless. Even without the effects of overindulgence.'

Her keen eyes flickered to my wine-stained mouth. My cheeks burned.

'I assure you—'

'Florence! George! Olivia!' the hoarse voice called.

'Confound the man. This house will be the death of me,' sighed Mrs Hayes, grabbing her skirts and hurrying away.

I stumbled back to my room and washed, dressing with as much grace as my muddled head and shaking hands would allow.

She is right, I thought, as I struggled to button my boots. *No doubt you made a fool of yourself and Dr Richmond is on his way to London with half a mind to source your replacement.*

The servants' stairs were at the end of the corridor leading to my room and I hurried downstairs to find the kitchen cold and piled high with last night's dishes. There was no sign of Marian and the range had not been lit. I poked at it, trying to decipher how it worked.

'I wouldn't bother.' Mrs Hayes bustled in from the long corridor to my left, her boots clacking on the flagstone floor. 'It's temperamental at the best of times. Marian has a way with it but this is her day off.'

I looked up, surprised.

'But surely she has not gone so early?' I said. 'It is not quite light yet.'

'She likes to get away,' said Mrs Hayes, her tone suggesting that she found this a great failing in a maid.

'Well no matter. I thought I would make some tea,' I said.

But Mrs Hayes had already disappeared back down the corridor again. Unsure of what else to do, I followed her.

At the end of the hallway, a smaller corridor joined. It held only two doors facing each other. The one on the right stood open. I stepped forward far enough to see that it was the kitchen pantry. That meant the door opposite most likely led to the housekeeper's quarters.

There was a brief sound of shuffling and muffled cursing from the pantry before Mrs Hayes emerged again.

'No medicine left,' she said. 'I should have asked Dr Richmond. Now the captain will scream the place down and Miss Olivia will have an attack of nerves because of it.'

'Does Florence Richmond not visit her father?' I asked, tentatively. 'I am aware there is some difficulty, but it sounds like it would soothe him more to have her here than any tincture or powder.'

Mrs Hayes gave me a strange look.

'Miss Florence?' she said. 'I don't see how she could. In fact, it would be quite impossible. Are you certain you are well? You are very pale.'

'My sleep was interrupted,' I said. 'Someone tried to enter my room in the night.'

Mrs Hayes paused. 'To enter your room?' she said. 'What an idea. No doubt you were dreaming. Or something of that nature.'

I lifted my chin. 'It felt quite real,' I said.

'And did you see the person?'

'No, but I noticed Olivia was awake at that time. Possibly she was unwell during the night and was looking for me.'

Mrs Hayes gave a breathy laugh, more like a sigh than a sign of merriment.

'That would be it. Miss Olivia becomes quite anxious when there is change or disruption. It causes her to become restless in the small hours and she tends to wander. She means no harm but some do find it unnerving. My advice is to lock your door if it is likely to disturb you.'

'She sleepwalks?' I asked, puzzled.

'It's all this talk of London,' said Mrs Hayes, over her shoulder as she turned back to the pantry again. 'It has quite put the cat among the pigeons. I hope for your sake you can deliver, Miss Pearlie, or we'll never hear the end of it.'

'I do not intend to disappoint,' I said, following her into the small room lined with shelves.

'No one ever does,' said Mrs Hayes, sorting through spices. 'Doesn't stop it happening though, and we have so little to go on with you.'

She turned to look at me. In the gloom, her face was thrown into shadow so that only the grey of her eyes could be seen, glinting with speculation like those of a wolf. 'Where was your last placement again?' she asked. 'Wasn't it Kent?'

A sudden chill went down my spine. 'Yes.'

Mrs Hayes nodded and turned back to the shelves.

'Shame what happened there with that politician's son,' she said. 'By all accounts the inquest was an absolute circus. Nasty business.'

It was so cold and yet I could feel a film of sweat on my skin.

'I did not know it had been reported here,' I said, my stomach turning.

'I have some acquaintances in Kent,' said Mrs Hayes, smiling in a way that made my breath catch. 'I should give them your name. Possibly we have people in common.'

My mouth was dry.

'We were quite far out,' I said, my voice weak. 'The nearest town was at least forty minutes away and most of the servants lived in. Not much coming and going, I'm afraid.'

'What? Not even tradesmen?'

'I'm afraid I didn't have much to do with that. That was all handled by Mrs – by the housekeeper.'

Mrs Hayes nodded, as though she was thinking. 'I see.'

She stepped past me and strode back up the corridor. I followed her into the kitchen. My hands were shaking and I squeezed them, joints cracking, to make them stop.

'Makes you wonder what the governess was even doing,' said Mrs Hayes over her shoulder. 'Leaving him alone to fall in and drown like that. It's the sort of thing that would make me fret about the river, except Miss Olivia won't go near it. Thank God.'

'Does Miss Olivia not like the river?' I asked, trying to redirect the conversation.

'I should say not.' Mrs Hayes lifted a tin and examined it. 'Well, we shall have to manage between us both today as we shall be playing nurses, it seems. Captain Richmond is having one of his days and Miss Olivia has come down with a chill and I've told her she's to take the day in bed.'

'If Miss Olivia is ill, I have the recipe for a mustard plaster that is very effective,' I offered, 'and I have always sworn by rosemary liniment. I am happy to walk into Fellwick for the necessaries.'

Mrs Hayes raised her eyebrows. 'Even in this rain?'

I glanced out of the window, which was misted and grey. 'It is just a drizzle,' I said. 'If I go now, I shall miss the worst of it. What about dinner? Without Marian we shall fend for ourselves, I take it?'

'There are cold meats and cheese in the cold larder,' said Mrs Hayes. 'I would be very grateful if you could also collect a sleeping draft for Captain Richmond from the pharmacy. There is also the matter of some St. Julian's tobacco for me. We have good credit so you won't need money.'

The wail began again but this time seemed to take on a new shape and meaning. The voice had a pleading quality.

'Florence. My girl. Where are you?'

Christopher's father had sounded like that, as he knelt on the lawn, the bottom of his trousers wet and clinging, his hands slick and cold where he held Christopher's head. I had stared down at the place where Christopher's temple had been crushed inwards and thought, *where is the blood? Shouldn't there be more blood?*

A small sound escaped me but Mrs Hayes was already gone. When the cry died down, the house once again seemed as empty as a tomb.

Plip...

I turned. A fresh water droplet gathered on the edge of the tap and dripped into the sink.

Plip...

As I stared at it, I became aware of a change in the air. I sniffed. It smelled of pondweed.

A bead of sweat trickled down my back.

'Juja?'

Was that voice in my head? It was so clear, as though it had been whispered in my ear. But it couldn't have been. Christopher was gone and Lucy was far away in Kent. There was no one here who knew the nickname they'd had for me.

Another cry rocked the house but I almost did not hear it. I was too focused on the shadow that appeared on the floor, as though thrown by a small figure.

I whirled around.

There was nothing there. But a small puddle of water had somehow formed on the floor.

The walk into town calmed me and steadied my thinking, but the rain grew considerably worse. By the time I crossed under the stone archway into Fellwick, the empty streets were a glistening silver and the hem of my skirt was soaked. Pulling my coat tighter around me, I hurried towards the main street, reciting my shopping list to myself: 'Mustard powder, turmeric, rosemary liniment, sleeping draught, calf's foot, bacon, tobacco…'

It was dawning on me that I had been so eager to volunteer I had not stopped to ask where to find many of the establishments I was to visit. What had not seemed a problem in a light drizzle was becoming a pressing issue in the heavy rain, which fell in unrelenting torrents.

Through the gloom I saw a rectangle of light and hurried towards it, splashing through puddles until I stumbled across the threshold, only to collide with someone who grabbed my arm and said, 'Miss Pearlie.'

A tall blonde woman looked down at me, the front of her grey dress stained dark from where I had become entangled with her. Her dark blue eyes crinkled in a reassuring smile as she steadied me. It was the cyclist I'd seen on my first walk to Mistcoate House. The reverend's sister. What was her name? Annie? Alicia?

'Alice Byres,' she said, as though reading my mind. 'Rotten weather, isn't it?'

'Yes,' I agreed. 'I do apologise for splashing your dress.'

'It is no matter,' she said.

I tried to step away but slipped on the tiled floor, nearly falling.

'Easy now,' she said, grabbing my arm. 'Come inside.'

As she led me into the glowing interior of the shop, I looked around at well-stocked shelves full of vegetables, spices and grains.

The greengrocer, a rangy man with a sandy-coloured moustache slung beneath a rather bulbous nose, gave us a nod as Alice led me to the counter and introduced him as Samuel Duncan. His beady eyes plucked at the buttons of my coat, the dressing of my hat and the lack of polish on my shoes like a raven pecking at a corpse. Behind him, a crouched woman with a worried face moved to and fro, fetching and carrying, pausing to listen to my list of groceries, and peering at me with quick, furtive glances.

'Mr Duncan is the village verger,' explained Alice, her attempts to sound jolly somewhat undermined by the breathiness of her voice, which was almost a whisper. 'Keeps us on the straight and narrow.'

'Thank you, miss, but only our Lord and Saviour can take credit for that,' said Mr Duncan, his moustache bristling at the compliment. 'I simply do my best on this earthly plane.'

'Nonsense,' declared Alice. 'Reverend Smythe absolutely relies on you both. Mrs Duncan is practically his stand-in housekeeper now that Mrs Wood is away to Norwich.'

The woman packaging the barley gave a fearful smile.

'Pride cometh before a fall,' intoned Mr Duncan, his eyes sliding sideways to his wife. 'We are all poor sinners. You're welcome to Fellwick at any rate, miss. I hope we will be seeing you in church on Sunday? It'd do that young lady and the doctor a world of good to have a proper Christian in their midst.'

He said 'doctor' in a tone usually used for 'child murderer'.

'I'm sure, if he is concerned, I could invite Reverend Byres to visit Olivia from time to time,' I said. 'I know he takes an interest in her welfare.'

'Aye, He's a hard-working man, whatever else one might say about him,' said Mr Duncan, shaking his head and then noticing Alice stiffening next to me.

'Oh, no offence, miss,' he added quickly. 'But you can agree he's lenient. Still, he does take the time and that's important. Still, even he's better off not going anywhere near that sinful place. It was bad enough with the other girl…'

He was cut off by his wife hurrying forward, passing over the goods she had wrapped for me. As I reached out to take the bundle, I noticed her square hands with bitten nails, reddened knuckles and dried skin.

Mine will soon be like that, I thought.

'Hopefully see you again,' she told me in a tiny voice.

'I'm sure we will, Morag,' Mr Duncan replied, giving me a significant look. 'Tomorrow at Sunday Service.'

'What a dreadful man,' I said, when Alice and I were out onto the pavement, the rain pattering against Alice's umbrella above us.

'Ed mostly works with him,' said Alice. 'Reverend Smythe has migraines so Ed takes on much of the work.' She paused. 'Since you have no umbrella, shall

I accompany you on the rest of your errands? I've a little time before the church meeting.'

'That would be wonderful. I must admit, I'm unsure where to find everything.'

'What are you shopping for?' she asked.

She slipped her arm in mine and guided me down the pavement as I recited my memorised list. Alice gave a wheezing laugh.

'So much!' she said, leaning in towards my ear so she could be heard over the rain. 'Mrs Hayes is getting her money's worth.'

'I don't mind,' I said. 'It is good to be useful.'

She nodded. 'Make yourself essential. That's the way.'

It heartened me that she seemed to understand. 'I am not saying Mrs Hayes makes it easy but I feel I shall get nowhere if I do not get her on my side.'

'You have made a good start with that,' said Alice, nodding towards the packet of tobacco that sat on top of my package of purchases. She pulled on my arm, tugging me towards the butchers. When we walked in, two women stood next to the counter, deep in conversation.

'He's been spotted up at Woodley's Copse,' one was saying. 'Bob Turner tells me they've been told in Little Woodle to keep a lookout.'

'I wouldn't let my Agatha out after dark with him around,' said the other, bristling under the thickness of her coat. 'Not for any amount.'

They fell quiet as I placed my order. Alice said nothing, but I could sense her disapproval.

'What was that about?' I said when we slipped out, calf's foot and bacon safely packed away.

Alice shook her head. 'Some unfortunate, confused man is making a nuisance of himself. People think him some sort of boggart. They're calling him the Shambler.'

'That awful man Sutton was talking about him,' I said. 'He's not some local then?'

Alice shook her head. 'Probably a vagrant – poor man. But that's not interesting enough for Fellwick. It needs to be something fantastical. As with Miss Olivia.'

This proved a prescient comment as we moved on to the pharmacy, where a woman in a severe purple dress and shocking orange hair worn in waves around her face looked down her nose as she informed me that Dr Richmond must send a letter ahead before someone new was to claim credit. Her eyes flickered to Alice's stern face and, then she conceded that a trickster would not come in with the reverend's sister, and handed over the sleeping draught and liniment I'd requested.

As we left, I heard her turn to the small man behind the scales and say to someone, 'So, the witch can sicken.'

'I shall report that to Dr Richmond,' I told Alice as we stepped out into lighter rain.

'Would it help?' She gestured at the small, damp lane. 'There is no other pharmacy.'

'Probably not.' I sighed. 'Possibly Dr Richmond is right. Maybe London would be better for Miss Olivia.'

'Is that the intention?' Alice caught my expression. 'Please do not worry. I am not a gossip. Takes too much breath.'

She laughed her wheezing laugh and then began to cough. Her hands flew about her for a handkerchief before seizing the one I offered her. It was over as quickly as it had begun and in moments she was composed, apart from her laboured breathing, which settled as we stood together. She went to return the handkerchief but I shook my head.

'Keep it. Are you recovered?'

Alice nodded and, seeing my concern, squeezed my arm. 'Do not distress yourself. It only sounds serious. The cold brings it on. And I went cycling yesterday. The doctor wants me on those.' Again, she indicated the tobacco. 'I cannot abide the taste.'

'Might it help? You must be careful. My father died of weak lungs,' I told her, before realising how thoughtless it was.

I was fourteen when it happened. By then he'd been too weak to cough. The doctor said that he should lie on his side so that the corruption could drain. Mother hid in another part of the house, while Anthony disappeared behind *The Iliad*. I lay in bed at night, making bargains with God: *If Father gets better, I will become a nun. I will be nicer to Mother.*

I looked up. Alice was watching me, her lips and cheeks a deep pink from the exertion of coughing, her eyes bright. She looked like an angel on a Christmas card.

'I'm sorry,' she said.

I forced a smile. 'Silly to think of it now really. It was so long ago.'

'Long deaths are hateful,' she said. 'My mother took about six months. Nothing to do but sit and watch. Better that Father went quick.'

'Like my mother,' I said. 'Was it his heart?'

Alice gave a derisive snort. 'I don't think he had one.'

'Alice.' The voice echoed off the rain-slicked buildings.

We turned to see Ed Byres striding towards us, his long coat billowing around his knees. 'What are you doing? You said you would only be gone for ten minutes. It has been at least thirty.'

'Edward, Miss Pearlie needed my assistance.'

'I am sure she did,' he said, drawing level with us. 'But that does not excuse you being out for this long and neglecting your health. You are needed. Please return to the church.'

'Reverend Byres, it is entirely my fault,' I began.

'I do not doubt it.'

I drew back. The reverend, who had been so careful and quick to reassure yesterday, was now stern and forbidding. Alice lowered her head and squeezed my arm. I was to argue no further.

'Good afternoon, Miss Pearlie. I do hope Miss Olivia feels better,' said Alice and then began to make her way towards the church.

Byres, who had been turning to follow her, paused. 'Miss Olivia is ill?'

'A chill,' I said. 'It is of no consequence. Excuse me, Reverend.'

But he hung back. 'Miss Pearlie, a word before you go.'

I turned. 'Yes?'

Byres' mouth moved silently, as though trying to form the right words. Behind him, Alice stood, waiting for him to join her. Rain clung to my hair and I wished I had worn a hat. Still the man did not speak and, not wishing to be chastised further, I tossed my head.

'Your sister needs you,' I said and strode past him.

His hand shot out and caught at my sleeve. I started. 'Miss Olivia should not go out at night,' he whispered.

I frowned. 'I beg your pardon?'

'She is known for going out on her own after dark. You must stop this,' he said, still holding fast to my sleeve. 'Please, Miss Pearlie, I do not wish to alarm you.'

'Then please let go of me.' It was my firm schoolroom voice, which brooked no refusal.

He released me as though I had grown white hot, and looked about us. There was no one in the street, no orange-haired lady at the pharmacy window. He shifted from one foot to the other.

'The nights are getting longer and darker,' he said, calmer now. 'It would be a good idea for Miss Olivia to stay indoors after nightfall. You too. But there have been reports of a vagrant—'

'I am aware of it,' I snapped.

Byres' eyes flickered to Alice who looked away, towards the church.

'I wouldn't wish Miss Olivia to encounter him in the woods. As her companion, I thought you should know.'

'What a sage piece of advice. Not something anyone has ever said to a young woman before,' I said, tartly. 'I shall do my best, Reverend, to keep her caged.'

He tried to speak again but I was already gone, following Alice towards the church and the graveyard, leaving Byres to kick the curb and mutter under his breath.

I had planned to return to Mistcoate House by the main road but was so flustered I found myself taking the same route as yesterday, through the graveyard. My head swam as I strode through the gate into the woods. The nerve of Reverend Byres, catching hold of me and scolding me in the street as though I was an errant schoolgirl, shirking her chores! What did the man mean by it? Of course, I mused, it was obvious cold, damp weather was not good for Alice. Possibly I should have insisted she returned to the church. But she was a grown woman, wasn't she?

And it was nice, wasn't it? I thought. *It was nice to run errands with a friend.*

So nice that I had let her gad about town with me in inclement weather, even when I knew her health was poor.

My cheeks burned with sudden shame. Possibly the reverend's ire had a point. It was, I realised, deeply uncomfortable to think that Reverend Byres thought me selfish. How strange. After all, what did I care what he thought? I had only just met the man. I was still mulling this thought over when I emerged from the trees to find the house in front of me. I had been so preoccupied I had given no thought to the dangers the woods might hold.

Not just selfish but foolish as well, I thought.

Mistcoate House was silent when I returned. My clothes were soaked through, and I left the shopping on the scrubbed wooden table top and climbed the back stairs, trying not to leave a trail of damp behind me. It was so cold in my room that I considered changing my dress, but I had so few dresses, this was an extravagance. I would take off what wet things I could and light the fire to dry myself.

As I placed the kindling, something moved outside my door. I could sense the pressure on the floorboards and hear the soft scuffling of footsteps. Turning from the mirror, I listened, waiting for the knock on the door. Nothing. Just the shuffle of footsteps, like someone pacing the floor outside my room.

Crossing the room in a few quick strides, I flung open the door.

The corridor was empty. There was no sign of anyone at all. I crept up the corridor, listening. The main landing was silent and still. As I stood in the doorway leading to the mezzanine, I realised I had never really been alone in a house before. It suddenly felt as though I was the only person living within miles. As if I could scream and no one would hear me except the whispering grass and dark trees.

'Miss Pearlie?'

I jumped. Mrs Hayes stood on the opposite side of the landing, the great open expanse of the mezzanine between us, her arms full of linen.

'You are back,' she said. 'Were you able to find everything?'

'Yes,' I said, smoothing my expression. 'I will bring the pharmacy things to Olivia. I can also help prepare dinner for everyone. I see you are busy.'

'Miss Olivia is asleep, as is Captain Richmond. I doubt much dinner will be needed.' Her gaze took in my wet hair and damp clothes. 'But you are soaked. You must take care; you will become unwell.'

'Thank you. I am perfectly well.'

'All the same, you look pale. Light the fire in your room and get warm. There is more firewood, coal and kindling in the kitchen,' said Mrs Hayes.

'That is very kind of you.'

I didn't quite manage to keep the surprise from my voice, and she gave a faint smile.

'Preserving servants' health keeps a house running, Miss Pearlie. We can't have you getting ill when you've just arrived. That would be a waste of everyone's time and give me more to do. Please get warm and get some rest.' She paused. 'And do remember what I said about locking your door.'

'Thank you, Mrs Hayes,' I said. I hesitated, and then plunged ahead: 'There is one thing. I spoke to Reverend Byres in town, and he said it is very important that Olivia does not go out at night. He was quite vehement about it.'

'My goodness, what a notion.' Her tone was light but her expression had tightened. 'Miss Olivia is going nowhere at night. You may thank the Reverend for his concern, but it is unwarranted.'

'He seems to think there is some danger,' I continued, determined to tell her all. 'And that she must be careful.'

'Come now, Miss Pearlie.' Mrs Hayes' smile was suddenly not so kind. 'What dangers could there be here?'

Before I could answer, she turned and was gone, vanishing into the shadows.

EIGHT

The High Priestess

My dear Anthony,

Anthony,
 ~~I have arrived in~~
 ~~I don't~~
 ~~How could you~~
damn

It was night when I woke, curled on my bed like a child, abandoned attempts at a letter to Anthony scattered around me. The darkness peered through the window like a single, unblinking eye. The dying light of the fire bathed everything in a warm, red glow.

I had done as Mrs Hayes suggested and rested. Now, I wasn't certain what to do. Was I hungry? Tired enough to go back to bed?

I swung myself off the bed and reached over to light the lamp balanced on the windowsill. As I did, I glanced out into the shadows, and my heart stopped. A dark figure was creeping across the lawn.

The lamp flared, blinding me. When I looked again, the lawn was empty.

You are imagining things, I chided myself.

Perhaps I did need to eat. I'd had very little food today.

The back stairs were in pitch darkness as I crept down, careful not to lose my footing in the dark. In the kitchen I lit the lamps, shivering in the cold, and found myself unexpectedly angry. What kind of place went a full day with no range? Nothing had been done. The shopping still lay on the table top where I'd left it. A search of the larder revealed half a loaf of bread already stale at the edges. No sign of the meat and cheese Mrs Hayes had mentioned earlier. A few slices with butter would have to suffice.

First, I needed water.

I lifted down an earthenware jug from the shelves and began to fill it at the sink. As I did this I glanced up at the window and saw myself reflected. My hair had come loose in my sleep and I still had the creases from the bedding on my cheek.

Then I saw him.

A boy stood behind me. The deep wound in his head, slick and wet as butchered meat, glimmered in the darkness of the glass. As I watched, a droplet formed on his hair and landed on the floor.

Plip...

I tried to cry out but it came out as a sudden rush of air. The jug slipped from my hands and smashed in the ceramic hollow of the sink.

When I looked again to my reflection in the window, I was alone.

My heart beat with such force that it pained me. I placed a shaking hand over it to try and calm it but I could not breathe.

'It's not real,' I said aloud. 'It's not.'

But even as I stared at the glass, daring something to appear, a shadow moved in the darkness outside.

It was difficult to make out their features, but that was no child. Someone was out there. Despite what Mrs Hayes had said, was it possible Olivia was wandering about outside in the cold and damp?

I should go to Mrs Hayes, I knew. I should tell her what I had seen. But then I remembered her face earlier, the way she so quickly dismissed my concerns. No, there was no good in telling her. I would have to handle this on my own.

A lantern hung by the door; matches were set close by. I lit the wick. The back door opened with no need of a key, letting in the sharp smell of rain-damp leaves and cold night air.

Locked at all times, indeed. I will be speaking to Mrs Hayes about that, I thought as I stepped out, the lamp casting a swinging light before me.

I walked in the direction I'd seen the figure move, keeping my eyes peeled for a pale figure wandering across the lawn. I could hear the low roar of the river in the distance. And the sound of gravel crunching under my boots.

Soon, though, the gravel gave way to a path that led through an archway of thick, bristling hedges, bordered by boxed flower beds that overflowed with sprawling greenery, their various colours indeterminate in the dark. Beyond that, stood a round, glass-panelled structure with a steeple glass roof. As I drew closer, I saw a dim light flickering.

Someone was in there.

I hesitated. If it wasn't Olivia, it could be dangerous. I had no weapon, although I could swing the lantern and run if need be. Either way, I needed to see inside.

I edged my way forward, peering through the glass door.

Olivia sat in a rattan-grass chair amid heavy, drooping plants. She wore a long white smock, and her hair hung loose about her shoulders. As the shimmering light of the candles played on her face, she looked the picture of a heathen queen in the deepest jungles. Her eyelashes fluttered like moths as she lifted her head, her features swirling and changing in the flickering dark.

She was not alone.

Four women were perched on wooden stools encircling a rough table, piled high with candles of various sizes. Some of them I knew. There was Sally Daly, the publican's sister who I'd met the previous day. Her wild mop of blonde curls betrayed her instantly. She sat facing another woman I recognised – Mrs Lewes, the red-haired schoolmistress.

I must have made a sound because she turned suddenly and peered over her shoulder.

I tried to duck out of sight, but gravel shifted under my feet and I lost my balance, falling through the open doorway. The lamp smashed against the floorboard, sending glittering shards of glass scattering. I threw my hand out to save myself and gave a cry as a sharp pain ran through my palm.

The women cried out and leapt from their seats.

Olivia, though, did not move. She watched dispassionately as I scrambled to my feet, clutching my bleeding hand.

'A blood sacrifice is nice but not necessary,' she said.

'Oh, you poor thing,' whispered a hushed voice. A small woman bent down next to me, wrapping a handkerchief around my hand. I started.

'Mrs Duncan?' I said, staring at the grocer's wife.

The woman smiled, like a shy child, happy to be noticed. 'Nice to see you again, Miss Pearlie.' Her voice was almost inaudible.

My hand wrapped, she retreated to her seat, as though embarrassed.

When no one else spoke, I turned to my charge.

'Olivia, what is this? What is going on?'

'Sit and see.' Olivia gestured towards an empty stool between Mrs Duncan and a hard-faced woman I had never seen before dressed in black bombazine, who was introduced as Mrs Horsch.

I didn't move. 'I have no idea what this is but Mrs Hayes said that you had a cold and yet here you are, in the middle of the night, outside. I doubt Dr Richmond would approve.'

Olivia smiled in a strange, knowing way. 'I told you I knew things,' she said. 'Now you'll see. It was meant to be. Sit. Please.'

I hovered in the doorway, still clutching my stinging hand. The other women regarded me with a quiet interest, waiting to see what I would do.

'Are we going to get started?' asked Mrs Horsch, with some impatience.

'Ladies, surely—' I began.

'Just sit,' said Sally Daly.

They waited. Reluctantly, I sank down onto a stool.

'Wonderful,' said Olivia.

Her hands disappeared into the depths of her skirts and drew out a large set of cards, bent and crumpled in places with old woodcut-style images. She shuffled them expertly with long, pale fingers.

I could not deny that something was happening in that close, glass room which smelled of warm, damp earth and the heavy wax of burning candles. The soft shuffle of the cards and Olivia's murmuring seemed to lull us, so that I found my shoulders sinking and my muscles relaxing. I leaned forward to hear her speak. She was telling the story of her cards.

They were a gift from Mrs Hayes, bought during one of her trips to London. Walking through the wet backstreets of the East End, she had spied them in the window of a small curio shop, with their beautiful colours and inviting texture.

'I was so unhappy,' said Olivia, shuffling the cards with a rhythmic whispering sound. 'I hated everything. Nothing amused me or made me happy. Some nights I cried until I thought I would die. Some days I did nothing but stare at my own four walls and wonder what the point was.'

Next to me, Mrs Duncan nodded, her face fixed in a fervent expression.

So it was that, standing in the streets of Shoreditch, thinking of the unhappy little ghost she had left behind, Mrs Hayes walked right in and bought them. It was an unusual extravagance, but one Mrs Hayes was hopeful about. True, Olivia's eyesight meant that it would be difficult for her to read them, but they could be a momentary diversion. Mrs Hayes would describe them to her and guide Olivia's sensitive fingertips over the delicate ridges of the woodcut.

'But of course,' said Olivia, 'it was fate. I lifted the first one and immediately understood the image I saw – and I did *see* it. It was as clear to me as I am to you. Now, I will share the cards' secrets.'

She slapped the cards down on the table, making everyone jump, and with a graceful sweep of her hand spread the deck in a line across the table top.

'Who would like to go first?'

There was a small cough. Mrs Duncan, twisting the material of her skirt in her roughened hands, shifted to the edge of her stool and looked ready to run from the room.

'Is it being read in front of everyone?' she asked, nervously. 'I didn't know that everyone would hear. I'm sorry, but this was a mistake. I should have come alone but I… I was too…'

She rose from her seat. Sally Daly reached out to delay her but Mrs Duncan was looking about, like an animal caught in a trap.

'Let her go and please let us get on,' snapped Mrs Horsch.

'Hush,' said Mrs Lewes. 'Morag, wait.'

'You will regret it.' Olivia's voice rang out.

Mrs Duncan turned, her eyes wide. 'I will?'

Without looking, Olivia selected a card from the row in front of her and held it at arms' length for Mrs Duncan's inspection. It was upside down and depicted a man sitting on a stone throne with a crown and a staff, peering out at us in haughty disregard.

'The Emperor Reversed,' Olivia intoned. 'The crumbling of authority. A loss of power.'

The women stared at her.

'How do you know that?' demanded Mrs Horsch, her voice doubtful. 'You didn't look at it.'

Olivia kept her attention on Mrs Duncan. The shadow of the card and the flickering candlelight played on her face, warping her features.

'You want to know more,' she said. 'I know you do. I can tell you, if you stay. We can do it another way. A private way.'

No one spoke. Then Mrs Duncan eased herself back down into her seat. Olivia replaced the card.

'If everyone would like to draw a card at the same time. Hold it to you, look at it, but show no one else. Then you can give it back to me, face down. I will place the cards on the table and read each one individually. Only you will know which card is yours.'

'Is it a magic trick?' Mrs Horsch sniffed. 'Like in the circus?'

Outside, a low howling rose as the wind carved through the dark of the woods. The candles flickered, dimmed and almost went out. I gripped my knees, sending a shard of pain through my injured hand. Why did I feel so watched?

'Do not insult the spirits again,' said Olivia. 'Terrible things can happen in the dark.'

Mrs Horsch made a scoffing sound but glanced over her shoulder at the blackness of the woods all the same.

I had intended to sit back, to watch the proceedings in order to give a full report to Dr Richmond later, but Olivia, with a prescience that was unsettling, turned to me and said, 'Miss Pearlie, as the last person to sit down, you can draw the first card.'

I hesitated.

'It is good luck,' Olivia assured me.

The other women gave me meaningful looks and Mrs Lewes nudged my arm. Finally, I slid a card out from the middle of the deck with my good hand, and held it gingerly between my fingers.

'Look at it,' Olivia prompted.

I made a show of glancing at it but could not bring myself to fully turn it over. The top of the card showed the hilts of swords and rain.

Sally Daly was next, biting her lip as she stared at her card, covering it with her chapped fingers. Mrs Duncan still held her thin, patched coat, her face twisted in indecision. Seeing her discomfort, Mrs Lewes squeezed Mrs Duncan's forearm before selecting a card from the array. That seemed to seal it. Mrs Duncan let her coat fall to the floor and chose her own card, peering at it and then pressing it to her chest.

After Mrs Horsch selected hers as well, Olivia gestured with one hand and we all handed our cards back, face down. She set the rest of the pack aside and shuffled our selection without looking.

In the quiet that followed I thought I heard the crunch of gravel outside. But when I strained my ears all I could make out was the wind, the whispering of the cards and the breathing of the other women.

My wound stung. I unwrapped the handkerchief long enough to see that the slice along my palm. It was long, but not deep. When I glanced up, Olivia had placed our cards face down on the table at separate intervals. Her hands hovered over them, as though reading them through her fingertips, then she reached forward and turned one over.

'Interesting,' she said.

The card depicted a man standing over a table holding cups of spilled wine.

'This suggests a warning about those close to you. They are not what they appear to be and should be treated with caution,' said Olivia, like a doctor prescribing medication. The certainty in her voice made her seem older than her seventeen years, and more confident than I had ever seen her. The other women watched her, entranced.

She flipped the next card.

It displayed a blithe young man about to step into a pit, not seeing the wide tree above his head that could offer safe passage.

'There is the potential here,' Olivia murmured, 'for change. A whole new way of living.'

The owner of this card would have to take a leap into the unknown if they were to seize this opportunity, she explained. But they needed to be careful of unforeseen difficulties. Everything must be planned carefully.

I felt something brush my shoulder and realised it was Mrs Duncan, leaning over the table, chewing her lip.

Olivia turned over another card. She was working faster now and swayed, as though caught in the current of something larger.

The third card showed a knight on a horse, holding a golden cup aloft. A charming young man who lures others in, Olivia explained.

'He is on a mission, slowly but surely approaching, never losing sight of his target, whoever she is. He is coming for her.' Olivia looked in my direction. In the candlelight her eyes were black and deep, as though something else looked out of them. Her voice deepened. 'He will never let go.'

Plip...

Something hit the window and I recoiled, nearly falling off my stool, and had to throw out a hand and grab Mrs Lewes. She shook me off, making a 'tsk' of frustration.

'It was a branch,' she said.

'I thought I saw something,' Sally said, but she was hushed by the others as Olivia turned over the fourth card.

A beautiful young woman, draped in rich robes, sat in front of voluptuous, blooming flowers. Her expression was one of worry and uncertainty, her mouth downturned, eyes staring into the middle distance. Possibly part of this was due to the fact that she was upside down. At the sight of her, Olivia's face crumpled and she bent over the table, pressing her cheek against the wood, and reaching out to stroke the card's face, as though in sympathy.

In the gloom, I could just read the title on the card.

The High Priestess.

'There are secrets here,' Olivia murmured, her voice plaintive. 'She is so lonely. So apart from everyone. What is she thinking? She probably is trying not to think of anything. She is so troubled. She is trying to hide so much. The problem is that it is clear to everyone. They can all see. It makes her feel like a fool.'

The room seemed to grow colder. Mrs Lewes gave a shaking sigh.

A damp candle wick, consumed by flame, crackled and spat. I shifted in my seat, feeling eyes on my back, knowing no one was there.

Olivia revealed the final card.

It was a heart, fat, richly red and dripping like a ripe plum, pierced by three swords, down the length of which, blood oozed like nectar. Behind it, a storm raged. In the flickering light of the candles, the heart seemed to beat. I felt my stomach lurch.

At the sight of it, Olivia drew back and writhed in her seat like a bedlamite, pulling her knees to her chest and rocking as she keened.

'It's hateful,' she muttered. 'It hurts. I hate it.'

'She is insane,' whispered Mrs Lewes.

Olivia made a spitting noise like a cat, causing the woman to flinch back.

Then Olivia bent forward, peering at the card as though it pained her to look at it. 'I see… I see disappointment. Rage. Vengeance. Grief. Hatred. So much… so much…'

Suddenly, she lifted her head and glared at me, her face contorted with hatred and fear. 'It's yours. Isn't it?'

The women turned and stared at me. My mouth went dry.

'This is nonsense,' I gasped. I could feel myself shaking as I stood, adjusting my skirts. 'Nonsense and playacting. Olivia, this has gone far enough. Stop it *at once.*'

Olivia gave a watery giggle at the back of her throat and began to sing. 'Row, row, row your boat…'

'I'm not staying here,' said Mrs Horsch, jumping to her feet.

'Please, I need to ask her something,' said Mrs Lewes.

'Gently down the stream…'

'Olivia, stop it,' I ordered.

'Morag, get your coat,' Sally Daly said.

'Let's throw Juja overboard and listen to her—'

A gust of wind blew the door open with a *bang*. Half the candles went out.

The women screamed and there was the sound of someone toppling from a stool.

'Olivia, *enough.*' I said, sharply.

But she only giggled, covering her mouth with her hands, a child with a secret, and whispered, 'He's here…'

Her eyes rolled back in her head and she slumped forward over the table.

I hurried to her, rolling her over. She was whispering something. As I moved her, her hand shot out and began to trace the cards. The night air blew in through the open doorway, bringing a howling cold with it.

Suddenly, I was terribly frightened.

What had she summoned? What had been called?

'This is over,' I said, raising my voice. 'Everyone must leave.'

'But I haven't asked,' wailed Mrs Lewes. 'I haven't even got to ask about the children. Please, what about the children?'

'Dead.'

We turned. Olivia continued to trace the cards, not looking up.

'All dead,' she whispered to herself. 'You can see it. Here.'

She tapped the High Priestess card.

'Here.'

She tapped the pierced heart and ran her finger over the Knight of Cups, muttering to herself.

'It's everywhere. All over, here and there. What did you do? What did you do, Mrs Lewes? What did you do, do, do… The cards are full of dead children. What did you do?'

Mrs Lewes rose from her seat, her face pale.

'This is disgusting,' she said. 'It is… it is a sham meant to upset honest people. I have done nothing – *nothing* – to warrant… And for her to suggest…'

She looked around at the others who did not seem able to hold her gaze, leaving her standing alone and shaking.

'What about your husband?' asked Mrs Horsch. 'The girl's right. You can hide it but we all see it.'

'What exactly do you mean?' demanded Mrs Lewes.

'Charlie Dewbury wakes sweating in the night,' whispered Olivia. 'He hears the whacking and can't jump up because he is so, so sore.'

Mrs Lewes gave a high, hysterical laugh.

'Gossip,' she gasped. 'Gossip and rumour is all this is—'

'The headmaster said he couldn't teach the little ones anymore,' whispered Olivia, staring at the table top. Then her voice changed, becoming deep and masculine as though someone were speaking through her. 'We won't dismiss you, but Felix Murray's father is out for blood and we would recommend—'

Mrs Lewes staggered a little, her face white and pinched. 'What? What did you say? How do you know about that? Who told you?' Her voice faltered and she looked about for support, finding none. 'Children need discipline,' she said, feebly.

Olivia's head rolled round to fix Mrs Lewes with her gleaming, pale eyes.

'That's why.' Her voice dripped with ice. 'They slip away inside you before they can grow big enough for him to take the cane and whack.'

Mrs Lewes stepped forward and slapped Olivia across the face. There was a moment of utter silence. Olivia slumped back in her seat, raising a hand to her cheek and then turned to me, her eyes glistening, confused and frightened.

'Miss Pearlie?' she said. 'What is happening?'

Mrs Lewes pointed a juddering finger at Olivia, her face contorted with rage and fear. 'It's her father who attends me,' she hissed. 'How do I know he hasn't done something? It wouldn't be the first time, would it? We all know about that too, don't we? Oh yes, we all know about high and mighty Miss Florence.'

'That is enough,' I snapped, stepping forward. 'I do not know what is happening here but it stops now. Miss Olivia is clearly ill and you, Mrs Lewes, should know better.'

'I'll go to the constable. Just you see if I don't.' Mrs Lewes' voice rose to a hysterical pitch. 'She can't go around making accusations like that. She's a fraud. She's nothing more than a little fraud.'

'What is going on?'

Mrs Hayes stood in the doorway, glaring around the room. Her eyes flashed as she took in the tableau of Mrs Lewes standing over Olivia, being held back by Sally Daly. Mrs Duncan was still on the floor and Mrs Horsch had retreated to a corner, watching it all with fearful fascination.

'What are you doing here?' Mrs Hayes' voice trembled with rage. 'How dare you come here and conduct yourselves in this manner? You should be *ashamed*.'

Sally Daly made a small noise at this, a grown woman reduced to a chastised schoolgirl. Mrs Hayes ignored her.

'Leave,' she said. 'At once.'

For a moment there was nothing and then, as if suddenly awakening from a nightmare, the women began to hurry from the room. Mrs Lewes was weeping and had to be helped from the room by Sally Daly. As they went past, Mrs Hayes' hand shot out and gripped Mrs Lewes's sleeve.

'It does not need to be said,' she hissed. 'But if I hear a word of this about the village, May Lewes, I will make it so that you and your spiteful little husband are both in the workhouse before the year is out. Do you understand? I will haunt you and sow disruption better than any poltergeist.'

Mrs Lewes nodded, wide-eyed, and stumbled away. Mrs Duncan followed, gazing at Olivia as she climbed through the doorway.

'Thank you,' she murmured. 'It was so very helpful. Very informative. I hope she's alright.'

She slipped through the doors of the glass house and disappeared across the gardens into the night. I turned to the housekeeper.

'Mrs Hayes,' I began.

She held up a hand, halting my excuses.

'It is late,' she said to Olivia. 'Get inside and go to bed. Now.'

'Does she need help?' I said.

'No,' said Mrs Hayes, barely glancing at me. 'She is perfectly well. Olivia. Bed.'

Olivia obeyed, her hands moving to guide her out of the room and into the night. I watched her go, terrified that some dark figure would appear and seize her. It wasn't until I saw her disappear towards the kitchens that I allowed myself to sink down onto a stool, head buried in my hands, ignoring the warm, throbbing sting from the slice in my palm.

'Now, Miss Pearlie,' Mrs Hayes' voice came from above. 'The first thing you can do is tell me what you were doing here?'

It was a good question. Why had I first come out here? It seemed a long time ago but I could not have been in the garden any longer than an hour.

'I thought I saw someone on the lawn and I wanted to investigate. There is talk in town of a stranger.'

Mrs Hayes sighed and rubbed her eyes with her thumb and forefinger.

'Please tell me they haven't started all that fuss about the tramp again.'

'They have. And I was concerned that someone was sneaking around the house.'

'And what would you have done if they were?' asked Mrs Hayes. 'You would have had your pretty little head stoved in and a fat lot of good that would've been to us.'

I started at her harsh tone.

'Did you see what Olivia was doing in here?' I asked.

'I saw enough.'

'Then you know this is unacceptable. Surely we should tell Dr Richmond?' I said.

'Don't be ridiculous,' Mrs Hayes said. 'We mustn't bother him with this. No. Not for a little flutter in the dark. That's all it was, after all.' Her voice grew quiet and thoughtful. 'Grown women, pushing her to tell fortunes. She just wants to feel included. It all got a bit out of hand is all. That sounds more like it. Nothing to worry him with.'

'Mrs Hayes, that may be so but we cannot allow these women to encourage her in this behaviour. Also, please consider that, even if we don't tell him, he will still find out. You saw the state of Mrs Lewes. Plus, Sally Daly was here. Between the two of them, it will be the talk of the town.'

Mrs Hayes glanced up.

'Do you think?'

'We cannot keep it from him,' I said. 'Please, I am trying to do what is best for Olivia.'

She gave me a knowing smile that was not pleasant. 'Forgive me, Miss Pearlie, but I'd say you're the last person who would know what's best for Olivia. I suspect you mightn't even know what's best for yourself.'

'Excuse me?' I stared at her.

Mrs Hayes pursed her lips and then, as though reaching a decision, picked up a flickering candle to relight some of those that had extinguished. Then she sat on one of the vacated stools across from me.

'Well, let's just say you run and tell Dr Richmond like a good little girl.' She fished around in a pocket and extracted a tin of cigarettes. 'Thank you for these, by the way.' She lit one on a candle and let out a stream of fragrant blue smoke. 'What's that going to do? Put more work on your plate for one thing. He's an exacting man. Trust me, I know. He'll want to know it's been stamped out. But then he'll think, here you were, watching it and did you do any stamping? I can't imagine any of this will look good in London. Wouldn't it be easier for Olivia to be sent to some sanatorium? But then, there's no London season and no work for you. Doesn't bode well, either way.'

I sought for something to say but found nothing. She was right. Seeing this, Mrs Hayes nodded.

'Much easier,' she continued in the same even tone, 'for you to return to the house and say nothing. Pretend it never happened. It would be best for everyone – yourself included.'

'What about...' I gestured at the empty chairs.

'The ladies? They will never admit they were here. It would be too incriminating,' said Mrs Hayes. 'I will speak to Miss Olivia. She is a good actress, as I'm sure you have noticed, and will have no problem hiding what happened here tonight from her father. Luckily for you.'

'You wouldn't tell him?' I asked.

'I wouldn't worry about me,' said Mrs Hayes. 'I'm good at keeping secrets. For instance, I've not said anything about that strange little reference you've got.'

Suddenly I could hear the blood pumping in my ears.

'What do you mean?'

'Don't insult me, Miss Pearlie,' said Mrs Hayes, her steely eyes boring into mine. 'I'm no fool. You said your last post was in Kent but your reference is from that woman in Finsbury Park. There's a story there, isn't there? I wonder, if I had a little look, what I could learn? I know all sorts of people. Housekeeping's like that. I'm sure if I poked around, I could find out all there is to know about you.'

For a moment a blind panic overtook me.

I worked to try and keep my face blank. Mrs Hayes exhaled a cloud of smoke and tipped me a wink.

'I don't judge. We've all got a past. It's the present I'm worried about. We all want what's best for Miss Olivia, but George Richmond is hot-headed. If he knew about this, he might make some silly decisions that are not what's best for anyone. So, you'd be advised to not go talking or I shall be forced to go looking. Understand?'

I stared into her eyes. She gave me the long steady gaze of someone telling the whole, unadulterated truth.

Slowly, I nodded.

'Good,' said Mrs Hayes. 'Well, we'll say no more about it then. I'd get to bed if I were you. Or, if you're too awake, you could finish your letters. I'm sure Anthony, whoever he is, is anxious to hear from you.'

I found I couldn't breathe.

How much does she know?

Mrs Hayes stubbed the cigarette out on the table and stood.

'Good night, Miss Pearlie. Remember what I said about locking your door. Lord knows what could happen in the dead of night.'

I slunk past her without looking up and hurried down the path. Realising she had not followed, I turned, just in time to see her bend to the candles and begin to blow them out, one by one, until she was swallowed by the dark.

NINE

Queen of Wands

From the Journal of Julia Pearlie

May 1889
Astor House, Kent

Christopher was sent home early – delivered by one of his masters. Lucy up in the night again. Won't say why. She appears at my door at the oddest hours and won't budge until I bring her into bed with me. Up at dawn to take her back down to the nursery so I am washed, dressed and ready to frighten the life out of the maid when she arrives to light the fire.

Breakfast of toast and the last of the raspberry jam. It is Christopher's favourite so I haven't broken the news that we'll be moving to plum tomorrow. Weather that storm when it comes. He's in a foul mood as it is. His papa is not coming home as promised. Again. According to Cook, there was an issue when he arrived in Liverpool so he's delayed. She always knows these things although I've no idea how. Maids all talking about it in the kitchen, irritable at all the cleaning going to waste. Christopher wouldn't eat a thing but Lucy supremely unconcerned. No mention of the night time visit or our strange sleeping arrangement. She hates to be babied. Hates the idea that Christopher might know.

She gave him her jam. Rather sweet really.

May 1889

Astor House, Kent

Disaster. Lucy has broken her arm in a game of Pirates. She is shaken – says she intended to swing on a rope from their tree house and lost her grip. Treehouse nearly ten feet up – horrors. Doctor just set it and she was very brave but she looks so small lying in bed with all her bandages. She has some nasty bruising on her other arm. Apparently, Christopher tried to catch her as she fell. Still, she won't cry and only complains a little. Bit sharp with the maids so I have to remind her of her manners but she is so sore and miserable, I'm not too insistent. Lots of tea and sympathy. Dinner taken with her and Christopher in the nursery – beef broth, poached eggs, and a jelly. Christopher would not leave her side since the accident. I've seen them talking with their heads close together all day but when I ask her about it, even indirectly, she is like an oyster tightly pinched around a pearl. I wish Anthony and I had been like that. We were close in our way but maybe it was different because of Father and all that happened afterwards. Doctor gave her laudanum for bedtime, which seems extreme but Lucy complains of such pain that I gave her the smallest possible amount and then played with her hair until she slept. Lots of stirrings below stairs today. Think the event has put everyone out of sorts. Maids are very fractious but shrug off my questions. Maybe I need to be firmer with Lucy about how she speaks to them.

May 1889

Astor House, Kent

The mystery of the furore below stairs is resolved. Mr Kemp has arrived, to minimal fanfare and great surprise this morning. It seems that, fearing another hitch in the plans, he contacted Mrs Morris ahead of time (the housekeeper is always a dark horse) and had everything prepared. He asked about me and the children. I asked after his time in Ulster and whether the trip home had been pleasant. You could see his relief at returning to Astor House. Poor man. Being without the comfort of one's own home and a family is difficult. I had to keep a straight face in front of the children – told them breakfast was ready and we would all be scolded by Mrs Morris if they took any longer. The squeals when they saw him!

I would love to see Father again.

June 1889

Astor House, Kent

I believe Mr Kemp plans to drive me mad. Since his return, I have been sent on the oddest of errands and feel very much like Hercules with his seven tasks. Every other moment, he wants Christopher and Lucy, then he sends them away again, then he decides they must appear in the parlour for dinner guests so I must dress them, and poor Lucy still has her arm bandaged. I am not permitted to attend these audiences although Lucy re-enacts them afterwards. Sometimes Christopher joins in and impersonates Mr Kemp's secretary, a rather serious man with the strangest accent I have ever heard – almost Scottish except not quite. Apparently this is how people from Belfast sound. He usually follows Mr Kemp around, looking almost pained with efficiency. It is sometimes all I can do to not to laugh at him and I admit that I do laugh at the children's impressions of him.

Aside from that, Mr Kemp keeps to his study except when he appears in the garden. Lucy and Christopher watch for him and the minute he emerges through the French windows, they're on him like a shot. He is game for it; I will give him that. Horse rides, pirate noises and pretending to be something called a Pookha – he says it's an Irish sprite that takes the form of a black horse and drags weary travellers off across the bogs on a wild ride. I don't discourage it. If Lucy with her broken arm doesn't fear such play – what harm can there be?

June 1889

Astor House, Kent

Must make a note to speak to the doctor. Lucy is coming out in such bruises. I've told her to be careful but she shrugs and carries on regardless. How she manages this, I will never know but it is hard to properly chastise her when I never see her do it. It's as if she waits until I'm out of the room and then launches herself against something. The size of them too! They must be painful but she brushes it off whenever I bring it up. I think a word from Doctor would make her be less careless. It is all this running around during holidays with Christopher, I am sure of it, for she never seems to have them as bad as this the rest of the year. She wants to keep up with him and do what he does, I should not be surprised if that is the cause. I would ask him to set a good example but he will only goad her further. He can be like that at times.

June 1889
Astor House, Kent

So tangled I cannot say. Spoke to Mrs Morris about Lucy. She says it is my job to turn Lucy into a young lady and that I can't have the doctor come and talk to her about bruises when I should be teaching her to be less clumsy. I could spit! Went for a walk to calm myself and bumped into John, as I am now to call Mr Kemp at his insistence. Hateful thing to have to be polite when seething but I caught him with a cigar in the library. He knows Mrs Morris discourages this in the house so he asked that I not tell. I was in no mood to tell Mrs Morris anything so I promised. Interesting to see him looking so relaxed instead of his usual, somewhat formal stance. Went to leave and he said, 'Are you in a funk too?'

'Not a funk, a rage,' I said (that's how cross I was), and of course, he – kind fellow – gets everything out of me and says he'll keep an eye on it, and winks but not in a gratuitous way. Almost like we were friends.

'It's hard, raising children, knowing what the right thing is to do,' I say.

'I know. I see the work you do,' he says. 'They are lucky to have you.' And he looks at me.

He has such blue eyes, you cannot imagine.

TEN

Two of Swords

The house was slow to wake the next day, with no need to be up and dressed for Sunday Service as Mrs Hayes had made it clear the family did not attend. My sleep had been deep but troubled, especially given the sharp pain in my still-bandaged hand that throbbed whenever I thought of it. I washed and bandaged the wound again, tearing up an old petticoat for wrappings, before clumsily dressing myself. Then I set about rearranging my room.

The night before, I had found my letters spread out on my bed where I'd left them and my tin box still stowed in my case as it should be. This gave me some comfort. At least Mrs Hayes had not gone looking through all of my things. Still, our conversation had unnerved me. It was clear to me that an old, cheap lock was no barrier to a determined woman. I would need to find somewhere else to put it.

After some thought, I'd decided to use the writing desk to wedge the case shut against the wall. At the very least, the noise would raise the alarm that someone was attempting to access my things.

But as I moved it, the heel of my foot went through a gap in the floor, knocking a loose floorboard to one side, revealing a space just big enough to hide the box. With the floorboard back in place, it was impossible to tell it had ever been moved. I moved the wash stand a little so that it stood over the boards, casting the whole corner in shadow.

It was a good arrangement. Mrs Hayes would have to look very hard indeed to find anything incriminating.

The kitchen clock read nine when I descended the stairs and found Olivia standing in her nightclothes at the table, looking cross.

'Where is everyone?' she said. 'Marian is not here yet and I cannot find Mrs Hayes. There is no fire and I am hungry.'

There was no sign of the possessed young woman from the night before, only a petulant girl who glanced about, as if expecting breakfast to appear out of thin air.

'Possibly Marian is running late.' I turned to the cold fire with a sigh. 'This is silly. The range cannot be difficult. Would you like toast?'

'Please,' she said, visibly relieved.

I bent down to the range, pulling open the grate to examine it.

Where could Mrs Hayes be? I wondered if she had gone to smooth things over in the village, but then what of Marian? What kind of house had a maid whose movements were so erratic? I said none of this as I laid the fire in the range, aware of Olivia waiting behind me.

'Do you want tea?' I asked, as flames began to lick at the kindling.

Olivia was sitting at the table, scraping long lines off the butter with a knife.

'The leaves are in the tin on the side,' she said.

I left the fire to build and pried the lid off the indicated tin, releasing a musty, aromatic scent.

'The damp has got into this,' I said, shifting the mulchy residue through my fingers.

'No, Mrs Hayes has Marian drain them and keep them there.'

This shocked me. 'You reuse your tea? At Mistcoate? Why?'

Olivia shrugged. Clearly the house's finances were not something she bothered herself with.

Cold fires, a locked-up house, one maid and reused tea leaves, I thought, setting the tin closer to the fire to dry out the leaves. *No wonder her father wants her married off. Good God, I'll be lucky to get any money out of this at all.*

'Did you sleep well?' I asked, in a voice that was much steadier than I felt.

'Fine,' said Olivia, not looking up from the butter. 'What were you doing this morning? I thought I heard something from your room.'

'I was stowing my case,' I said, turning away lest she should read something in my face. 'Now that I am settled here.'

'Oh,' said Olivia. Her gaze landed on my bandaged hand and I thought she would ask how I managed to stow anything or even just ask if it hurt. But all she said was, 'Can I have jam as well?'

I strode into the pantry, my jaw set so tightly it ached, and fetched the bread wrapped in wax paper as well as a jar of home preserve. Olivia did not look up when I set everything down on the table. Her indifference rankled me.

'I just asked you how you slept. It is polite to return the question,' I said. I tried to slice the bread but it was painful to curl my palm around the knife. I slid it and the loaf across the table to her. 'And you can cut this since I am sore after that nonsense last night. If you can use a fish knife, you can use this.'

Taking the knife, she said, in a feigned show of propriety, 'Excuse me, my lady Pearlie, but might I inquire if you also slept well?'

It was as though the night before had never happened, that it had been a dream concocted in my head. It made me feel insane.

'No,' I said, shortly, watching her hack at the bread. 'I did not. I was very much disturbed.'

'By your hand?'

'Among other things, yes. I have half a mind to tell your father and give my resignation the moment he returns. I cannot prepare a girl for London who is playacting in the garden in the middle of the night.'

I regretted it the moment I spoke the thought aloud but, at the mention of London, the smile died on Olivia's face. She said nothing as I handed her the jam and watched her spread it, not even to point out that she had wanted toast or to ask about her tea. Instead she took the plate and began to eat without comment, eyes downward. For a moment there was nothing but the ticking of the clock. Then Olivia broke the silence.

'Well, I did say I could do it,' she said.

I gave a sigh and allowed myself to sink into the chair opposite her.

'You did,' I said. 'Do you often upset people with your readings?'

Olivia thought for a moment before answering.

'Not always,' she said. 'Mrs Lewes was angry before. I could feel it when she walked in. She's not been sleeping. It's the babies. She sees them when she sleeps and then she wakes up hearing them. They hang around her, crying, and she can't pick them up.'

'And where did you hear that from? We need to talk about how you know these things. Have you been listening at your father's door?'

Olivia gave me a look of disgust.

'Papa doesn't treat anyone at the house,' she said. 'No one will come. I told you. I *see* these things.'

'That is impossible, Miss Olivia,' I said, although I wasn't sure how much I believed this myself. 'No one can see such things.'

'*I* do,' she insisted. 'Four babies. One is from when she was young, before Mr Lewes. It didn't take. She was grateful then but now she wonders if she brought it on. Cursed herself by being happy about it.'

'Did she?' I said and then wondered why I had asked. 'Actually, I do not wish to know. This cannot continue. Whatever this is. What will you do if she asks for her money back?'

'Oh, I don't charge,' said Olivia. 'Epidemius St. Joseph says that it muddies things.'

'And how do you know that? Come to think of it, how did you ever hear of Epidemius St. Joseph?'

'I have ways,' said Olivia, looking smug. '*And* he says you should see the truth, not what people pay you to see.'

I raised an eyebrow. 'Don't be naïve. How does he make money to live then?'

She flipped her hair off her shoulder. 'Mrs Hayes says that talent attracts money.'

Before I could respond to this, there was a clattering at the back door and Marian entered, flushed with the cold, her arms full of packages. She dumped them onto the table, shrugged off her shabby coat and hung it on a nail by the door then stopped short at the sight of us.

'Miss!' she said. 'I'm sorry I'm late. It's been the strangest morning.'

'Have you brought the Saturday post?' asked Olivia.

'Oh, yes Miss Olivia. There's one there for you.' Marian shot me a nervous glance. 'Is Mrs Hayes here?'

I shook my head and saw the relief in her face.

Olivia snatched up the large envelope, tearing at it to produce a newsletter.

It was printed on cheap paper, the kind where the ink rubs off on your fingers in greasy black smears. The title read *The Inner Eye,* and beneath it was a picture of a young man with a shock of long, white-blond hair curling about his shoulders. The headline said: *Speaking with Ghosts: Epidemius St Joseph, Whitechapel's White*

Wizard.

'It's him,' Olivia whispered, her hands running over the picture. 'I can feel it. Read it for me.'

She thrust the newsletter towards me but I made no move to take it.

'This is absurd,' I said. 'I am not going to encourage this.'

'Fine. Marian?' When the maid hesitated, Olivia made an impatient gesture. 'Come, it shouldn't be too difficult. They don't use big words to save space on the page,' she said, unkindly.

Marian's face flushed a deep, wine red under Olivia's attention, which was as cold and unblinking as a snake. Fuming at her cruelty, I snatched the newsletter up and flicked through to the page featuring pictures of crowded theatre halls, where people hung over the side of the balcony to watch St Joseph sitting at a table on stage.

'Would you mind making tea, Marian?' I said, as I skimmed the article. 'I shall need it once I am done with this nonsense.'

As Marian turned towards the kettle, I began to read.

'*Epidemius St. Joseph appeared on Saturday last to a packed house at The Britannia in Hoxton. The celebrated Whitechapel Wizard delighted, amazed, and shocked the crowds as he called forth departed spirits and read the minds of the audience. Numbers attending were at an all-time high, despite attempts by the local council to ban him from performing. It certainly helps, this reporter muses, that St Joseph has the support of the London theatres, who enjoy the income from the crowds St Joseph and his compatriots attract. But what of the assertion made by officials and church leaders that Spiritualism is merely a game played by fraudsters and those willing to trick the gullible?*

'"*There are those out there,*" *St Joseph admits.* "*But a true medium is not made; they are born and when they appear, it is a sin to deny them their art. Make no mistake, what I offer is real and that is what people pay to see.*"'

Olivia gave a shiver of delight and wrapped her arms around herself in a tight embrace.

'You see?' she said. 'It is a sin, he says, not to share my gift.'

'I don't think Dr Richmond would agree.' I tossed the newsletter onto the table. 'Or Mrs Lewes. From what I have seen, you could cause serious harm.'

'I *don't*,' said Olivia. 'I help. Ask Mrs Hayes. She'll tell you. When she first came here, you could hear her crying at night—'

'Olivia, that is Mrs Hayes' business.' I glanced around at Marian, who had turned her back as she worked.

'But I helped her,' Olivia insisted.

I held up my bandaged hand. 'Just because these things seem obvious to you, it doesn't mean they are any of your business and it certainly does not mean that you are allowed to share them with other people.'

'You're just saying that because you're scared of what happened before.' Olivia sulked. 'That is why you want to stop me.'

'That is ridiculous,' I snapped. 'What do you think I'm afraid of?'

'You're afraid of what happened with Lucy and—'

I slapped the table hard with my good hand, making Marian jump.

'I do not want to hear another word,' I said, rising from my seat and punching the air with my finger. 'This is not a game. There are people out there who have suffered, who are in pain and your intention is to cheat and fool them.'

Olivia leaned back in her seat, her eyes wide with reproach.

'I *don't*. I will help them,' she said. 'Ask Mrs Hayes. You ask her.'

A ragged, enraged voice rang out across the lawns: 'Richmond? George Richmond? You come out here!'

'What in God's name?' I said, looking up.

Marian turned, her eyes wide. 'Fred Duncan,' she breathed.

I was confused. 'Who? The greengrocer?'

Marian set down the cup she held and hurried forward, speaking in a low, rapid tone.

'It's what I was saying when I came in, miss. Reverend Smythe didn't take the service today, which was odd but everyone thought it was probably his headaches, which he gets these days, and that was fine because Reverend Byres was doing it and he's quicker and more interesting anyway, only he usually has Mr Duncan helping him. But today there was no Mr Duncan. Nor Mrs Duncan. And I thought maybe Reverend Smythe was very ill, only there was no Mrs Lewes either. Just Mr Lewes looking all sore at something, and *that* doesn't bode well for the young ones tomorrow.'

'Marian, you're going too fast. What exactly has happened?' I said.

'I'm trying to tell you, miss.' Marian twisted her apron. 'We were walking past the Duncans' place on our way to the church and there was such shouting, Ma thought we'd have to call the constable. Mrs Duncan was saying something was ordained by God because miss Olivia foresaw it and she didn't need to answer to Fred Duncan or anyone.'

Olivia did not move. I could see her from the corner of my eye, gripping her newsletter in pale, shaking hands.

'Richmond!'

The voice was louder now. Gravel crunched outside. He was coming towards the house. I rose to lock the back door as Marian kept talking.

'Then we saw Sally Daly after the service and Ma asked about Mr and Mrs Duncan and Sally got the funniest look on her face. She said she wouldn't be surprised if Mrs Duncan and Reverend Smythe had been up to no good; that she went to deliver something for the harvest festival a few weeks ago and walked in on Mrs Duncan caught up in Reverend Smythe's cassock.'

My hand flew to my mouth. So, Sally Daly had thrown Mrs Duncan to the town-gossips. What was it Olivia had said last night? *Be careful of someone close to you, they are not who you think they are.*

Olivia's chair scraped back and she fled from the room.

'Olivia!' I called after her, but Marian put her hand on my sleeve.

'Leave her, miss.'

The maid moved over to the back door and took the key from my shaking hands.

'I'll deal with this, if you go tell Mrs Hayes,' she said.

'But she is not here.'

Marian muttered something under her breath and wedged a chair under the door handle.

'Marian, perhaps this is unnecessary,' I said. 'Whatever is happening, Mr Duncan is not going to offer us violence. I am certain that with the right approach, he will be meek as a lamb.'

'Are you, miss?' Marian didn't hide her disbelief, and I deflated in the face of her scepticism.

'No,' I conceded. 'But I will not hide from the greengrocer. You go and check on Captain Richmond. I will see about this.'

Fred Duncan was almost at the top of the driveway by the time I had made my way through the house to the front porch. His steps were unsteady and he had bandaged his forehead in the haphazard manner of someone unable to see what they were doing, one eye covered in a way that would have been comic were it not for the force of his rage, which was palpable even from the top step. His waistcoat hung open, flapping in the breeze that shook the trees behind him and he carried a half full brandy bottle in one hand.

God help me, I thought. *He's drunk as well.*

'Mr Duncan,' I said. 'Good morning.'

'Richmond!' he shouted at the house behind me. 'Hiding behind a woman again, I see.' He focussed on me and slurred, 'You tell him to come out here.'

'If you mean Dr Richmond, he is not here,' I said, evenly. 'He is in London and will not be back until tomorrow. Can I help you?'

'You've done enough.' the greengrocer said, eyes glinting with malice. 'You and that harpy charlatan in there. I knew it the moment I first saw you. Mild as milk on the surface but you're no better than the rest of them.'

He staggered forward, his face contorted in an ugly leer. 'I always knew Morag was a weak, foolish woman. I thought I could guide her, keep her on the Lord's path but she allowed herself to be taken in by that witch in there, to be lured into that viper's nest.'

He lunged at me with sudden speed. I stumbled back but he snatched my dress, pulling me down towards him into the fug of brandy.

'We should have known after the older one – that Florence girl,' he said. 'Her with her looks and her money but she was no better'n Morag. She was at it as well. You all are.' He gave a savage, mirthless laugh. 'Oh yes. She thought she was a cut above and look what happened to her – God punishes, oh yes. God punished Florence Richmond and he will punish Morag for walking into this den of whores, witches and ghosts. It corrupted her. But no more. The Bible is clear. Exodus 22:18. "Thou shalt not suffer a witch to live".'

He gripped my arm, squeezing so that I almost cried out.

'For God's sake, stop!' I said, struggling.

'Or what?' he hissed, the sour smell of old brandy and venom overwhelming me. 'What will you do? Call the constable? Report me to the reverend? You can scream all you like but there's no one here to help you.'

'And why would I need help?' I said. My voice was too high, too frightened.

'What exactly are you going to do, Mr Duncan?'

In the distance, the trees whispered in the wind. The breeze was cold but that was not why I was trembling. Fred Duncan stared at me, his watery grey eye pale and distant as his jaw worked.

'God's work,' he said and smiled. 'He has spoken to me and will act through me. He came to me. She didn't foresee that. Adulterers and witches cannot understand God's power. She meant to kill me, I'm sure, but instead she sent me into the darkness and allowed Him to come to me.'

He threw me from him, pushing me away from the house and onto the gravel. I threw out my injured hand to stop myself and whimpered as the wound reopened.

'Nothing good in this place anymore,' Fred Duncan muttered. 'There's only ungodliness and degeneracy here.'

He was unwrapping the bandage from around his head and stuffing it into the neck of the brandy bottle. His head had a large welt along the back and a swollen cut where he had been hit with something heavy.

'Vengeance is mine, I will repay, sayeth the Lord,' he muttered, tucking the bottle under his arm and fishing around in his pockets until he produced a small book of matches.

'Oh my God. No!'

My legs tangled in my skirts as I launched myself at the swaying grocer.

'Mr Duncan, please stop. This is not the way.'

'This is the only way!' he roared, a hand at my throat.

'Olivia! Marian!' I shrieked, trying to grab the bottle. 'Get out! Help! Police!'

A voice rang out over the lawns. 'Fred!'

I turned to see Ed Byres racing up the driveway on his bicycle. Fred Duncan pushed me from him again and I raked my nails across his mouth and neck as I fell. Furious, he turned and spat at me lying on the ground. That was when Byres struck him. The brandy bottle smashed on the driveway. Both men landed on the gravel with a heavy thump but Byres was up first.

'I am sorry, Mr Duncan.'

Before Fred Duncan could move or protest, Byres landed an audible blow on the greengrocer. The man slumped and was still.

We watched him, Byres shaking out his hand and wincing, until Mr Duncan gave a loud, resounding snore. Byres nodded to himself and turned to me.

'Apologies,' he said. 'Are you hurt, Miss Pearlie?'

I allowed the reverend to pull me to my feet, both of us covered in dust and fighting for breath. I could see a bruise forming on his cheek.

'Are you harmed?' he asked.

I was too shaken to feel pain. 'I don't know. Only my hand, I think.'

Blood was seeping through the bandages, staining them.

'You shall need to have that cleaned,' said Byres, turning my hand over in his to examine it. His fingers were rough and calloused, like a labourer's. So different from Dr Richmond's hands.

A window opened overhead and Marian leaned out.

'Are you alright, miss?' she called.

'I shall need to go for the constable,' said Byres.

'Please don't go,' I pleaded, convulsively gripping his sleeve. 'What if he wakes up? Mrs Hayes is out, and there is only us here.'

'Still?' He looked puzzled. 'I passed her in the woods on my way here. All the same, we must send someone.'

'Marian?' I asked, turning to look up at the maid. 'Marian, Miss Olivia can deal with her grandfather while you go to town for help.'

Marian nodded and disappeared. I realised Byres still had my injured hand in his. As if reading my thoughts, he gently released me.

'I am sorry I could not get here sooner,' he said. 'I left as soon as I realised where he had gone.'

I shook my head.

'No, no thank you,' I said. 'Truly. I dread to think what he might have done if you hadn't come. Did Mrs Duncan do that to his head?'

Byres sighed and nodded, running a hand through his hair. 'I am afraid so. The kitchen skillet I believe. We are still looking for her but it is complicated.'

'Is Reverend Smythe also missing?' I guessed.

Byres started.

'How on earth did you know that?'

I relayed what Marian had told me. Byres' face grew darker and more drawn as I spoke.

'That must be what Smythe meant when he said he was ill. All those times he had me meet with Duncan, getting us both out of the way... I am such a *fool*.'

His hair had fallen over his forehead again. He looked so upset with himself that I found myself fighting the urge to reach up and sweep it away.

'Miss.' Marian reappeared at the window, pale and frightened. 'It's Miss Olivia. I've searched the whole house but there's no sign. She's gone.'

Byres pointed into the distance. 'Look there.'

I turned in time to see a white figure pause at the boundary of the woods, listening.

'Olivia!'

The figure bolted into the trees.

'I will go,' said Byres.

'No. You must be here if Mr Duncan wakes up. Marian,' I called up at her. 'Go quickly and get the constable. I'll find Olivia.'

Without waiting for a response, I lifted my skirts and ran into the forest.

ELEVEN

The Moon

Sound fell away as I broke through the tree line and saw the vanishing figure of Olivia ahead.

She slipped through the trees like a ghost. Bracken did not impede her, she did not slide over wet, dead leaves as I did. Every so often she stopped, her hands outstretched to touch a tree, her head extended forward, turning her face to find the light through the gaps in the leaves. Then she would race off again. I trailed behind, slower now, pulling my skirts free from branches, stumbling over tree roots.

The further we went into the trees, the more I worried about whether we would find our way out. The walk from Fellwick had not given the full impression of the forest's depth, but now I could see that someone could wander in here and become quite lost.

I followed her along the dirt path until the rush of the river drowned out the whispering of the trees. But then we turned the corner in the track and found ourselves faced with a sudden, sharp incline, studded with tree roots and rocks. The only way forwards was to scale up it.

I cupped my hands around my mouth. 'Olivia! Come back please. It's too dangerous.'

But she just reached down to tuck her skirt into the top of her boots and began to climb, gripping an exposed tree root and using rocks as footholds, feeling her way forward with her hands. When she disappeared from sight, I had no choice but to follow.

It was difficult to climb quickly. It was not a surprise, therefore, when I hauled myself over the top and found myself alone, lost and panting.

'Damn it all,' I whispered.

I was on a large land shelf overlooking the raging river below. The ledge itself was flat and featureless apart from a small wooden shack, which stood alone, looking sullen and resigned to intrusion. Its walls had grown green with mould and, other than a single window, it had no entry besides the partially open door.

The wind shook the trees, cold raindrops pattering. The view was calm, lush and green.

Something moved inside the hut.

It had to be Olivia, surely. But then I thought of a shambling man, a walking ghoul, appearing in the door.

'Hello?' I said.

The movement stopped.

Was he waiting inside, this stranger, waiting to see if I made suitable prey? But if he was in there, where was Olivia? She could not have disappeared so entirely.

'Miss Olivia?' I called, edging forward. 'Come out please. So we can talk.'

The door, which had stood ajar, began to close slowly, as if pushed with great difficulty from the inside. The rusted hinges and swollen wood made the action difficult. I hurried forward, trying to jam my foot into the gap.

'Come out now,' I insisted.

'No!' The voice was hers.

I pushed the door hard. It hit against something with a groaning of metal on wood, and would move no further. I moved over to peer through the single window. Olivia had blocked the door with a small, metal bed frame.

'This is ridiculous,' I said. 'You cannot stay here all night.'

'Why shouldn't I?' she demanded.

'Well,' I said, 'for one thing you will catch a chill. Mrs Hayes said you were ill already, although I doubt that now. And, if I am honest, I do not like the thought of it. I would worry.'

There was a pause. 'Are you going to tell Papa?'

I chewed my lip. I hadn't had time to consider that yet.

'I should,' I said. 'I want to.'

'Then why don't you?' came the petulant reply.

'I don't think it would help,' I said. 'The damage is done, I'm afraid.'

'It is not my fault,' Olivia insisted. 'I just read the cards. I never told Mrs Duncan to do those things.'

A fat, cold raindrop hit my forehead and ran down the bridge of my nose. More rain pattered on the leaves overhead.

'I know,' I said. 'And I will tell Dr Richmond that, but I can't leave you here or he will probably sack me and then you will have no one to tell the truth.'

'He will blame me anyway. He will lock me away and leave for London and forget me again.'

I leaned against the wall of the hut, trying to shield myself from the rain.

'He will not,' I said. 'Of course he will not. Isn't he paying me to prepare you for London? Why would he do that if he was going to abandon you? Please, Miss Olivia, it is quite wet out here. Open the door.'

'You will tell him. He will threaten to sack you and you will tell him.'

'This is silly,' I said. 'I am not having this conversation in the rain through a door. I am coming in.'

'No!'

I heard Olivia throw herself onto the bed but she was too slow. I had shoved my shoulder against the wood and the door, weakened by damp and rot, buckled and pushed the bed frame backwards. This left a gap just wide enough for me to squeeze through, the dirt of the shack sticking to my dress.

I was obliged to climb over the foot of the bed and the odour of damp and rot rose to meet me as my foot sank into the horsehair mattress.

The dank room held signs of other visitors: discarded bedding speckled with autumn leaves; a snapped shoelace. Mysterious messages – 'A + W' and 'I see you' – had been scratched in furious, large letters on one wall. Long clusters of ivy had trickled through a hole in the roof, brushing the top of an old chest, which bled sinister patches of blood red rust onto the floor.

Olivia sat on the bed, knees pulled up to her chest. There was a thin rime of sweat on her forehead and her eyelashes glistened. She was still in her nightdress but, in addition to her boots, she had fastened a large, hooded garment around her; neither a coat nor a cloak.

'How did you find this place?' I asked.

'I come out for walks,' said Olivia, sniffing. 'When Mrs Hayes is busy or at night when everyone is asleep. It's meant to be a secret place.'

'Secret places are not always safe. And they make it hard to find you.'

'That's the point.' She squeezed her finger, making the joints crack.

'Is that why you came here?' I said. 'To hide?'

Olivia shrugged but her mouth drooped at the corners. I placed my hand over hers. She twitched as if to retract it but didn't.

'Everything will be fine, you know. Mrs Hayes and I have already agreed that Dr Richmond does not need to know about this. If you come back now, we can have everything settled. But – and I mean this, Olivia – you must stop these readings. I am not certain it is safe.'

'But Epidemius St. Joseph—'

'He is not working within a small community where he must live with the consequences of his readings,' I reminded her sharply. 'Plus, we have London to prepare for.'

Olivia bit her lip.

'I have been doing readings about it.'

'Oh?' I said, a little exasperated. 'What do they say?'

She began to cry in earnest, shoulders shaking like a child.

'You see?' I told her. 'This all just upsets you.'

'It will be a disaster,' she wailed. 'I will ruin it. The cards say it.'

'Nonsense,' I said. 'How can they know that?'

'They know,' she sobbed. 'They told me about the boy I saw.'

'I am not terribly sure that you *did* see a boy,' I said. 'I think it is more likely that you have been snooping.'

'No.' Olivia shook her head. 'I did a reading of you the first night. Look.'

She drew the pack of cards from last night out from the folds of her clothing. I shrank back but Olivia did not notice. She started to shuffle the desk, selecting cards and dropping them onto the bed.

'You see? The Moon card. Fear, uncertainty, deception. I also drew the Nine of Swords, the Two of Swords, the High Priestess.'

'You did a reading of me? Without my knowledge?'

Olivia stopped, caught off guard by the edge to my voice.

'You would not give answers,' she said, uncertainly. 'You know all these things about me and I know nothing about you.'

'I do not have to tell you things that are none of your business,' I said. 'And you didn't ask in the first place. Please tell me that you did not repeat any of this to Mrs Hayes.'

Olivia did not reply. She shuffled the cards and shoved them back into her pocket.

'This is exactly why it all needs to stop.' The floorboards creaked as I stood. 'Come. We are going straight back to Mistcoate and you are telling Mrs Hayes that any nonsense you have passed on is just that.'

'It is not nonsense. You flinch whenever I mention him.'

'There is no *him*.'

'There is,' she insisted. 'I see him.'

Her eyes, always vague and directed elsewhere, now focused on a point just over my shoulder.

'He is here now,' she whispered.

A coldness spread over my back, as though someone was reaching towards me. I twisted to look, but no spectral form of Christopher Kemp awaited me.

'You see?' Olivia's face glowed in triumph. 'You looked. There *is* a boy.'

I sank down onto the bed. For a moment neither of us moved but sat listening to the rain beating against the roof.

'Who is he?' said Olivia.

She was regarding me from under her dust-coloured eyelashes. I was too exhausted to hide my distress. My hand throbbed; my head ached. I felt as though, should I go to bed, I would sleep for a week. And to think, I had arrived just days ago expecting nothing more than awkward dancing lessons and disagreements over dresses.

'You tell me. You see all these things.' I pressed my fingertips to my eyes, trying to ease the sting of fatigue.

'He won't explain it,' said Olivia. 'He is sad and so angry. Like when you stub your toe and then want to destroy the table.'

I gave a dark, breathless laugh. 'Yes, that sounds about right.'

'He keeps on calling you "Juja." But I don't know if you can hear.'

Juja. They had both called me that. Christopher had a way of saying it that made it sound like his own private joke. Lucy said it the way other children would say 'Mama'. No one had had a pet name for me since Father. And of course, later,

John.

'Who is he?' asked Olivia again.

She was looking straight at me now, all vagueness gone. It was disconcerting but also, somehow comforting. Her face was calm and open, with no judgement, only curiosity. For the first time, it seemed as though she was interested in who I was.

'His name is Christopher,' I heard myself say. 'He is – *was* twelve. He drowned.'

'So did Florence.'

I almost missed it over the noise of the rain. I drew in a breath, but Olivia had turned her face towards the light of the window, lost in her own thoughts. I envied that. I did not trust myself to think of Christopher. I dared not think of him now in case she somehow managed to syphon the ideas out of my head.

'Your father said she ran away,' I said. 'I thought she had married without his permission.'

Olivia shook her head.

'Florence never married. She was going to but then he said he didn't want to. Father was so angry and she… I couldn't talk to her about it. Then she…'

She broke off, her eyes red-rimmed and shining. I thought of my first night at Mistcoate, when I found Olivia in front of the portrait.

'Is that why you speak to her picture now?'

'Not just her picture. She speaks to me. She sends me little things. Sometimes I think I can see her, wherever there is deep water.'

In my mind's eye, I saw Florence Richmond submerged in a bathtub, her dark hair billowing, lips parted like a sleeping fairy tale princess. Then her lids snapped open, revealing white orbs. I shuddered.

'How did Christopher drown?' Olivia had turned so that she was sitting a little closer to me, her legs hanging off the bed.

I shook my head to rid myself of the mournful image of Florence.

'He went out on a boat that he should not have. There was a big pond on the estate and he fell in and hit his head,' I said. 'He was forever doing that sort of thing. Stupid, really.'

'Florence fell in the river,' said Olivia. 'Papa wasn't here. He's never here. It happened not far from here, I think. After that, all I had was Mrs Hayes. Until the cards.'

A memory flickered in my mind. 'What about Emily Towers?' I asked, trying to keep my voice light. 'I hear you were friends with her for a time?'

Olivia shook her head irritably.

'Emily was a fool,' she said. 'She did not understand what we were doing.'

'And what was that?'

Olivia turned to me. Her mouth twisted into a small, knowing smile. 'Practising.'

Something hit the side of the hut.

Olivia jumped.

'It will be a branch,' I said. 'The wind is picking up.'

Another thump resounded against the flimsy wooden walls. Then came a voice, muttering something I could not quite make out.

I remembered the talk of the man roaming the wilds, violent and aimless. What was it Bert Sutton had said?

Terrible one for the ladies, is the Shambler.

Motioning for Olivia to stay quiet, I eased myself up off the bed, but the rusted springs gave a whine. The shuffling outside stopped.

'*Julia…*' Olivia gasped.

A shadow fell across the gap in the door. Suddenly I was aware of a smell: the pungent musk of unwashed clothes and the sour tang of old sweat and rust. I gripped Olivia's shoulder, pulling her off the bed. She stared at the door, eyes wide.

There was a throaty chuckle and the door started to ease open. I shoved the head of the bed with all my strength against the doorway, ramming it shut. From outside, we heard muffled swearing and the thud of something heavy hitting the door.

'Push with me,' I commanded Olivia.

But she was frozen, staring unseeing in the direction of the door. Another blow rocked it and a piece of wood chipped off. The bed began to creak backwards, shoving me against Olivia, who gave a high, wild scream.

The creature outside let out a snarl of laughter and shoved harder on the door, forcing me back.

'Come out, come out, Winnie…' it crooned.

'Get away, damn you!' I shouted and pushed the bed again.

The pressure on the door stopped. I waited, ready for another attack but nothing came. Suddenly remembering the hole where the ivy climbed, I looked up, half expecting to see a yellow, staring eye looking down on me like something from a penny dreadful but there was nothing.

'Whoever you are,' I shouted, 'Reverend Byres is set to follow us and should be here soon. Get away!'

There was no response. Only the sound of twigs crackling and the rain beating on the roof.

'Hold this,' I said to Olivia, motioning to the bedstead. 'Be ready to push.'

She gripped the iron frame so hard her knuckles looked ready to break through her skin. I crept over to the window and looked out. Nothing. No sign of anyone.

I turned to her. 'Did you see who it was?'

Olivia shook her head.

'Whoever it is, he's gone now,' I said. 'We'll wait another minute.'

'He will come back,' she said. 'Please, let's go now.'

'We should wait for help,' I said. 'We will get lost.'

She gripped my hand. 'I won't. I know the way. Please, Julia, let's go.'

I glanced from Olivia, trembling and terrified, to the empty ledge outside.

'I will go first,' I said.

Cautiously, I eased the door open and peered out. Rain fell in great grey sheets across the stony ledge. We were completely alone. Whoever had been out there earlier, there was no one now.

I turned to Olivia. 'Stay close,' I said. 'We must be careful.'

There was no weapon I could see in the hut. If it came to it, we would need to run. Olivia clung to me as we stepped out into the storm.

'Can you see anything?' said Olivia.

'No,' I said. 'I think we—'

A great roar went up from the trees to our right, causing birds to take flight in a panicked *whoosh*. Olivia gave a piercing cry and bolted.

'Olivia!'

I reached out to grab her but she slipped past me. I called out again but the rain deadened the sound, filling the air with the rush of water so that Olivia must no longer have been able to hear the river.

'Olivia, that's the *wrong way*.'

She was running too fast on the slick ground. It all happened so quickly; I almost missed it.

As if sensing she was too near the edge, she turned back, but the rock under her foot skidded out of the mud. She lost her balance and began to slide down the slope towards the racing river.

As her feet slid out from under her, she screamed. 'Julia!'

But I was already there, throwing out my arm to catch her. Her flailing hand grabbed my injured palm and squeezed. I cried out from pain, but held tight and pulled her back.

More of the waterlogged ground crumbled beneath me, making us both slip further towards the river, until the water seemed to lick at her boots, soaking the edges of her skirts. I could feel the slow drag of it on her feet as I pushed at the slick earth, which started to give way under me.

'Grab that rock,' I shouted, above the roar of the water.

It was to her left, jutting out of the dirt. She wrapped her arm around it.

'Be ready to push yourself up. Ready? Push.'

She dug in her heels and launched herself at me. I pulled her back up, over the slope.

We collapsed on the ground and lay, gasping for breath, Olivia sobbing.

'It's alright, I have you,' I murmured, holding her to me. 'Are you hurt?'

'I hate it,' she said, burying her face in my shoulder. 'I hate it. I hate it. I hate it.'

'Shush now,' I murmured, stroking her mud-streaked hair. 'We have to go. Can you take us back? I know some of it but I'm going to need your help.'

I stopped. I could feel a prickling over my skin. The hairs on the back of my neck lifted in a way that had nothing to do with the cold.

'What?' said Olivia, as if she could sense it too. 'What is it? Are they back?'

There was a dark figure on the other side of the river, standing between two of the trees. As I stared, it turned its squat, square head to look at us – to look at *me* – and then it was gone in a rustling of leaves.

TWELVE

Ace of Cups

'What in God's name?'

Mrs Hayes was already running towards us as we emerged from the trees. Olivia no longer needed my help to walk, but her eyes had dark circles under them, and she shivered violently. She did not resist when Mrs Hayes grabbed her shoulders.

'Look at you. You're soaking. What happened?'

'Olivia had a bit of an accident in the woods,' I said, trying to keep my voice light. 'No harm done.'

Mrs Hayes scowled and pointed towards the house, where a carriage stood in the front drive. Reverend Byres and the constable were manoeuvring Mr Duncan into the back. I allowed Mrs Hayes to take a hold of Olivia and usher her round to the back door. By then, Byres was already up and into the carriage, the constable climbing up onto the box behind him. The bent remains of the bicycle had been strapped to the roof. I called out, but my voice was swallowed by the crack of the whip. I watched the carriage trundle down the gravel drive until it was gone. Then, shivering, I hurried after Mrs Hayes and Olivia.

When I reached the kitchen, Marian was pumping water into kettles to place on the range, a soft hum of heat emanating from it. She made a shocked sound when I walked in, bleeding and covered in mud.

'Are you hurt, miss?' she asked, as I entered.

'Have we any bandages, Marian? It's just my hand. And I would dearly love that tea we planned earlier.'

Marian nodded and held out a large soup pot full of hot water.

'I'll just take this for Miss Olivia's bath. Mrs Hayes' rooms are the warmest right now so she is having her bathe down there.'

'I'll take it,' I said, waving away her protests. 'I am fine. Please, the tea and the bandages.'

Reluctantly, Marian handed me the large, steaming pan, and I carried it down the corridor to the housekeeper's rooms, ignoring the pain in my hand.

The door was open and all the lamps lit. The first and largest room was her study. It made me think of Mrs Morris at Astor House, with the busy-looking desk, stuffed with papers and ledgers, the collection of accounts books, the pretty rug by the fireplace, the display of china and the old carriage clock. Beyond that was her bedroom. The door was ajar.

Through the gap I could see Olivia standing with her back to me, shivering, as Mrs Hayes pulled and fussed at the soaked, muddy clothing.

'Promise me,' she was saying as I entered. 'Promise me.'

'I promise,' said Olivia, her teeth chattering.

'It's bad enough that you—'

I tapped the door with my foot, causing Mrs Hayes to jump.

'Miss Pearlie,' she said, recovering, and gestured at the pan in my hands. 'Bring that in here.'

The room was larger than I expected and very warm, containing a double bed with a broderie anglaise coverlet. There were bookshelves, a fireplace, a chair. A fire crackled, and a hip bath had been pulled up in front of it. Olivia, now down to her stays and pantalettes, did not register my presence but stood, compliant. She was trembling, and her breathing was deep and laboured.

'I will have Marian make up your fire,' said Mrs Hayes, pulling at Olivia's stays. 'Oh but you have mud everywhere. It's a wonder you weren't killed.'

The walls of her room were decorated with old music hall posters, some dating back to when I lived in London with Mother and Father. I read the names printed in large letters – George Lassiter, Edwina Stern, Harry Cartwright... I found one – Iphegenia Miller – who sang a song about an angel appearing in someone's back garden, which Father used to hum to make Mother cross. She hated Father's quiet enjoyment of Music Hall, although now I wondered if his pleasure in it wasn't more to do with her irritation.

'Miss Pearlie,' Mrs Hayes called, bringing my attention back. 'The bath, if you please.'

I poured the water into the hip bath, steam rising, then said, 'I can start the fire in my room. Marian is busy.'

'Marian is always busy,' said Mrs Hayes, running her fingers through Olivia's hair. 'You will also need a bath. Olivia, make yourself bath-ready please.'

Olivia glanced at me and I began to gather her clothing.

'I can take this with me for washing,' I said.

There was a splashing as I left the room and a small, muffled sob. Embarrassed, I stooped to pick up Olivia's abandoned boots and her discarded cloak. Behind me, Mrs Hayes whispered soothingly, and the sound of weeping quieted. In the silence, I stopped, relishing the sudden absence of screams, creaking, and raised voices that had been such a part of Mistcoate since I arrived. Then the music started.

A mellow, honeyed voice sang *O Mio Babbino Caro*. I glanced behind me. Olivia sat in the bath, her thin frame a startling shade of white. Her shoulders protruded sharply through her skin, as though she were about to sprout wings. She wrapped her arms around herself, knees pulled up to hide her nakedness. Her eyes were shut as Mrs Hayes combed the thick mud from her hair, singing.

She had a good voice, better than good. A little out of practice possibly, but even I could tell that this was more than just everyday talent. Mrs Hayes had a gift.

I thought of what she would say if she saw me watching from the doorway and ducked out of sight, just as her voice cracked on a high note. The song died, leaving a ringing silence.

'You had it for longer,' said Olivia, quietly. 'Maybe it is coming back?'

'I don't think so, my dove,' said Mrs Hayes, a whisper of regret. 'I don't think it works like that.'

Marian told me to leave the clothing in the side room that held the copper. I was turning out the pockets when my hand closed on Olivia's tarot. I had forgotten about the cards. So had she, it seemed. Where did she keep them? Usually they were always on her person but they must go somewhere when she slept. Under her pillow? By the bed?

Into the fire, I thought.

'No.'

I jumped at the sound of my own voice, but there was no one to hear. No, I couldn't destroy them; I knew that much. They were, after all, only tools. If I destroyed them, a new deck could easily be sourced. It would be much better, I reasoned, to convince Olivia that she didn't want or need them at all. One way to do that was to show her life without them.

Despite their size, they fit easily into my pocket. I felt their accusing weight against my thigh all the way to my room, where it took moments to move the washstand and hide them under the floorboards in my tin.

As I stood back to assess my handiwork, I caught sight of myself in the mirror. Eyes made puffy and dark from exhaustion set in a pale, pinched face beneath my muddy, rain-soaked hair.

'The respectable Julia Pearlie,' I murmured.

'Excuse me?'

Mrs Hayes was standing in the doorway.

'Mrs Hayes,' I said, turning. 'Is Olivia well?'

'She is drying off.' Mrs Hayes stepped into the room. I noticed that she had a piece of bracken stuck to the bottom of her mud-splashed skirts. 'I wish to speak to you before she comes up. I am aware that I was out of the house this morning but I, perhaps foolishly, trusted that everyone would behave as they should. Apparently, that was not the case.'

'I…' I began, but she cut me off.

'Olivia has told me everything so I would not waste your time.'

The clock ticked on the mantle. Mrs Hayes cleared her throat. Could she sack me? Where would I go? I could not return to Anthony and I had only met Alice Byres once. I could not ask her for help on such a short acquaintance.

'Olivia has asked me to apologise to you,' said Mrs Hayes, finally. 'She's too embarrassed to do it herself. I said I would pass it on. She takes full responsibility for leading you into the woods, ignoring when you called and especially for going too near to the river. She admits that she was showing off.'

'She told you that?' I said, astonished.

Mrs Hayes' brow knotted.

'Of course. Olivia does not lie to me.'

'No,' I shook my head. 'No, of course not.'

Mrs Hayes continued, 'With that being said, I wanted to ensure that this has had the effect of reinforcing our agreement last night. I think we can both agree that the events of the last twenty-four hours have been trying, but there is little to be done about it now. Olivia will be the one to suffer if Dr Richmond hears of it. I hope you see that now.'

'Yes,' I said.

'Good. I also hope that this has been illuminating for you, Miss Pearlie. Olivia is much more delicate than she will admit. That is why we keep her so close.'

'I understand. Really. I do.'

Mrs Hayes seemed to accept this.

'Thank you, by the way,' she said. 'For everything you have done today. I appreciate that I was not here. I had thought I was being useful by walking to the village and smoothing things out after last night but I…'

She broke off and cleared her throat. Her eyes were glistening and her face looked drawn.

I frowned. 'Mrs Hayes?'

When she spoke there was emotion in her voice. 'That girl… she's all I've got now. If anything happens to her, I don't know what I'll do.'

I hesitated. 'I take it Mr Hayes is…?'

Mrs Hayes snorted.

'He's been dead these past two years,' she said. 'And we're all better off for it, let me tell you.'

My eyes were drawn to the long scar that marked her face, pulling at her twisted mouth.

Mrs Hayes gave a grim smile. 'Married bliss ain't for everyone,' she said, her Bermondsey accent suddenly thick. 'Especially with a demon like he was. I'd already rebuilt myself as my own woman long before he copped it. I didn't mourn him. Just nice, not having to look over my shoulder the whole time. Sometimes it's the best thing. It sets us free, doesn't it?'

She looked at me from under her eyelashes, a long, hard look. It made me feel cold.

Uncomfortable in her gaze, I changed the subject. 'You have quite the collection of posters.'

The deflection worked. Mrs Hayes blinked and then smiled in a way that wasn't altogether happy.

'Souvenirs from a past life,' she said. 'From a long, long time ago.'

I thought of the cracked voice singing but said nothing.

'Olivia will need to go to her bed,' said Mrs Hayes. 'I can't imagine she will be much use before tomorrow morning. Take some rest yourself. You have earned it.'

Mrs Hayes turned to go and then paused.

'Everything I do is for Olivia,' she said. 'She trusts you, which is a surprise. It's not like her. I hope you're worth it. She's been through enough and she takes disappointment very hard.'

I stared at the nape of her neck, not daring to let my eyes flicker to the spot where Olivia's stolen cards resided.

'I will do all I can for her,' I said. 'I promise you.'

Mrs Hayes disappeared through the door.

I watched her go, then sank down onto the chair and buried my head in my hands.

THIRTEEN

Six of Swords

Monday morning dawned, sharp and bright. I rose early and slipped out of the house without notice. In daylight, I felt safe in the woods, but I hurried all the same. Despite the hour, Fellwick was bustling as shopkeepers unlocked shutters, women scrubbed their front steps and scolded children who ran, slipping and laughing through the greasy water, down towards the school building, where Mr and Mrs Lewes waited. The two stood side by side, the fiery red of Mrs Lewes' hair a sharp contrast to her husband's short, dark crop.

Duncan's Greengrocers remained dark though, the shutters locked in place. The bright November sun cut through the trees as I walked under the stone archway on the edge of town towards the grey stone church.

I'd had time to think about what had happened in the hut. A part of me thought I should tell the constable, but then I remembered the officers who had interviewed me in Kent, and the way they had confused details and misinterpreted what I said. No, I would never trust the police again. But I must tell someone what had occurred.

Alice had told me her brother was taking an interest in the Shambler, so I'd decided to speak to him. I'd been surprised to find the idea gave me great comfort.

There was also Olivia to consider. Soon she would notice her cards were missing. I needed to have something ready to distract her when that moment arrived.

I was just passing the Hive and Honey when a shriek went up from the schoolhouse. Around me, everyone paused in their work to see a boy, stumbling backwards out of the school door, followed by Mr Lewes, his hand raised as if to strike him.

'Started early today,' someone observed darkly.

But before anyone could act, Mrs Lewes appeared and grabbed her husband's shoulder. Mr Lewes swung around as though he might strike his wife as well, but the schoolmistress gave him a sharp shove. He stumbled, hands flailing, before tipping over backwards and landing on the cobbled street. The children raced past him, through the open door into the school house. As I watched, stunned, Mrs Lewes followed them, and pulled the door shut behind her.

Mr Lewes scrambled to his feet, schoolmaster's robes whirling and tangling about him, but he was too late. The door closed and though he pulled and pounded on the wood, it did not budge.

'Someone should call the constable,' said a woman behind me, but no one moved. Instead we stood, watching Mr Lewes shouting and beating upon the schoolhouse door.

I thought again of Olivia's warnings that night in the greenhouse.

You cannot be certain this has anything to do with her, I told myself, but my heart gave a strange, dark fluttering as I made my way first to the bakery and then to the Byres' house.

When I knocked, Alice Byres came to the door of the little thatched cottage, a canvas apron smeared in paint wrapped around her.

'Hello there,' she said. 'I hoped you would drop by.'

I held up the parcel of warm buns I'd bought on the way. 'I apologise for calling so early but I had hoped to catch Reverend Byres before he left for the church.'

'Oh, I am sorry,' said Alice. 'He's gone to Cambridge to speak to the bishop. He will be gone all day.'

'All day?' I tried to hide my stricken expression but did not succeed. Alice watched me for a moment, her gaze flickering to my bandaged hand, and then stepped aside.

'Come in. Please.'

I followed her through the narrow hallway up two flights of stairs to a large, airy attic room. In other households it might have been used for a nursery, but here it had been painted a fresh, clean white and was filled with canvases, paper, and two battered chairs that made me wonder how they had ever got them up the narrow steps. An easel was set up by a window, next to a small table that held tubes of paint and a saucer which was clearly being used as a palette. On the opposite side of the room stood a dressmaker's dummy and a large wooden table covered with sewing tools and patterns. Baskets of fabric were stacked in one corner while others held piles of books.

'Apologies. It is not quite visitor-ready,' said Alice, setting my box down on her cutting table. 'Have a seat. I will bring tea.'

I sank down into one of the chairs. There was no fire but the heat of the cottage seemed to fill the room, making it snug.

A short while later Alice climbed the steps, holding the tea tray as though she were the maid. I rushed over to help but she laughed and said,

'No, you will unbalance me. I am perfectly accustomed to it. I was in service for many years.'

This shocked me. 'You were?'

She nodded, smiling. 'It has been helpful in my role as spinster of the parish,' she said and winked. 'Sit, sit.'

As I took my place, I tried to imagine Alice as a servant. She moved with a slow grace, pouring with her fingers splayed over the teapot lid, as though completely unaware of the heat of the porcelain. I could not imagine a housekeeper doing the same.

'Now,' she said, not taking her eyes off the hot amber arc of tea. 'We have tea and time. And you are troubled. What is wrong?' She looked up and smiled.

All of a sudden, my eyes stung and I could feel my throat burning.

Lie or she will turn on you in a moment, I thought.

She watched me, puzzled. 'Miss Pearlie? Julia?'

I pressed my fingertips to my eyes and began to speak and then, to my embarrassment, to cry. Alice listened, head tilted, as I told her about what had happened in the greenhouse, and my experience with Olivia in the woods the day before. I did not look up again until I was finally finished and a great well of silence had opened up beneath me.

'My God, you must have been terrified,' said Alice, breathless in a way that had nothing to do with her health.

'It was awful,' I agreed, wiping my eyes.

'I'm glad you're safe. Everyone is concerned about this man, and I hope they find and help him soon,' she said. 'Now tell me, what did you do with the cards?'

'I hid them under the floorboards.'

She smiled. 'How very Edgar Allen Poe of you.'

'Am I dreadful?' I asked, leaning forward, watching her expression.

'Of course not,' said Alice, firmly. 'Not at all. But what will you do?'

'That is what I need help with,' I said. 'I must come up with something to distract her. Help me. What do young ladies enjoy?'

'I hate to be somewhat obvious,' said Alice, sipping her tea, 'but aren't you a young lady?'

'Well, yes,' I conceded. 'But I was never a young lady like Olivia.'

Alice nodded, gazing out of the window behind me.

'Do you know Mr Rogers?' she asked. 'The local magistrate? His daughter Suzanne is having a birthday celebration in three weeks' time. Ed and I have secured an invitation. I could get one for Olivia, if you think it would be helpful for her to have some society.'

'After all the rumours?' I asked, my voice doubtful. 'Would they even want her?'

'The right dress and the right attitude will do wonders. That is what Dr Richmond wants to see. It could be an excellent opportunity.' She sounded very confident but I wasn't convinced.

'But what about the community? What of the Duncans?'

'You need not worry about that,' Alice assured me. 'It is possible that Olivia has done some people a service. Mr Lewes has a temper and Mr Duncan is... Well. If Olivia has saved Mrs Duncan and those boys from misery, so much the better. I would not be surprised if others think so too, even if they do not say it.'

I wasn't sure everyone would agree, but the idea of this distraction appealed.

'She will need something to wear,' I said.

Alice's hand swept around the room, encompassing the cutting table and materials. 'It can be arranged. I can even make *you* something.'

'Me?' I laughed, despite myself.

'Well, she will need a chaperone,' said Alice.

'Do your powers extend that far?'

'I shall ensure they do,' she said. 'There, now, never say that I am not good to you.'

'You are being so good to me, Alice,' I said. 'Better than I deserve.'

Alice smiled, blushing, and said, 'Well. That settles it. I can ride over to Weatherall House right now if you would like to secure the invitation?'

She began to rise in a pantomime of efficiency, her apron tangling in her legs and catching on her saucer, tipping it so that she had to bend down to catch it.

'Horrors. This is why you are better off at that party than me.' Alice laughed. 'I always said I was a maid, not a dancer.'

'My mother made sure I had lessons when I was younger,' I told her. 'Back when she thought I might still get married.'

'Maybe there will be someone at the party worth dancing with,' Alice said, with a smile.

'I shall have my hands full already. What about you? Are there no eligible men you have your eye on?'

'I very rarely have my eye on anyone,' she confessed. 'Your Dr Richmond would probably be the closest thing to eligible, although I have never warmed to him. I cannot say the same for some though.'

My cheeks flamed. 'He is not *my* Dr Richmond.'

'No, of course not. I suppose Ed will be invited now that Reverend Smythe is gone.'

I looked up in surprise. 'He's gone?'

Alice stopped, her cup halfway to her lips.

'You have not heard? I would have thought the village would be full of it.'

'I have heard nothing. What happened?'

Alice made a noise of irritation. 'Please do not repeat this but, while Mr Duncan was indisposed, Mrs Duncan took the opportunity to abscond with Reverend Smythe. They were both seen in the postal carriage yesterday afternoon. Word is that they've run away to Brighton of all places.'

'*No...*' I sat back, stunned.

'That is why Ed has gone to Cambridge,' she said. 'It is likely he will have to act alone as curate now, which I admit would be welcome. Ed works so hard. I would like him to have the recognition. He has done so much to support me...'

Her voice drifted off, and she looked away.

'It's hateful, isn't it?' I said, guessing at her thoughts. 'Owing him so much and knowing you will never be able to repay him?'

'Yes. And no. Ed saved me. Were it not for him, I would still be... oh, I don't know.' She caught my gaze and gave me a wan smile. 'Would it shock you to know that I am a miner's daughter?'

It did shock me. With her neat dress and elegant movements, I could no more envision her as a coal-smeared miner's child than I could see her as a maid.

'Truly?'

Alice nodded, and then told the story as though she were recounting the church meeting minutes. It was all sketched out in the briefest of sentences, but it was so easy to see. The small cottage in a mining town. The couple whose children withered and died, until the twins who thrived where their siblings had perished. The father, coated in grime and coal dust from the pit. The mother, her fingers calloused and eyes weakening from years of close stitching in poor light by the fire.

Alice and Ed Byres had attended the local church school and were noted for their abilities. The vicar wanted Ed to go to the boys' school but their father was adamant he was to work in the mine, just as all the boys did, so the vicar loaned Ed his own bicycle so he could make money acting as a delivery boy instead. Their father returned the bicycle and would hear nothing about entrance exams or scholarships to schools.

Ed hated him. So did Alice.

Driven by embarrassment and resentment towards the two children who had grown up to be smarter than was good for them, their father seemed determined to force them both into the shapes that were available in that world.

In their free moments, Alice and Ed would go for long walks, where they would plan their escape from the valley and the mine. But they both knew it was unlikely. Even if Ed did get into the boys' school, he would have to leave Alice.

Then their father died.

'So Ed went to school after all,' she said. 'I went into service to help my mother. I spent my time polishing silver and dusting. We wrote to each other, of course. We even made trips home when possible.

'Finally, one day, we arrived and the house was empty. Old, moulding soup was on the range and her shoes were by the door, but my mother was gone.' Alice drew a breath. 'We found her out in the fields and, you know, she didn't even recognise me. She was so thin – we both knew it was the beginning of the end for her. By then, Ed had received his first posting as a chaplain here in Fellwick so he could send some money. When she died, he asked if I wanted to come with him.' She glanced up at me. 'So you see, we did get to run away after all.'

I clutched my cup, which held the dregs of now cold tea.

'You are so accepting of it,' I said. 'Did you not wish to go to school?'

'There's no point thinking of that,' said Alice. 'Ed made sure I had all the books and learning I could want once we were away, and Ma taught me to sew, which is something. I make myself useful. I'm lucky, really. What if I'd had no Ed? Or what if he'd been a different person – someone who would have gone off and not given a backward glance? I've a lot to be grateful for, really.'

We lapsed into silence. How different it would have been, I thought, if Anthony had been more like Ed. But there was no point in thinking about that, either. 'If we go to this party,' I said, returning to the problem of Olivia. 'Will you please come too?'

'You will be using my invitation, remember? That alone will be enough of a surprise. We get the etiquette invitations because of who we are, but no one expects us to attend. I doubt Ed will. He is not as good as I am at pretending he enjoys these things. Although, I think if you are there, he would find much more diversion in it.'

She smiled and I felt the blush rising as I stammered a response.

'I am not fit for... I mean to say... I'm not what a man like Reverend Byres would be...' Embarrassed, I lowered my head and considered the depths of my teacup.

Alice sat silent and watchful for a moment before saying, 'Whoever he was that put that look on your face, he was unworthy of you and, as your friend, I urge you to forget him immediately.' She squeezed my hand.

I forced a smile. 'I will do my best.'

'Now,' said Alice, setting her cup down. 'We must begin our plans. Your dress, what do we think?'

We had finished the buns and were on a second pot of tea at the cutting table when we heard the front door open. Alice looked up, pencil paused over a sheet of paper where we were drafting a second Season dress for Olivia.

'Ed?' she called down the stairs.

'It is like a circus out there,' he said in reply.

I followed Alice to the staircase, pausing in the hall, listening to her greet her brother.

'I got caught by Mrs Pomander. Did you hear about this morning?' Byres sounded breathless as he moved about the kitchen.

'Mr and Mrs Lewes? Do you need to go out again?'

'Well, the last time I saw Mrs Lewes, she had locked herself inside the schoolhouse. I tried to speak with her but all she said was something about 'that girl'. We know what that is about.'

I covered my face with my hands.

'Ed, Miss Pearlie—' Alice began, but he was still talking.

'It's quite alright. The children have been let out. Mrs Lewes saw sense there, at least.'

'But she hasn't come out?' Alice asked.

'She's locked herself in again with Mr Lewes. If they don't appear by tea time, I think we shall have to send the constable over. Let us hope she talks some sense into him in the meantime. By the way, aren't you going to ask?'

'You haven't given me an opportunity,' Alice told him. 'Well?'

There was a pause and then Alice gave a high-pitched squeal.

'Are you in earnest?' she cried.

'I can't promise things will be much better but it's a step,' said Byres.

I decided I would creep away and leave them to their celebration. However, as I turned to retrieve my things, the stair gave a loud, treacherous creak.

Byres said, 'What was that?'

'Oh, yes – Miss Pearlie is here. I was trying to tell you.'

I came the rest of the way downstairs. Ed Byres stood in the kitchen, his face flushed from the cold, still in his outdoor coat.

'Miss Pearlie is going to be attending the Rogers' party,' Alice said.

'Wonderful.' Byres began to shrug off his coat, smiling. 'Well I thought it was going to be rather dull, but we shall make it a merry party, the four of us. I am taking it that this is for Miss Olivia's benefit?'

'So you will go, too?' Alice said.

'Certainly. We cannot let Miss Pearlie loose on Fellwick without a guide,' he said.

Alice gave me a fleeting, almost gloating look.

'You are right, of course,' she said. 'I shall speak to Suzanne on all our behalf. Oh, that reminds me. You wanted to speak to Ed, didn't you, Miss Pearlie? What was it about?'

Ed was smiling at me, his eyes the colour of the ocean.

'It's no matter,' I said, shaking my head. 'No matter at all.'

FOURTEEN

Three of Cups

I had just let myself in to Mistcoate House through the back door when there came a crash from the floor above, followed by raised voices.

Fearing for Captain Richmond, I hurried to the stairs.

However, when I reached the landing, I discovered the commotion was emanating from Olivia's room. It was, if possible, in greater disarray than usual. Pillows lay on the floor, the sheet had been torn off the bed, boxes had been turned out, drawers ripped out and emptied. Olivia, still in her nightgown, was pacing the room, her hair clinging to her tear-stained cheeks.

'I don't remember where I last saw them,' she said, breathless from weeping.

'Well, we will find them,' said Mrs Hayes, who stood in the middle of the devastation like a lighthouse in a storm. 'But you must *calm down.*'

'You think I'm losing my mind but I am not,' Olivia insisted, through her tears.

'What is going on?' I asked, despite already knowing.

'My cards are gone,' sobbed Olivia.

'You haven't seen them, have you?' Mrs Hayes turned to me, her gaze fixed and burning. But I was used to this sort of thing by now.

'No,' I told her, firmly. 'Have you checked your pockets, Olivia? The last time I saw you with them, you put them there.'

As I had known it would, inspection of various garments showed no sign of the cards.

'Someone has taken them,' Olivia muttered. 'That maid—'

'Marian has been with me for most of the morning,' Mrs Hayes said. 'Have you perhaps placed them somewhere without realising? You know you sleepwalk.'

Olivia stopped in the act of shaking a pillow from its case.

'Maybe I took them to Grandfather's room?'

'We can check once you're dressed,' I said. 'Actually, I am glad to have found you as I have some news. We are invited to a party.'

Mrs Hayes' eyes narrowed. 'A what?'

'Miss Byres called it a *soirée*, but I imagine that isn't much different to a party,' I said, smiling at Olivia. 'We have been invited to Weatherall House.'

'They invited *me*?'

Olivia looked like a child given an unexpected and very expensive present. It was so comical to see her looking so disconcerted that I allowed myself to laugh a little. Mrs Hayes' face stiffened as though she had been slapped.

'Yes,' I said. 'Both of us are invited, actually. It is in three weeks, so we will have plenty of preparation time.'

'What has Dr Richmond said?' Mrs Hayes interjected, coldly.

I faltered. Truth be told, I hadn't considered asking Olivia's father.

'I will speak to Dr Richmond once he is returned,' I said. 'I'm sure the matter can be arranged.'

'He is home now,' Mrs Hayes informed me. 'He arrived while you were gone.' She turned to Olivia. 'You must not raise your hopes too high, my love. You know these things over-excite you.'

'How could they, when I haven't been to one in years?' Olivia dropped the pillow she'd been holding, her cards momentarily forgotten. 'He cannot stop me going if Miss Pearlie is with me. But I shall need to have a new dress. I have nothing that looks suitable. Shall we speak to him now?'

'What about your cards?' asked Mrs Hayes.

'They will turn up,' I said, quickly. 'I'm sure they have not gone far.'

'No,' said Mrs Hayes, looking at me. 'I'm sure they haven't.'

My breath caught in my throat. I turned away so Mrs Hayes wouldn't see how my cheeks flushed under her accusatory gaze.

'I think you might get dressed first, and this room needs tidying,' I told Olivia. 'I shall ask Marian to come up. Would you like me to arrange your hair before we speak to Dr Richmond?'

'What are *you* going to wear?' said Olivia, now breathless with excitement.

'Once you're ready, then you can help me choose,' I said.

Olivia laughed and ran off to her closet, pulling out dresses and wraps.

'Possibly you could wear the burgundy?' said Mrs Hayes.

'It's too small. I cannot do a thing in all this,' said Olivia, gesturing at the room as though the devastation were nothing to do with her. 'Mrs Hayes, would you go and get Marian? Then I think Father will want you.'

Mrs Hayes' eyes flashed, her mouth setting in a tight line as she responded, 'If you like, my dove.' But Olivia had already turned back to the closet and scarcely noticed.

Mrs Hayes gave me a strange look as she strode out of the room.

As Olivia picked up her garments, all thoughts of tarot were forgotten. I sat on the bed and watched her discarding her clothes, claiming that they were all either unfashionable, inappropriate or did not fit. She was still searching when Marian arrived to tell me Dr Richmond wished to see me in his office.

Olivia's father was unfastening his cufflinks when I entered and did not look at me. His shirt, I thought, looked new. Its crisp whiteness stood out against the dark varnished wood of the office and, though he was unshaven, he seemed more energised than during our last meeting. However, his mouth was set in a grim line, which twisted in a look of distaste when he looked up at me.

'Ah, Miss Pearlie. Good afternoon.' He sat down in his chair. His lack of invitation or instruction meant that I remained standing.

'Mrs Hayes has been informing me of your progress since I left for London.'

His eyes flickered to a point behind me. I glanced over my shoulder and gave a start. Mrs Hayes was on the sofa, leaning forward, her eyes glittering in the gloom. Her expression was hard to read but she was watching me with the intensity of a waiting predator. She was so still that, for a moment, I thought I was imagining her but then she blinked and shifted her weight and a different kind of uneasiness settled on me. I turned back to Dr Richmond, whose eyes were hard with quiet, cold fury.

'At what point were you planning to tell me about the circus that took place here on Friday?'

My stomach gave a terrible flip. 'Sir?'

'Do not play ignorant, Miss Pearlie. Mrs Hayes says that she discovered Olivia holding some sort of gathering on Friday night where she indulged in all sorts of nonsense, making a mockery of this house and this family and you – Miss Pearlie – were in attendance. Is that not so?'

How could I deny it? Mrs Hayes had betrayed us.

'Yes, sir.'

'I cannot see then, how I can do anything else but terminate your services with us,' my employer declared.

Was I shaking? I felt like I must be but it was impossible to tell. The beat of my pulse thundered in my ear, overpowering everything else and it was all I could do to keep breathing. She had said she would not tell. We had made promises.

You promised not to tell, hissed the icy voice in my head. *She never did...*

But why? She had said herself that it would do no good. Oh God, what do I do? Then the answer struck me.

I squared my shoulders. 'And Mrs Hayes? She was also in attendance. Is she also leaving your service?'

There was a soft sound behind me.

'Mrs Hayes did not act in complete contradiction to my instructions,' said Dr Richmond, clearly caught off guard.

'Neither did I,' I said. 'At no time in our correspondence or interviews were séances ever mentioned. Miss Olivia's interest in spiritualism was not outlined in our interview. I was not informed of any of this.'

'It was not necessary,' said Dr Richmond, after a moment's pause. 'Girls go through something of this kind, and I believe she will grow out of it.'

'If that is the case then you must concede I had no way of knowing what was taking place in the garden house,' I said. 'How could I? But, having discovered the gathering, yes – I did stay but only in order to protect Olivia. There was something happening that I needed to see in order to understand. It was like an... Oh, I do not know what doctors call it, but it must have a name?'

'An observation exercise,' said Dr Richmond.

'Yes,' I nodded. 'After all, how am I to help her if I do not know the full extent of what she's been doing? I could not walk out of that garden house any more than I'm sure you could walk away from one of your patients who presents with a specific and peculiar symptom.'

Dr Richmond leaned forward, his forearms pressed on the desk.

'And what did your observation tell you?' he asked.

I felt the muscles around my lungs relax a little to let me breathe. 'That she is not beyond help. She takes instruction when told to stop.'

'She does not always.'

'Sometimes is better than never, sir.'

Dr Richmond pushed his spectacles up onto his forehead, rubbing his eyes.

'And you, Mrs Hayes?' He spoke without looking up. 'What did you observe? Apparently, your attendance was more than first suggested.'

I didn't dare turn to look at the housekeeper. 'Mrs Hayes was very much the cavalry,' I said. 'She arrived at the end to calm things and send the visitors home. Throughout the whole experience, she expressed nothing but concern for Olivia. I can only imagine that that is why she has brought this to your attention.'

With effort, I glanced behind me. The housekeeper's face was a deep pink.

'It is for exactly that reason,' she said, her voice a little too high. 'Miss Pearlie has proven that she is incapable of protecting Miss Olivia from our neighbours and now she wants to take her to a party full of them.'

I was ready for this. 'If she is to attend the season, she must have practice,' I said. 'And not just that, but she must have a spotless reputation. At the moment all she is known for is being the Mistcoate Witch.' Dr Richmond winced. 'But if she is brought into society appropriately – as guests of the vicar – this could change.'

'After all he has done…' Mrs Hayes began but she was silenced by a sharp look from Dr Richmond.

'Olivia is a bright girl with too much time and not enough outlet,' I said. 'She needs a redirection of energies and a chance to practise her dancing and her etiquette.'

Mrs Hayes gave a snort of derision.

'I must admit, I share Mrs Hayes' concerns that it is too soon.' Dr Richmond's brow furrowed. 'This is not the first time Olivia's behaviour has had consequences, but it is increasingly hard to manage and, if I am honest, it worries me. There are times when it is difficult to tell if Olivia's fantasies are due to whimsy or a deficiency of the mind. I have wondered if perhaps she would be better placed elsewhere for a time. I admit that this has provoked that thought again.'

There was a rustle as Mrs Hayes rose from the couch. 'We agreed before Miss Pearlie arrived that the hospital was not necessary.'

'That was because we believed Miss Pearlie would prove effective,' Dr Richmond said.

'Sir, I have only had a few days,' I reminded him. 'Surely that is not enough time to undo the habits of years? Olivia does not need doctors, in my opinion. She needs company closer to her own age. If she truly thinks she can see things, I must find out why and convince her that she doesn't. That work will take longer than a week.'

Dr Richmond rose from his seat and moved to the sideboard and the bottle of whiskey stashed there. I felt the warm bulk of him brush past, the scent of shaving oil and soap lingering in his wake.

A downpour outside had begun in earnest, voluptuous as a monsoon. Somewhere in the house a door slammed and I turned, as though expecting Olivia herself to appear in the doorway, but there was no one.

'It was not so bad at first. She only spoke of it within the family. It does not escape me that this all began after Florence left.' Dr Richmond spoke without looking at either of us. He poured a neat measure of whiskey, knocking it back.

'I took it as grief but now she seems to revel in this nonsense. She is either wilful to the point of ruination or her delusions have progressed to the point that she is dangerous. Either way, it seems that I may have no choice but to settle Olivia somewhere where she can be properly administered to. It is no fault of yours. So little is known of her condition, its pathology and effects. It may all be down to the blood. This entire family may simply be cursed.'

He sounded defeated.

Mrs Hayes took a step towards him. 'Do not say that,' she said. 'Olivia is like any girl – she needs attention, a chance to show off. In any case, it is not necessarily the party I object to. Merely the chaperone.'

I met her gaze, burning inside with indignation.

'If I were to go with her...' she began.

'You would teach her quadrilles, would you?' I let sarcasm linger in my tone. 'Waltzes? You would make introductions and teach her how to eat finger food properly? Possibly you would help her source a new dress?'

Mrs Hayes opened her mouth but, for once, words failed her. I didn't wait for her to find a response.

'What if I could prove that she is not dangerous? Or delusional?' I turned to Dr

Richmond. 'If you are convinced that Olivia needs medical attention, I cannot say otherwise but I am guessing it would take you time to make arrangements. Give me some of that time. I will prove to you that Olivia can be changed. People can change, can't they? Illnesses can be healed. Isn't that what doctors do?'

Dr Richmond paused. 'Yes,' he said. 'But normally that would take place in a hospital.'

'At great expense and possible scandal,' I said. 'The party will happen regardless. It is an opportunity. Let us try it and then we may talk again.'

Mrs Hayes' jaw moved, as though practising what she would like to say and then she leaned in close to Dr Richmond.

'Please,' she whispered. 'Don't send Olivia away.'

Dr Richmond turned to her and for a moment they were close enough that, if he leaned forward, they could embrace.

But then he looked up at me, his face so drawn and tired that I felt a strange guilt.

'I would need to see a great deal of change,' he said. 'More than I think it is fair to expect you to create.'

'But if you saw it, you could be convinced?'

'It would give me pause.' He strode back to his seat. 'As it happens, my latest excursion to London has borne fruit. A colleague of mine, Peter Joyce, has a promising new study, and I will be helping him deliver a presentation to the Royal College in a month's time. Peter has requested that he have my full time and attention until then.' He met my eyes. 'I will give you a month, Miss Pearlie, and after that we shall see.'

FIFTEEN

Seven of Swords

There was a knock on the door and Olivia looked in at us.

'What on earth are you all doing?' she demanded. 'You have been gone for an age. Are you talking about the party?'

'Ah, Olivia. Come in.' Dr Richmond motioned for her to enter.

'Please say I can go, Papa,' pleaded Olivia, whirling over to him. 'Miss Pearlie can teach me to dance and Marian will make me food to try so I know what it all tastes like, and look.' She held out a women's newspaper, folded open to an advertisement. 'You don't even have to have dresses made now, you can buy them as they are. So they take no time.'

Her eyes were bright and a fetching colour had risen in her cheeks replacing her usual pallor. Instead of a drab shift dress, she wore a worsted wool skirt and linen blouse that made her appear somehow healthier and more mature. She had even braided her hair.

I could see Dr Richmond noticing this.

'Time is not the issue,' he said. 'It is more a matter of cost.'

'Julia has said that Miss Byres would make a dress for us so it may not cost much. Please, Papa, none of my dresses are suitable for dancing.'

'And what of your behaviour?' he asked. 'Recent and future?'

'I have been good. Mrs Hayes, haven't I been good? Miss Pearlie?' She didn't wait for us to answer. 'And I will listen very closely to Miss Pearlie and do everything she tells me. Only, I shall have to learn to dance. Miss Pearlie, can you teach me to dance?'

'I imagine that if you twirl enough and do as your partner shows you, you'll do alright,' said Dr Richmond before I could respond. 'That's what I do.'

Olivia gaped at him with the comic disbelief of a child. 'You don't go dancing.'

'You don't know what I do when I go to London.' A small smile played on his face.

Olivia giggled behind her hand, her usual ethereal aloofness and cold self-assurance gone. Suddenly, she was a pretty, happy girl of seventeen.

The effect was not lost on Dr Richmond, who seemed to soften at the sight of it.

'I suppose you must also think of your chaperone,' he said. 'You wouldn't be going anywhere if it weren't for Miss Pearlie. What is she to wear?'

'I have a very serviceable dress,' I told him, surprised at the question.

'I hope you're going in something that is more than *serviceable*,' Olivia said.

I laughed. 'Well now it seems that it will have to stand up to your scrutiny. I can help you to have a look at it if you like. See if it meets your standards.'

She turned back to her father. 'But what of *my* dress?'

'We could always alter something for you,' I suggested. 'Take something apart and put it back together anew. I'm sure Miss Byres could arrange something.'

'I will go and choose one then,' said Olivia. She slipped from the room, a pale ghost flitting about the house, before Dr Richmond could remind her he had not yet given permission.

He stared after her. 'I stand in amazement.'

'I fear she will hound you until you give in about the dress,' I said, with a grim smile.

'It is the first time she has been interested in one,' said Dr Richmond and then added ruefully, 'It seems your theory about her may have had some merit. I cannot think of a time when she has been more bright and alert.'

Mrs Hayes folded her arms, her face thunderous. 'And what are we to do when she has cut up all her dresses? Her mood changes so quickly. What pleases her now may vex her later.'

'It is often the way with young girls but I think you can see her capacity for change,' I said.

'I will admit, you have remade her,' Dr Richmond said. 'I fear I must commit myself to the cost of a new dress. Mrs Hayes, would you mind fetching her back please?'

'I would have thought that would be Miss Pearlie's arena,' she said stiffly.

'Of course,' I said. I didn't mind. My point was already made.

I arrived at Olivia's room to find her examining two dresses.

'Which one do you think?' She held them up. 'I suppose I could take the lace trim from this one and add it here. But do you think that would be terribly old fashioned?'

'I think if you go downstairs and ask about new dresses again, you may have better luck,' I told her.

She brightened. 'Really?'

'Really.'

'Can I see what you are going to wear?' Olivia asked. 'Then at least I shall know what to aim for.'

I knew myself that I was no longer a good judge of what constituted a fashionable dress but I led Olivia to my room. She pressed her lips together when I showed her my choices.

'Have you nothing else? I could not bear it if people laughed.'

'Well, thank you,' I said, replacing the dresses. 'I can only imagine what you would have said if they were ugly rather than just plain. Come, I'm sure once we go downstairs and speak to Dr Richmond you will feel differently.'

We descended the main staircase, so engrossed in our own conversation it wasn't until we reached the study that we realised we'd walked into the middle of an argument. I opened the door in time to hear Dr Richmond say sharply, 'I have told you before that that is none of your concern.'

Mrs Hayes stood rigidly. Dr Richmond's neck and ears had turned a patchy red.

'Papa?'

Dr Richmond turned at the sound of his daughter's voice. For a moment, he looked ready to continue shouting but then seemed to catch himself and clapped his hands together in an attempt at bonhomie.

'Ah, Livvy. After thinking it over, I've decided you should have a new dress. You can go into town and speak to Miss Byres about it tomorrow, if she is willing to make one for you.'

Olivia ran to him, throwing her arms around his neck. 'Thank you.'

'Fine,' said Mrs Hayes, through clenched teeth. 'We shall have to be up and out early tomorrow.'

'No,' said Olivia. 'Julia must take me.' She turned to me. 'Won't you?'

'Of course,' I said.

Mrs Hayes looked as though the ground had shifted under her feet.

'Fine,' she whispered. 'Fine.'

She walked from the room, her shoulders tense.

I'd expected Olivia might feel a moment of regret, but she was talking excitedly with her father and didn't seem to notice.

A small figure in white bled into the corner of my vision.

Do you remember that day? whispered the memory, in the soft voice of a child who feels unloved. She was so close I could almost smell the horse dung, unwashed bodies and soured beer. *Do you remember that day when he told you it was all a lie? It was all over and it felt like you were falling off a cliff?*

My stomach knotted. The memory felt like missing a step on the stairs and pitching forward. John had been standing there with his soft, rueful expression, trying to look anywhere but at me while asking, 'Where are the children?'

That was when the screams had started.

This is not the same, I told myself.

The memory child said nothing but the smell and the sick feeling lingered.

'I'm just going to check in with Marian,' I said and hurried out.

When I stepped into the hallway, Mrs Hayes was walking from the kitchen, a bottle of tincture for Captain Richmond in her hand. She swept past me as though she had not seen me, and began climbing the stairs.

'Mrs Hayes?' I called.

'Do not follow me please,' she said without looking back.

'I just want to see that you are well.'

She spun on her heel to face me, her mouth twisted in a vicious snarl. 'I will be well if you leave me in peace.'

I ignored this. 'I am sorry that Olivia was callous – she does not mean it.'

Mrs Hayes gave a low, humourless laugh. 'Save your good intentions. If you really want to help, you can tell me where you've put them.'

My brow furrowed. 'Put what?'

'You know exactly what I mean,' she said. 'I don't know what you've done with them but I will find them.'

There was a pause.

'I am not your enemy, you know,' I said. 'There was no need to do what you did today. I would have kept to our agreement if you had. And you must be able to see that Olivia needs friends.'

Mrs Hayes began descending the stairs. For a moment I feared that she was going to strike me but she stopped an arm's length away.

'Do not lecture me, Miss Pearlie. You do not even begin to understand what you've done. Have you considered what happens when she goes to that party and they stare? Or whisper? What happens when people refuse to stand next to her or touch things she has touched? It has happened before. Are you going to explain to her that people think she is a walking disease? A freak? A misfortune waiting to happen?'

I swallowed hard. 'I am hoping to prove quite the opposite.'

'How noble.' The housekeeper's tone was icy. 'Except people don't see her that way. What happens when this party is over and no-one calls on her? Have you got something else waiting in the wings? No. I can see you haven't.'

'She cannot continue as she is,' I insisted.

She took a step towards me, bristling. 'You think you're the only one who knows what's best for Olivia? I have spent *years* considering how that girl will cope with adult life. You don't care about her at all. You're just a liar with light fingers and an empty head who is out for what she can get. You may have fooled them but you don't fool me.'

'Please, I thought we had an understanding,' I said.

'The understanding was that you kept your mouth shut and did not upset things.' Mrs Hayes' voice echoed off the hard walls. 'I have spent too long putting things in place for you to come along and destroy it now. My eye is on you, Miss Pearlie. Rest assured, I know what you really are, and when that false character breaks, I will be there. If, that is, I do not break it for you.'

SIXTEEN
Two of Wands

Julia,

Invitations have arrived. I have everything planned. Your first dress appointment with me is this Saturday at midday.

Alice Byres

'How is it that you are here less than two weeks and already you have a friend?' said Olivia, pouting. 'You make it look so easy.'

It had been just over a week since our meeting in Dr Richmond's study and, after a dry, sunny morning, we had decided to walk to Fellwick for our first dress meeting. Refusing to don her protective hood, Olivia instead held a lace-edged parasol to shield her sensitive skin from the sudden, unseasonable sun. She also wore a pair of round, smoked glasses to protect her eyes, and the combination gave her a somewhat jaunty air.

As we walked, the townspeople we passed followed her with their eyes, but if she noticed, she made no sign of it.

When we passed the church, a jovial voice called out, 'Good morning, ladies!'

We turned to see Ed Byres descending the stone steps of the church dressed in a long dark cassock that made him look taller somehow.

'Out causing a stir, I see,' he observed, glancing meaningfully at a couple who had stopped to stare at us. This made Olivia giggle, and he smiled at her. 'Well, who wouldn't stare at two such delightful ladies?'

The giggling intensified into an excited hiccupping as Byres gave her a small bow and said, 'It is lovely to see you, Miss Olivia. I hope you are well?'

'Very well, thank you,' said Olivia, from behind her hand.

Byres' face showed no guile. If anything, he was looking at Olivia so earnestly I felt the need to break his gaze lest she die of delight and embarrassment.

'We are on our way to call on your sister,' I explained. 'She is doing some sewing for us.'

'New dresses,' Olivia beamed. 'For Suzanne Rogers' party.'

Byres seemed to be keeping back a smile. 'How exciting. It is a shame I am in demand, otherwise I would have escorted you, but if I stir too far the ladies on the committee will know and come to find me. Then I will need you for protection rather than the other way around. Enjoy your afternoon, ladies.'

I gave a nod and steered Olivia away.

'He's a dear,' whispered Olivia as we bustled off. 'He has always been so nice.'

'I didn't think you would know him well,' I said. 'I heard Mistcoate doesn't get involved with the church.'

'No,' said Olivia. 'But he and Florence were, once.'

I stopped so suddenly that Olivia stumbled. 'Involved? Reverend Byres and Florence?'

Olivia nodded. 'Florence always denied it but he used to come up to the house quite often to help her with the flowers. Florence loved gardening. The reverend would come and they'd go on long walks. Then he stopped coming and then… then she died and that was that.'

Her face clouded.

I squeezed her hand and started a conversation about dress trimmings, disguising my shock. Why had Alice never mentioned her brother having an attachment at Mistcoate?

When we arrived at the cottage, Alice had left the front door ajar and we let ourselves in.

'Step into my parlour,' she called down from the top of the narrow stairs, where she waited in a long, high-necked smock with the sleeves rolled up.

'I have spread out some material,' she continued as we climbed up to meet her. 'See what you like. Hello, Miss Olivia, I see you're interested in the brocade. It is beautiful but may be too old. You are looking for something that will make you appear like a dream. Am I right?'

Olivia nodded. Alice made a small, satisfied sound.

'I have a roll of silk and a swathe of lace that I worried would never be used. Now I see that they were only waiting for you. I don't know why I didn't think to bring them upstairs. One moment.'

She hurried away.

Olivia flitted between fabrics, touching them softly, but I was still thinking about Ed Byres and Florence. I didn't know what to make of it. But there was no chance to discuss it with Alice, who reappeared with a large, folded square of stiff silk striped with white and a very faint duck-egg blue.

We helped Olivia up onto a stool where she stood while Alice draped, pinned and tucked. Olivia flushed when she saw herself in the mirror, standing so close that her breath misted the glass.

'It's perfect,' she said, softly.

'It will take a few days to finish it,' said Alice. 'I just bought one of those machines with a pedal and that should speed things up a bit.'

She turned her speculative gaze on me. 'Now. What to do about you?'

'I don't really need anything,' I said.

'She'd like something dark and plain,' said Olivia, still looking at herself in the mirror.

'Olivia…' I chided.

'If I'm to look this lovely, you must at least match,' she said.

I turned to Alice and found she had completely vanished.

'Olivia, you cannot speak for me like that,' I scolded.

'I don't see why not.' She smoothed her pinned skirt. 'You won't say anything and it needs to be done.'

A rustling indicated that Alice was climbing the stairs again, this time with an armful of deep, blood-red satin.

'A little fast, perhaps,' she said, pulling out a section for us to see. 'But I could not leave it to rot in that dusty old haberdashery.'

It was a beautiful fabric. It lay on the counter, as sleek and smooth as the surface of a pond. I could not stop myself from running my fingertips over it, feeling the rich heaviness of the material, how soft and silken it was.

The colour rippled under my touch, turning from red to burgundy to black and, when Alice pulled more, it spilled into a languid puddle on the floor.

'I think with the right tailoring – a modest cut – nothing too low at the neck or high at the arms, it could be glorious,' she said.

It looked shatteringly expensive.

'How much would that be?'

My voice sounded choked.

'Don't be silly,' said Alice. 'I had no thought of charging.'

I knew how much it cost to make a dress. For Alice, it was more than a gift, it was charity.

'But it's so much time and energy.'

'You can have George Richmond put some money into the church funds,' said Alice. 'And you can get me some more paint. That will be a fair exchange.'

I pinched my lips together, shifting from one foot to the other.

'Even then,' I said. 'I couldn't. He would be paying for me.'

'Well.' Alice kept her gaze on the red silk. 'Why don't you pay me for half the fabric then?'

'How much was it?' I asked.

She told me, and I tried not to wince at the number. It was not as much as I had thought but still more than I could afford.

'Thank you,' I said, retracting my hand from the material with reluctance. 'I will consider it.'

Alice looked as though she wanted to argue the point, but I turned away. She left me to stare longingly at the fabric while she unpinned Olivia.

It is a strange feeling one experiences when you have been close to something that you want and may not have. I thought I had grown used to it but now found myself feeling bitterly disappointed. My mood must have been clear, for even Olivia abstained from enthusing about her dress, while Alice began to ask me tactful questions about what I might do with my hair and which shoes would be most comfortable as we didn't want to spoil the evening with blisters. I tried not to think too poorly of my own dresses, hanging up in my room. I had been delighted when I first bought them, so proud to have found dresses made of durable, attractive fabric at such good prices. Now, I would have burned every one of them and lived the rest of my life in castoffs if it meant that I could afford that red satin dress.

'You had a lighter dress, didn't you?' said Olivia. 'A green one?'

'My Sunday dress? I confess I had not thought about it,' I said. 'Is it not a bit simple?'

'I think we should bring it for Miss Byres to look at. With your hair and eyes, you would look wonderful in green and I think we have some camellias in the glasshouse that would look beautiful pinned on you. And pearls as well.'

'I could definitely spin it into something if you were happy,' offered Alice.

'That sounds wonderful,' I said, trying to muster the appropriate excitement. 'Thank you, Alice. This is so generous.'

'Nonsense. It keeps me out of trouble. Now, I promised you lunch. It is exactly one o'clock. Let us go.'

She served a restorative lunch of cold chicken, fresh bread, and a salad of potatoes, leeks and beetroot dressed in oil and made fragrant with herbs. Olivia had to be encouraged to take as much as she liked and confided to me, as we walked home, that she had held back on pain of looking too eager, just as I had taught her.

'Do you think we should practise dancing?' she asked, as the house loomed into view. 'I hope I do not make a show of myself. I have never been to a proper party before.'

'Neither have I,' I said, and winked.

Olivia laughed. 'Don't tease.'

We clattered into the hallway, shrugging off our walking capes and stowing away Olivia's parasol.

'I am sure that it is step together, step together,' I said.

'Isn't that all dances? Anyway, the timing is different for a waltz.'

'Are you sure you're not thinking of a hornpipe?'

'Will you go and get the dress now?' said Olivia. 'I shall go and collect some camellias so we can experiment.'

'If you like. Please take your boots off when you come in.'

Thinking back, I do not know what it was but, as Olivia made her way out to the gardens, I suddenly had the very real sensation that something was terribly wrong.

I looked around the hallway. Nothing had been moved. The house was a little more still than it should be, but it was often quiet. Everything appeared fine.

And yet my skin prickled with the certainty of some misdeed at work.

Standing still, I looked up towards the mezzanine above me, half expecting some dark, silent spectre to be standing there, watching.

Nothing.

'Julia?' Olivia hovered by the door, watching me with confusion.

'Hush.'

As I spoke, a noise came from upstairs. I waved a hand to silence Olivia and then gestured towards the stairwell. It was foolishness, I was sure, but then I thought of that dark, hulking figure who had tried to force his way into the hut. What of the creature who had watched us from the opposite side of the riverbank? Could it have gained access to the house while we were gone?

It is nonsense, I thought. *Dr Richmond is at home. Nothing could happen.*

And yet…

'What is it?' whispered Olivia.

I didn't want to frighten her. 'I think your father must be sleeping,' I said, quietly. 'The house is so still. Let us creep upstairs and check in on that dress. Stay close now.'

Olivia nodded and we climbed the main stairs, taking the doorway to the servants' corridor.

As we tiptoed down the hall, I could see my door was ajar. Suddenly, I felt cold. I had closed it before fetching Olivia from her room that morning, meaning to keep the warmth of my morning fire in. Marian did not clean the servants' rooms. There was no reason for it to be open now.

I signalled for Olivia to stand behind me and pushed on the door. We gaped at what lay before us. My room was in devastation.

Bedding had been ripped back and the mattress pulled halfway onto the floor. Pillows and blankets littered the floorboards, where the rag rug had been tossed aside. Clothing spilled out of drawers, which had been torn from the dresser. The doors to my armoire lay open and the clothes were scattered everywhere.

'Julia,' gasped Olivia, gripping my arm. 'Your dresses…'

They were soaked in soap scum and dirty water. The bowl and jug from the washstand, now cracked and chipped from being thrown into a corner, had been emptied onto them. Scuffmarks covered the skirt of my green dress and part of the lining had torn away as the interloper had clearly walked straight over it to move about the room.

We stood like that for a moment, a tableau from a melodrama. There was a feeling like an inhaled breath.

'Papa!' Olivia cried, and raced down the hallway.

A door opened with a creak.

'Olivia?' Dr Richmond's voice came from downstairs.

'Come quickly.'

'What's this?' Mrs Hayes' voice rang from the kitchen stairs. They creaked under her weight as she started to climb.

'We've been robbed,' Olivia announced.

'We don't know that,' I said, although my eyes lingered a moment on the floorboard beneath the washstand that held my little horde of shameful treasures. Did it look like it had been disturbed?

I heard the sound of feet down in the hall, then pounding up the main stairs. There was a swish of skirts as Mrs Hayes stepped aside to let Dr Richmond past and then he was next to me, pressing against me, a comforting hand on my arm as he looked about the room.

'What in God's name…?' he murmured, surveying the damage.

'Did you see anyone, Mrs Hayes?' said Olivia, who had returned to the doorway.

'I was in the kitchen, my dove,' the housekeeper said. I noted she showed no real surprise. 'I'm sure I didn't hear or see a thing.'

'No?' I said, glaring at her over Olivia's shoulder. 'Not even with furniture being moved and crockery smashed?'

The housekeeper stood in the hallway and folded her arms. Her sleeves were rolled up and she had the gleam of exertion on her brow and at her temples.

'I was wringing laundry in the yard,' she said, sourly. 'Once you buy dresses, someone has to wash them, Miss Pearlie.'

'They might still be here.' Olivia shivered and drew closer to us.

'Calm yourself, Olivia, please.' Dr Richmond's tone was commanding, but even he seemed at a loss as to what to do. 'Miss Pearlie, look to see if there is anything missing while I make a search of the house. I believe I shall have to go to Fellwick and fetch the constable.'

'What? For a bit of a mess?' Mrs Hayes sounded surprised.

'Hardly.' Dr Richmond gestured at the damage. 'At the very least it's wanton destruction of property.'

'My cards,' cried Olivia. 'Someone stole my cards and now Julia's room. Mrs

Hayes, have you lost anything lately?'

'Of course not.' Mrs Hayes' reply was instant.

'Papa?' Olivia turned to her father.

Dr Richmond's brow furrowed. 'I have been looking for those old cufflinks – the ones with the diamond chips. I thought I had left them back at the Peppermint Club back in Mayfair but no luck.'

'Mrs Hayes, you should go downstairs and check your room,' insisted Olivia, aglow with the drama. 'We could have a thief indoors.'

'Aren't you meant to keep her from becoming too heated?' Mrs Hayes said, from the shadows of the corridor. 'You know what her imagination is like.'

'This isn't imagination,' I said, my voice rising in fear and frustration. 'Someone did this.'

'And how do we know it wasn't you?' said Mrs Hayes, her voice as silken and sharp as a drawn dagger.

I drew in a shocked breath, so stunned that I could find no words. I turned in the doorway, staring at Mrs Hayes, who was closer now than I had realised.

She watched me, her face smug and knowing.

'Why would Julia destroy her own room?' Olivia asked.

'Why does anyone do anything, my dove?' said Mrs Hayes, placidly. 'She'll have some reason. There's some who can look right as rain one minute and flip their lid the next.'

'Eda...' Dr Richmond chided.

'But Julia has been with me,' said Olivia. 'All day.'

'That may be, but what about before?' Mrs Hayes asked.

'I do not appreciate the tone of this conversation.' My voice trembled. 'Why would I destroy my own things?'

'I have no idea but it's nothing the constable won't ask.' The housekeeper's voice held amused malice. 'He's not a stupid man. He'll say to himself that it's a funny thing for your room to be the only one touched and no one else's. Almost like they were looking for something. Have you something to hide, Miss Pearlie? Something you're not telling us, perhaps?'

Plip...

Dr Richmond was speaking but I could not hear. My ears filled with the sound of dripping water. Something dark bled into the corner of my vision; a small figure at the foot of the bed, just out of view. Everything felt so cold.

Olivia shuddered.

'Olivia?' said Dr Richmond, turning to her with difficulty as we all stood, huddled in the doorway to my room.

Her eyes were locked on the foot of my bed, and then her gaze turned to me.

'Do you see him?' Her voice was a high, fearful whisper.

Mrs Hayes's eyes narrowed. 'Who? Who do you see?'

Olivia's eyes were wide, her breath coming in wheezing gasps.

'He's here,' she gasped.

I refused to turn my head as the small, dark figure at the edge of my vision took a wobbling step forward. There was the distinct sound of a wet footstep.

Olivia's eyes flickered from it to me, a moth between two flames. I gave a tiny nod of the head.

'It's fine,' I said, though my hands suddenly felt numb. 'Nothing to worry about.'

I could hear the sucking of the thing's lungs, just a whisper above silence.

'What is it?' Mrs Hayes seized the front of my dress in her fist. 'What are you playing at?'

'Eda,' snapped Dr Richmond. 'Enough.'

Ignoring him, Mrs Hayes tightened her grip. 'What is this?' Her voice had lost its certainty. It creaked with fear. 'What is happening?'

'You can hear him,' Olivia whispered. 'You can smell him…'

'Stop it!' Dr Richmond insisted, gripping his daughter's arm. 'You're scaring everyone.'

'*Juja…*'

Did I hear that or was it in my head? I couldn't be sure. Maybe it was merely a memory, a relic from back when Christopher was little. Except now it bubbled up from a swollen chest, through a throat made ragged from suffocated, underwater screams. Yet, the voice… it was still his voice, crooning in that horrible way it would when they played hide and seek and he wanted to scare Lucy.

Plip…

'*Juja…*'

I could bear it no more.

'Please,' I gasped, a tear rolling down one cheek. I squeezed my eyes shut.

'Please...'

I felt the air change. The clamminess was gone and instead there was an oppressiveness that left me winded and brought sweat to my brow.

A floorboard creaked. Mrs Hayes gave a shuddering cough and made a small sound, almost like a wail.

'What is this?' she repeated, pulling me towards her as though to use me as a shield. I was so close, I could feel her arm pressed against my ribs, her thigh pressing against mine through her skirts.

'Is it Archie?' she whispered. 'Please, no.'

I opened my eyes. 'Who?'

Her eyes were wild, her hands shook.

'What is happening?' she wheezed, as though choked. 'What have you brought here?'

'That is *enough*. Mrs Hayes, you will release Miss Pearlie this instant.' Dr Richmond's voice cut through the silence.

I felt the housekeeper's grip relax on my dress and she allowed some breathing space between us. But she was still furious.

'This is you, this is,' she said, pointing a shaking finger at me. 'Ever since you got here, things have been strange.'

'Miss Pearlie is here because I employed her,' Dr Richmond reminded her.

'And just who is she?' asked Mrs Hayes. Her voice shook, wildly. 'You've brought her here into our home and we know nothing about her. She's hiding something. Why are you so blind?'

'You forget yourself.' Dr Richmond's voice made us all flinch. 'I have endured more than is fitting from you but this is far beyond any possible bounds of propriety.'

'Propriety?' Mrs Hayes made the concept sound ridiculous.

'Yes,' said Dr Richmond. 'I admit, our household is not like others but there needs to be a limit. This is enough.'

Mrs Hayes stared at him. Her mouth opened and closed as though she were trying, and failing, to form words in her defence.

Somewhere down the corridor, the muffled sound of a plaintive voice started, the words made senseless by distance and doorways.

'My father requires assistance,' said Dr Richmond, stiffly. 'Call Marian to come and see to this.' He gestured at the room. 'Then we will see if I can trust you enough to have you continue as housekeeper at Mistcoate.'

'I've been here for nearly ten years,' Mrs Hayes reminded him. 'The things I know—'

'Would be dismissed as the ravings of a bitter ex-servant who was jealous of the new staff,' said Dr Richmond. 'Because that's exactly what they are.'

The distant voice began again. 'Florence?'

No one moved.

'I could see to him,' I said.

Mrs Hayes shoved me hard against the wall, and strode down the hallway.

I closed my eyes and leaned back.

'Are you ill? You look as though you are about to collapse.'

Dr Richmond spoke with such tenderness that I presumed he was speaking to Olivia but when I looked up, he was so close I could smell the scent of his rosemary soap. Behind him, Olivia leaned against the wall, shaking and sweating. Her father did not seem to have noticed.

'No,' I said, though I was still trembling. 'Thank you, sir.'

Dr Richmond followed my gaze and turned to Olivia. 'And you?'

'My arm,' said Olivia, cradling it.

'Yes. I'm sorry about that.' He moved as though to embrace her and then, at the last moment, lifted her arm to examine it instead. 'Is it painful?'

'No.' Olivia shook her head. 'I still think we should search the house.'

Dr Richmond sighed.

'I do not think that will be necessary.' He glanced at me, searching for the right words. 'I can see that it may be that Mrs Hayes—'

The doorbell rang. The three of us stared at each other, mystified.

'Marian will get it,' I said.

'I think, considering the circumstances, it is best if I go.' Dr Richmond patted Olivia's shoulder. 'To put your mind at rest.'

When he'd gone downstairs, Olivia reached over and grabbed my hands.

'You saw him, didn't you?' she asked. 'The boy?'

My stomach gave an uncomfortable lurch and my head swam as though I had drunk too much wine. Olivia was looking up at me, expectant and excited beneath the clear exhaustion on her face.

You cannot let her believe it, I thought. *You cannot believe it.*

'I don't know what I saw,' I said. 'I was overexcited and upset.'

Olivia looked disappointed in me.

'You're lying,' she said, sullenly. 'Even Mrs Hayes saw it.'

'Please.' I dropped Olivia's hands. 'I do not want to talk about Mrs Hayes.'

There was a great shout from downstairs, causing us both to jump.

'What on earth is happening now?' I said.

The sound of male voices carried up from the entrance hall. Then came laughter, voices co-mingling.

'Come along,' I said, stroking her shoulder. 'Let's go and see who has arrived.'

Olivia glanced back at my destroyed room and bit her lip.

'It is fine,' I said. 'I can put it all right later.'

'It's not that. It just all feels so strange. Someone was here.'

'I think we know who did it,' I said, tartly.

Olivia shook her head. 'But it couldn't have been Mrs Hayes. She wouldn't do that. It must have been someone else.'

I could see no point in arguing with her.

'If it distresses you, I could check the house once we have seen who is here?'

Olivia nodded her agreement and followed me down the stairs.

The main hallway was a flurry of activity. Dr Richmond was standing with a thin, red-headed man, who was shrugging off his coat so that Marian, her hands gripping the lapels, could take it. They all looked up as we descended.

'Ah, ladies,' said Dr Richmond, turning to us with a tight smile. 'This is my good friend, Dr Peter Joyce. He has saved me a trip to London by visiting us for a few days. Dr Joyce, this is my daughter, Olivia, and Miss Pearlie, her companion.'

Dr Joyce turned his pointed face up to us. He had the same, impish features of a Mr Punch doll and, like Mr Punch, it was hard to tell if this made him appear comical or sinister.

'Good afternoon, sir,' I said and turned to Olivia who, in her confusion over manners, tried to bob a curtsey on the stairs.

Dr Richmond raised his eyebrows but Dr Joyce seemed to enjoy the gesture.

'Well trained, isn't she?' he said.

'Will you need a room made up?' I asked, turning to Dr Richmond.

'Mrs Hayes will see to it,' said Dr Richmond. 'Peter, can I get you a drink?'

'What? No tour of the old pile?' said Dr Joyce, looking around. 'I say, old man, you weren't lying when you said it was a grand place. Mina will be very sorry she missed it. I'm sure she'll want to hear all about it when I'm back.'

He tipped a wink at his friend, whose smile became, if possible, more rigid.

'I am afraid it is our regular maintenance day, Dr Joyce,' I said, thinking quickly. 'You will not see everything to its full advantage until the evening.'

Dr Richmond gave me a grateful look. 'True enough,' he said. 'Come, I believe you still owe me a game of billiards to win back that wager from last time.'

'Which is still unpaid, by the way,' said Dr Joyce.

'Let's see,' said Dr Richmond, leading him into room to the left. 'Marian will bring us drinks and then we'll see who owes who what.'

As they turned into the room, I heard Dr Joyce murmur, 'A housekeeper and a companion. Lucky boy.'

SEVENTEEN

The Devil

The weather was turning cold again. A curling mist had rolled in from the fens, obscuring the woods at the end of the gardens. My breath formed wispy clouds as I hurried to the glasshouse, a shawl wrapped around me. To placate Olivia, I had helped her to search the house and had my own suspicions confirmed when we found nothing untoward. At one point we walked in on Mrs Hayes preparing a guest room. She ignored us both, shaking out pillow cases and smoothing down the coverlet as if we weren't there at all.

Now there was only the garden house to check. Olivia let me venture out into the cold by myself, happy to wait in the kitchen by the range. I did not argue. It was a relief to be alone with my thoughts.

The greenhouse door was unlocked, although the handle was stiff from the damp. Glass still littered the floor from the jagged edges of the smashed lamp, the remnants of Olivia's séance.

It all looked as it had been left that night. Clearly, no one ever came here except Olivia. I picked up a fallen stool and sank down onto it to think. Outside a bird chirruped and another gust of wind shook the grass on the lawn.

Mrs Hayes was the culprit behind the destruction of my room, of that I was certain. But what to do about it? And what of her reaction to the presence in my room? Who was Archie? It seemed to me Olivia knew more than she was telling, and I would make it my business to find out what.

At least it proved one thing; I had been right to choose my hiding place and wrong to trust Mrs Hayes. She knew I had taken the cards and she would search again. She had so little to lose now. I wondered if a new hiding place was needed. I considered giving them to Dr Richmond but that would feel as though I were asking him to finish something I had started.

It was cold, and I pulled my woollen shawl tighter about me. Many of the plants looked withered and listless. I thought of what Olivia had said about Florence Richmond's love of flowers and imagined her working in here, savouring the same solitude I now found.

I plucked at a faded leaf and wondered what Florence had thought of Mrs Hayes. Had she bullied Florence as she did me? I could imagine Mrs Hayes gossiping about her mistress, making snide comments about her being nearly forty and no better than her niece's nursemaid. No wonder Florence would have escaped to the garden house, to grow flowers and plant seeds, and smile as she looked up, seeing Ed Byres striding across the lawn.

Olivia had once told me that Florence had hoped to marry someone but he had refused the idea. Had that been Ed?

And now nobody came out here at all, except Olivia when she was looking for a place to hide.

To hide…

I straightened, looking around me. Yes, this would be a perfect hiding place for anything you wanted to keep secret. I could hide the tarot cards here and if they were ever found, everyone would think Olivia had forgotten them here.

I began to check in boxes and under shelves for a perfect location. As I searched the potting table, a pot overturned, revealing that it was not one large pot but two, stacked together. When I lifted the top pot, I noticed a small, velvet pouch purse, sandwiched between the pots. I lifted it out, surprised by how heavy it was. I pulled on the drawstring and opened it. When I looked inside, my breath caught.

It was filled with money. Rolled notes, guineas and half crowns. It was impossible to tell without counting but, judging by the notes, it was possible there was more than a year's wages.

I dropped the bag quickly. Who could have left this here? Could it be Olivia's? Or possibly Florence's, hidden here for some reason, and forgotten after her death?

But the money looked too clean to have been here for that long.

'Miss Pearlie?' It was Olivia, calling from the garden.

I just had time to shove the purse back and set the pot upright before the door opened and Olivia looked in, her hood hastily thrown over her head.

'Did you find anything?'

'Nothing.' I resisted the urge to glance back at the pots and their secret hoard.

Olivia looked disappointed. 'Papa says we are all to dress for dinner and Marian is asking if you might help with service.'

'Of course.' I followed Olivia out of the garden house, pulling the door shut behind me.

Until I discovered who owned that money, I would not feel safe to hide anything there myself. My treasures would have to stay under the floorboard.

As soon as we were inside, Marian came clattering down the back stairs, her arms full of fabric. She looked red-faced with either exertion or embarrassment and nodded at Olivia, saying, 'That's done there, ma'am.'

'What is done?' I said, looking around for a spare apron.

'I asked Marian to straighten your room,' said Olivia. 'And I can dress myself tonight so you can help Marian.'

Seeing I was about to argue, Marian held up the bundle, which I now recognised as my clothing, smiling in reassurance.

'I've touched nothing that wasn't out of place, miss. I'll put these aside for cleaning and mending. Really, it's not as bad as it looks. I think most of them can be saved.'

'See?' said Olivia, as Marian bustled into the laundry room. 'Everything is well. The house is safe, and you need not worry about your room. Marian needs you. I don't think we've had a dinner party since before she arrived, and Papa is keen to impress his friend.'

She hurried up the back stairs, and I looked after her, surprised by this change in her.

But there was little time to think about it. I tied an apron on and turned to Marian.

'How can I help?' I said. 'Please, keep me busy.'

Watching Marian cook proved to be an education. She was not much older than Olivia but worked with a confidence I would have expected in a more experienced servant. It occurred to me, as we moved about the kitchen, that in my two weeks at Mistcoate, I had utterly failed to notice Marian's industry. In the time it had taken for Olivia and me to search the house, she had inspected the larders, tidied my room, and compiled a menu, in a scrawling hand.

The first course was to be something called Clear Gravy Soup, a concoction made of vegetable stock and Madeira, a bottle of which I was dispatched to fetch from the parlour. This was followed with Huntington Fidget Pie, which was layers of onion, bacon and softened apple, sprinkled liberally with salt and pepper before being covered with a pastry lid. Marian instructed me to add two bay leaves, a sprinkle of sage and some nutmeg, which filled the kitchen with a heavy, delicious scent as it cooked in the oven. The main course was to be sole fillets, fried in an egg and breadcrumb batter, served with a brown butter, vinegar and tarragon sauce.

'Where on earth did you learn to cook like this?' I eventually asked.

Marian smiled as she stirred the soup.

'Mam always said that a woman who cooks well will never have trouble finding work or a man.' Wisps of hair had escaped her cap and her face was flushed, but her apron was still clean.

'Well, I think you are a marvel,' I said, and she blushed with pleasure.

Mrs Hayes did not appear for dinner, as I delivered the various courses to the dining room and refreshed glasses. Olivia had dressed herself in a blue silk gown I had never seen before. It gaped a little at the bust and I wondered if it was an old dress of Florence's. She sat next to Captain Richmond, who was dressed and upright for dinner.

I had barely seen Olivia's grandfather since the night I had helped him back to his bed. He looked pale and shaky but pleased to be in company, I thought. He smiled at me vaguely whenever I walked into the room.

'My word, it's like being at the Ritz,' laughed Dr Joyce, as I poured wine. 'Although I do not find their waiters half as charming.'

He smiled at me in a way I suspected he thought was charming.

'It's a wonder you come to London at all, Georgie,' Dr Joyce joked, reaching for his glass. 'When there's so much comfort to be had here.'

'Comfort and freedom rarely go together,' observed Dr Richmond, downing the dregs of his wine and holding out his glass for a refill.

The dinner continued without much incident. I had thought Olivia would wish to stay at the table and find out more about London but, as soon as the meal finished, she rose and gave her grandfather her arm, leading him back up the stairs to his room.

The two doctors retired to the parlour. Marian and I cleaned the kitchen and ate our supper in front of the range, chatting about the evening. We'd never spent time together before, and I found I liked her.

'Thank you, by the way, for tidying my room earlier,' I said.

'It was no trouble, miss.' Marian's smile dimmed. She glanced at the servants stairwell behind me and lowered her voice. 'Have you any idea who did it?'

'None at all,' I lied. 'I'm sure there was no real malice involved. For all I know, it was the captain, in some kind of fit.'

'You don't believe that, do you miss?' She looked concerned. 'Captain Richmond is a lamb, and how could someone with his health get a room into that state?'

'You're right.' I rose, lifting Marian's bowl from the table to put it into the sink. 'All the same, please don't let it worry you. I'm quite sure in my own mind that it will not happen again.'

'It does give me a turn though to think of someone sneaking about,' said Marian.

There was a pause, as she seemed to struggle with her thoughts. 'I'm sorry, miss. I probably should have said about the back door before but I thought it was just me being daft.'

Something in her tone made me look up.

'What about the door?'

'Have you not seen? It's all scuffed around the bottom and the handle's all loose,' said Marian. 'Like someone's been trying to force it.'

I hurried over to check, letting cold night air flood the kitchen as I crouched down to look at the exterior handle.

She was right. On the bottom of the door were fresh scuff marks, as though someone had kicked it. I reached up and jostled the handle. It rattled loosely. Around it, some of the wood had splintered.

A shriek rang out across the lawn, making me jump.

A fox, I told myself, although my nerves were shaken, and I shut the door hastily.

'Well?' said Marian as I seized the key, testing the lock still worked.

'It will be fine for tonight,' I said, affecting a nonchalance I did not feel. 'But tomorrow I will speak to Dr Richmond. Perhaps it is weather damage.'

It isn't though, I thought.

At bedtime, I allowed Marian to carry the lamp with her to her room on the second floor, and forced myself to walk down the passage to my own room in the dark.

When I reached the door, I realised I did not want to go in. I had not let myself think about the thing Olivia and I had both seen at the foot of the bed. I did not want to think about it now. All the same, the room had to be faced.

I twisted the handle and stepped inside. A candle burned low on the window sill, casting a faint glow. True to her word, Marian had set things back into order and I was relieved to find that the physical damage was minimal. A quick inspection of my underfloor hiding place showed nothing had been disturbed, although a look in the armoire was less encouraging. Nearly every dress was missing, taken by Marian to be mended.

The mattress and bedding had been put back onto the bed, the cracked ewer and washbasin replaced with an undamaged set, and the heat from our industrious kitchen below meant that the room felt quite snug. I closed the door, sliding the bolt firmly into place.

The damaged back door gave me much to think about. Marian had seemed relieved by my suggestion the damage was due to weather but neither of us had been truly convinced.

What if it hadn't been Mrs Hayes after all? Could someone have crept into the house and done this?

But why my room only? I thought. *I have nothing of value to anyone except for my secrets.*

Of course, there was the possibility that Mrs Hayes had damaged the door herself to lay blame on a burglar, but this didn't seem right. All the same, I determined that I would go to Dr Richmond tomorrow for advice. I worried still about Mrs Hayes. She was proving to be a very dangerous enemy.

I was readying myself for bed when there was a soft knock at the door.

I straightened at the wash basin, water dripping from my face onto the floor. Realising it was most likely Olivia, I felt my way to the door, eyes partially shut, and drew back the lock bolt.

'Come in, Olivia,' I said, walking back to reach for a cloth.

Behind me, I heard the door open and someone step into the room. However, the step was much heavier than Olivia's.

I looked up to see Dr Richmond standing in the doorway.

'Sir.' Hastily, I lifted my wrap from the peg where it hung and pulled it around me. 'Is everything well? Is Olivia in need of me?'

'She is fine. Although Peter gave her too much wine at dinner.' He smiled and his teeth were stained dark. 'I am afraid you may find her rather unhappy in the morning.'

I tightened my grip on the wrap, hoping it would cover the lack of stays beneath. 'At least she is not upset,' I said. 'It has been a trying day.'

Dr Richmond shuffled into the room, leaning a little on the wall for guidance.

He is drunk, I thought, as my employer sank down onto the end of the bed. I chose to remain standing near the open door.

Dr Richmond ran a hand through his hair and fixed me with a bleary look.

'I don't like him much,' he said. 'Peter.'

'I do not—'

'He's an ass. But he has been good to me.' Dr Richmond regarded his hands and, for a moment, looked like a schoolboy. 'I owe him a great deal. Especially now. But his arrival was unfortunate. It has not allowed us to discuss much.'

He paused, waiting for me to speak. When I refused, he continued.

'Olivia showed excellent manners at dinner. After her episode in your room today, I worried. But she has recovered quicker than I might have imagined. I hope she didn't scare you. She even had me thinking I saw things.'

But there was *something there*, I thought, surprised at my sudden certainty. *I saw it. I felt its presence.*

'She is very convincing,' I said, cautiously. 'But she is quick to move on, I feel.'

He nodded vigorously. 'It is thanks to you. The idea of the party helps, as you suspected it would.' He glanced at my open armoire, mostly empty now. 'Olivia intimated to me that your wardrobe is rather the worse for wear.'

I could not deny it. 'They will all need repairs. Marian and Alice Byres will help me.'

Dr Richmond pressed his lips together 'I will ask Mrs Hayes to help.'

I stiffened. 'With respect, sir, I would rather have little to do with Mrs Hayes. Under the circumstances.'

He tilted his head as if to help him focus on me. 'I fear that I have not managed this situation as well as I might have. Mrs Hayes is a woman of passions. Not many want that in their staff but, for Mistcoate House to remain a haven for my daughter and my father, I need someone of a loyal and devoted disposition. In fact, it is something I see in you.'

He watched me closely, as if to ascertain whether the compliment had flattered me. 'We have not had anyone new in the household for quite some time and those who have been here have proven to be unsuitable. I think Mrs Hayes has become over protective. What she did today was inexcusable, and yet I hope you will forgive her. I am sure she is very sorry for it and will, of course, make a full apology.'

I do not want it, I thought, and tensed my jaw to ensure I did not blurt out the words. Instead I said, 'Forgive me, sir, but it sounded as though your intention earlier was to dismiss her.'

Dr Richmond rose from the bed, springs clinking as he did so. 'I spoke without thinking. Retaining a new housekeeper is not so easy for an old widower, you know, and Mrs Hayes knows how we do things here. It gives a degree of comfort, although I appreciate that is not currently apparent. What I can guarantee though, Miss Pearlie, is that you will have no more interference from Mrs Hayes. You have my personal guarantee on that.'

I was furious. Surely, the man could not believe that he could keep Mrs Hayes under control? I had never seen a housekeeper behave the way she did and yet she seemed to have the entire house in her thrall.

Tightening my jaw, I made myself give a curt nod. 'Yes, sir.'

He seemed to have grown more sober, standing and walking towards me without wavering.

'You are unsatisfied.' He spoke softly, a note of regret in his voice.

'I am not in a position to be satisfied or unsatisfied, sir. You have given me a very reasonable explanation and I am grateful you took the time to speak to me about it.'

I lifted my chin and met his gaze directly. The light of the candle highlighted flecks of gold in his eyes and hair, and I could smell the cologne clinging to his shirt collar.

'We are very lucky to have you, you know.' His voice was a low murmur. 'What Eda did today was a fit of madness. But I should hate to think of what would happen if you decided to leave us.'

I was uncomfortably aware of how alone we were in my rooms. He could just reach out and touch me if he wanted to, I realised, standing here with the household asleep, and no one to see.

I kept my tone cool. 'I would not get far without my reference and my pay, I assure you.'

'Still,' he said, 'I would be happier knowing that I had left you satisfied.'

He leaned towards me.

Something creaked in the hallway; it sounded like footsteps. Dr Richmond sprang away from me and stepped to the door to look out into the dark corridor.

'There is no one there,' he said, as though to reassure me.

'It does that,' I told him. 'Especially at night.'

He hesitated in the doorway, unsure whether to retreat or return.

'Thank you again, sir,' I said. 'Goodnight.'

His brow furrowed and then he gave a stern nod.

'Goodnight, Miss Pearlie.'

And with that he was gone, shutting the door behind him.

EIGHTEEN

The Sun

15th July 1889
Astor House, Kent

He smiles at me when he thinks no one is looking. I thought I was imagining it but now the maids have noticed. They giggle whenever they see the two of us together. The new girl, Margaret, was impertinent enough to make a sly comment in the kitchen. I asked Mrs Morris if she allowed the staff to make insinuations like that.

20th July 1889
Astor House, Kent

Hottest day so far. Took the children to the pond to wade for the afternoon. Bit naughty but what is the harm if I am with them and watching closely? Lucy refused to wear a bathing suit and it is too warm to argue with her. Gave her an old dress and a set of long bloomers instead. I'll never understand it. She's casual enough about the bruises when I ask about them, then she's embarrassed later. Christopher frolicked like an otter. His papa will be lucky if he doesn't go for a sailor. Never happier than in the water. Says his father has promised to take him river swimming although I know that John is far too busy these days.

The unrest in the north of Ireland disturbs John greatly. I'm glad I'm ignorant of it all – I'm sure he must think me a dreadful bore. No matter how much he seeks me out.

Today he slipped away from the house and the man-servant who keeps him on such a tight rein, and sat on the grass with the children and I. *Taking a break from politics and land,* he said. When he leaned back to watch the children wading in the pond, his hand covered mine and he did not move it until Christopher called out to him.

1st August 1889
Astor House, Kent
Horrible day. Violently hot and Mrs Morris has had to dismiss Margaret, which I am not sorry over, but she did cry and carry on. Apparently, she has been stealing from the other servants and failed to return a small item Mrs Morris had hidden in one of the sitting rooms. She denies it, but several missing items were found in her room, although Mrs Morris' own watch that she was given by the late Mr Morris is still missing. I think it has pained Mrs Morris greatly. I brought the children out of the house so they would not have to hear Margaret weeping, but she made a show of herself from the moment she was confronted until she was out on the road.

It very much upset Lucy. I suspect Margaret was in the habit of slipping her treats. Christopher thinks it's wildly funny. Of course.

8th August 1889
Astor House, Kent
Found Mrs Morris' watch. Margaret must have hidden it and forgotten about it but what she was doing with it in the nursery, I have no idea. She must have thought no one would think to search the children's dresser but she should have known that I would find it. No matter. I have returned it and all is well. Also found a gold earring, of all things, under Christopher's bed. I threw it out of the window.

I am glad that that Margaret creature is gone. Now that will be the end of it.

16th August 1889
Astor House, Kent
John says we must enjoy civilised company while we can, which I agree with. We sit in the library together once the children are in bed. He reads and I sew. It is oddly domestic. I wondered aloud what I would do if he had to return to Ireland – probably have to sit in the kitchen with the grooms and the maids, drinking beer and playing whist. John said he did not think that would be so bad but he did not

like the idea of the grooms.

I said no one likes the idea of their governess getting married. He said that was not what he meant. Would have pressed his meaning but Lucy arrived at the door in one of her moods and I had to take her straight upstairs. I think she was still half in a dream, she said she's afraid of her room. I said *why on earth are you afraid of your room? Isn't Christopher there with you?*

John was rather formal and distant when I returned. I think I was impertinent, mentioning marriage. Possibly he thinks I have my eye on someone?

3rd September 1889
Astor House, Kent

Everything is so different. I am different – changed – a new woman. A full, complete, enjoyed and appreciated woman! I cannot share what has been – it cannot be told but I am so happy. So complete and so happy!

9th September 1889
Astor House

Played hide-and-seek in the gardens with John and the children. He found me in the arbour. Stayed for some fifteen minutes together in secret while Christopher searched for Lucy outside. Composed ourselves in time for Lucy to start crying over something Christopher said. Really, she is too old to be so sensitive to her brother's teasing.

I know I should worry in case someone should see us, but if John does not care why should I?

18th September 1889
Astor House, Kent

John has had to return to Ulster. The children are miserable. All of us out of sorts. Christopher is like a spitting cat and Lucy clings to me. I say they are both too old for these tantrums, which just makes it worse. Mrs Morris and Cook at a loss for information or a return date. I can't bear it.

23rd September 1889
Astor House, Kent

He is a hateful little demon. I do not believe it was an accident and I do not believe he is sorry, no matter how innocent he looks. He is leaving for school tomorrow and we are all glad of it. I shall write to John and request that he is made to stay there if he is not careful.

29th September 1889
Astor House, Kent

He is gone. Maybe we shall have some quiet until Christmas. Lucy seems quite settled but I think loneliness will drive me mad…

NINETEEN

Eight of Swords

I woke in the night to the sound of laughter. Somewhere someone was playing a waltz on the piano. It made no sense. Who could be playing music in the middle of the night?

I sat up, the blankets falling off me. 'Olivia? Marian?'

Nobody replied.

I struggled out of bed, tripping over the rag rug in the dark. The room was freezing. Pulling my wrapper down off the back of the door I slid back the lock and stumbled out into the corridor.

I could see light spilling from the mezzanine landing as the waltz echoed around the house.

I'd reached the main landing when I felt the strange stillness take me.

Was it darker here? Colder?

The music stopped abruptly. All was quiet.

Why had I imagined there'd been light? Everything was in shadow, with only a shaft of pale moonlight drifting through the windows.

You fool, I thought, taking a step back. *You were dreaming.*

I was turning to go back to my room when I heard a soft sound, almost like a sigh.

A chill crept down my spine.

I turned to look again but nothing was there. Only the darkness, watching me.

But no. I was wrong. Something moved on the other side of the mezzanine.

There was a small shadow there, deeper than the others.

'Who is there?'

It came out as a choked whisper, too hoarse and low for anyone to hear.

Again, came that breathy sound.

My heart stopped.

There was a face in the gloom.

Olivia was standing on the gallery level opposite me, the opening to the hallway below in between us. I could have sworn she had not been there a moment ago but the white of her skin seemed to soak up the moonlight, making her face and hands starkly visible against the gloom.

She stood, as still and poised as a statue, her dust-coloured eyelashes resting gently against her cheeks.

She was sleepwalking.

'Miss Olivia?' I whispered.

She made no move.

I started to make my way along the hallway, ready to guide her back to bed. 'Miss Olivia – it is time that you went to your room.'

I froze, mid-step.

Behind Olivia, two shadows moved. Their bulk tensed and shifted and suddenly I realised that they were not shadows but figures. Dark figures, obscured in the gloom, flanking Olivia. Towering over her.

My breathing stopped. My arms broke into goosebumps so urgent that they were almost painful. All sound died except the pounding of my own heart in my ears.

Olivia, seemingly unaware, turned and started to make her slow, methodical way down the hall towards Captain Richmond's room. The figures followed, echoing her rocking gait. I stood, transfixed, until they passed through the arched doorway and were disappearing down the corridor. She was leading them to her grandfather's room.

'Miss Pearlie?'

The voice startled me so completely I gave a cry and almost sank to the floor but managed to steady myself on the handrail.

The lamps were lit. The eerie darkness of the house was gone. Olivia was nowhere to be seen. In her place stood Mrs Hayes in her nightclothes, hands on her hips. She stared at me as though I were an animal at the botanical gardens who had begun to worry at itself.

'Are you unwell?'

'I... I saw... I thought that I...' I couldn't seem to find my words. I tried to look composed but I still gripped the railing and I could feel a fine needling of sweat on my brow.

'I thought I heard something. Music,' I said, finally. 'But possibly not. Was it you playing that music? I did not know you played.'

'Miss Pearlie, you are unwell,' announced Mrs Hayes.

'I am fine,' I insisted.

'Poor thing,' said a voice. I turned to my left and saw her in a corner. The Soho witch-child, a dark ribbon of blood unfurling from her nose. She had never had that before, had she?

Maybe in my nightmares but not really. Not really.

'Poor thing,' she wheedled again. 'She's imagining things.'

'I think she might be mad,' agreed Mrs Hayes.

I turned from one to the other. No... surely they could not see each other?

'Yes, quite, quite mad,' said the witch-child and grinned, exposing irregular rows of rotting teeth covered in a dark, slick film of blood.

'I would also advise against meetings with Dr Richmond at improper times,' continued Mrs Hayes, as if there was no bleeding child in the corner. 'Possibly it was not a cause for concern in previous positions.'

'Not for you,' giggled the witch-child, slurping at her teeth.

'But Dr Richmond has a reputation to uphold and it would not do for people to hear of him hosting the lady's maid.'

'Companion,' I heard myself say.

'Whatever you are. It is improper for you to be alone with him in your bedroom. People talk.'

'But I haven't done anything,' I said.

'No?' said Mrs Hayes and suddenly there was the smell of the pond in the air.

'*Juja...*'

I looked down. Something was standing at the bottom of the stairs. A small wet figure.

Plip...

I bolted upright in bed, my scream unformed as the nightmare drained away, shaking and sweating with the force of it.

Around me, the house sighed.

TWENTY

The Lovers

'Did you hear anything at all last night?' said Marian, the next morning.

'Dr Richmond came to see me at one point,' I said, eyes on the breakfast trays. 'He wanted to talk about yesterday.'

'No,' she said, darkly. 'I didn't mean talking.'

My queasy dreams of laughter and music from the night before stirred in my memory.

'You didn't hear music, did you? Or laughing?'

'Some laughing, yes,' said Marian and shook her head. 'But that's not what I mean either.'

'What do you mean, then?' I said. 'Did you hear someone in the house?'

'Oh, I heard plenty,' said Marian, savagely slapping the dough she was kneading.

It suddenly occurred to me that Marian's rooms were on the side of the house, above the guest bedrooms. I peered at her and then found my gaze drawn in the direction of Mrs Hayes' rooms.

Marian continued to abuse the dough. 'She'll do anything to get her way. She'll use anyone. If it were me, miss, I'd suspect her before Captain Richmond for what happened in your room.'

I gave her a puzzled look. 'What exactly did you hear last night?'

But Marian wouldn't say anything more and I didn't feel comfortable pressing her. As I carried the breakfast tray up the back stairs, I wondered what she might have overheard. What could Mrs Hayes have done or said?

I discovered the housekeeper in the corridor outside Olivia's door. I waited in the shadows, not wanting to confront her.

'Olivia,' she said, her head inclined towards the door. 'Please, my lamb, I must speak to you. I don't know what that awful girl has said but you cannot keep me out. Olivia?'

She paused, pursed her lips and whispered, 'Just tell me – was it him? I need to know or I'll never rest. Livvy?'

When no answer came, she gave a breathy sob, her hand flying to her mouth, smothering the sound. She glanced down the corridor and for one awful moment I thought she had seen me but then she turned and started towards the captain's room.

I waited until she was out of sight before hurrying over to knock on the door.

'It's Julia,' I whispered. 'I have breakfast.'

'Oh, good.' Olivia opened the door a crack. 'Come in.'

Her room was more orderly today, and the dirty plates had been cleared. Olivia took the toast while sitting on her bed, still dressed in her night clothes.

'You will get crumbs everywhere,' I warned.

She shrugged and continued to eat as I opened the curtains and lifted the sash.

'It's bad for you to always keep the windows closed,' I said. 'You must have fresh air.'

'That's what *she* says.'

'Oh? She's "she" now, is she?'

'Surely you're not going to defend her?' Olivia said, her mouth filled with bread. 'After all the things she did?'

'Well. She was very upset just now,' I said.

'I shan't be softened by it,' Olivia decided. 'All that tosh about you hiding something. So what if you are? It's not like she's not done things.'

She shook her head, as if trying to rid herself of a thought.

'Come,' I said. 'Let me arrange your hair before you get dressed.'

I waited until she was sitting in front of me, the glass angled so I could see her face, before I said,

'Olivia, are *you* hiding anything?'

Her eyes flickered but would not meet mine in the glass. 'What do you mean?'

I began to brush her hair in long, slow strokes, cradling the buttery white strands in my hand.

'What we saw the other day,' I said. 'Mrs Hayes seemed very troubled by it. She mentioned "Archie". Who was that?'

Olivia shrugged.

'I have an idea that he might have been her husband,' I said, in the voice I'd used when Lucy was being difficult, the one that sounded as though I were talking to myself. 'She mentioned to me that her husband was dead. She did not seem overly fond of him. I imagine she would not like to think he was haunting the halls of Mistcoate.'

I peeked in the glass. Olivia was looking at me from under her pale eyelashes.

'He used to beat her,' she revealed. 'So badly she couldn't walk sometimes.'

'And did she tell you that or is it like with Mrs Lewes?'

Olivia flinched as though I had struck her. I pretended not to notice, continuing to work until the tangles of sleep were smoothed out and I could start braiding.

'She told me,' she said, after a moment. 'She had all these bruises everywhere. Not real ones but still. I could see them. They're not as clear now but she still feels them. Then there's the baby.'

'Baby?' I met her eyes in the mirror.

Olivia paused and then said, 'She thought he might stop when the baby came. He promised he would but he got drunk and angry. He hit her with the poker and she fell.'

Her voice trailed away.

That explained the scars, then. I despised the housekeeper, but she hadn't deserved that. Nobody did.

'Poor woman,' I said, resuming brushing. 'No wonder she is protective of you. What happened to him?'

'There was a fire.' Olivia's voice was flat.

'And then she came here?'

'No.' She tried to shake her head but I held her still. 'She was already here when it happened.'

'Then who told her about it?' I said.

'I did,' said Olivia. 'I saw it one night. During a reading. She was frightened. Not sleeping and she asked about it and I saw it. The flames and him inside, screaming.'

She fell silent. I looked into the mirror. Her eyes were reddened and her mouth was trembling.

'Do you think I'm wicked?' she asked, in a tiny voice.

I wrapped my arm around her shoulders and kissed the top of her head. 'No,' I said, as two fat tears spilled down over her cheeks. 'I don't think you're wicked at all.'

'Sometimes,' she said, 'sometimes I think I might be.'

'Why do you say that?'

But she shook her head and would not say anything more.

I left her dressing and took the plate down to the kitchen. As I exited the room, I saw Dr Joyce and Mrs Hayes in close conference in the hallway, their heads bent together.

'Don't fret. I'll talk to him,' Dr Joyce was saying.

'I am really very grateful,' said Mrs Hayes.

'Oh yes?' he said with a smile. 'How grateful?'

Mrs Hayes gave a low chuckle. The door clicked as it closed behind me. They snapped apart, Mrs Hayes shoving what looked like a piece of paper back into her pocket. I carried on down the stairs, pretending I had not noticed them.

It was a relief when Dr Richmond announced a trip into Fellwick that would keep him and Dr Joyce out for most of the next day.

'I've always said, it's easier to get things done about the house without men in the way,' said Marian as we dried the dishes later. Her mood seemed to have improved since breakfast. 'Except Captain Richmond, of course.'

'Is Mrs Hayes with him now?'

'Not on your life,' said Marian. 'The post arrived while you was upstairs and she's all dithery over some letter. Hasn't asked a thing about his breakfast or anything else. Not to worry though, I have it in hand.'

I busied myself helping put away the breakfast things but I could not shake a distinct feeling of unease. What could be in a letter that would get Mrs Hayes so excited?

She loathed me so; I feared her plotting.

'Marian,' I said. 'You didn't happen to see what the letter was about?'

'Nothing except a London postmark, miss.'

'Could it be from family?' I asked. 'Her mother, perhaps?'

'Couldn't be her mother, miss,' said Marian. 'She's been dead these past few years. Dr Richmond took her to the funeral himself.' She gave me a curious look. 'Is anything wrong, miss?'

I smiled at her. 'Thinking too much about things that don't concern me, Marian. Nothing that can't be fixed by a dance lesson with Olivia. If you wish to indulge in a moment's folly, you can look in on us in the breakfast room.'

The next day dawned with a steady, sullen downpour that continued all through the morning.

'Take the carriage to your dress fitting today,' Dr Richmond told me at breakfast. 'This rain will do Olivia no good.'

Just as we were about to climb up into the cab, though, Mrs Hayes appeared in the doorway in her bonnet and capelet.

'Will you join us, Mrs Hayes?' I asked.

She gave me a cool look and set off down the drive without a backwards glance.

'Leave her to sulk,' said Olivia, sounding so much like Mrs Hayes herself that I had to suppress a smile.

We arrived in Fellwick early, so I made the driver take a detour to Meadow's Tea Shop to make use of the spending money Dr Richmond had allotted to us. As I climbed down, I noticed there was someone new behind the counter in the greengrocers next door – a rather large, red-faced man whose jovial voice boomed into the tea room through the dividing wall.

'He's a bit of a caution, that man,' Mrs Meadows said, as she handed me my box of iced buns. 'I never know where I am with him. Has me laughing one minute and pulling my hair out the next. Still, he's an improvement on Old Duncan. He went off to Cambridge, you know. He's a street preacher, I heard, telling the educated about their sins.'

She leaned closer and lowered her voice. 'Have you heard the latest? Little Emma Woodson got attacked by the Shambler last night. She's unharmed, it seems, but shaken, bless her. I swear, the minute they catch him, we'll all rest easy.'

I hurried out into the rain to find Olivia standing there, clutching an umbrella.

I gave her a puzzled look. 'What are you doing?'

'I sent the carriage away,' she said. 'I thought we could walk. I love walking in the rain.'

'It loses its allure very quickly,' I warned. 'Come then.'

Linking arms, our string-tied parcel swinging precariously, we strode down the lane towards the Byres house. The roof was practically in sight when Olivia gave a disgusted cry and lurched into me so hard, I nearly lost my balance.

'What are you doing?' I asked.

'I slipped in something.' She squinted down at the road, soiled boot raised.

I looked down and stiffened.

It was a rabbit carcass. At least, I thought it was. It was hard to tell without the head. It lay stretched out on the road, legs stretched out as though still in flight. The body seemed to be intact but the wound about the neck was ragged and raw. Blood had sprayed across the verge and was now black and congealed. The head was nowhere to be seen. Olivia's fingers dug into my arm, a strangled noise emitting from her throat. She had looked long enough to decipher what it was.

'Something has been hunting,' I said, pulling Olivia away from the gruesome sight. 'Do not let it upset you.'

'It's like at the hut,' she muttered.

'Nonsense, we saw nothing like that at the—'

Realisation dawned. I stopped and turned to face her. 'Olivia, please tell me that you have not been back there by yourself?'

She blinked at me. 'Only once.'

'*Olivia.*'

'I won't go back anymore,' she promised. 'I just wanted to see if my cards were there. There were bones on the bed and blood on the mattress. It was horrible. Why would an animal drag something up onto the bed to eat it?'

'Promise me you won't go back again,' I said.

'I promise.'

'Good. Come along.'

I pulled her along with me, trying not to think of the hulking figure that had watched us that day.

I had worried that Alice would be standing waiting for us at the door, but when we reached the house, everything seemed quiet. When I rang the doorbell, there was no reply.

'Did we get the wrong day?' asked Olivia, her voice rising over the patter of the rain on our umbrella.

I knew we had not. It was not like Alice, I was sure, to miss an appointment. Something had to be wrong.

'Wait here,' I said, passing her the parcel from the tea house.

I hurried around to the side gate. The lock was stiff but after some struggling it slid back and I slipped into the garden. I followed the small path to the back of the house, hoping to find her in the kitchen, perhaps unable to hear the door.

As I rounded the corner, I froze.

A man was in the garden. At least I thought it was a man. All I could make out through the sheets of rain was a hunched figure in an oversized coat, hacking at something viciously. My mind filled with the image of the mutilated animal on the road, the damaged back door, my destroyed room. The danger I'd felt surrounding us for days.

My heart pounded in my chest.

'*Police*!'

My voice cut through the rain, bouncing off the trees. The figure jumped, the spade in his hand landing in the mud with an audible slap. He turned.

It was Ed Byres. His hair was saturated, rivulets of rain running down his face. His coat hung open, revealing a soaked shirt, open at the neck and a pair of old trousers tucked into boots. He had not been hacking at anything living. He was digging a runoff ditch next to a vegetable bed.

He blinked the rain from his eyes. 'Miss Pearlie?'

'Reverend Byres. I am here to see Alice,' I stammered, suddenly aware of my own rain-bedraggled appearance.

He looked as confused as I felt. 'Is she not—'

'Edward James Byres, what *are* you doing?'

We turned to see Alice standing at the back door, Olivia peeking over her shoulder.

'The whole cabbage row would have been drowned,' said Byres, gesturing at the bed behind him.

Alice looked from her brother to me. 'So will you both if you don't come in now. Honestly, Ed, you're meant to be at the church offices.'

Both visibly mortified, Ed Byres and I shuffled into the warmth of the kitchen.

'You are soaked, both of you,' Alice scolded. 'Wait here. Miss Olivia, please go upstairs and try on your dress. It is hanging in the studio.'

Alice followed Olivia. Reverend Byres and I stayed behind as he pulled off the coat and hung it on the back of the kitchen door.

For a moment neither of us spoke, and then he turned to me. 'My apologies if I startled you.'

'No, I am sorry I shouted.' I laughed. 'Oh, it is too ridiculous.'

He smiled, a droplet of rain dripping off a strand of hair. 'You did not think I was our resident bogeyman, did you?'

'And who could blame her?' said Alice, reappearing with her arms full of towels.

There was a pink tinge to her cheeks and she had a somewhat manic quality to her. She gave a cough and Ed took a step towards her but she waved him away.

'I admit that I did,' I confessed. 'How is Emma Woodson?'

'He just scared her, I think,' said Byres, glancing reproachfully at Alice before taking a towel and moving over to the kitchen range.

'The poor girl was still shaking an hour later.' Alice's voice seemed strained and quiet. She wiped her lips with a handkerchief and gave a shuddering sigh before turning to her brother. 'You say the Shambler is harmless but I cannot agree. Harmless men do not accost young women. You should call a council meeting. People are worried.'

'I have,' said Byres, sounding weary. 'Tomorrow. I need today, Alice. You know that I always need today.'

The pleading in his voice made me look from Byres to Alice. What was special about today?

'You will not always be able to have it,' said Alice.

The box of buns we had brought was on the countertop next to the sink. She lifted them and reached for the kettle but Byres was there first.

'Yes, but until then, I will,' he said, placing it on the range top.

Alice made a face and handed me the box. 'Eat these. Stay here. Get warm. I will call you once Olivia is ready.'

Byres and I sat close to the range, the buns balanced on a stool between us.

Byres selected one and took a large bite, chewing thoughtfully.

'Is it too much? Taking over the parish with Reverend Smythe gone?' I said, taking a bun for myself.

Byres shook his head. 'No. In fact, in many ways, it is easier. I can make decisions on my own now.' He met my eyes. 'I am truly sorry I frightened you out there.'

'It is nothing,' I said.

Another raindrop had collected at the end of his hair, where it had fallen over his face. Quite without thinking, I reached over and plucked the droplet from the strand, the water coating my fingers. He reached out, a kitchen towel from the range wrapped in his hand and covered my fingers in warm, scratchy linen, rubbing to dry them.

'I am a lucky man,' he said. 'To have such a friend.'

As he said this, another droplet fell from his hair and landed squarely on his mouth, running over his lips. He was still holding my hand in his, our skin separated by a tea towel. I at once felt the thrill of proximity but also a great sense of peace, as if there was no world beyond the two of us in front of the fire. We were so close. I could lean over and rest my head on his shoulder. I imagined the comforting, warm weight of his arm around my back and then, without warning, an image of us against the table, frantically clutching at each other, gasping and hungry. It filled my mind so entirely that I pulled my hand away in shock.

'There was something else,' I said, to cover my confusion. 'Something happened on the road.'

I recounted the story of the rabbit and then, feeling I could hardly leave it out, I told him about the hut. By the time I was finished, he looked troubled and more tired than before.

'It is just becoming more and more apparent that I am an utter fool,' he said.

'I cannot say I believe that.'

'Then you are kinder than most, but there will be several people who will share my opinion. Possibly I should have let the constable run the Shambler out when he first appeared. It seemed unfair to demonise someone who simply wished to avoid the workhouse – but now, all this...' He waved one hand. 'I cannot think why, but it is clear that his intentions are not as innocent as I had hoped.'

'He mentioned the name Winnie,' I said. 'Does that mean anything to you?'

Byres shook his head. 'Nothing. But, if the man is unwell, Winnie could be anyone. Or she may not even exist. No, it is as Alice says. I cannot help everyone.'

'It is quite heroic to try though,' I said.

'Sadly, it is atonement, not heroism.' He gave a thin smile. 'Apologies, Miss Pearlie, I am not pleasant company today. It is the anniversary of my father's death.'

So that was what he had meant earlier.

'I'm sorry. Alice had mentioned him. She said that he was killed in a mining accident?'

Byres gave a snort.

'That, and shame.' He searched my face. 'Have you ever been in a mine, Miss Pearlie? Of course you haven't – stupid of me to ask. But I'm glad, because it's hellish. Imagine a cramped, wet tunnel smelling of decay where men crawl around under tonnes of earth. I hated it. But my father was determined. I mean, there were lads younger than me working. Sitting in little tunnels with the canary. I was thirteen. Old enough.'

He gave an involuntary shudder. I noticed his hands were shaking. He gripped them to stop the trembling and addressed the fire instead of me, his Yorkshire accent becoming thicker as he spoke.

'I couldn't do it. I didn't want to do it. I wanted fresh air and a garden and books. He didn't understand. I was meant to start work that day but instead I was taking my entrance exams to the boys' school a few towns over.' He paused, looking down at his hands. 'I wasn't there, so my dad went down the pit without me. One of the men hit a soft wall, releasing fire-damp that ignited one of the torches. Alice told me they could hear the noise of the explosion all the way to our cottage. We never did find him. Even with us all digging for days. Probably nothing to find.

'After that none of the men wanted me near the mine and Ma would barely look at me, never mind speak to me. When I was offered the scholarship, I left. I never even thought twice about it. So you see…' He looked up at me, eyes wet and red-rimmed. 'It is more proper to say that it is cowardice that drives me. Not heroism.'

I shook my head. 'I don't think that is true. Cowards do not, as a rule, have people relying on them. It makes them feel burdened. Someone who cares and who does not feel that saving someone makes them a burden? That is heroic. At least, I think so.'

I lifted my hand and laid it on his cheek. It happened quite without my meaning to. He turned into it, his nose, cold with rain, pressed against my thumb and the subtle heat of his mouth against my palm in a gesture that was not quite a kiss.

'Maybe,' said Byres, lifting his face from my hand. 'Thank you.'

'Julia!' Olivia's voice startled me so I rocked backwards on my stool.

'Coming.' I began to gather my things and left the confused clergyman, still clutching the tea towel, as I rushed from the room. There was a glass in the hall and when I caught sight of myself, face red, hair wild and frizzed from the rain and wind, it was all I could do not to sob.

'*Who do you think you are?*' The witch-child sat at the top of the stairs, sneering at me. '*If he knew the truth about you, he'd not even acknowledge you in the street.*'

I turned from my own reflection and ascended the stairs, quivering, burning and ashamed.

Alice and Olivia were in the attic room.

Olivia stood on a stool gazing at herself in the glass, standing so close her breath misted the surface. Her skin was milky and pure against the delicate duck-egg stripes.

'I wish I knew where my cards were,' she murmured. 'Then I could ask them about romance before we go.'

'This dress will tell you more about possible romance than any cards,' said Alice, her mouth full of pins. 'It is the only oracle you need.'

'It really is stunning,' I said, smiling at her. 'I cannot imagine how you have managed to produce so much in so little time.'

As Olivia hopped down to the floor, Alice turned to me.

'Would you pop up onto the stool for a moment?'

'Me? Why?'

Alice made an irritated sound and urged me towards the stool. I did as I was told. She disappeared for a few moments and then stepped back into view, holding what looked like sections of a dress, all made in the beautiful dark red satin.

'What is this?' I said, staring at the fabric, my heart fluttering.

'A little birdie suggested that it would be very much appreciated if I were to find something for you. I was promised a heavy compensation.'

'Olivia?' I turned to her, but she shook her head.

'It wasn't me.'

'No,' said Alice. 'This little birdie arrived in a carriage yesterday accompanied by a… I'm not sure, possibly a weasel? Come to think of it, he was not so much a little birdie. More an eagle carrying a bar of gold.'

'Alice…'

Ignoring my tone, she continued blithely, 'I've had to be quick so it's a very plain cut and style but it should do.'

As I stood on the stool, she worked nimbly, nipping, tucking, and pinning until finally she stood back.

'There now.'

Olivia sighed in pleasure and I surprised myself by smiling.

Even just pinned to me, the fabric flowed over my body, emphasising my hips, cinching my waist. For the first time in a long time, I felt beautiful.

In that moment, the horrors at Mistcoate seemed far away. There was no witch-child, no ghostly Christopher Kemp. I wasn't some drab governess in cheap dresses. I had friends, I was going to a ball and suddenly, amazingly, I was the happiest I had been in a long, long time.

Outside, the clouds broke apart, the sun shone through the attic windows, illuminating my reflection in the mirror. Unable to resist, I twirled until the silk swished, and the room was full of laughter and light.

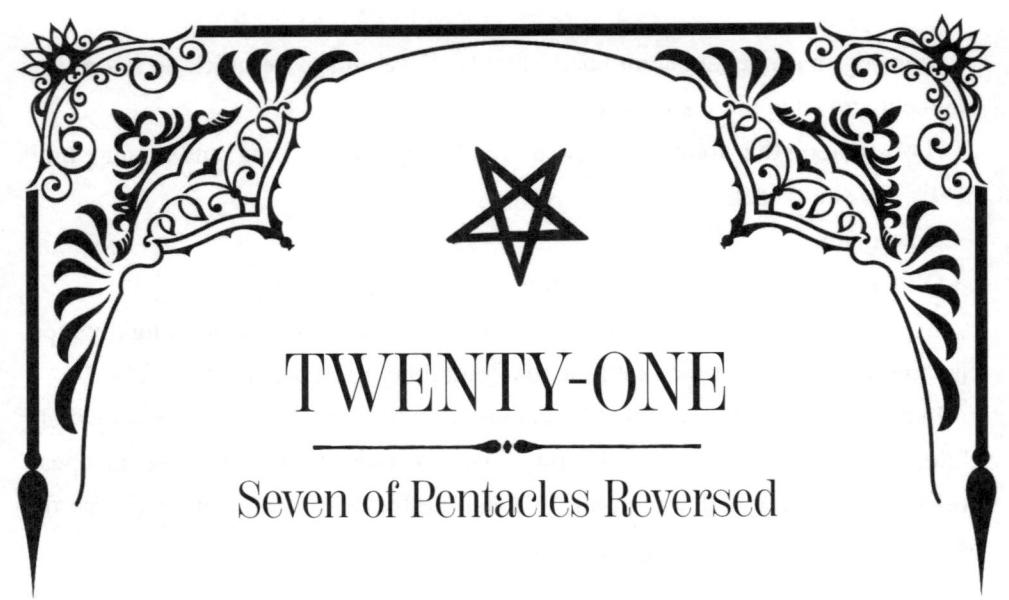

TWENTY-ONE

Seven of Pentacles Reversed

Captain and Mrs Rogers request the pleasure of Miss Olivia Richmond's company to celebrate the birthday of their daughter, Suzanne. This shall take place at Weatherall House on Friday 28th November at 8pm. Music and dancing.

Dr Richmond
  We have received your letter and would be delighted to extend you and your guest an invitation. Suzanne is delighted your daughter will be in attendance. We should be pleased to have you there also to watch over dear Miss Richmond.
  Very kind regards,
  Mrs Rogers

G: Everything is in place. She is keen for the night ahead. Do send word about how it goes. E.

Looking back later, it was clear to me that the week before the party had been full of warnings.

On the Monday and the Wednesday, Olivia and I had two more appointments with Alice and Dr Richmond gave us the carriage, citing the freezing winds that were now blowing from the fens as November was about to turn to December.

Olivia became more fractious with each visit, but she seemed to enjoy Alice's company. They waltzed around the attic so Olivia could get used to dancing in her dress, laughing as they did.

In truth, it was Alice I was concerned about now, not Olivia.

The week before the party, she descended into a violent and frightening coughing fit, which thankfully passed as soon as it started.

'It is the cold weather,' she insisted, waving away our concerns. 'Let me sit a while and I should be fine.'

We said nothing more, but it worried me.

It was after this visit that we spied Mrs Hayes sitting in the graveyard with Mrs Horsch as we walked home. I had not seen the latter since that night in the garden house many weeks ago, and the sight of her surprised me.

'I did not know they knew each other,' I said, when we were out of earshot.

'Eda seems to know everyone.' Olivia shrugged. 'She's got all sorts of friends.'

'What an odd place to meet though,' I said.

'I suppose they thought no one would interrupt them,' said Olivia.

The women looked over sharply as we passed and though we kept our distance, pretending not to have seen them, when I looked back, they were both gone.

Despite my excitement over my new dress, I had been unable to approach Dr Richmond about his generosity due to the interminable presence of Dr Joyce, whose visit had now stretched to two weeks and seemed to be without end. The pair spent most of their days in Dr Richmond's study, where I believed they were preparing for their presentation to the Royal College in London, although none of us knew what the nature of this presentation was.

Dr Richmond's presence meant that I was shielded from Mrs Hayes, who had largely ignored me for the past fortnight. But Dr Joyce made me uneasy. Especially the way he looked at Olivia. It was not the gaze a man uses on a woman, which I supposed was some mercy, but rather of a man appraising a piece of furniture, looking over it for signs of a bad investment. I hoped fervently that she was not the reason for Dr Joyce's prolonged stay with us.

If Olivia noticed, she gave no sign, but she avoided him, and even chose Mrs Hayes' company over being left alone with him.

It was during one of these moments that Mrs Hayes must have made an apology to her, because on the Wednesday I entered Olivia's room to find the two of them deep in conversation. Olivia was in bed, cradling her knees to her chest, as Mrs Hayes perched on the edge of the mattress, saying, 'Stop worrying. You don't need them.'

They both jumped when they saw me, standing in the doorway, breakfast tray in hand.

'Thank you, Miss Pearlie. If you put it there, I'll have it in a minute,' Olivia said.

I raised my eyebrows at her but did as she bid me, not allowing myself to look at the smug expression on Mrs Hayes' face.

Mrs Hayes seemed to have many secrets these days. I avoided collecting the post now, weary as I was of having it snatched from my hand. I had decided that I did not care who her mysterious letters were from. I was much more taken up with watching her conduct with Dr Joyce.

Evenings now had an enforced social hour in the parlour where we all gathered, possibly to give Dr Joyce some semblance of society and, though his conduct was unimpeachable, there was something about the way he smiled at Mrs Hayes, and the way he lingered when accepting a drink from her, or even simply standing next to her, that suggested an insidious intimacy. It was impossible to pinpoint, though, and I would have thought it the workings of my imagination were it not for Dr Richmond's sudden stiffness when the two were together. He never said anything but the room would take on the oppressive, suffocating atmosphere of something present but unspoken.

Then there was the night when, having gone to the kitchen for water, I spied Mrs Hayes slipping into Dr Joyce's bedroom on the landing upstairs.

I decided it was time to ask Marian what she knew.

'Has Dr Richmond called for Mrs Hayes lately?' I asked, as we prepared breakfast the next morning.

She gave me a puzzled look. 'Why, miss?'

'I just thought that she had been less busy with him recently,' I said, carefully.

'Well, I think we can guess why that is,' said Marian, casting a glance to where Dr Joyce could be seen through the kitchen window, smoking a cigar out on the overgrown lawn.

So it was as I suspected.

'Is she just flattered by his attention, do you think?' I asked.

'She's getting something out of it, miss, one way or another,' Marian assured me.

'Dangerous for her, though.' I glanced at the corridor to the housekeeper's room, but all was still and silent. 'Dr Richmond might take offense.'

She gave me a significant look. 'Dr Richmond seems to be of the opinion that he doesn't care anymore what Mrs Hayes does.'

I thought about the night the doctor came to my room, drunk. He'd never done anything like that again. Still, I wondered if he had expected to simply replace his housekeeper with his daughter's companion. If so, he'd been disappointed. And I intended to keep it that way.

When the night of the party arrived, Alice sent a note to say that she would collect Olivia and me at seven o'clock sharp.

My dress hung from the beam across my window, the colour rippling in the evening breeze. It had taken all my willpower not to touch it every time I passed nearby.

Alone in my room, I dabbed *eau de toilette*, borrowed from Alice, onto my wrists and neck, and dressed my hair with a soft, cream-coloured camellia.

I stepped into the gown, pulling it up over my shoulders. At the sight of myself in the mirror, I gave a sigh of wonder and pride. To my surprise, my eyes pricked with tears.

The dress was very simple, with a small bustle at the back and a long sweeping skirt. The neckline was a neat, straight line that showed off the rounded tops of my shoulders. In an unexpected nod to fashion, Alice had made it sleeveless but added in a pair of black satin gloves that reached up to my elbows and matched the buttons on the back of the gown.

It was as though I had stepped into another life, a world of what might have been. Here was Julia Pearlie if her father had lived, if her circumstances had not been so reduced, if she had not been discarded. The Julia Pearlie that should have been.

Mother always said that pride was a sin but I found I could not agree. Surely it was not a sin to feel so happy? No one could look at me and see a woman disgraced or impoverished.

When I was ready, I went to Olivia's room and found her sitting at her dressing table. She gave an audible gasp when I stepped into the room.

'Julia,' she breathed, squinting hard at me. 'You look like some dark queen from a fairy-tale.'

I laughed and moved over to check on her dress, which hung from the door of her wardrobe.

'Then I suppose you will be the princess. Are you ready to be dressed?'

Her dress, too, was a triumph. The second she stepped into it, the pale blue stripes seemed to make her skin colour richer, more like ivory, and the snug sleeves emphasised her delicate wrists and hands. The neckline was square with a chiffon tucker. On someone else it might have looked old-fashioned, but on Olivia, who had such an otherworldly appearance, it was charming. Alice had not bothered with any kind of bustle, and so the skirts hung from her neat hips, made voluminous with petticoats.

As we stood side by side in the mirror, I couldn't help but laugh a little.

'What a stir we shall make,' said Olivia and clapped her hands.

By then, we could hear the sound of horses and the crunching of gravel from outside.

'It is time,' I said.

Olivia fetched a wrap and we headed down to the entrance hall.

Dr Richmond and Dr Joyce stood in the hall with Mrs Hayes and watched as we descended the stairs. I could feel my skin turning fiery red at Dr Richmond's gaze, and I cursed myself. I would look like some ridiculous schoolgirl instead of a confident woman.

'Well, I must say—' Dr Joyce began, but he was interrupted by the doorbell.

When Marian opened the door, Alice was standing on the doorstep, resplendent in a light mauve tulle. Ed Byres stood beside her, looking distinguished in a black suit with his white collar gleaming at his throat. His smile faltered a little on seeing me.

I didn't know what to think. Did he disapprove?

'Your carriage and escorts await,' Alice announced, beaming.

'I thought—' Dr Joyce began, before he was hushed by Dr Richmond.

Glancing at them, Alice smiled in a way that did not quite reach her eyes.

'We meet again,' she said. 'Will you be accompanying us?'

Her voice, I noticed, seemed particularly breathy tonight. She had a fur coat wrapped around her to ward off the chill. I worried it was not enough.

'We will make our own way there,' Dr Richmond said and then, seeing it could not be avoided, he nodded at the reverend. 'Byres.'

'Doctor.' There was no mistaking the strained look on Ed's face.

'Well, I hope you enjoy yourself,' Mrs Hayes told Olivia. 'The dress is at least better than I had thought. Now, just you remember…'

She pulled Olivia into an embrace, whispering into her ear.

As I watched them, my brow furrowed, I noticed Marian standing in the shadows on the far side of the stairs, her eyes wide; Cinderella, watching everyone else go to the ball.

I hurried over and took hold of her hands.

'I will bring you every good thing I can,' I whispered. 'I shall fill my purse and drag a prince home if need be.'

Marian smiled.

And then we were out the door and into the freezing night. Our breath seemed to freeze in the air as we walked, and even under the wraps, I felt the ice of it against my skin as Olivia ran ahead and seized hold of Byres' outstretched arm.

'She's chosen her escort then,' Alice told me, threading her arm through mine as we walked to the coach. Her voice sounded weak. 'I shall try not to be insulted. Is that frightful man coming to the party?'

I knew without asking that she was talking about Dr Joyce.

'I'm afraid so.'

'That's fine, we shall make a game of avoiding him,' said Alice and pressed the back of her gloved hand to her mouth, suppressing a cough.

'Are you feeling well?' I said, watching with concern. 'You look a little pale.'

'Right as rain,' she insisted, and pulled me towards the carriage.

Before I climbed up, I glanced back at the house. The door was open and Dr Richmond stood watching us, the stub of a cigar pinched between his lips. His eyes remained fixed on mine until Mrs Hayes closed the door.

When our carriage arrived, Weatherall House seemed full to the rafters. Servants took our wraps and shawls in the large stone entryway where two fires burned, and we were led up a flight of stairs into the main salon, where groups gathered, some sitting on circular settees before an imposing fireplace. To the right, French windows opened up onto a walled, stone balcony where couples walked, young ladies gossiped, and men stood smoking together. Ahead, one could make out a brightly-lit dining room, where tables groaned under the weight of cold meats and cheeses, sandwiches, preserves, trifles, a whole dressed salmon gleaming on a platter, vivid fruits and golden pastries, glistening jellies and glasses of cold champagne. On our left was a grand ballroom, from which the sounds of a piano and stringed instruments floated in a rousing waltz.

We lingered near the door. 'Now that I'm here, I have no idea what to do.' Olivia sounded nervous.

'Well, first we must take a turn about the room,' Alice told her. 'We must see and be seen. Then we should locate our host.'

Byres joined us, now free of his coat and hat. I noticed a few strands of hair, though combed and waxed back into some sort of neatness, had still managed to escape and fall over his forehead.

'For my part, I should like to explore the dance floor,' he said.

I expected Olivia to leap at the opportunity but instead she stood next to Alice, clinging to her arm.

Some of the guests had noticed Olivia and were whispering and nudging each other; it was all I could do to not stand in front of her, blocking her from view.

'Oh, I have just spotted Captain Rogers,' exclaimed Alice. 'Come, Miss Olivia, they will want to meet you. It is good manners to greet the hosts. And there is Suzanne, as well. She is quite the socialite and can tell you all about the season in London.'

They were gone into the throng of people before I could say anything, Olivia drawing glances both shocked and admiring as they passed.

What if Mrs Hayes was right? I worried. *What if I have made a spectacle of her?*

'Olivia will be fine,' said Byres, who had been watching my expression. He held out his hand. 'Shall we?'

His grip was firm and the warmth of his skin was comforting through the satin of my glove. The quartet had just started a light, springing waltz, which we joined as a space opened up between the twirling couples. I felt more than a little awkward.

My last dance partner had been Lucy and we had usually made stumbling circuits of the carpet in the nursery, laughing at our own clumsiness. It gave me a pang in the chest to think of it, to remember Lucy giggling as she tried to stand on my feet and then her squeal of delight when I carried her along.

But that was the past. Now Byres guided me in smooth circles across the polished oak floor, making clear signals as to footfall and speed so that following him soon became a matter of ease, and I was not thinking about it at all.

'There we are,' he said. 'Like we've been doing it for years.'

'I'm afraid I am not a natural dancer,' I admitted.

'Me neither,' said Byres, placing his hand on my waist to spin me. 'So long as we don't crash into anyone, we should be fine.'

'Oh, please don't,' I said, skipping sideways in time to the music. 'I already feel as though everyone is staring.'

'Olivia looks well,' said Byres, looking over my head as we turned. 'Alice has her in hand. They're laughing.'

'Thank goodness,' I said, feeling the tension ease in my shoulders. 'Alice did a wonderful job on the dresses.'

'You have done a good job too,' he said. 'With Olivia, I mean. She's quite the young lady. I'm sure Dr Richmond must be pleased.'

'I'm afraid that changes with his mood,' I confided. 'Like at the house. What happened between the two you? You were both so strange.'

There was a pause as we twirled across the floor, our feet now moving in sync. 'We do not know each other that well,' he said, after a moment. 'I imagine what you noticed was simply a natural reserve.'

I studied his face. It had set in such a strange way, becoming as impassive as a locked door.

'Olivia mentioned that you and Florence Richmond were friends.' I tried again.

'Yes,' he admitted. 'At least I thought so. Florence always had so many responsibilities; I think she appreciated a listening ear. I don't think she got one much. I don't think she ever got much of anything really.'

He sounded so bitter; it was a shock to hear it in his voice. But there was something more, something he was not saying.

'Her death must have been very difficult. I believe it was unexpected. Do you miss her?'

I wasn't sure what made me ask the question – only that I suddenly felt a deep need to know the answer. I felt his grip tighten around my waist.

'Not as much as I used to. She had changed so much from the woman I thought I knew.'

The waltz came to an end and I dipped my head and curtseyed. Byres gave a polite bow. The band struck up again, a slow, sweeping number, and Byres slipped his hand around my waist, pulling me in, more gently than before.

'Is that comfortable?' he murmured, his lips near my ear. 'Not too tight?'

His breath sent a shiver through me, and I nodded, not trusting myself to speak.

I did not mention Florence again, not wanting to ruin this new comfort we had found together.

We would have danced a third but the room was becoming crowded and Byres was obliged to greet people, make small talk and introduce me: 'Have you met Miss Pearlie? She was recently in Kent but is living at Mistcoate.'

When I felt him tiring of the conversation, I feigned a desperate interest in various dances, none of which I actually knew, and he would pull me towards him and whirl me around so that we were breathless, our faces flushed and smiling.

'Please,' I said, at last, as the band's crescendo again died to ripples of applause. 'I really must have some refreshment now or I shall expire on the spot.'

Byres laughed and escorted me into the salon where we found Alice and Olivia speaking with three young women. Two were dressed in a light tulle, while the third girl, a small, curvaceous creature with shining dark hair and a mischievous smile, was dressed in a jewel-blue tartalan. Olivia, I saw, was desperately trying to focus on them, rather than over their shoulder or at a spot above their heads. As we approached, the middle girl said something that caused them all to break into peals of laughter.

'Here they are,' said Alice, waving to us. 'Ed, Miss Pearlie, this is Miss Suzanne Rogers, our hostess, and her cousins, Miss Allegra and Anna Howeth. Ladies, allow me to introduce Miss Pearlie, our woman from London. She is preparing Miss Olivia for her coming out.'

Byres made polite conversation and then peeled away to fetch drinks.

'We had hoped to introduce Miss Olivia to some friends,' said Suzanne, gripping Olivia's hand. 'We shall whisk her away and bring her right back.'

'Please return her directly to us,' I began. But Olivia quieted me with a desperate frown. I bit my lip as they bore her away amidst much whispering and giggling, with not a single backward glance.

'Don't,' warned Alice, seeing my pained expression. 'She must have some society of her own. It is good for her.'

'I do not want her getting into trouble,' I said.

'She is in excellent and very appropriate company,' Alice reminded me, her voice tightening. She pressed her hand to her chest. 'You worry so…'

But her words were drowned out in a flurry of coughing. People turned to look, as Alice doubled over.

I searched my bag for a handkerchief, rubbing her back. 'Gracious, Alice. Are you well? Shall I fetch Reverend Byres?'

Alice waved a hand, gasping for air. Pink spots sat high on her cheeks and a fine bead of sweat formed on her head.

'I am fine,' she gasped, after a moment. 'Too much excitement. I must just sit quietly for a moment.'

'I knew it was too much,' I said, guiding her to a chair. 'It's my fault. You've been working yourself too hard on our dresses. I shall require you to have a long holiday after tonight.'

'I promise,' she said, sinking back into a seat, taking slow, laboured breaths.

After a few minutes, her breathing seemed to steady. She gave me a sudden piercing look.

'I was just thinking,' she said. 'Has he told you that you look lovely? He probably won't, but you do.'

'I don't know what you mean,' I said, blushing.

'Contemptible little liar,' said Alice. She was grinning, but her smile faded as she looked past me. I turned to see Dr Joyce and Dr Richmond standing behind us, eyes shining with whiskey and mischief.

'Who's a liar?' Dr Joyce asked, grinning.

'Where is Olivia?' Dr Richmond looked about the room, his eyes too bright.

'Some of the young ladies took her to meet their friends,' I said. 'I thought I should let her go.'

'Indeed? I wonder, Miss Pearlie, if this dance was for Olivia's benefit or yours,' said Dr Joyce, winking in a knowing way that made my stomach knot itself.

'I assure you, sir—' I began but Dr Richmond cut me off, clapping his friend on the shoulder.

'Stop teasing her, Peter.'

'Well, Miss Pearlie, at the very least you must promise George a dance. He should get the chance to see your new dress to its full advantage.' Dr Joyce grinned wickedly at Dr Richmond, who turned away from us, fiddling with his left cufflink.

'I'll look for Olivia now. And I must say good evening to Rogers,' Dr Richmond said, gruffly. 'Excuse me.'

'Yes,' said Alice, 'I must see where my brother has got to and find out if he will accompany me outside for my lung medication. I had thought to give Mrs Hayes' tobacco habits a try.'

'Anything I can help with?' asked Dr Joyce. 'I am a trained medical professional, madam.'

She glanced at him politely. 'If you have matches it may very well make you the man for the job.'

He offered his arm and Alice rose, her breathing now steadier and fuller. I watched them go and then peered through the doors of the ballroom, to where Olivia stood with Dr Richmond, chatting with a group of young people.

'Poor Alice has lured away that awful Dr Joyce,' I said, when Byres appeared at my elbow, carefully balancing three coupes of champagne. 'I am certain she deserves some form of medal.'

'A toast to our fallen friend,' said Byres, handing me a glass.

The bubbles fizzed in my nose, the taste both sweet and vaguely metallic.

We passed the time by concocting theories about the other guests. One elderly gentleman performing circuits between the dining room and the patio was hiding from his wife, who hated both his preference for cigars and rich foods. A waif-like young lady was a secret heiress, enjoying a night of anonymous diversion. A short, dark, middle-aged man was a spy for the Queen.

'It does make you wonder, what would people say if they saw us?' I mused at one point.

'Old married couple,' Byres decided. 'There is no doubt. You are shrewish and I am shy, retiring and hen-pecked.'

'*Reverend Byres*,' I scolded, laughing.

'You see?' He held out his hands innocently. 'I am much put upon.'

'If you insist on this role then you can follow me to the ballroom.' I set my empty glass on a passing tray.

The dance floor was now heaving. I tried to keep a look-out for Olivia as we dipped and spun amidst the mass of twirling bodies. First she was with Miss Rogers, then dancing with a dark-haired young man, who kept throwing glances that I did not like to two grinning friends. When I looked again, they were all gone.

There was no sign of Alice. Dr Joyce stood with Dr Richmond in one corner, trying to entertain two young ladies with some drunken tale although Dr Richmond seemed more concerned with my dancing than anything.

'He believes I am neglecting her,' I told Byres. 'Let me go find her.'

'I also should go and find Alice,' he said, as we walked off the dance floor. 'She can find these things overwhelming and may be hiding somewhere.'

A circuit of the ballroom revealed no sign of Olivia. She was not in the parlour either, and when I stepped out onto the balcony it was empty. The cold night air felt good against my skin and I paused to take a breath.

'Miss Pearlie?'

I spun around to find Dr Richmond had followed, and stood watching me from the French windows, which had been opened to let cool air into the overheated room.

'Are you taking the air?' he enquired.

'I'm looking for Olivia, sir,' I said. 'I have not seen her in some time.'

'Please,' said Dr Richmond, stepping closer. 'Let us not be 'Sir' and 'Miss' for a moment.'

His movements were steady, but it was clear this was only due to great concentration on his part. How much whiskey had he and Dr Joyce had, before taking the carriage to Weatherall? His eyes had a strange look about them, a focus and a steeliness that made my stomach squirm with nervousness.

'I really must find Olivia,' I said, taking a step towards the door, only to find he was blocking my way.

'She is fine. A dance under the stars first? You can hear the music from here.'

He seized my hand and pulled me into a waltz position, the firm trunk of his body pressed against mine, the smell of alcohol mingling with the scent of his cologne. I forced myself to smile as he began to turn me across the balcony.

This felt different to dancing with Ed Byres. Clumsier. I had to think harder about it.

'I must say I am surprised to find you without your chaperone,' he said.

His face was too close. The sharpness of his whiskers scratched against my ear and he was holding me too tightly.

'Miss Byres is nearby, I think,' I said.

'I didn't mean *Miss* Byres.'

My steps faltered but Dr Richmond held me closer.

'I would be very careful before becoming too close to Ed Byres,' he whispered. 'He is not what you think he is.'

'Sir?' I leaned back, trying to pull away, but he held me tight.

'I gather you have been asking about Florence?'

There was a new edge to his voice.

'I'll admit I was curious,' I said, cautiously.

'Then you must also know…' Dr Richmond squeezed my hand so hard I winced, but he did not seem to notice my discomfort.

'It is perhaps *impolite*,' he spat the word, 'to mention it, but I suppose you must also know that when Florence died, she was—'

'Miss Pearlie?' Ed Byres stood in the doorway, silhouetted against the light.

I wanted to step away from Dr Richmond but he continued to grip my waist. We stood in a ridiculous tableau.

'I am afraid I must enlist your help,' Byres said, in a strange voice.

'Is something wrong?' Relief was evident in my voice.

'My sister and Miss Olivia both seem to be missing,' he said. 'There are some areas of the house it would be imprudent for me to intrude on. Would you mind?'

'Of course not.' At last, I wrenched myself free of my employer. I straightened my skirts, ran a hand across my hair and then hurried inside.

I felt Dr Richmond's gaze on me as I followed Byres through the glass doors and into the ballroom.

'I apologise for the interruption,' said Byres, stiffly, as he led me through a set of double doors and out into the corridor to the top of the large staircase that led down to the huge entrance hall. 'One of the young ladies said that she heard coughing from the women's parlour.'

'I will go and look now,' I said, cheeks flaming under the sudden coldness of his gaze. 'And it was no interruption. Dr Richmond has had much wine, I think.'

Byres said nothing but led me down the stairs.

'It is through here,' he said, gesturing to a dark corridor behind the stairwell.

A door opened, spilling light into the shadows and a young woman emerged, the sound of loud wheezing behind her.

'Is there a doctor?' she asked as I raced inside. 'She seems to be in some difficulty.'

'Alice!'

I found her hunched over on an ornate chair, coughing into a handkerchief. Her face was a bright pink, curls clinging to her forehead. When she took the handkerchief away, her bottom lip was slick crimson.

I sank down beside her. 'Oh no. Alice? Can you walk?'

'Not yet.' She buried herself once again in the starched linen, body wracked with coughing.

'What happened? Was Olivia with you?'

Alice shook her head and took a long, shuddering breath, her face contorting as though it pained her.

'Those girls… she ran off…'

'With them or from them?' I asked, feeling my scalp prickle with nerves.

'With. Something… something… happening… I couldn't follow…'

Her coughing fit began again.

'Please don't speak,' I told her. 'Ed is in the hall. Let me help you up.'

It took three attempts to get her onto her feet. Eventually she managed it, leaning against me. Staggering a little, we made our way to the doorway.

Byres hurried forward at the sight of us, clearly having waited in anxious anticipation.

'Alice, my God – I should never have let you come. I knew this would be too much.'

'Shall I have a carriage brought round?' I asked, still holding her gloved hand in mine.

'I asked the young lady who passed us to speak to one of the servants about it. I'm going to take her home,' Byres said.

'Of course.' I gave Alice a worried look. She seemed so weak. 'Olivia has got herself into mischief and I must find her. Alice, which way did they go?'

Alice turned to point at a doorway opposite.

'There,' she gasped and her thin body shook as she gave another rattling cough.

'I must get her home,' Byres said.

'Go, I will call on you,' I told them, before heading in the direction Alice had indicated.

The first open door led to an unlit billiards room. It was empty and dark. Had Alice been confused? How could they be in here? But as I turned to go, I noticed part of the ornate oak wall panel was somehow standing ajar. There was a flickering light behind it.

Perhaps it was a servants' corridor of some sort. A perfect place for young people to hide.

I crossed the room soundlessly and slipped into a candlelit gloom.

The room beyond was a large hidden library, bounded on all sides by tall mahogany bookshelves. Candles burned in a window alcove where a hushed group of young people was clustered. As I stepped closer, two young ladies in front of the fire rose to meet me.

'Are you here for the meeting?' whispered one.

'I am looking for Miss Olivia,' I said.

'You are not too late then,' said the second, in a low voice. 'Isn't it too thrilling? They've only just started. How clever of Suzanne. Who else would have thought to invite the Mistcoate Witch?'

TWENTY-TWO

Page of Swords

Olivia sat at a card table, surrounded by a motley collection of partygoers. Suzanne was on her right, while the young man Olivia had been dancing with peered over her shoulder. There was nothing on the table except Olivia's hands, which were splayed flat against the wood. Her eyes had a distant, unfocused look and she seemed to be staring at nothing.

'Are you here?' she said.

Her voice sounded deep and rough in a way that I had never heard before. Her head jerked back, as though shocked by some sound and a girl next to me grasped the hands of her friend.

'Who are you?' Olivia gasped in a guttural tone, her eyes rolling back in her head.

The room was deathly silent, the music seeping in through the ceiling. Olivia's head lolled and then snapped forward. Her eyes locked on mine.

'There you are, Juja,' Olivia hissed.

The other young people looked from me to Olivia in confusion. Was I part of the show?

A candle flame guttered and flickered. For a moment in the wavering light, I thought I saw the witch-child behind Olivia's shoulder. She smiled, her teeth slicked with a film of brown blood. Jerking as though she were not used to movement, Olivia raised a finger and pressed it to her lips.

'Remember?' she said.

'*Stop it*,' I demanded, but my voice sounded like that of a frightened child, too high and too uncertain.

All the candles dimmed at once. Someone shrieked. When the candle flames flared again the witch-child was gone.

Olivia's face contorted into a wicked leer, but her eyes were glassy.

'It's so cold,' she said, her voice wobbling. 'So cold in the water…'

'Stop it,' I whispered, and then forced my voice to be louder. 'This is silly, stop it.'

My hands had begun to shake, and I clenched my fists hard.

'I can't,' she said. A heavy tear spilled onto her cheek but still the rictus grin remained. 'He won't let me. He's here again. He wants to talk to you.'

She tilted her head, as though listening to someone whispering in her ear.

'There is no one here,' I insisted.

'He wants you to say that you did it,' said Olivia, as if I hadn't spoken.

I don't believe this, I told myself. *I don't believe in any of this.*

Then why are you so frightened? said an icy voice in my head.

My mouth was dry. My heart hammered in my chest. But all I said was, 'You are making a fool of yourself.'

'Just *admit it*.' Olivia slammed her fists down on the table.

The group reeled back from her.

'My head,' Olivia moaned, gripping her forehead, hair tangling in her fingers. 'It hurts. It hurts so much.'

She began to tug at her hair, pulling at it with such violence that hairpins scattered across the floor. Then she stopped abruptly and stared at Suzanne. The dark-haired young woman stared down at Olivia, eyes wide and cheeks pale.

'That's where it hit her,' Olivia whispered. 'Isn't it? The vase. One of Mama's favourites.'

Suzanne's skin was suddenly pale. 'What do you mean?' she asked, although I could see that she already knew.

'You were on the first floor and she was walking below. You took the vase and you put it on the bannister and when she went under you, you knocked it off. Didn't you?'

'Suzanne, this is too much. Make her stop,' pleaded a young man. But before anyone could do anything, Olivia began to bang her hands on the table, a loud, rhythmic beat.

'Row, row, row your boat gently down the stream...' she sang, in time to the banging, in a voice that suddenly sounded horribly familiar. 'Don't peek over, see what's there or it will make you—'

A young lady to my left screamed. Then another. But they were not looking at Olivia. They were looking at the window behind her.

A dark figure stood outside. Hot breath misting the glass as he watched us.

His face was mostly covered by a dark woollen cap and moth-eaten muffler, stolen, no doubt, from a washing line or an ill-attended cloakroom. What was visible was broken and angular, like that of a bare-knuckle fighter, allowed to live into disfigured maturity. One dark eye stared out, whole and perfect and angry while the other was white and blank as milk. The strips of skin on his cheeks had been roasted away to reveal flesh that was thin and stretched, deeply pink and almost shiny under the strain of covering the essential meat beneath. His lips had been seared into dry blisters and struggled to meet, fixed, as they were, above a jaw that had clearly been broken and never properly healed. A concave dip could be seen in one cheek where the bone had shattered. The nails on the hand that pressed against the window were split and caked with mud, dried blood and a yellow spongy substance that suggested mould.

'The Shambler,' someone whispered in horror.

Seeing us transfixed at his sudden appearance, the creature gave a muffled, phlegmy chuckle and crooned through the glass, 'I see you. I see you now.'

He lifted his fist and beat upon the window. Everyone scattered, nearly upending the card table. The candles went out. I heard screaming and weeping. Only Olivia remained in her seat, sobbing as though she were being murdered.

The hidden panel doorway was crowded with people trying to escape. Others stood, frozen in horror, staring at the figure through the window. I saw the familiar figure of Mrs Horsch disappearing through another secret door, and I wondered how many people had stood watching in the shadows.

'Julia!' cried Olivia. I followed her terrified gaze, to see the man outside lifting a large stone above his head.

There was a heavy wooden chair beside me and, without thinking, I seized it, pulled it back along the floor and, with all the strength I could gather, hurled it at the window.

The glass shattered on impact, the chair legs buckling underneath it as it struck the walkway outside. Cold winter air flooded the room.

At that moment, hands clamped onto my upper arms and Dr Richmond's voice spoke in my ear.

'We must leave.'

He ran forward, wrapping his arms around a sobbing Olivia, who fought wildly against him as he dragged her from the room.

I followed them out through the doorway into the billiards room, past the crowds of partygoers who had clustered around those emerging from the secret room. Everyone was talking excitedly and gesticulating, and men ran out the door to search for the intruder.

Dr Richmond escorted Olivia through the throngs, out into the driveway. I followed on their heels.

Olivia fought like a cat to free herself from her father's grip. I didn't understand why she was so angry.

'Doctor, please leave her.' I hurried down the steps to her side and reached for her hand. 'Olivia, are you injured?'

No sooner had Dr Richmond released her than she stooped down, grabbed a handful of gravel and threw it straight into my eyes. The dirt and grit stung like knives and I gave a cry, my hands flying to my face.

Blinded, I heard a noise like a sack of dry meal being hit, and a gasp. Next to me came the sound of a high whistle and, moments later, the crack of a whip and the crunch of horses' hooves.

'Help, please,' I called. 'I cannot see.'

I began to weep, the stinging of the grit intensifying with the salt of my tears.

'Miss Pearlie?' It was Dr Joyce's voice. 'Come with us.'

A hand gripped my arm and guided me into the carriage, which pulled away with a lurch.

Something was pressed into my hand. A handkerchief.

'The crying should rinse the grit out.' Dr Richmond's voice opposite me. 'Blink your eyes as much as possible and dab the tears. Do not rub your eyes. We'll examine you properly back at the house when we have light.'

I nodded, still weeping, although it was more for the pain in my eyes than anything else.

'Olivia?' I asked.

'Is here.' Dr Joyce said. 'She is resting.'

The pain had lessened by the time we pulled up to Mistcoate House but I still needed help climbing down from the carriage. I could see now through a stinging haze that Olivia was unconscious, cradled in her father's arms. There was a livid red mark along the side of her face.

The front door opened and light spilled out.

Marian stood back as Dr Joyce and I followed Dr Richmond and Olivia into the entrance hall.

'I shall need to examine her,' Dr Richmond said, over his shoulder. 'She may have had some sort of episode. Miss Pearlie, what the hell happened?'

'She…' I began, but Dr Joyce stopped me.

'The girl's blinded, Georgie,' he said. 'Let the maid see to her eyes first and then we can find out what's what. I should like to speak to you if we can. This could be very interesting.'

'Where is Mrs Hayes?' demanded Dr Richmond. In his arms, Olivia made a soft sound.

'She's with Captain Richmond, sir,' said Marian.

'Very well.' Dr Richmond's eyes darted to Dr Joyce. 'Send her to me when she finishes.'

He turned and continued down the corridor.

Olivia had begun to stir and I heard Dr Joyce say, 'Best to give some laudanum for now.'

'Let me take you upstairs, miss.' Marian reached for my arm but I waved her away.

'Thank you, I'm fine, really,' I said. 'I can make my own way.'

Marian peered at me. 'Are you certain?'

'I'll be fine,' I insisted, climbing the stairs.

A headache was beginning at the back of my head. My temples were pounding. I would go to my room and put a cold cloth on my neck. I just needed a moment alone.

When I reached the landing, I found my bedroom door open. It had been closed when I left, but now light spilled into the dark hallway and a scrabbling sound came from inside. I crept forward and peeked in.

Blinking back painful tears, I saw that the washstand had been dragged aside and the carpet kicked back, revealing an empty hole in the floorboards.

Mrs Hayes stood in the centre of the room, a tall, dark blur, shuffling a set of cards.

She didn't look up as I entered but continued, as though counting to make sure they were all there. When satisfied, she glanced my way, as if she had summoned me to her.

'You're back early,' she observed. 'I haven't even had time to clean up.'

My mouth went dry. 'What are you doing?'

'I just needed to look more closely,' she said. 'Still, it's gratifying to know I was right.'

I tried to focus on her face. For the first time she looked at me and paused. Her voice, when she spoke, sounded deeply satisfied.

'Well, what happened to you? Did the ball not go well?'

I wanted to slap her and had to grip my hands together to stop myself.

'I will scream,' I said. 'Dr Richmond is just downstairs.'

'Please.' Mrs Hayes made a theatrical gesture towards the door. 'I would be very interested to hear what he had to say about the rest of what I found.'

My stomach lurched. The diary. I had been so fixated on the cards I had forgotten the diary. I looked around for it but could not make out whether it was there or not.

'Where is it?' I said, stepping into the room and closing the door behind me.

'What?' said Mrs Hayes. Her voice was smug. 'Must be important. You wouldn't look so pale otherwise.'

My eyes burned.

'Give it back.' I could not stop the tears escaping and running down my face. 'You have no business taking things that are not yours.'

She waved the cards. 'That's a bit rich coming from you, isn't it? No one likes a thief, Miss Pearlie. I think it's best if things are returned to their owners.'

'Does that include my notes?'

'Notes? I didn't find any notes. Just this.'

From her pocket, Mrs Hayes drew out a newspaper clipping. The paper had been cheap to begin with and it had been folded so many times that the creases showed light through them when she opened it, with a flick of her wrist.

'I knew there was more to you but I never thought this,' she said, her face suddenly stern as she read the headline. '*Governess Beat Politician's Children, Inquest Hears.*'

I lunged forward, hands outstretched but Mrs Hayes had been expecting this. She spun away so quickly that I tripped on the rug and fell against the dressing table, sending the mirror rattling. She was on me in an instant, gripping my chin, the edge of her hand pressing into my throat. She squeezed, her fingertips digging into my cheeks, holding me still.

'Hush now – we wouldn't want everyone coming up and hearing this, would we?'

I reached out again but she balled up her fist around the tarot and punched me to the floor. As I fell, the heel of her boot landed on my knuckles and pressed. My fingers crunched and I stifled a cry.

Standing there, crushing me, Mrs Hayes continued to read as though reciting a story for children:

'*Today's hearing saw an examination of Miss Lucy Kemp. The doctor found young Miss Kemp to be covered in bruises, which she confirmed were caused by her governess – Miss Julia Pearlie. This was repeated by Miss Kemp during the hearing, who also said, "She did not know what to do with us and there were often beatings. Both our doors had locks."*'

She pressed down harder on my hand. Something cracked and a shooting pain went through one finger. I pressed my face into the rug to silence my cries. '"*But she was hardest on Christopher. That's why we snuck away.*"'

At last, she removed her foot from my fingers. I lay on the floor, staring at the dark bruises already rising to the surface on my hand. My breath came in great, silent sobs and tears coursed down on my cheeks as I tried to bend my fingers and found I could not; not without such violent pain that I thought I would be sick.

'No wonder you didn't have references,' said Mrs Hayes, disgust dripping from every word. 'And to keep a copy of such a thing? Like you're proud of it?'

'I didn't do it.' My voice was so faint I could barely hear it. I could barely breathe. 'I didn't do that. I loved Lucy. I don't know why she said it.'

Mrs Hayes lifted her foot and gave another brutal stamp on my fingers.

I cried out into the rug and there was a pause as we both listened, me panting and afraid, Mrs Hayes watchful, to see if anyone would come. When nothing stirred, Mrs Hayes bent down, her face cold and impassive, as though she were looking at an insect.

'It's disgusting, really,' she said. 'That people like you are allowed to go around hurting others. I can't allow that, I'm afraid. So you are going to clean yourself up and you're going to go to George Richmond and say that you can't go on. That you're leaving.'

'I will tell him you did this,' I warned.

'No you won't,' she said flatly. 'Because then I'll show him what I found and you'll be out with no reference and no pay. We know each other too well, George and I, to be silly about these things. He hasn't exactly covered the family in glory, and I don't just mean the failed medical career. So I doubt he'll be as helpful as you think.'

I raised myself up and stared at her through my tears. 'Why are you doing this?'

There was a pause before she replied. 'I've been looking after Miss Olivia for a long time. I know what's best for her. I don't need that to be upended by someone hoping to use her to get to the master.'

There was the sound of footsteps on the stairs. Mrs Hayes raised a finger to her lips.

'There you are, miss – let's get you into bed.'

It was Marian's voice, down the corridor, conciliatory and gentle.

'Where is Julia?' Olivia sounded sleepy and confused.

'Miss Pearlie is in her room,' Marian told her. 'Oh please, Miss Olivia, don't cry now.'

Olivia's bedroom door clicked as she and Marian disappeared inside.

'Olivia's so trusting,' Mrs Hayes observed. 'And to think of how you've been using her.'

'I am not interested in George Richmond,' I said, cradling my wounded hand.

'But you wouldn't say no,' Mrs Hayes sneered. 'You'd be a fool if you did. Maybe he would even consider it. And, from what I've read, it wouldn't be the first time you've let a master use you. Still, I doubt he'd be in any rush to commit himself to a girl with three dresses to her name, no friends and no references. Now, Reverend Byres, on the other hand. He's less particular.'

She looked down at my fingers, which were now visibly bruised and swelling.

'Dear, dear, dear,' she said, in a voice that was almost motherly. 'They look like they might be broken. Not nice, is it, when someone hurts you? Miss Florence found that out. Oh yes. High and mighty Miss Florence who liked everything just so. Constantly answering to her, I was. Meanwhile she was up to all sorts. Did you know she was five months gone when she died? She hid it with oversized dresses and wraps but it was plain as day when you knew what to look for. When they fished her out of the river… Well. There was no hiding it then.'

I stared at her. Her eyes were huge and dark in the lamplight, glassy as a doll's. 'What are you talking about?'

'Florence Richmond was pregnant,' said Mrs Hayes, bluntly. 'And your Reverend Byres wanted nothing to do with it. That's why she did it. *That's* why she threw herself into the river.'

'No.' I shook my head.

But she went on. 'And here you are, bringing him to the house and shoving him in George's face. That's why I think it would be best if you gave your resignation. Save us all some heartache. Including Miss Olivia. How is she going to feel when she finds out you stole her cards and beat your previous charge? She'd never trust anyone again.'

She watched my face and gave a wide, warm smile, like I was an errant child who had finally pleased her.

'That's a girl,' she said, dusting off her skirts.

'Where is my diary?' I demanded, desperately. 'You don't have to take it. I won't tell anyone.'

'Don't you worry about that,' said Mrs Hayes. 'You can have it back once your resignation letter is handed in. You see, if you were to change your mind, I might feel it my duty to let him know everything. The thing about George is that he doesn't like it when someone else gets there first. Makes him feel a bit stupid and if he's been thinking that maybe you were fighting feelings for him, and then he reads that it's an act – that he's just another fool, I doubt he'll be too happy.' She looked down at the tarot deck in her hands. 'I must go and give these cards back to Olivia. She'll be delighted.'

I remained crumpled on the floor, defeated and battered, as she swept from the room.

I heard her knocking on Olivia's door further down the corridor.

'My lamb? Look what I found.'

I lay back, my hand blackening, tears rolling freely now, listening to Olivia's small cry of delight and the click of her bedroom door shutting her in with the housekeeper.

TWENTY-THREE

Two of Cups Reversed

18th November 1889
Astor House, Kent

John is writing a little. He says I should destroy the letters but I can't always bring myself to. I will burn them in the fire before he returns home but until then, I shall keep them at the bottom of my sewing box to reread when needed.

1st December 1889
Astor House, Kent

I have suggested that Lucy now have her own bedroom and her papa has agreed. It will be her Christmas present and I am having a devil of a time organising it without her seeing. I wondered if I should unveil it before Christopher is home, but it will only be a few days between his arrival and Christmas Day. I don't know why but I'm so worried of him ruining it.

12th December 1889
Astor House, Kent

Christopher returned from school with a message from the headmaster. He is not to go back. Apparently, letters were sent to John but there was no reply. They say he has become too wild and unruly. What is the good of school if they cannot tame children?

25th December 1889
Astor House, Kent

Christmas Day. John sent a turkey and we played games in the afternoon. Children sad not to have him here – myself, also – but we made the best of it. Christopher has a new boat, which I have forbidden him to be in without permission, and Lucy has her new room. Poor dear was quite overwrought and cried. Christopher said little, even when shown his own room. I think he is quietly worried about sleeping alone but he will soon get used to it.

1st February 1890
Astor House, Kent

Mrs Morris says she will leave if I cannot get Christopher under control. John will not answer my letters. Lucy has decided she now hates her room and will only sleep in my bed with me. No word from John since Christmas. Worried.

7th March 1890
Astor House, Kent

John returned. So grateful to have him back I nearly cried. He says he received none of my letters, which I find astonishing but he was surprised to find Christopher still with us so possibly this is true. It does not explain, though, why none of his letters came either. He brought presents, a lace dress for Lucy and a pen knife with a blackthorn handle for Christopher. I cannot imagine this will end well. Harrison the gardener has already made complaints about the rose bushes. Apparently, Christopher kicks them flat when he thinks no one is looking. That or picks off the buds. I cannot imagine what he will do with a pen knife but John will not hear it. I am certain Christopher sneaks about the house at night. Told John this evening that I heard something outside the office door. He said I was imagining things but I am not sure.

2nd April 1890
Astor House, Kent

We have had a mishap with the laundry. Lucy's clothing – including her Irish lace dress – has returned with slashes through the material. It must have been Christopher. It is too clean to be a rent from the mangle and the kitchen maid says that everything was pristine when she packed it into the basket. I have it in mind to take the knife before he does real damage. I have done my best to make repairs but Lucy refuses to even try it on. I brought letters to John and tried to speak to him about it. He receives so many these days and not all of them business. Some smell of Lily of the Valley or rose water. It reminds me that I should burn ours, but he is so distant these days I cannot bring myself to do it.

13th May 1890
Astor House, Kent

John has been so strange. He says it is stress and I try to be helpful and keep the children out of the way. He doesn't call for me as much and avoids my gaze. I don't know what I shall do. I had Harrison install a sliding bolt on Lucy's door, he is much more accomplished with tools than the footmen. He has been no fan of Christopher since the War of the Rose Bushes and was happy to help. Hoping this will give the child some peace of mind.

24th May 1890
Astor House, Kent

Christopher took Lucy out on the boat. It was a foolish and dangerous thing to do but John says no harm was done. Mrs Morris has complained that Christopher has been scratching his name into every piece of furniture in the house and his father has finally taken the pen knife from him. I'm glad and said so. John agreed that he had been too lax. He has said to come to his office tonight. I am blushing just thinking of it.

23rd June 1890
Astor House, Kent

It could not last. I do not know how Christopher got hold of his pen knife but I have assured Lucy that her hair will grow back. I swore I would never raise a hand to a child but what could I do? He is to be locked in his room for now. Even John agrees that it has all gone too far. Lucy will not leave my side.

12th July 1890
Astor House, Kent

Christopher now allowed out of his room. Lucy clings to me. It would be so much easier if John would propose and we could stop sneaking but he says it is not the right time. I can't help but think it would be the right time if we didn't have all this mess to deal with.

23rd July 1890
Astor House, Kent
That child is hateful. We would all be better off without him.

6th August 1890
Astor House, Kent
Christopher is dead. God help me.

TWENTY-FOUR

Three of Swords

'Well, Miss Pearlie,' said Dr Richmond, turning my resignation letter over in his hands. 'I think we can both agree that our experiment has not gone as either of us had hoped. Both Olivia and you showed a staggering lack of judgement last night.'

In the silence that followed, the carriage clock on the mantle chimed. It was eleven o'clock. I'd barely slept after my encounter with the housekeeper. I'd washed the dirt from my eyes with shaking hands, and spent the night staring into the dark, in too much pain to rest. When I did sleep, I had nightmares in which I could hear children crying, as the Shambler lumbered towards me.

By dawn, I'd known what I had to do.

Winter had arrived in earnest overnight. Outside, a thin layer of silver frost covered everything. Inside, a fire crackled in the grate. It would have been cosy but for the tension that hung in the air between myself and Dr Richmond.

Clearly, he too had experienced a difficult night. His haggard expression betrayed his lack of sleep and I could see from the way he massaged his temples that he had a headache. I looked no better, I was sure. My eyes were clearer but still reddened, and my hand had swollen so much, and was so tender, I was barely able to scrawl my resignation letter before creeping up the stairs to Marian to beg her to bind it for me and ask me no questions.

She had agreed but her face was pinched and lips pressed together as she worked. It had been necessary to fashion a sling for me and my hand now nestled against my chest. I had told Dr Richmond that it had been injured in the incident with the Shambler the night before. And he, irritable and lost in his own thoughts, had not questioned this.

He had not offered me a seat so I stood in front of his desk, feeling as though I were swaying on the spot.

'I am sorry, sir,' I said, lowering my head. 'My intention was to scare the brute off.'

Dr Richmond held up a hand. 'And now, to compound matters, you are trying to quit my service at a time when you might actually prove to be useful. It is insupportable.'

I blinked. 'Sir?'

'After our return yesterday evening, I had an illuminating conversation with Peter Joyce. He has some concerning insights as to Olivia's imbalance and has suggested she be presented to the Royal College. I will now be taking her to London at the soonest opportunity.'

Dr Richmond pulled a sheet of paper towards him and made an annotation without looking at me. 'For now, she will need to have appointments with me, twice a day. She will also need to be put on a strict diet.'

He handed me the list. I took it, feeling awkward using my left hand. It was quite short, consisting mainly of clear broths and the lightest of meals. The sight of it worried me.

'It is very plain,' I said.

'It was recommended by Dr Joyce,' Dr Richmond said. 'He has extensive knowledge in cases such as these.'

It seemed to me he spoke as though Olivia were a stranger.

'Excuse me, sir, but what cases are those?'

At this, Dr Richmond met my gaze directly for the first time. His eyes had a coldness to them that I had never seen, not even last night on the balcony. He was, I realised, both utterly furious and, somehow, hopeful. I thought of Olivia and felt a swoop of fear.

'Hysteria nervosa.' His voice grew clipped. 'An anxious disorder of the mind that manifests in hallucinations and hysterical behaviour, such as last night. We are only at the beginning of our understanding of it, but many experts on the subject have suggested it is due to overstimulation. I believe you yourself suggested something of that nature?'

'Forgive me, sir, I never suggested she was ill. Merely bored and over-imaginative.'

He waved a hand, dismissing my point. 'It is natural that you would not be able to consider anything deeper than that. I confess I did not even spot it myself. We are lucky Peter was here to witness Olivia's behaviour. Knowing what I know now, it would be remiss of me, as Olivia's father, to allow her illness to continue. I must act and you have responsibilities, which you will honour. You have said you would like to resign at my convenience and my convenience is after I have news from the Royal College regarding our presentation.'

Relief made me light-headed. Surely, this meant I could stay? After all, Mrs Hayes could not force me into leaving if Dr Richmond refused my resignation?

'I understand, and I'm happy to stay on as long as you need me,' I said, humbly. 'Also, I could stay at Mistcoate and look after Captain Richmond if Mrs Hayes is to accompany Olivia to London.'

He gave a curt nod. 'That's exactly what you will do.'

I looked down at the paper with its list of bland foods. 'When will you tell Olivia?'

Dr Richmond studied me shrewdly. 'Naturally I do not wish to cause my daughter undue distress. I will be keeping the real reason for our trip to London private. I shall explain it properly in the fullness of time but for now, I think it best if she believes it is a social call. A repayment for Dr Joyce's stay with us. I'd appreciate it if you told her nothing.'

I did not like the idea of lying to Olivia.

'I confess, sir, that may be difficult,' I said. 'She is an intelligent young woman.'

Dr Richmond's stern glare froze me in my place.

'She is a sick child who does not know the living from the dead.' His voice had a steely edge. 'Your role now, Miss Pearlie, is to make yourself useful in whatever way you can. But know that if I find you have disobeyed my instructions and breathed a word of this to her, you will be out of this house without reference and without pay.' He picked up his pen. 'Now. Please send in Mrs Hayes. It seems I have much to discuss with her.'

I found Mrs Hayes pretending to tidy the parlour, with Dr Joyce loitering in a nearby chair. He had been reaching out to her, the edge of her skirts caught in his fingertips when I walked in. She did not try to hide the flirtatious smile as she turned, last night's unwashed glassware in her hand.

'What?' she said, barely looking at me.

'Dr Richmond has asked for you.'

'I'm sure he has,' said Dr Joyce, in a tone that made me feel queasy.

He grinned, as Mrs Hayes set the glasses on the sideboard and smoothed her skirts.

'Take those out for me,' she told me, and then made a show of noticing my bandaged hand. 'Nasty-looking wound there. Did you fall over?'

I nodded, eyes on the floor, hating myself.

'Good girl,' she murmured as she swept past.

I turned to go but heard Dr Joyce call out, 'Miss Pearlie?'

He was lying back against the chair, one foot up on the centre table. His shirt was undone at the neck. I felt as though I had caught him undressing.

As if reading my mind, he grinned wider and gestured at the sideboard. 'The glasses.'

I hurried forward but my injured hand made it impossible to hold the tray. Instead I gathered the glasses up with my good hand, fingers pinching the rims. There was a rustle behind me as Dr Joyce stood up.

'Too much champagne last night?' he said.

'Sir?'

'Your hand.' He gestured. 'Let me see it.'

I paused, not wishing to turn round and face him.

'Come, come, I am a doctor.'

Left with no arguments, I set down the glasses and turned to face him.

He was closer than I had expected. I gave a small flinch of surprise and he chuckled.

'I don't often have that effect on women.' He slipped my hand out of its sling, unwrapping the bandages to examine my bruised and swollen fingers.

He let out a low whistle.

'How did you manage this? You will need to bandage it better than that,' he said. 'What is this? Old petticoat? We shall have to see if Georgie has anything.'

'I'm sure Marian can do it again,' I demurred. 'Dr Richmond is so busy.'

I tried to pull my hand away but Dr Joyce maintained his hold, rubbing his thumb along my fingers, feeling how tender they were.

'Preparing for the big trip to London, yes. I'm glad he's finally seen sense. Have you ever been to the city?'

'Yes, I was there before I came here.' I desperately wanted to get away, but forced myself to stay still.

'We shall have to swap hot spots,' Dr Joyce teased. 'I'm sure you know a thing or two.'

'I shall write to my sister-in-law,' I said, aware of the mild but uncomfortable pressure Dr Joyce seemed to be applying to my hand. 'She knows all the fashionable places. I am somewhat behind the times.'

'Yes, I imagine it's easy to fall out of touch, squirrelled away up here.' He turned my hand over, making a show of considering the underside of my palm. 'This is a nice old pile, although Georgie was somewhat generous in his description of it. I'd always suspected he was a bit hard up but he kept going on about this place. Of course I don't blame him, a man must keep up appearances but it's hardly Chatsworth, is it? I am sure he will be glad to be rid of it.'

He ran his thumb up my palm, pressing into the skin, not seeming to notice me flinching.

'It seems there's quite a lot Georgie wasn't forthcoming about,' he mused. 'I imagined him up here in the wild acting as a sort of hermit but, in fact, he seems spoiled for delightful company. He might have said. I wonder what I could do to convince him to share? Especially now that I have made an investment.'

I frowned at him, searching his face to decipher what he meant.

'Sir?'

He took a step closer, still examining my hand. He was so close now that I felt almost trapped. I couldn't discern if he was unaware of my discomfort or savouring it.

'Georgie didn't tell you?' he said. 'Well, he will probably wring my neck for this. But Old Man Rogers was none too pleased at a chair going through his window. He sent a man down first thing this morning with a demand for payment.'

My eyes widened. 'He did?'

Dr Joyce laughed. 'Put Georgie in a bit of a spot, since he didn't have the funds ready. Lucky I was there, really. Still, what are friends for, eh?'

My heart pounded as I realised what I'd done. How much had my rashness cost? No wonder Dr Richmond had looked so angry.

But Dr Joyce was waiting for a response.

'That was very good of you, sir,' I said, weakly.

'Not at all.' He gave a modest smile and began wrapping the bandage back around my hand with easy skill. 'But I shall have to give some thought as to repayment. We shall have to think of something.'

He gave my hand a light squeeze, just enough to elicit a gasp of pain, and leaned in so close that I could smell the cigar smoke on his breath. 'I am sure we will be seeing a lot of each other. I know my sister is very keen to see George again. Not too sure how keen Georgie is, to be fair. But, knowing Mina, she'll get what she wants. Georgie always said he'd never marry again – says he's not the marrying kind. But who knows? He might feel he's out of other options.'

He tipped me a wink and slid away, leaving with me a peculiar queasy feeling. As though my mouth were coated in thick oil.

TWENTY-FIVE

The Hierophant

I took special care in the coming days, especially at night, when I bolted the door and shoved my chair underneath the handle for added safety. Mistcoate felt very unsafe now.

There were two occasions when my door rattled in the night and, imagining Olivia, barefoot and shivering, I had moved to open it before pausing. The door had rattled again, and there had been a thump and low, muffled swearing.

I burrowed under the bedding and waited until Dr Joyce was gone.

During the day, I went for walks in the cold air, avoiding Mrs Hayes as best I could. A part of me wondered what would be said about me. I did not know if I was still considered Olivia's companion and was, therefore, neglecting her. But Olivia seemed to be living in seclusion, keeping to her room and admitting only Mrs Hayes.

On the Sunday following the party, I walked to Fellwick to check on Alice, but no one came to the door. My notes had gone unanswered and even Mrs Meadows had no news when I enquired at the tea shop.

'The Reverend took the service this morning as usual. Why do you ask?' she'd asked. 'Is there something wrong?'

'Nothing at all, Mrs Meadows,' I lied, and hurried out of the shop.

So they were continuing as normal. Then why hadn't they responded to my notes?

The idea that they might both be avoiding me brought tears, and I walked back to Mistcoate feeling more alone than on the day I first arrived.

A week after the party, Dr Joyce left Mistcoate aboard the nine o'clock postal coach to Ely. His departure immediately changed the atmosphere. It was like breathing after breaking the surface of deep water.

As if he missed male company, Dr Richmond began taking his meals in Captain Richmond's room. The low rumble of their voices carried up the corridor and, though it was nice to see him take more interest in his father, it all had a secretive air that made me uneasy.

He also began a series of appointments with Olivia, which left her tearful and pale afterwards.

Mrs Hayes was an integral part of these appointments, often spending an hour locked in Dr Richmond's office. She kept an even closer watch on Olivia than before, monitoring her food, her appearance, and spending long stretches in her room.

As the days passed, Olivia struggled to sleep and grew lacklustre in her lessons. I could not understand it.

'I have been here nearly two months and you still cannot play a single tune,' I scolded her one afternoon, as she sat at the piano. 'Londoners will not know what to make of you. Please try.'

'Has Papa said I must impress them?' she asked.

'*I* have said it.' I turned over the music sheet to a new score. 'Now, let us try…'

I stopped mid-sentence. Her sleeve had slipped, revealing a round bruise on her arm. It was the size of a thumb print, and a deep, angry puce. Olivia sat, silent, as if daring me to comment.

'How did you do this?' I asked, touching the bruise lightly. 'It looks painful.'

She looked away. 'I suppose I fell.'

'Olivia, are you going out at night again?' I gave her a stern look. 'I will paint your window shut if I find out you have. You know it's not safe.'

'I am not.' She pulled at her sleeve, covering the mark. 'Now what do I need to play?'

But I wouldn't give up. 'Where did it come from then?'

Olivia shrugged and pressed a key. Its shrill note echoed around the room. I'd rarely seen her this subdued.

'Sometimes I wake up with bruises after my appointments.' Her voice was flat. 'Papa gives me something on my tongue and it makes me sleepy. Then I wake up and I'm sore.'

My insides went cold. It was as if I was sitting with Lucy again, listening to her lie.

I cleared my throat. 'Are you in pain now?'

Olivia shook her head and hit another note. Lower, more mournful.

'Mrs Hayes gives me something before bed sometimes so it doesn't hurt.'

Anger flared and I struggled to hide it from her.

'It's called laudanum,' I said, and began to pick out notes from *Moonlight Sonata* with my left hand. My right, though healing, was still bandaged. 'It's not good for you.'

Olivia sat with her hands on her lap, watching me play. 'But I have such horrible nightmares. Almost as bad as you.'

'How do you know I have nightmares?'

'I see you there,' she said. 'With Christopher.'

I stumbled on a note and the mistake was left to hang in the air.

Later, I steeled myself and went down to have a word with Mrs Hayes. We had not spoken alone since the night in my room. The housekeeper relayed her orders through Marian.

If the kitchen maid had guessed at the cause of my wounds, she said nothing. However, judging by her sullenness whenever Mrs Hayes spoke to her, and the way she found a reason to squeeze my arm reassuringly or stand in front of me when the three of us were alone in the kitchen, I felt that she knew. And I was grateful to her.

Now, though, I felt I had no choice but to deal with the housekeeper directly. I had no wish to speak with her, but if it could help Olivia, I was willing to try.

But when I found her sitting at a desk in her office, she showed little interest in my concerns.

'It's nothing for you to worry about,' she said. 'Dr Richmond has been kind enough to explain it all to me in detail but it is very complex.'

I noticed that she avoided looking at me directly and busied herself arranging folders and putting away notebooks as she spoke.

'I'm worried about her,' I said. 'She is losing weight and her hair…'

'Her father is a trained professional,' Mrs Hayes informed me, curtly. 'He knows what is best. However, if you are interested in arguing the point with him, please do. Now, go and help Marian with the washing, there's a good girl.'

I despised her triumphant smile.

Still, as I walked out, I thought all was not lost. Among the papers on her desk, I'd observed a small, leather-bound book that could well be my journal.

I vowed that, the next time she left the house, I would go back and recover it.

After that, I did not know what would become of me.

But Mrs Hayes did not leave the house as the days passed, and the chill of December grew. Almost nobody did. Mistcoate became even more shuttered and secretive. I had imagined that, after so long in the country, Dr Richmond would leave for London soon, but instead he stayed, issuing a list of times that Olivia was meant to appear in his study as his research intensified.

At this point, Olivia's lessons with me ended completely. Aside from sessions with her father, she was never outside her room and Mrs Hayes seemed constantly on guard. Days went by when we didn't see Olivia at all.

Marian and I whispered in the kitchen, but we could do nothing, despite our growing concern about what was happening.

As Christmas drew nearer, post arrived more frequently. Here, again, Mrs Hayes was a step ahead, always there to collect the letters and packages before I could look at them. It was the only time she left Olivia completely alone.

One afternoon, I waited until the housekeeper went outside to collect her deliveries from the bottom of the gravel path. As soon as I heard the door thump shut, I raced into Olivia's room. I found her in bed, eyes ringed with dark circles, her thin pale hair limp and straggling. She peeked out from under the stale, sour-smelling bedding as I entered.

'Just me,' I said, brightly. 'Shall we go for a walk?'

'I am not feeling well,' she said, listlessly. Her voice was thick and hoarse.

I sat down on the edge of her bed. 'I'm worried about you,' I said, smoothing the damp strands of hair from her forehead. 'Is it the appointments? Are they too much?'

'I've been reading my cards,' Olivia murmured, tiredly. 'But they won't tell me.'

'Tell you what?'

Her pale eyes glistened. 'What is happening to me.'

She looked so worried and small, I found myself lying down next to her, pulling her towards me like I had for Lucy, breathing in the mustiness of her unwashed hair. She gave a sigh as she settled against me.

Then she said, 'I've been thinking. Maybe I should not go to London? Papa would have a better time without me and I could stay here with you and Grandfather.'

For one wild moment, I wanted to agree. To say, 'No, of course you don't have to go.' Except, I remembered, it was not really a social trip.

'Why don't you want to go to London?' I asked instead.

'I do not want…' she began and then she took a deep, shuddering breath. 'I do not want to embarrass Papa.'

She was lying.

'You will do no such thing,' I assured her.

'But what about at Weatherall?' she said, her voice low and frightened.

'What happened there, Livvy?' I asked. 'Tell me the truth.'

'Nothing went right,' came the muffled reply. 'I ruined everything.'

'What do you mean?' I said. 'What were you meant to do?'

'I wouldn't have done it, only she said it was why I had been invited, and that I had to.'

'Who told you that?' I asked. But she seemed not to hear me.

'We weren't really invited by Suzanne's family,' I said, giving her a squeeze. 'We were guests of the Reverend and Miss Byres, and they're not upset, I don't think.'

At the mention of their names, I suddenly remembered my unanswered notes, and I wondered if anything I was saying was true.

'But I *was* invited,' said Olivia. 'Look.'

She stood unsteadily, and I nearly gasped at the sight of her. Her nightdress floated loose around her body; her limbs were so very thin. She advanced towards her dressing table, located a drawer and drew out a cream-coloured square card.

I stared at it.

'Why didn't you tell me?'

'Mrs Hayes said it would embarrass you,' she said. 'You could only go as someone's guest, but I had been properly invited. She said, if I told you, you would be angry.'

'I am not angry,' I said. 'But I thought these readings were going to stop.'

Olivia shook her head.

'I can't,' she whispered. 'I can't stop.'

'You don't need it, Livvy,' I told her. 'It's not the only thing you can do.'

'It's not that. It's—'

We both heard the footsteps in the same instant. Someone was coming up the stairs.

Olivia looked at me, her eyes wide with fear.

'Oh no,' she whispered.

I reached out and pulled her back towards the bed, speaking hurriedly.

'What is it, Livvy?' I said. 'What is happening? What are you frightened of?'

Before she could reply, the door opened.

'Are you awake?' Mrs Hayes stopped short at the sight of me, her back stiffening.

'What are you doing here?' she demanded.

Without waiting for an answer, she directed her attention to Olivia. 'My lamb, Dr Richmond wishes to see you for an emergency appointment.'

Olivia's voice was almost a wail. 'But we already had one today. I feel too ill.'

'Dr Joyce has called him to London tomorrow and he needs to finish up his notes,' said Mrs Hayes, calmly. 'You know this is important for him.'

'Julia, please,' Olivia pleaded, turning to me.

'It's no good you saying anything to Miss Pearlie. She has no more say over it than you do,' Mrs Hayes cut her off. 'If you want to go to London, you need to cooperate.'

Still, Olivia clung to my arm.

'Go speak to him, Julia,' she begged. 'He listens to you.'

Mrs Hayes gave a sharp little laugh at this.

I rose from the bed. 'Wait here. I'll have a word with him.'

'I wouldn't if I were you,' Mrs Hayes said, but I was already out of the room and descending the staircase.

I found Dr Richmond standing at his desk, shirt sleeves rolled up, sorting through a buff folder of different writings. He turned, removing his spectacles.

'Miss Pearlie? Is Olivia on her way?'

'She has sent me down to beg your pardon or, at the very least, to request some gentle handling,' I told him.

'She has done *what*?'

His voice was soft and dangerous. I smiled, trying to soften the tension that filled the room.

'She is somewhat concerned about the bruising and discomfort that occurs from your appointments and has asked me to intervene.'

But Dr Richmond was striding past me and down the corridor, into the main hall. I stumbled after him, my soothing words unheard as he shouted up to the mezzanine floor above.

'Olivia Richmond! Come down here at once.'

'Dr Richmond, please,' I said.

'Who do you think you are?' he snapped, rounding on me. He grabbed my arm, gripping my wrist so fiercely I nearly cried out. 'How dare you interfere with my work?'

I was speechless with shock. He looked deranged. Was he drunk? No, there was no tell-tale sign of alcohol; just a manic look in his eyes that suggested stress and insomnia.

'You know nothing about what I am trying to do here,' he continued. 'I was already in enough debt to Peter Joyce before you... And now you are trying to impede me in the only worthwhile thing I can offer him after he has given me a place on his research team. Can you not understand what this might mean for my family?'

He was sweating and his breath smelt acrid.

'She merely asked me to—' I began, but he shook me, his fingertips digging into my flesh.

'You are not here to do as she tells you. You're here to do as *I* tell you. Is that understood?'

'Yes, sir.' I stumbled as he pushed me away, knocking into the grandfather clock so that it tipped a little before righting itself with a dull thud. As I stepped back, I noticed Marian hovering in the kitchen corridor, watching with worried eyes.

'Olivia!' Dr Richmond roared.

There was a moment and then Olivia appeared on the stairs with Mrs Hayes behind her.

'Ah, you have decided to participate.' Dr Richmond was panting now, perspiration beading his forehead. 'How good of you.'

'Please, Papa,' Olivia began, almost tearful, but he spoke over her.

'If you have decided to no longer take part in preparations for this trip, you can stay here and not go to London at all. Would that be preferable?'

Olivia said nothing and then, slowly, nodded. Dr Richmond's eyes bulged. When he spoke again, it was through clenched teeth, the quiet of his voice more terrifying than when he had been shouting.

'Come here and get up onto the table. Miss Pearlie, you are dismissed.'

Without waiting, Dr Richmond turned and stomped back down the corridor, flexing his fingers as though he should like to hit something. Above me, Mrs Hayes marched Olivia down the stairs. As they passed, the housekeeper turned to me and said, 'Make yourself useful and go into Fellwick. There's a list in the kitchen.'

I listened to them disappear down the corridor and heard the door to the study close. After that I heard the faint sound of plaintive weeping and harsh words.

I stood alone, clenching and unclenching my hands.

What are you going to do?

The Soho witch-child sat on the floor of the hall, curled up in a corner, knees drawn up to her chest, the way Olivia often did. I stared at her.

Or will you do nothing? she hissed.

Behind the study door, the sounds stopped. Somehow, that made everything worse.

TWENTY-SIX

Six of Wands Reversed

I couldn't stand another moment in Mistcoate. I pocketed Mrs Hayes' shopping list without reading it and pulled on my warmest wraps for the walk into Fellwick. The sky was slate grey as I stepped out into the cold. In the distance, the clouds promised snow.

The woods were silent as I strode through them, head up, watchful for any sign of movement. There had been no talk of the Shambler since the party at Weatherall but this did little to comfort me. I had seen him. I knew what he was capable of. And they had not found him.

As my feet grew numb with cold, I wondered if my life would always be so filled with worries and pain.

When I reached the town, I noticed with a start that bright decorations had been erected in the square. Garlands hung in shop windows and wreaths brightened doors and windows.

But of course, it was the second week of December. Soon it would be Christmas. I had almost forgotten.

There was none of this at Mistcoate, which seemed to exist in its own dark time and place.

An icy wind sent my coat fluttering around me, and I hastened towards the steamy glow of Mrs Meadows's tea rooms, where she had even gone so far as to put up a Christmas tree in one corner.

'Bit of Christmas cheer for all,' she said, when I admired it. 'Will you be needing any Christmas goods, miss?'

'Only what's on this list, please,' I said, handing it over.

'Got you running around for her then?' Mrs Meadows observed, recognising Mrs Hayes' handwriting.

'I find it best not to argue, Mrs Meadows,' I said, not bothering to hide my bitterness.

'She's a tough one, is Eda Hayes,' she said, packaging up my items. 'Did you know she used to be in the Music Hall?'

Somehow, I could not imagine the scarred, angry Mrs Hayes glittering under a spotlight. She put me more in mind of a prize fighter, all gristle and sinew, ready to beat her opponent into submission. Wasn't that exactly what she had done to me?

How could I protect the girl against such a person?

What was going on in that room right now and why didn't Mrs Hayes stop it? Couldn't she see that Dr Richmond had lost perspective? His focus should have been on the presentation to the Royal College but his fervour over Olivia was growing into an obsession. He'd looked like a madman, shouting and grabbing me.

'Are you well, miss?' The shopkeeper gave me a curious look. 'You see seem miles away.'

'Forgive me,' I said, forcing a smile. 'I'm lost in thought. I meant to ask, is there any more news on the Shambler?'

'Nothing certain but...' Mrs Meadows leaned forward. 'They say they found a body in Woodley's Copse that they think might be him.'

'Really?' I felt something like relief, tinged with doubt. How could that monster have just died?

'It's these cold nights, miss,' Mrs Meadows confided. 'They're no laughing matter. Especially if we get a strong enough wind to bring that sharp air in off the broads.' She shivered, her many layers of clothing rustling. 'I shan't say I'm sorry if it is him. And I'm sure we'll all sleep better in our beds; but that that's no way for a man to die. Frozen and alone out in the wilds.'

She handed me the package wrapped in brown paper. 'Is that all, miss? Only, if you're stopping by the Byres', Reverend Byres said not to let anyone bring refreshments.'

'Why did he say that?' I asked.

'Well, they'll be away for a bit and – did no one tell you? Miss Alice is being taken to hospital. She's… Miss Pearlie, don't forget your things!'

Minutes later, I hammered on the door of the Byres home, refusing to stop until I heard footsteps on the other side.

Ed Byres opened the door. He wore an over-large woollen pullover that made him look like a little boy. His eyes were puffed and his cheeks so hollow for a second I wanted to wrap myself around him, and then I remembered why I was here and the longing turned to acid in my stomach.

'Miss Pearlie.' His tone was as cold as the air around us.

'I am told Alice is being sent to a hospital,' I said breathlessly. 'Why did you not send word? I called and sent notes, did you not receive them?'

'I have not had time for letters. Alice has needed constant care since her attack.'

His tone chilled me. It was so clipped and disapproving, and he would not meet my eyes. I blinked, hurt and confused.

I had thought often over the last weeks of what Mrs Hayes had said about Florence Richmond's pregnancy. I had believed it something malicious, said only to cause me further pain, but his change in demeanour made me wonder.

'Well, I am here now,' I said, keeping my voice steady. 'Tell me how she is.'

'She is weaker. The doctors are worried. We are leaving for the hospital as soon as the coach arrives.' Despite his demeanour I could hear the worry beneath his voice.

I bit back tears. I had been a poor friend to Alice. Why had I allowed this distance to form? Why had I not broken the door down to check on my friend?

'I didn't know,' I said.

'No.' He looked me full in the face, his expression a mixture of hurt and censure. 'Perhaps you have enough to keep you busy.'

'I don't know what you mean,' I said.

'Well, you certainly seemed to enjoy dancing with Dr Richmond. And you and he have been little seen since that night.'

'I also danced with you,' I reminded him, stung.

'And now we both know that meant nothing.'

I flinched away from his cutting tone but the unfairness of it riled me. Had he not seen that my employer forced me into that unwanted dance? Did he not see my struggle to get away? How could Ed believe for a moment I had wanted any of it?

'There is much to do. I must go,' said Byres stepping back.

'I haven't done anything wrong, Reverend Byres.' I met his gaze directly. 'I asked for none of this.'

There was a long silence; I could see the doubt on his face.

'Well,' he said. 'Just be careful of him. He has a reputation.'

'He is not the only one,' I put meaning in my voice. 'And I am heartily sick of being given these vague, ominous warnings as though I were some silly girl. If there is something you wish me to know, I would thank you for saying it.'

'I could say the same to you,' he said. 'You clearly have something on your mind.'

'Why did you not tell me the truth about you and Florence Richmond?' The words came out in a rush.

Byres' brow furrowed. 'I did. I told you we were close.'

'No,' I said. 'You didn't. You told me nothing of the baby. Or of Florence's suicide.'

Byres winced and stepped out towards me, his voice hushed and rough. 'That was not my story to tell. And I would ask that you do not judge her.'

'I do not judge Florence Richmond,' I said. 'It is not her fault that she was abandoned by those meant to protect her.'

'She made her decisions,' said Byres, his face rigid. 'It was not my place—'

'Then whose place was it?' I demanded.

'Her family? Her father? The very people who put her out of the house in the first place? What else was I meant to do?' His voice broke and he looked away, his face carved with weariness. 'I cared for Florence but, in many ways, she was naïve to the point of recklessness. She made some very poor decisions and would accept nothing but a fairy tale ending.'

'So you abandoned her?' I said.

'She was not mine to abandon,' Byres insisted. 'I offered what I could. But it was not what she wanted. I was a young man, just starting out in Fellwick. I could not become any more embroiled in the scandal than I already was.'

'And what was that offer?' I demanded, my voice rising. 'A damp bed in a dormitory full of other unwed mothers? The chance to raise her child in poverty or not at all? If she had given it up, would she have been allowed to return home?'

I had forgotten the cold now, warmed by my anger. Was this what men were? Did they all take what they could and then abandon the women they were meant to love?

Byres' face hardened. 'I am sure, I do not know. I could have completely turned my back, and I would have been right to, but I did not. And now I am made into the villain for not doing the impossible?'

Furious now, I took a step towards him. 'I would never have thought you to be one of those men who cast aside those so you could have an easier life.'

Byres seized my shoulders and pulled me into the seclusion of the porch.

'If I wanted an easy life, I would never have followed you into that graveyard.' His voice was low and tense. 'I would not have encouraged your friendship with my sister, or helped her to buy fabric, or allowed her to stretch herself to exhaustion, nor even would I have attended that damned party. Do you understand that I became a subject of gossip through our association? People have noticed how I look at you and they talk about that too. But I invited it all, to help you.' He held my gaze. 'Believe me, Miss Pearlie, if I wanted an easy life, I would never have allowed myself to care for you. But I did.'

I was trembling now. Byres' hands dug into my arms, but with urgency rather than the intent to hurt. My eyes stung with tears but I would rather die on the spot than allow myself to cry.

When I spoke, my voice was hoarse and choked. 'All I can say is if you are likely to be offended by keeping company with people who make poor decisions – people like Florence Richmond – then you might find it is just as well to keep your distance from me. I am not perfect, Reverend Byres, I have made many mistakes. Love and rationality are often at odds. So if it is a safe, rational woman that you seek, please look elsewhere.'

I held his gaze, daring him to argue further. He set his jaw and released me.

'Fine.' His tone was suddenly formal. 'Would you like me to give Alice a message?'

It was as if a great, black hole had opened beneath me. My hands shook. But all I said was, 'Tell her I'm sorry she is unwell. I will call again.'

The knocker rattled as he shut the door in my face. I gave a long, shuddering sigh and turned to go, tears now falling.

A movement drew my attention. Alice looked down at me from an upstairs window. As I raised a hand to her, she placed her palm against the pane of glass. I pressed my gloved fingertips to my lips and blew her a kiss.

Alice turned, as though called from within the house, and disappeared from view.

TWENTY-SEVEN

Nine of Wands Reversed

I woke in darkness to a strange sound. It was a kind of scrabbling of claws on wood, the sound an animal would make when worrying at a door, trying to get in. As my eyes adjusted to the gloom, I heard my door shivering a little at the hinges. Something *was* trying to get in. But I had locked the door… hadn't I? As I tried to remember what I had done before bed, I realised that the door was already open. Yes, even as I looked at it, it stood ajar.

And yet, the scrabbling continued, but slower, more purposeful. It was accompanied by a guttural bubbling sound, as if someone was struggling to breathe. I tried to push myself up in bed, but I couldn't move. I could only lie there, staring, as around the corner of the bed came a creature, moving on all fours.

It was a child, and yet not. The limbs were too long, the hands scaled and nimble. It was naked, with slick, dripping hair and long, yellowing fingernails, caked in filth.

It crawled on its hands and knees, fingers scuttling across the floor, searching as it went. All the while a watery, rattling breath came out of it as it began to hiss and whisper.

Its voice was the same deep growl that Olivia's voice had been in her trance during the party at Weatherall.

'Where are you?' it muttered.

Water pooled on the floor as it crept across the dark room, its head down, hands searching.

I held my breath, lying stiff and still, not daring to move.

It gave a watery chuckle and spoke again. 'I can smell you…'

I could feel the sweat at the nape of my neck. My hands prickled with fear. I strained to leap to my feet, to vault over the end of the bed and flee into the waiting dark of the corridor. But my body would not respond. I could only lie there, barely breathing, even my screams unable to escape, and watch as the creature came closer, its long, drenched hair covering its face.

The horror of it choked me. I made a small, involuntary gasping sound. And the thing on the floor froze.

For a second it was still, so still I thought it was not a child at all but a trick of the light or a piece of furniture that I could not see clearly. Then it lifted its head. Part of its forehead was missing. The skin around the deep gouge in its skull was ragged and wet, as though nibbled by fish. I became aware of a very particular smell – the tang of blood and the rot of pondweed.

A broad, dark, glistening ribbon of blood seemed to cover the side of the creature's face and as it lifted its head, I was horrified to see that its – *his* – eyes were gone.

'Christopher?'

His dark, mottled lips parted in a vile grin.

'There you are, Juja,' he said.

His back legs tensed, like an animal's, and he leaped at the bed. I pulled the covers over my head, startled into motion, and felt for a moment like I was falling backwards, through the mattress. I squeezed my eyes shut.

A weight landed on my chest and pinned me down. I could hardly breathe and through the darkness of the blankets I heard a low watery chuckle. A hand curled over the edge of the bedding and pulled it back, long ragged nails scraping gently against my skin.

I opened my eyes. A white face appeared, inches from my own.

The witch child smiled down at me. She was sitting on my chest, her knees bent up to her ears, her sweetly foul breath, like rotting meat, tickling my nose.

As I stared up at her, her lips slowly parted in a smile, showing two rows of jagged, broken teeth. Her pupils were so pale they were nearly white and when she pressed a finger to her lips, I could see that her nails were yellow and overgrown.

I wanted to reach up and move her hand away but I couldn't move. Around us, the walls of the room seemed to be undulating like the rhythmic pulse of a beating heart. I screwed up my eyes and now it was not the witch child but Lucy Kemp looking down at me, her skin blackened, her nose bloodied, the way she had been that day when they pulled her out of the boat. Her breath rattled in her chest as she bore down on me.

'Lucy?' I whispered.

'Juja,' she said. A dark, thick trickle began to ooze from her nostril. It collected in a round, heavy orb on her lip and then dropped onto my face.

I woke with my scream dying in my throat.

When I opened my eyes, Olivia was standing next to the bed, looking down at me. I gave a small cry but she did not seem to notice. She stood, swaying, her eyes half open and unfocused. As I pressed my hands to my mouth, trying to quell my panic, she lifted the blankets and climbed in, her body pushing against mine, shoving me to the cold, empty side of the bed.

We lay there together. Me, pinned next to the wall, her giving a sigh of contentment as she settled into the warm space where my body had been. As the nightmare receded, my breathing slowed. Gradually, I allowed myself to get comfortable, accepting that Olivia would probably be there for the night.

As lay there, I realised I was grateful for the slowly breathing presence next to me. It was a comfort that I hadn't felt since Lucy used to climb into bed with me.

Suddenly overwhelmed, I buried my head in my pillow and silently sobbed.

A week later, Dr Richmond took Olivia to London. The travelling party left before daybreak. Lamps flickered as the coachmen dragged cases out into the freezing darkness and lifted them onto the roof of the carriage.

I stood in the doorway, breath misting in the early morning air, watching as Mrs Hayes ordered the coachmen about. She was dressed like a lady, in a smart coat, leather gloves and broad-brimmed hat.

'Is everything on?' Dr Richmond asked the coachmen, who nodded.

The doctor looked taller in his dark wool great coat. He had tucked a burgundy scarf across his chest and was pulling on a pair of leather gloves. In deference to travel, he had opted for a black, felted hat with a small adornment of feathers tucked into the band.

The night before, Olivia had come to my room again, pleading to stay at Mistcoate. I had held her close whispering, 'Livvy, I'm sorry. It's beyond my control.'

'I understand,' she said, with dull acceptance. 'Mrs Hayes likes to have me to herself.'

Olivia ran to me now and hugged me tight. She wore a thick wool coat and a fox fur stole. She looked so pale and fragile. I longed for some way to keep her safe, but I had no power.

'You have all you need?' Dr Richmond strode towards me, his expression as cold as the weather. 'Mrs Hayes has taken you through everything?'

I straightened, but kept a hand on Olivia's shoulder, unwilling to let her go.

'Yes, sir,' I said, meekly.

He gave me a dismissive glance. 'We will discuss your situation on our return.'

I watched helplessly as he ushered Olivia into the carriage and climbed in after her.

Mrs Hayes followed, her haughty manner making my stomach sour and my mind rage. The carriage door shut. Then the driver cracked the whip and they were off with a jangle of reins and a rattle of wheels, the breath from the horses creating a trail of vapours.

I stood for as long as I could bear it, watching the carriage roll down the driveway until the fog engulfed them and they were out of sight. Even then, I lingered, until there was nothing but the silence of the trees.

When I reached the kitchen corridor, the heat from the range thawed my frozen skin. Marian had lit the lamps, bathing the kitchen in a warm glow as she stood, neat and industrious in a fresh blouse and clean, white apron, making a pot of tea.

Hearing my steps, she turned and gave me an encouraging smile over her shoulder, dimples appearing in her round cheeks, her hair hidden beneath her white cap. I found myself smiling back, despite my misery. How could I ever have dismissed her as a slovenly maid-of-all-work? Her eyes shone with intelligence and, with her resourceful, resilient manner, she was, I realised, the only real ally I had at Mistcoate.

'So how will you do, miss,' she asked, turning back to her task, 'spending Christmas in this big place on your own with Captain Richmond?'

'I am trying not to think about it,' I admitted, sinking into a seat at the kitchen table. 'I'm just glad you're still here now.'

It occurred to me that Marian had taken no days off since I'd injured my hand. Without a word of complaint she'd worked seven days a week to make up for my indisposition.

'I'll be going to Mam's for Christmas Day, but I should be back the next day so you'll not be alone for long,' she said, unaware of my thoughts.

'That will be nice,' I said vaguely. But Marian shook her head.

'Mam is a penance at the moment with her sudden fits of temper and getting overheated at a moment's notice. She can't bear to be near the range so I'll be doing most of the cooking, and then Toby's getting to that age where he could eat a horse and still be hungry, so he'll be complaining there's not enough on the table. My other brothers will be in the public house before it gets dark. If anything, I think I shall be glad to get back to Mistcoate.'

'That does not leave much time for you to relax,' I said.

It was obvious to me that she deserved more. I was selfish to want her to stay with me so I would not be alone in the house.

I made a spontaneous decision.

'Marian, I would like you to take today off.'

She turned, the kettle still in her hand. 'But Mrs Hayes said—'

'Mrs Hayes is not here,' I spoke over her. 'You have been such a help recently while I have been injured. Finish whatever you are doing and then go and have a day to yourself. Captain Richmond and I can manage. Go see your mother and Toby.'

Marian was still doubtful. 'I was going to start on the Christmas menu.'

'Then go into town and see what ideas strike you,' I said. 'As Mrs Hayes is in London, I am authorised to charge groceries to the Mistcoate account, so you may order what you wish. Of course, we could not be extravagant.'

'We would not need to be, miss,' said Marian, almost breathless with excitement as she realised I was in earnest. 'Set me an amount and I shall make such things with it!'

'Wonderful, now let's have some tea. As soon as it is light, out you will go to be a lady of leisure.'

Marian beamed, blushing with pleasure.

After Marian left, I built up the fire in Captain Richmond's room and brought his boiled egg and toast.

I had expected to find him still in bed, but he was sitting up at a small writing desk dressed in navy blue silk pyjamas and an embroidered dressing gown, a small pair of glasses perched on the end of his nose. The fire crackled in the grate and I was pleased to find that the room had a comfortable warmth to it. I wondered if he would remember me, seeing as he had only seen me when serving dinner during Dr Joyce's visit, but he barely looked at me, instead glancing at the tray in my hands.

'Ah,' he said. 'Over here, if you please.'

His voice was hushed and steady, though his hand shook a little as he moved a stack of papers out of the way. When I placed his breakfast in front of him, he rubbed his hands together in anticipation. They made a soft, papery sound that was not unpleasant.

'Would you like me to see to anything, sir?' I said. 'Tidy anything away for you?'

He looked up, a piece of toast with egg balanced neatly on it in one hand.

'Why?' he said. 'Is the girl not here?'

'She's just gone into town for the day. And of course, the others have gone to London.'

He fixed me with a shrewd look, much sharper than any scrutiny I had received from him before.

'They have gone?'

'Yes, sir.'

'And Olivia with them?' he said.

'Of course,' I said.

'Blast,' he said. 'We shall have to call the constable.'

'Sir?' I blinked at him.

'I expressly forbade him to take her to London.' He made an irritated sound and sat back in his chair, breakfast abandoned in front of him. 'He will make her an exhibit. Him and that *roué* he brought here.' He shook his head, staring into the fire. 'She didn't want it. She said so. What am I good for if not to protect her?'

It was the most cogent I'd seen him, and his words so echoed my own helpless thoughts, that I found my eyes welling.

'I fear for her, too,' I told him. 'But I do not believe a constable can help. I fear we are too late.'

We both fell silent, considering our personal failures. The sound of the crackling fire seemed suddenly loud.

I swiped the tears away and forced a smile. 'The gloom in here is making us maudlin. Here.' I pulled the curtains apart, filling the room with a cold, austere winter light. I eased the sash open enough to let out the fug and bring in the sharpness of the air. Then I began to straighten the room. Putting books back on shelves and straightening the bed covers. He watched me work.

'They don't tell you about it, you know,' he said, suddenly.

'No, they do not,' I agreed.

He gave me an interested look, as though surprised at the feeling in my response.

'You don't even know what *it* is,' he said. Then he paused to consider. 'Neither do I.'

The focus he'd displayed earlier was gone, and that air of confusion had returned.

'I know, sir,' I said, moving over to tuck a blanket around him.

He watched me work. 'How she screamed when she was born. You could hear it all over the house. Louder than Florence or George. Then the nurse came and there was so much blood.'

He turned to me, his eyes wide and brimming with tears, a man peering out at me from the depths of his own personal hell.

'George wasn't even here. Can you imagine? He left her here – his own wife – while he went to that damned club in London. And she slipped away alone, leaving this… this *imp*. But she became such a sweet child and what was she to do, with such a feckless father? Now he has taken her and will parade her for all to see. Oh, Florence… My Florence. I have failed you.'

He buried his face in his hands and wept like a child. I stooped down next to him, taking his wrinkled, soft hands in my own.

'Hush,' I whispered. 'Of course you haven't failed her, sir. Please do not distress yourself.'

He looked down at me, his eyes blank, as though he had never seen me before. For a moment his features creased as he tried to formulate a thought and then, coming to a conclusion, he smiled and reached out to stroke the side of my face.

The pads of his fingers were soft.

How long had it been since I had been touched by someone who did not want something from me? I had not realised how much I had missed it, but now I felt ready to break from the pain of it.

'There,' he said. 'There you are now, my girl. What have you been up to?'

It was the look that did it. I had not seen one like it for many years. Not since Father died.

'Oh, sir,' I said, biting back a sob. 'They all think I did something awful that I didn't do but what I *did* do was still terrible. And I am so worried about Olivia.'

'Secrets are poison,' said Captain Richmond, gripping my hands in one of his. He was calmer now. 'I should have done things differently. But they do not teach you, you see, about being a father. You can only piece it together for yourself, and we were already so steeped in tragedy and infamy. Olivia's mother died in that petty, bloody way. What if the same happened to my Florence? I could not bear it. Better to not see it at all. So I turned her out. And then she took herself to the river.'

I looked up and stared into his face. Once more, it had the sharp, keen expression of a man in control of his faculties. I felt the blood rush from my face.

He turned his gaze to me.

'I'm sorry...' he breathed.

Then he was gone again. I could see the distance in his eyes.

'I never thought of you as a flighty girl,' he chided, giving me an indulgent smile. 'What were you thinking? You know Byres had hopes of you? True, he was a younger man but at your age, you should be grateful. And yet you threw him over the first chance you got for that rogue.'

My breath caught, and I willed him to continue.

'You and that lawyer. Did you think no one noticed? Not everyone is as blind as me, young lady.' Captain Richmond stared into the fire, grumbling to himself. 'Disgraceful.'

'Sir?' I said, placing a hand on his arm. 'Sir, who was the lawyer?'

He cowered from my touch. 'What are you doing?' he cried. 'Who are you?'

He was gone again, but I had to know more. Nobody would tell me the truth about Florence and Ed Byres, and it was maddening. I had to know. I kept my voice calm.

'It is me, sir, Miss Pearlie. I'm sorry to startle you.'

After a moment, I rose and began cleaning again. When I saw calm return to his countenance, I spoke with a casual tone. 'You've just said something that confused me. You were talking about Florence. You see, I had thought her condition was due to Ed Byres.'

His face became guarded. 'Her condition, as you put it, madam, was due to a young upstart from Hampshire who should never have been admitted to the Bar. I shall have Mr Alder…'

But what he would have had Mr Alder do was taken up in a fit of coughing. I hurried over to pour water from the ewer and brought it to him. He gulped it like a man dying of thirst, his hand gripping my wrist, before sinking back into his chair, his breathing laboured for a moment. When it had eased, he opened one eye and regarded me.

'I kept your letter,' he said, gasping for air. 'I fetched it from my diaries. Look. I am not so heartless.'

His shaking hands rustled through the papers still on the desk, pulling out a page, much folded and refolded, written in a cramped, rounded hand, which he held out to me.

I took it and began to read.

Dear Father,

I write to you in the throes of desperation. I hoped to make this appeal to you in person but Mrs Hayes informs me that you are not available. Frederick is yet to answer my letters and I fear now that he may never do so. Please know, dearest Father, I have only behaved as I have through the natural feminine hope to have a home and family of my own. Such were the promises that Frederick made and which, I regret to say, I believed. Do let me come back, dear Father, and you will see your foolish daughter rendered infinitely wiser and more resilient to the ways of the world. I beg you. If you do not relent, I cannot see what else I can do.

Florence

Carefully, I folded the letter and slipped it back among the papers on the desk. The captain had closed his eyes, and I draped the blanket around him.

'I so enjoyed our walk, Florence,' he murmured, vaguely. 'Shall we take another tomorrow?'

'Of course,' I said. 'First thing.'

I moved slowly from the room, but my mind was racing.

Mrs Hayes lied. Ed Byres was not the father. I rejected him for something he did not do.

TWENTY-EIGHT

The Hermit

Leaving the captain to sleep, I walked numbly down the kitchen stairs.

Florence betrayed him, I thought, as I built up the fire in the parlour. *He told me he was not responsible and I did not believe him. He said he did all that he could, and I did not believe him. Oh God, what have I done?*

Even as the sun reached its noon height, the fog was thickening in the woods, and it seemed to make my thoughts darker. I could not sit and think about my mistakes and what they had cost me. I had to stay busy.

I lit the lamps until Mistcoate blazed like a lantern. I could not bear the idea of things lurking amid the trees. I filled my arms with books from the bookshelves in the parlour – a battered copy of Darwin, the latest Gissing, some neglected-looking copies of Dickens, Richardson's *Clarissa,* a few editions of *The Yellow Book* – and carried them upstairs to fill Captain Richmond's shelves as he slept.

I worked with a speed that almost suggested mania, the burning of my limbs distracting from the feverish thoughts that roared, constantly.

Mrs Hayes lied to me. About everything.

All at once, it struck me: with Mrs Hayes gone, I might be able to discover the truth. I'd seen her desk, and I knew where she kept things. There was no-one here to stop me.

Before I could change my mind, I hurried down the long corridor to the housekeeper's rooms. But when I reached out a tentative hand, the handle wouldn't turn.

My shoulders sagged. Of course it was locked. Mrs Hayes was careful.

But there had to be a way. Mrs Hayes always kept the house keys with her, I'd often seen her pull the jangling ring from her apron pocket. Surely she wouldn't have taken the keys to London?

No, she must have left them here for Marian to use. But where?

I raced to the kitchen, where Marian's apron hung on its peg. Hurriedly I felt the fabric, squeezing the soft cotton in my hands.

Instantly I felt the weight of them. I wrenched the ring from her pocket and ran back down the corridor to the housekeeper's room.

I did not know for certain that the key to her own room would be with the others on the ring, but it stood to reason that it would.

But which one? There were dozens of keys on the ring. I recognised the front door key, but the others were a mystery.

One by one I tried the keys, and each refused to turn. Even though no one was there, my hands trembled, clattering the keys against the brass casing.

I had almost given up when, at last, a small silver key slid smoothly into the lock. My hands shook as I twisted it. It turned easily. There was a satisfying click as the lock released.

I exhaled and opened the door.

I had heard stories in other houses of housekeepers laying traps in certain rooms to reveal if the staff had been snooping. Some tied a strand of hair around the door knob or left trifles balanced in a certain way so as to be knocked over when a person entered. Something told me that Mrs Hayes would consider this sort of thing fanciful, but I was careful all the same as I eased my way into her chambers.

The air was ice cold and stale, as if she'd been gone for days instead of a few hours.

I felt odd, like a burglar as I crossed the floor. I flung open the curtains to let in light. Everything had been left tidy. The floor had been swept, and the grate dusted.

I wanted to search everything in this room, to try and understand why Mrs Hayes despised me so. But I knew the facts must be found in the letters that had poured into Mistcoate over the last few weeks. Those were what I needed.

The desk folded open to reveal stacks of papers as well as drawers and several promising-looking compartments. Most were locked. One small drawer opened to reveal a series of clippings from various newsletters and magazines. I flipped through them, hurriedly.

All were on the same topic: spiritualists.

'One may never know when a talented new medium may emerge...'

'She was discovered when her mother called her to commune for guests in the living room...'

'Currently touring in America as part of the...'

'London audiences have been crying out...'

I returned them to their hiding place and turned to the other drawers. Two locked, one empty, one with an envelope holding a series of letters, packed together, written in the most incomprehensible handwriting. I could only make out certain sentences: '...*I can speak to him before you come, but you must do the promotion yourself... No sign but I shall keep a look-out, why do you ask?... She is not happy but says she'll ask him. Don't expect much...*'

Beneath those, was a small leather-bound ledger that looked so familiar I gave a cry of relief as I picked it up. But it was not my diary. It was in Dr Richmond's neat hand.

22nd November 1890

Subject presenting some anomalous symptoms following our recent tests. Interesting though that this is previously unheard of from Subject and correlates with the test matter. Must investigate. Subject appears disturbed which proves promising.

11th December 1890

Began physical exploration of Subject today. Found a dose of laudanum with some chlo. added works best. Some nausea presented afterwards – must be mindful. Everything presents as statistically 'normal' – E there to assist. Commented on enlargement of labia – must investigate if this is congruent with control subjects.

The words created an unpleasant queasiness in my stomach and I did not know how much more I wished to discover. I flicked back to earlier pages.

15th December 1889

Visited Mollie in Soho. Paid 5s for examination and 5 more for services after.

Examinations of both her and Bella have shown little physical correlation so possibly their susceptibility is cognitive or otherwise internal. P suggests it is through choice and that makes me feel somewhat better but what of F? Does that mean it was all due to poor choices or to a sickness in the family blood? It would explain O and, I admit, myself. But then that raises the question of parentage and who introduced this to the line? Must investigate. Mollie was exemplary, as usual, though coughed too much.

20th December 1889
Mollie ill. Saw Dora instead. Mollie will charge for questions but Dora much more forthcoming. Was offered other services but refused, considering state (see sketches). Strange – I also felt E might not like it. P invited me to dinner with his sister. Would rather take Dora to the Ritz. Would be less painful. Glad to get back to Mistcoate. O tiresome. E very attentive.

I closed my eyes, my stomach writhing.

Of course I was aware that men visited such women, I was not a fool. But the idea of Dr Richmond doing so, of him sitting with his studious expression sketching them in the most intimate way… Why on earth was a folder of such things in Mrs Hayes' rooms? Was she blackmailing Dr Richmond as well?

I had learned enough. I closed the ledger and pushed it back into the drawer, turning back to the locked compartments. I tried the smallest keys on the keyring, but nothing fit. No, she would not have been that careless. She was more likely to have hidden the key.

But where?

I sifted through the unlocked drawer, removing every paper, my fingers searching the sides. Finding nothing, I tried other dressers in the room, moving from drawer to drawer.

In the drawer of an occasional table, I noticed a small protrusion under the green felt, and I plucked at a corner. It was a round, raised piece of wood, almost like a button. I pressed it, suspecting that it would be useless, but suddenly a slim, inconspicuous compartment that spanned the top of the desk above the space for the legs slid out, revealing my diary and a small photograph.

I seized the book, hugging it to my chest. Whatever Mrs Hayes might say on her return, she would never again use my own words against me.

I slipped it into my pocket and was about to leave when my gaze fell on the photograph. I picked it up to examine it.

It held the image of a younger version of Eda Hayes. She was dressed in the kind of dresses Mother used to wear when I was young, and sitting in a padded armchair against a curtain, laughing, her face slightly blurred as she struggled to keep still, one hand clamped to her stomach, which protruded just enough to suggest the new life within. At her shoulder stood a man. He leaned over, as though he had just whispered in her ear but, like Mrs Hayes, his face was blurred from movement. I turned the picture over.

Family picture. 1879

From the kitchen, I heard the distinctive sound of the back door slamming.

'Hello, miss. It's only me!'

Marian had returned early.

'Hello!' I shouted back.

Hastily, I dropped the picture back into the drawer and locked it. Then I pushed the compartment back so it clicked into place and put the papers inside the desk.

In a last-second decision, I pulled out Dr Richmond's ledger. I had no idea what I would use it for, but something told me it was safer to have it. I was just closing the drawer of the bedside table when a glint of gold caught my eye.

'You'll never guess what I learned,' called Marian from the kitchen.

Tucking the doctor's notebook under my arm, I crouched down and tugged at the gold piece with my fingernail. It came up easily and I held it between my finger and thumb.

It was a cufflink that had fallen and become trapped in the gouge between the floorboards. It was engraved with three diamond chips in one corner and bore two initials.

G.R.

George Richmond.

I thought of the times I'd seen him murmur to her, the hours alone in his office.

'*E very attentive...*'

Bile rose in my throat, my suspicions now utterly confirmed.

The cufflink fell from my hand and I left it on the floor. I fled the room, not bothering to lock the door behind me, trying to calm myself as I strode along the corridor into the kitchen.

'He is dead,' Marian announced as I walked in. 'The Shambler. Mrs Meadows says the constable has confirmed it. We'll all sleep easier now, I'm sure.'

'Well, I cannot pretend it is not a relief,' I said.

I slipped the house keys into the pocket of her apron as she put the groceries away, chattering excitedly about the town gossip. My hand dropped occasionally to my pocket, where I carried the two little leather-bound journals.

Marian made a dinner of a small roasted peahen with bacon and greens, and the last slices of a rather stale Victoria Sponge cake, softened with custard. We ate with Captain Richmond at the table in the dining room. Marian had taken some convincing about this but after all, I said, what would we have her do? Eat alone in the kitchen?

I lit the fire and set the table so it was quite comfortable, and had Marian take her apron off and brush her hair. Captain Richmond, who took a sly delight in wearing pyjamas at the dinner table, called for us all to have a glass of wine to toast the excellent dinner. I thought of Olivia, of how much she would have enjoyed this upending of the home's hierarchy, and I hoped she was safe in London. I did not like to think about what Dr Richmond had planned for her.

I could not bear to leave my diary unattended again. It was as though the malignant presence of Mrs Hayes was still with me, ready to snatch it back again. I kept it, safely in my pocket, feeling the reassuring weight of it throughout dinner.

As Marian and Captain Richmond laughed and talked, I found my mind turning to my next steps. And I knew I would not slink away as Mrs Hayes wished me to. Not now that I had evidence of her wickedness. No, I was going to stay.

I would find a way to set things right. I would apologise to Reverend Byres. I would confront Dr Richmond. And come what may, I would have justice.

TWENTY-NINE

Five of Cups

That night I slept better than I had in months and woke to a world covered in white.

It snowed on and off for five days. We did not go into town during that time. We slept, walked, cooked, read and ate. In the evenings, Marian and I washed dishes together, sometimes laughing, sometimes in companionable silence. We fell into a comfortable daily rhythm that seemed to suit Captain Richmond, making him more alert and livelier than I had ever seen him. In the evenings, he told stories of his youth that made me roar with surprise and laughter, and in the mornings, we took a walk through the snow to the bottom of the long driveway.

'Mistcoate is really starting to feel quite like home,' observed Marian as we sat in the kitchen one evening.

'Yes,' I agreed, hardly aware that I was smiling.

I did not think about what awaited us when Dr Richmond returned. Now that I had decided to fight for my place, I somehow felt more at peace. The witch-child had been silent for days.

It felt as though things were changing.

On Christmas Eve, Marian and I ventured into town for supplies, and found everywhere filled with holiday cheer. We each had a glass of mulled wine in the inn, and barely noticed the cold on the walk home.

Christmas Day arrived dressed in a mantle of frost. The lawns glistened, as though studded with diamonds, and the sky was the clear, cold grey of freshwater pearls. I let Captain Richmond sleep late and built up the fires myself, as Marian left early to see her family.

Breakfast was taken in front of the fire in Captain Richmond's rooms, after which we read *Romeo and Juliet*, which Captain Richmond pronounced 'a maudlin little romance, but not without beautiful imagery.'

'It is customary for us to take a walk before lunch,' he told me, at the end of Act Two. 'Come, Florence – let us not be idle.'

He often called me by his daughter's name and I did not correct him. It suited us both and, I fancied, gave us both some comfort.

Marian had left us an elaborate picnic complete with cheeses, roasted and sliced meats, mince pies, two different kinds of potatoes, fruits, and even oysters, which Captain Richmond cheered at when they were unveiled.

After the meal, plates abandoned at the table, I played piano rather poorly, due to my fingers, which were still stiff. Captain Richmond sang in a voice that would once have been an impressive tenor, as the snow resumed outside.

It was a comfortable and, dare I say, happy time. But it was not to last.

The weather caused us to neglect our walk on St Stephen's Day, and the next day Captain Richmond was keen to be out in the fresh air.

'Just think of how wonderful it will be to have a warm fire and fresh scones waiting on our return,' he said, as Marian laced his shoes.

'You should come with us,' I said, as Marian waved us off.

'But then the scones would not be made,' she reminded me with a laugh, and we struck out into the cold.

The snow was still unspoilt and Captain Richmond took a boyish delight in leaving footprints on clean drifts, clinging to my arm and sighing 'wonderful', as his boot made a satisfying crunch. Our breath escaped us in gentle white puffs and the crispness of the air turned our cheeks and noses pink. The scene was so quiet and restful that we lapsed into companionable silence, with nothing but the crackle of snow under our feet.

We had just made a circuit of the lawns and were striking back towards the driveway when we heard a cry from the direction of the house. At first it seemed like a bird, high and otherworldly, but then it came again, clearer and more familiar.

My chest tightened.

'Marian!' I cried.

I started to run but Captain Richmond could not. I turned to him desperately, and he released my arm and pointed in the direction of Mistcoate.

'Go,' he ordered, in the tone of a military man. 'I will follow behind.'

I lifted my skirts and ran towards the house, my heart pounding and blood racing in a way that had nothing to do with my exertions.

I arrived to find a struggle taking place at the front door. Marian, her cap askew and her face wild, was wrestling on the doorstep with a man dressed in shabby clothing.

'Let her go!' I demanded, throwing myself at him and managing to grab a handful of his coat.

Twisting around, the man locked eyes with me and I felt my heart seize. His face, which had been covered by his collar, was blistered and shining with scar tissue. One milky-white eye stared out at me, unseeing. The other gleamed with malice. The shock rendered me immobile and, seeing his chance, he shoved Marian hard to the ground. I heard her elbow give a crack as she landed. Then he wrenched himself free of my grip and fled across the lawn.

For a moment I could not move. I could not breathe.

The Shambler, I thought, wildly. *But they said he was dead...*

Beneath me, Marian lay, clutching her elbow, weeping and breathless. Her distress brought me to my senses and I bent to help her to her feet, leading her into the hall. She trembled violently, whimpering as she sank down on the bottom stair. I removed my coat and draped it round her shoulders, ripping my gloves off so I could rub her icy fingers.

Captain Richmond arrived a few minutes later, puffing but in one piece. He bolted the door, made certain Marian and I were well, and then, in a sudden fit of independence, tottered off to check the rest of the ground floor for intruders before returning.

'He... is... gone,' he announced, pausing between words to catch his breath. As he stood beside us looking furious, I suddenly saw the resemblance he had to his portrait, which hung at gallery level above us. Here was Captain Richmond as he might have been in his army days, decisive and focussed.

'I'm s-s-so cold,' Marian whispered.

'Come. Let us move to the parlour.' I helped her to her feet.

When we'd retreated to the warm room, I built up the fire and, at Captain Richmond's insistence, we all had a small glass of brandy 'to steady the nerves.'

'Now, girl,' he said, turning to Marian, who cradled her glass, 'what happened?'

'Sir, I hardly know.' Marian's voice shook. She fought back her tears, trying to speak up. I placed a soothing hand on her shoulder as she struggled to explain what had occurred.

'I was making the scones when someone knocked at the door,' she said.

She believed we had abandoned our walk and returned. Instead, she found a man, his face covered by his collar, along with a threadbare scarf and hat, waiting on the doorstep.

'I thought he was a gypsy,' she said. 'They come sometimes and on the way through they'll offer to do bits and pieces for us. I told him, if it was work he was looking for, he'd need to look somewhere else.'

'And what did he say to that?' asked Captain Richmond, watching her intently.

'I don't like to repeat it,' said Marian, shuddering. 'I never heard such language. He demanded to know where Winnie was. Then I saw his face – his face—'

I felt my own shuddering and forced myself to stay still.

'What happened then?' I pressed.

'I told him there was no Winnie here and that was when he tried to force himself into the house. He kept shouting that name, "Winnie! Winnie!" Did you not hear him?'

I shook my head. We had walked too far and had only heard Marian because she had screamed.

She blinked back tears. 'Oh miss, what if he comes back? What do we do?'

I didn't have an answer for her. Was there no end to the fear in our lives? Were we never to be safe? The thought filled my head, almost making me reel. But this was what happened, wasn't it? Every time there was a bright spot, a moment of hope, something came in and destroyed it. *Well*, I thought grimly, *not any more*.

Possibly I had brought darkness and danger down on myself and that was fine, but I had always tried to do the right thing and Marian – Marian had done nothing to warrant being attacked on the front step by a stranger. It was all too much. I had allowed it for too long, but I would not allow this. I would not allow Marian to become yet one more person I could not protect. I clenched my hand into a tight fist and took a deep, steadying breath.

'I will walk into Fellwick and tell the constable,' I said.

'Oh, miss, please don't go.' Marian's face looked pale. 'He could be in the woods. Waiting.'

It was unnerving to see our resourceful, capable maid suddenly so nervous.

'There is no one else to do it,' I told her, easing my coat off her shoulders and slipping it on. 'You stay here with Captain Richmond. Lock all the doors.'

I strode out into the hallway, Marian and the captain following in my wake. My gloves lay where I had abandoned them on the stairs and I stooped to retrieve them.

What will you do? You are all alone now.

The witch-child stood in the corner by the door. I did not look up from my gloves, I did not want to see her. I had been blessedly free of her for days and now I was to be haunted again.

Suddenly furious, I yanked my gloves on with such force my healing fingers ached.

'I will not sit here like a rat in a trap,' I said, angrily. 'I am tired of it. I am weary of men tormenting whomever they choose. I cannot allow it anymore. I shall go mad.'

'I just wish I knew why,' Marian whispered. 'Why must he come here? And who is he?'

'I think I know,' I said, not wanting to say more lest I terrified her further. 'But we must be careful. Keep your eyes open. I have such a strange feeling.' I opened the door. 'I must hurry if I'm to be back before dark. Once I am gone, lock everything.'

The walk to Fellwick was bitterly cold. The air had teeth in it, biting into my cheeks and the end of my nose. By the time I reached the stone arch leading into town, it had started to sleet, shards of ice thudding against my hat. It was a relief to step into the comparative warmth of the police station.

'Well, we'll send someone out, miss,' said the chief constable, when I'd told him about the attack. 'But there's a snowstorm coming. It's likely we won't get much done before then. That being said, the weather may solve the problem for you, if you catch my meaning.'

'I heard that they confirmed the remains at Woodley's Copse,' I said. 'If so, I believe it is possible that there may have been some mistake. It might not be the Shambler's body.'

The constable's expression darkened.

'I don't see how,' he said. 'Sergeant Combs is an experienced officer with an unblemished reputation. If he says it is confirmed, it is confirmed.'

But I could not accept that. 'Did the body have burns? On one side of his face?'

'You have seen him, I take it?' guessed the constable. He was a short, round man with an impressive moustache, and his face was not unkind. 'I must say, until now no one mentioned any burns. There was a beard, a scar, even an eye patch, if you will believe it. Every description we receive is different. It's like chasing a ghost.'

I hesitated, and then said, 'That night at the party at Weatherall House, I looked him straight in the face. The man I saw was covered with burns.'

'That party is where many of our other witnesses came from.' The constable smoothed his moustache thoughtfully. 'Leave it with us. We will send someone out to Mistcoate this very day if the weather holds.'

There was nothing more to be done.

I trudged back along the forest road towards Mistcoate, replaying that conversation in my mind.

The constable wasn't wrong about the weather at least, dark clouds were already gathering overhead again, shuddering with snow.

What if it cuts us off completely? Who will help us then?

The thought enraged me all over again. There was no one else. *I* would have to protect us from this wretch and, God help me, I would do whatever I must.

A twig snapped and a wood pigeon took off, wings thrashing, sending snow hissing down to the ground. I would not stop, would not look back, even though I could sense it again. That feeling of being watched. Of being followed.

Bracken crackled to my left and still I strode on, tears of fury in my eyes. I would not run.

Seconds later, something cut through the forest on my right. And I heard a sound of laughter that chilled my blood.

'I am not playing your game,' I told the shadows around me.

Emboldened by the sound of my own voice, I turned to confront the forest behind me.

'Do you hear me?' My voice rang out, bouncing and echoing between the trees. 'We are done with that. So come out! Let me face you now.'

Nothing. Just the sound of ravens in the distance and the wind whistling through the forest.

Still, my heart raced inside my chest and I sped off down the path, back to the safety of Mistcoate House.

My eyes snapped open in the dark. Something had woken me. What was it?

It was late. At ten o'clock, seeing Captain Richmond dozing, I had forced him and Marian to go to bed and had sat up for hours by the fire in the parlour, clutching a poker. At some point I must have drifted off.

Now I stayed statue-still, listening to the roar of my own blood in my ears, straining to hear what had woken me.

At last it came again. The sound soared across the lawns: a long howling wail.

I stood slowly, willing my breathing to quiet, aware of every creak as I crept towards the window and pulled the curtains aside.

Light streamed from the full moon, picking out the gloomy shapes of the trees and the wide shadowy expanse of the garden. At first, everything seemed normal.

But then something moved at the edge of my vision. A dark figure, hunched and slow, ran among the trees. Holding my breath, I watched it pick its way, stumbling and heavy, along the edge of the forest.

Moments later, it emerged from the bracken, closer now, and still moving. Shivering, I watched its shambling progress around the house, stumbling and pausing to gaze up at the windows, as though searching for a way in. Suddenly, it stopped and lifted itself up, as though sniffing the air. Then it turned its head and looked straight at me.

I could not see its face but I felt its gaze, the way a small rodent knows when it has been spotted by a snake. We stood, frozen, staring at each other.

The creature began to run towards the house before cutting to one side, out of sight.

The back door.

I had locked it, but would it be strong enough?

There was no time. Still clutching the poker, I raced from the room, the cold and terror turning my skin to gooseflesh as I skidded into the kitchen, which stood dark and silent.

The door was shut tight. I let out a shuddering breath.

Then came a slow, soft sound. The door handle began to twitch, up and down. There was a dull thump from the other side and the door rattled on its hinges. The wood groaned, as if a weight was against it. And then silence fell.

As I stared at the door, a hand slammed against the window beside me, so hard I thought the glass might break. I leapt back, nearly dropping the poker; a small, frightened, noise escaping my lips.

In the sharp silence that followed, I clearly heard the sound of someone walking on the gravel path around the house.

He's circling us, I thought.

Something moved in the hallway, and I turned just in time to see a shadow roll across the light spilling out of the hallway, where a lamp still burned.

'Marian?' I whispered.

Nothing. But there it was, a small shadow, on the edge of my vision. I drew in a sharp breath.

Surely he could not have got in so quickly. I had heard no glass breaking.

I crept out into the main hall and gave a soft whimper as I stepped in something that splashed. In the glow of the lamp, I could see a puddle of water on the floor. As my eyes adjusted, I noticed another, then another. They led around the stairs towards the entrance hall and Dr Richmond's study, where the shadows were deepest.

Plip...

I took a step forward, my foot landing in another puddle. The cold and damp seeped into my bones.

As I rounded the foot of the stairs, the shadows seemed to reach out for me. A scuffling sound, a rustling. I think I knew what I was going to see as I approached, but still I could not stop myself.

'Who's there?' It came out as a gasp.

He stepped out of the shadows.

It was Christopher.

His hair and clothes dripped inky water, creating another small puddle on the floor. His eyes were over-large and dark, ringed with blue circles. The breach in his skull glistened wet in the moonlight with blood and pond water. Dark, congealed rivulets ran down the side of his face, obliterating one, shadow-ringed eye, which stared past me, unseeing.

'Juja...'

I sagged, my shoulder and the side of my arm pressed against the bannister. I still gripped the poker but my hands were sweating.

'Where are you, Juja?'

Water spilled out of his mouth, as though flowing from overfilled lungs. I gave a dry sob.

The one clear eye snapped round to me.

'There you are...'

He leapt.

I screamed and ducked back behind the stairs, the poker useless in my hand. Something thudded against the window in the parlour.

'Marian!' I cried.

I heard the sound of wheezing breath behind me, a coldness by my ear, a feel of clammy skin next to mine.

'Please,' I whispered, not daring to turn. 'Please, no...'

A freezing hand closed around my neck.

'Marian...' But my voice was barely above a whisper now.

Icy fingers squeezed my throat. I dropped the poker and heard it clatter on the floor.

There was a thud against the front door and male voices. A light appeared on the first floor.

'Miss Julia?'

The hands on my throat loosened and yet still I could not move.

Footsteps on the mezzanine above my head. The wheezing breath receded, leaving only the ice in my veins.

I heard a shout from outside and another thump against the door.

'What's happening?'

Marian appeared, hanging over the railing of the floor above, looking down at me, a candle in one hand and a carving knife from the kitchen in the other, her hair coming loose from her braid.

'Help me up,' I whispered, tear-stained and damp with fear. Marian raced down the main stairs and pulled me to my feet, just as a hammering began on the door.

I snatched up the poker again.

A voice cried out through the door. 'Julia?'

I knew that voice.

I ran to the door, wrenching it open. Ed Byres, wrapped in a heavy coat and scarf, blood streaming down his face, stumbled into my arms.

THIRTY

Judgement

'He came out of nowhere,' Byres said. 'I can see why he was called a ghost.'

'Marian, help me get him into the kitchen,' I said.

We each put one of his arms around our necks and guided him down the kitchen corridor, blood dripping onto the floor which, I could see, was dry and without puddles. The grandfather clock, as we passed, read half past six. Morning had come before the dawn.

Byres gave a groan as we eased him into one of the kitchen chairs, a hand lifting to his bloodied head.

'Did you see what he hit you with?' I asked, removing his scarf and unbuttoning his coat as Marian moved to and fro, fetching water and a cloth before hurrying off to check on Captain Richmond.

We set the poker and the knife on the table. Byres had not commented on their presence, but I could see him snatching glances at them as I cleaned his wounds.

'An old clay pot, I think,' he said, wincing as the cloth touched the cut. 'He broke it over me and ran.'

'Which way did he go?'

I looked up, half expecting a dark figure to appear at the window but Byres shook his head, wincing at the motion.

'Back into the woods,' he said. 'He will not risk attacking the house again.'

'Can you see?' I asked, cleaning the blood from his eyes.

'I shall be fine. As I say, it was an old pot. The thing was falling to pieces before it hit my head. But you are shaking.'

'I am doing no such thing,' I insisted, even though my hands visibly trembled and my voice wheezed with anxiety. 'Not that I am ungrateful but how are you here?'

'I couldn't sleep. I saw the constable yesterday. He said you had reported an incident and that you seemed uneasy. I said I would come and check on you all but then the day got away from me... I decided late was better than never.'

'Thank you,' I said, and it did not seem enough to say.

'You can thank Alice.' Byres flinched as I picked a piece of clay from his hair. 'She made me promise to come and speak to you. That it was our Christian duty.'

The sudden stiffness in his voice worried me. I tried not to look at him but he stared into my face as I took the cloth and rinsed it.

With Marian out of the room, I knew I could speak freely.

'How is Alice?' I said. 'Please. I want to know.'

Byres sighed. 'Much the same. She must rest. The doctor says she has been doing too much. He is having to keep her in the infirmary. After that, we shall see. It seems as though it may only get worse.'

The thought of Alice having spent Christmas in a sanatorium proved almost more than my overwhelmed heart could bear. My lips felt dry and tight. I licked them, tasting their metallic tang, which caught in my throat.

'I miss her,' I said.

There was a moment's pause and then Byres said, 'She misses you. She said so.'

'Please do not be kind to me.' I rose from my seat, lifting the bowl of bloodied water, so he would not see my eyes fill. 'I am not sure I can bear it.'

'I am afraid that you do not get to tell me how to treat you.' There was a new edge to his voice. 'And, if I am honest, it helps me that it pains you. That my kindness still means something to you. See?' He reached out and gripped my hand, forcing me to turn and look at him. 'I am not so impressive after all.'

'What were you thinking?'

The witch-child sat on a stool in the corner of the room. I could just see her behind Byres' shoulder. She looked dishevelled and vicious, like a stray cat that has just fought off something bigger and is now feeling spiteful and furious. She bared her teeth at me and they were slick with blood.

'*Coward,*' she spat. '*There is no peace for cowards who run away and lie and pretend. You can't protect her – you can't protect anyone. You're useless. You always get it wrong.*'

A large tear brimmed in her eye and rolled down her gaunt, pale cheek. At the feel of it, she shuddered and curled in on herself, sobbing.

'*He hurt me,*' she said.

Instantly, I could smell it all over again – the soured beer, the ripe stink of horses, the smog of the city. In my mind's eye, a tiny pale figure was selected by a grown man and disappeared into the darkness of that tumble-down building while I, dressed in my new coat and sturdy winter shoes, could only watch.

'I'm sorry,' I whispered.

'Miss Pearlie?'

Ed looked at me oddly. Suddenly I was aware that I was crying. I gripped the bowl and cloth, carrying them to the sink, trying to regain some control of myself. Shock ran through my limbs, causing my arms and voice to shake. A tear hit the porcelain.

Plip...

When I looked up, Byres' reflection in the window was staring at me. He sat, a slit carved into his lip and his coat unbuttoned, blood staining his shirt collar. He looked more like a back-yard pugilist than a country vicar. His hands hung between his knees and his head tilted to one side, looking at me as though he had never seen me before. No wonder. I could see for myself that my hair was coming undone, his blood was on my shoulder and my face was mottled with tears and exhaustion. What would Anthony say? That I was having a tantrum, probably.

'*You can't always explode like that, Julia. It would not kill you to hold it in.*'

Except that it was. It was killing me and now I was talking and there was no way I could stop.

'I owe you an apology,' I said, my back still to Ed. 'I have been wrong. I thought that you had fathered a child and that you were the cause of a woman's death. I thought you felt that this was acceptable and that the fault lay with Florence and it made me angry. But it also made me think that, if you knew the full extent of my own foolishness and cowardliness, you might abandon and blame me. I could not bear that. I now know that this was not the case. I wish I'd had enough faith to believe that you would never be capable of such things, but I have believed that about people – men – before and been wrong. I am not a very good judge of character.'

I paused, listening to the tick of the clock in the hallway as I addressed myself to the sink.

'I fell in love with a man called John Kemp. My employer. There was no mutual feeling but I didn't know that. I didn't know anything. I didn't even know I was lonely until he spoke to me, told me things, wanted to know what I thought. Nobody had wanted that for so long. I became infatuated. I thought if I behaved as his wife, he would treat me as such. I had been caring for his children, helping with the house, I loved him in that stupid, little girl way. I thought that was what men wanted. It never occurred to me that respectable, widowed fathers wanted nothing more than a dalliance with the help. I was foolish.'

Byres spoke at last. 'I wouldn't say foolish; naïve, maybe.'

I gave a harsh laugh. 'At my age it was the same thing.'

'What ended it?'

My nose was running. I wiped it with the back of my hand, not caring how it looked.

'He met someone else. Someone more suitable. And decided to dismiss me. The day it happened, I was meant to take the children out into the grounds for a picnic and he asked me to come to him. He said we had something important to talk about. I thought he was going to propose. But when I got to his office, he told me it was all over. That I couldn't have expected anything else. He made me feel so *stupid*…He said he was taking the children to Ireland and I would not be needed any longer. But then Christopher – his son – drowned. They pulled him out of the pond and I should have been there but I wasn't. I was in John's office having my heart broken while Lucy…'

Her face swam in front of me and I gave way to sobbing. I heard the scrape of a chair and Byres' hands clenched around my shoulders, squeezing them as I shuddered and wept.

'She killed him.' It came out as a snuffling whine. 'Her own brother.'

'Stop, Julia…' he whispered.

But I couldn't stop. Not now. 'I was so wrapped up in myself that I didn't see how he brutalised her. I didn't *want* to see it, and even when I did, I was too much of a coward. When they pulled her out of the boat, he had clearly beaten her – her lip was split and her eye was black – and I knew. I knew she had done it. She hit him or pushed him or maybe she just fought back and it was an accident.'

I felt a hand press down on my waist, the other against my cheek but I could not lift my face. His hand was so warm and soft. I wanted to bury my head in his shoulder.

'Is it any wonder she blamed me at the inquest?' I whispered. 'If they'd known it was Christopher, they would have suspected her but she said I gave her those bruises and I may as well have. I was supposed to protect her.' At last, I looked up at him. 'What is wrong with me, Ed? What in God's name is wrong with me?'

Byres' voice was in my ear, low and kind and urgent. 'Nothing. There is nothing wrong with you. You just wanted what everyone else wants, that is all.'

'You would not have done that,' I said, wiping at my eyes with my sleeve. 'You even tried to help Florence after she—'

'I failed Florence.' He cut me off, his voice flat. 'As a friend and a person in need. The last time I saw her, she didn't just want my help; she wanted kindness. Oh, I made practical offers but what she wanted was compassion. I was too angry, too hurt. I tried for a long time to tell myself that I did nothing wrong, that many men would have done less, but sometimes you need to step out of your own world and strive for something bigger. I am going to do my best but it is hard doing that alone.'

He stood so close to me, I could feel the heat of his body through his shirt. He smelled of herbal pomade and mint. I was surprised to see his eyes as tearful as mine. His hand shook, where it rested on my hip.

'At least you have Alice,' I said, my voice low.

He leaned in, his hair brushing my forehead.

'You are being obtuse,' he whispered. 'It is maddening.'

The sound of wheels and hooves on gravel broke the silence of the room. It was faint at first but growing louder. Someone was coming.

Byres gestured to me to stay where I was and went to the hall to look through the front door.

'It's Dr Richmond,' he called.

By the time I reached the front door, a coach was drawing up in front of the house and Marian had appeared on the stairs. The driver jumped down and opened the doors. Dr Richmond helped Olivia down and rang the bell.

Marian and I looked at each other. Where was Mrs Hayes?

The bell rang again. I hurried to open the door.

'In what world does a man have to ring twice to enter his own home?'

Dr Richmond strode in, the scent of whiskey on him, leaving the coachman and a shivering Olivia in his wake. I was horrified by the sight of her. Her cheekbones jutted from underneath her overlarge, watery eyes. Her wrists looked like they would snap if gripped too hard.

I pulled her to me, feeling her icy hands.

'It's warmer in the parlour,' I told her. 'Go. Marian will fetch something for you to eat.'

The coachman was waiting for his payment. I darted back up the hall to speak to Dr Richmond, who roared, 'Take it, damn you!'

A shower of coins clattered around me on the floor.

'Really now,' chided Byres.

Dr Richmond twisted round to face him, staggering a little against the door frame. He didn't seem to notice the blood still on Byres' face, or the wound.

'What the hell is going on here? Miss Pearlie, what is the meaning of this?'

His voice was a growl. When he turned his burning gaze on me, I flinched away from it.

'I do not want to consider what has been going on in our absence. But that will be the end of it. Do you hear me?' He strode down the hall to his study. 'I have had enough of feminine interference and the ill-bred, unwashed charlatans of London. If I recall, you gave your notice before we left, is that not so?'

'I am in no hurry,' I said, following him. 'I am happy to stay until Mrs Hayes returns. I take it she will be spending longer in London?'

Dr Richmond's eyes glinted, his mouth twisting in fury. The office door slammed. From the floor above, Captain Richmond gave a cry and Marian disappeared with a swish of her nightdress.

'He is drunk,' said Olivia, in a small, fragile voice from the parlour doorway.

'Yes,' I said. 'I see that.'

'You gave your notice?' She looked at me, her expression hard to read.

'It is complicated, we will talk about it later. Come. Into the parlour with you.'

'I had better go,' Byres murmured.

I paused in the doorway. 'Will you be safe getting back?'

'I will avail myself of the coachman. Will you be alright here?'

I nodded.

'Ed,' It was strange how comfortable it felt to use his first name. 'Thank you, again. For coming to check on us.'

'I am glad I did. Even if I did have a pot cracked over my head for the privilege.'

Byres lifted his hand as if to touch my face, but then faltered. I followed his gaze. Olivia was still watching us.

'Good day, Miss Pearlie,' he said. He pulled the front door closed behind him.

Marian had put together a plate of bread, cheese and ham in the kitchen. She gave it to me to take into the parlour, where I found Olivia lying crumpled on the carpet in front of the fireplace.

I set the plate in front of her, as one would for a skittish animal, and went to the drinks cabinet to pour us both generous measures of port.

'Here,' I said, handing it to her. 'Your grandfather swears by it for the nerves. Eat a little. You will feel better.'

Olivia did as she was told and the shaking soon stopped.

'Are you warmer?' I asked.

Suddenly, she began to shake and weep again. I pulled her towards me, wrapping my arms around her shoulders. She did not resist, but allowed her head to rest on my chest.

'What happened, Livvy?' I asked, gently. 'Where is Mrs Hayes? What is going on?'

THIRTY-ONE
Nine of Swords

It took some time, but as we sat by the fire, Olivia told me what had transpired in London.

On their arrival at Liverpool Street Station, Dr Richmond had flagged a cab and sent his own bags to the Peppermint Club, before leading Olivia and Mrs Hayes east of the station. They were not staying with the Joyce family, as Olivia had expected. Instead, he had booked them into a hotel in Cheapside.

This appeared to be news to Mrs Hayes, who had not hidden her disappointment.

The landlady barely looked at them but pocketed Dr Richmond's money. Their shared room, Olivia said, was much smaller than her own and had two single beds, a wash stand, a chamber pot, and a rather greasy-looking screen to change behind. The curtains were made of cheap, yellowing lace and the floorboards creaked underfoot.

Dr Richmond came up to join them, rubbing his hands and asking how the ladies liked their accommodation.

'I'm sorry it's not Claridge's,' he said, with a tense smile. 'But we were lucky to get rooms at such short notice.'

Mrs Hayes looked as though she wanted to argue but she said that she and Miss Olivia would do just fine here, which was clearly what he'd wanted to hear. He said he would be busy all day, but he left them the funds for dinner and an evening's entertainment.

Olivia had watched through the window as he was swallowed in the throng of bodies making their way back towards Bishopsgate, carried off in a stream of strangers.

She was intimidated by the crowds, but Mrs Hayes seemed full of energy.

'Shall we go see what London has to offer?' she suggested.

The day was a blur of crowded omnibuses, and pies eaten, salty and steaming, as they stood in the street. The crush of Covent Garden and St-Martin-in-the-Fields, where they drank bitter, dark coffee from the cart of a vendor who was a real Italian. They walked along the river, Mrs Hayes pointing out sights she remembered from her girlhood, her eyes seeming to search every face in the crowd.

Olivia, of course, drew a few glances herself, dressed as she was in her hood and smoked glasses, but no one said anything. If anything, they seemed to regard her attire as an affectation rather than an oddity.

When they passed a poster for one of the music halls, Mrs Hayes announced, 'There we are!' and took them to catch the omnibus. They bought seats at the door, sitting in the balcony so they had to lean over the railing to see the acts.

First there was a comic, dressed like a fishwife, who told a story that Olivia only half understood and blushed at because of the way the audience – the men, especially – laughed. Then there had been a pair of girls dressed in glittering costumes, who sang a series of duets and blew kisses to the jeering crowd. There was a juggler, a short comic farce, and even an emotional monologue from a young lady, her face blackened with soot and rouge used to create false bruises, who told a plaintive story about loving the wrong man and hurrying into a violent marriage.

Mrs Hayes seemed less impressed with this act. She watched with one hand covering her mouth.

Finally, there was a spiritualist, his dark hair oiled so that his handsome features stood out starkly against the lights. Olivia watched him stalk across the stage, his body moving under his cheap suit material, the way a tiger's muscles might.

His act mainly consisted of speaking to dead loved ones of audience members. He told a man where he might find his father's old smithing hammer (in the attic next to the third beam); he told a young woman not to lose heart, change was coming soon, and received a watery thank you. When he had an older, sharp-faced woman's dead aunt knock three times on the underside of her seat, the theatre was in uproar.

'That could be you, my dove,' whispered Mrs Hayes, so close to Olivia's ear it made her start.

By the final act, Olivia was exhausted. They took a Hansom cab back to Cheapside, and she was asleep before Mrs Hayes had turned down the lamp, her head full of dreams of dark suits and harsh laughter.

Her father had come to collect her the next morning. Mrs Hayes had looked very put out not to be included in the expedition but Dr Richmond had firmly told her that her presence was not required.

'Dr Williams is most excited to meet you,' he said to Olivia as they made their way to the Royal College.

Dr Williams was the head of the programme under which he was working. A large man with a protruding stomach and a thick, bristling beard, he asked Olivia a series of questions about her appointments with her father. She was also given a tour of the college, which she pretended to be interested in, as her father walked behind her, as proprietorial as the owner of a well-trained, thoroughbred dog.

Afterwards, they took a cab to the Joyces' home in Mayfair, where they were greeted by Peter's sister, Mina. She was a tall girl with broad shoulders and more teeth than a mouth should possibly contain. She did not try to hide her audible gasp at the sight of Olivia.

'I would say radiant but it's more *reflective*,' she had breathed, gazing at Olivia's skin. 'Like the moon.'

She said she was glad Olivia had not dressed up too much for lunch. Olivia spent the rest of the meal trying to make polite conversation whilst worrying about her clothes.

However, Miss Joyce seemed more concerned with Dr Richmond's company and directed most of her comments to him, not noticing how stiff and distant his smile became when he turned to her. He deflected her attempts at coquetterie by drinking too much, and so was quite flushed by the end of lunch.

It occurred to Olivia that some sort of interrogation was being conducted of her father. At first, Miss Joyce's questions were about his research, then Mistcoate, and even the state of Olivia's condition, as though Olivia were not in the room or could not understand.

When her father spoke about Mistcoate being ideal for his research and allowing himself to be devoted to Olivia's care, Dr Joyce interrupted with a laugh.

'Come now, Georgie,' he teased. 'You make yourself sound like Francis of

Assisi when in reality you're surrounded by women.'

'Oh?' said Miss Joyce, her eyebrows rising.

'The staff,' George clarified. 'The housekeeper, the maid and the person responsible for Olivia.'

'But surely,' Miss Joyce purred, 'that is such a lot of expense and management when a wife would do just as well?'

'I would not expect my wife to do the work of a servant,' Dr Richmond snapped.

Mina Joyce's arrogant smile melted into a look of confused resentment. In a bid to not be outdone, she asked Olivia how she did for company out in the wilds.

'I speak to the dead,' said Olivia.

Miss Joyce's startled laughter filled the room.

Olivia had returned to her rooms in Cheapside to find Mrs Hayes peering out of the window.

'Did you see anyone out there?' she'd asked, nervously.

'Lots of people. Why?'

Mrs Hayes shook her head. 'This place is making me rattled.'

Olivia was not invited back to the Joyces' for dinner after that.

The next day they went to a matinee show. Once again, they saw the dark-haired medium, Olivia's eyes following his every movement. That night, they retired to an inn for their evening meal.

As Mrs Hayes ate, her gaze moved around the room. For a woman who had often said that she did not miss London, she seemed to be constantly on the lookout for something. It was almost a relief when she excused herself from the table.

Glancing over her shoulder, Olivia saw a large man in a long, battered coat standing at the bar, the great protrusion of his stomach hanging over his belt. He held out his arms to Mrs Hayes, who gripped his hands and engaged him in earnest conversation.

Olivia went back to her meal. It was a bland mush that promised fish somewhere but, so far, she'd been unable to find it. She thought longingly of Marian's baked ham with creamy leek sauce and fluffy, mashed potatoes with butter and milk. She longed for her own soft bed and the clean, sharp air of Norfolk.

She had brought her cards with her, and she slipped her hand into her bag and ran her fingers over the ridges of the printed engravings until a man appeared at her elbow.

'Anything else, miss?'

She shook her head. The man lingered for a second, as though trying to draw her eye but, when she refused to look up from her plate, he drifted off. When a hand gripped her shoulder, she recoiled, thinking he was back, but it was Mrs Hayes, her jaw set in a thin line.

'Come along.'

When they slipped out into the dark, wet night, Mrs Hayes' arm clamped around Olivia's.

'Is anything wrong?' enquired Olivia.

'I just need to get you back in good time. It's the big presentation tomorrow, isn't it?'

It was true. Her father was calling at seven o'clock. Olivia felt her stomach flip.

Mrs Hayes squeezed her arm. 'Don't be nervous,' she said. 'I've got a surprise for you tomorrow.'

'What is it?' Olivia asked.

'Just you wait,' said Mrs Hayes.

They were woken by a knock at the door. Rain battered the window pane as though it were trying to break into the room, and a cold wind snaked its way under the door. Still groggy with sleep, Olivia was only aware of a padding of feet and a sudden light across the room.

'Is she ready?' a voice asked.

'Five minutes.' Mrs Hayes told them. Then, to Olivia, 'Hurry. We are late.'

A fumbling in the dark to find clothes and washing with cold water because there was no time to call for warm. Ten minutes later, Olivia stepped out into the hallway to meet a soaked, anxious Dr Richmond who directed her to the cab with a flick of his hand. He did not speak as they made their way to the Royal College, so Olivia watched the raindrops race each other across the panes of the coach door.

'Will there be more interviews?' she asked.

'Mostly,' said her father. 'Just follow my instructions. It shouldn't be too taxing.'

They had to dash from the cab to the entryway, the rain soaking their heads and shoulders. The black sludge of the street smeared the tiled hallway as they hurried through the college. Her father seemed to barely care whether she was following or not until he paused to usher her into a cramped office.

'You can change in here,' he said, indicating a screen, behind which there was a white linen gown folded neatly on a stool.

She looked at it, puzzled. 'Do I wear this for the interviews?'

'Please, Olivia,' he said, running an impatient hand across his wet hair.

She'd changed without further comment, retaining her chemise and under-drawers. Then they were back down the corridor and into a wood-panelled anteroom to wait.

'Now, just answer the way you always do,' Papa instructed. 'I will be back for you shortly.'

He slipped out, leaving Olivia to wait, shivering a little. She tucked her cold bare feet under her, irritated that she hadn't been told to bring slippers, her stomach fluttering.

Somewhere a bell rang and there was the sound of footsteps and voices.

After the voices died down, there were the sounds of two men speaking in the adjoining room – the first one she thought was Dr Williams and the second one was her father. After a while, a porter in a stiff white high-necked coat emerged and ushered her into the adjoining room.

It was like a large amphitheatre, lit from all sides by gas lamps. If she squinted she could see that, beyond the lights, men in dark suits were sitting, watching the stage with some faint interest. Olivia felt her stomach flutter again. No one had told her there would be anyone else here.

Her father told her to sit on a stool. He asked questions, which she answered and then he spoke to the dark, bristling audience behind the lights about what she had said. There was a glass of water by her and she was encouraged to drink it. In truth, she was quite glad of it. The lights were hot and nervousness made her throat dry. The water didn't taste right in London. It was too hard. This glass, in particular, had a sharp, chemical tang.

Possibly it was the warmth of the lights or maybe the early hour that she had woken, but she found herself beginning to feel fatigued. She was horrified to find that she felt as if she were on the verge of sleep. What would her father say if she just nodded off in the middle of his presentation?

Thankfully no one seemed to have noticed, and then the porter was there, guiding her up and onto a table. Her father continued to talk, so that was a mercy.

She had not ruined anything, and was quite grateful for the bed and the opportunity to shut her eyes without anyone seeing. Then the bed was tilted and the lights hit her in the face, burning her through the lids.

Something was happening around her ankles; the hem of her gown was being gathered and lifted. She opened her mouth to protest – or she thought she did, but no sound came out.

The waistband of her drawers was pulled. Someone said something and there was a ripple of indulgent laughter. Then someone was lifting her leg by the ankle, pressing her foot against a wooden block so her legs draped open. She wanted to close them, to cover herself, but everything felt so heavy and her body would not respond.

A strange rumbling chatter filled the room, *sotto voce* conversations lighting like torches in the dark.

Her father was still speaking.

'I must therefore consider that the physical irregularity may extend to... if we are to examine the... but of course, external can only tell so much – speculum please...'

Then there was cold and pain and nothing more.

She woke on a chaise longue in a warm office, a dressing gown laid across her. Her father was sitting in front of a desk, his head in his hands.

'Experimental work is always a risk,' said Dr Williams, filling a pipe. 'Unfortunate, but give it time. The college just doesn't understand the angle of your work. It is a shame but there you have it.'

'That's all there is, then?' her father said. 'It's all over?'

'Come back with a new thesis and we'll try again,' Dr Williams advised. 'You're not without friends. Joyce has a good head on his shoulders. I'm sorry you didn't listen more to him when he advised you against this, but...'

Dr Richmond went still. 'I beg your pardon?'

Williams frowned. 'Dr Joyce advised against this experiment.'

The colour left Dr Richmond's face. 'That is not true. Peter Joyce *suggested* this line of experimentation. He has been reviewing my notes for weeks. He encouraged this.'

Dr Williams cleared his throat, fingers toying with the lid of an ink pot. 'An attempt to help a friend, I'm sure. His influence may yet be helpful. I suggest you speak to him. Apologise for not listening to his good advice. Come back with something brilliant and we shall see. A smaller audience next time, maybe. A more select group.'

Olivia felt sick to her stomach and gave a small groan. Her father turned to her, his eyes bleary.

'Is it over?' she said.

'Yes. Everything is over,' said Papa, bitterly.

He took her back to the hotel in a cab. She would need to pack, he said. They would be returning to Mistcoate at the soonest opportunity.

Her tongue felt too big for her mouth, her lips would barely form words, so she stumbled silently upstairs.

Mrs Hayes was not there when they arrived so he helped her into bed and left, locking the door behind him with a key he obtained from the landlady.

Olivia was still in the linen robe he had made her wear. It scratched her skin and smelt of chemicals. She sat up long enough to pull it off before burrowing under the damp sheets that now, after several nights of sleep, were beginning to smell like her. She must have slept because when she next opened her eyes, it was dark outside and Mrs Hayes was standing over her, holding a candle.

'I don't feel very well,' Olivia murmured, thickly. Her stomach churned and her head pained her.

'You need some fresh air, you do,' said Mrs Hayes. 'Come, I have something exciting planned.'

'We're going home,' Olivia told her.

'Not just yet, silly thing.' Mrs Hayes began gathering clothes and pulling garments from suitcases. 'Come on. The white dress, I think.'

'Please,' said Olivia. 'The chamber pot.'

Mrs Hayes got to her just in time. Olivia threw up thick yellow curds of bile, the acid stinging her nose and throat, until she sobbed.

'Too much, possibly,' said Mrs Hayes, almost to herself, when she'd finished. 'You need water and air.'

Dressing was a slow process. Her stomach ached as she moved and when she sat, the most private part of her burned. Her fingers felt so heavy and clumsy that Mrs Hayes did most of it, brushing her hair so that it hung down her back, gathering the sides into plaits as though Olivia were a mediaeval maiden.

'There,' said Mrs Hayes. 'Now you look the part. Come along.'

There was a cab waiting outside. The air smelled of cabbages, smoke, and horse dung. It made Olivia feel nauseous again and she was glad of the cool night air that ruffled her hair and eased the sweat on her brow. She dozed during the ride and when she woke the streets were different. The buildings, though tall, looked derelict and bleak.

'Where are we?' Olivia asked, rubbing her eyes.

'Whitechapel,' said Mrs Hayes with odd cheer. 'We'll be at Mile End soon.'

The names meant nothing to Olivia, but she was too tired to ask questions. Eventually they stopped at a large house, sandwiched between two others in a low row. As Mrs Hayes paid the driver, a short, stout woman appeared in the doorway, dressed in a high-necked black dress.

'You're late,' she grumbled.

'Does them good to wait,' said Mrs Hayes, guiding Olivia to the door. 'Builds anticipation.'

'Is this her?' The woman eyed Olivia with interest.

'No, it's my lady's maid,' Mrs Hayes' humour felt brittle. 'Of course it is. Miss Olivia, this is Mrs Adworth.'

'Well she looks the part, I'll give you that,' Mrs Adworth said. 'How'd you get her so white?'

She had reached out to tug at Olivia's pale hair, and Olivia flinched back. Mrs Hayes just chuckled.

They walked into a narrow hallway that smelled faintly of spices, and picked their way towards a doorway through which she could hear the rumble of voices.

In a way, it was horribly similar to the college earlier that day, and Olivia's stomach flipped.

'Now, just you wait here,' said Mrs Adworth, before disappearing into the room.

'What is this?' asked Olivia. The pain in her head was growing, and she pressed her fingers against her brow.

Mrs Hayes ignored the question. 'Here, you'll need these.' She held out Olivia's tarot cards.

Olivia just stared at them, uncomprehending.

'You know what to do, my lamb,' continued Mrs Hayes, pressing the cards into her hands. 'You're not like the crooks who pretend to fool the gullible. You've got a gift. You've got to share it. Imagine what we could do? You showing people the way and me helping.'

Olivia looked from Mrs Hayes to the door as the haze began to lift.

'What's behind there?' She pointed at it, her voice growing stronger.

Mrs Hayes smiled. 'People. Now, all you have to do is what you do at home. Like what you did at the party.'

Before Olivia could argue, Mrs Adworth had opened the door and intoned in a much deeper, more dramatic voice than she'd used earlier: 'Mistress Livia. Enter.'

Mrs Hayes gave Olivia a push and, against her will, she stumbled into the crowded room.

There was a faint gasp as she stepped into a dimly-lit living room, complete with antimacassars on the back of the armchairs and porcelain figurines on every surface. It was full of people, positioned around a circular table in the middle of the room where a series of candles burned. She had to make her way towards this slowly, her free hand outstretched, as voices whispered around her.

'Is it a spirit?'

Someone giggled nervously. A hand reached out and touched Olivia's hip. She slapped it away.

'Not a ghost then,' said a young man in the gloom. There was another bubble of laughter.

The chair, when she found it, was a cold, wooden affair that had been dragged in from the kitchen. She sat down, careful not to touch either of the bodies that pressed in on both sides, aware that she probably still smelled of vomit and chemicals. Again there was that pain beneath her and she had to concentrate to not think about it.

She stroked her cards with her thumb to distract herself and set them on the table.

The room was hushed and watchful as she cut and shuffled the cards, trying to concentrate, but her head ached fiercely and it was difficult to focus.

'Shouldn't we ask a question?' said a female voice and was hushed.

She set the cards out in a simple three card spread. That would start her off at least. She ran her fingers over the engravings.

The Struck Tower. The Nine of Swords. Death.

There was a shiver around the table. Somewhere, Mrs Hayes sucked in her breath through her teeth.

Olivia intoned in her usual low monotone the reading of impending disaster and betrayal, but before she'd finished, the woman next to her spoke eagerly over her, 'I was hoping to ask about a young man.'

Olivia drew the cards to her, reshuffled and laid them out again. The Six of Wands upside down, the Devil, Ten of Cups upside down. Arrogance. Failure. Disharmony.

'Well, that does sound like my Gregory,' said a laughing female voice.

There was some laughter.

'This is all rather *bleak*,' observed another.

Across the room, a dark-haired man sitting in the corner lit a cigar and said nothing. Olivia felt his eyes boring into her. Something about him seemed familiar. She did not like the feel of his gaze.

'They say, Mistress Livia, that you can speak with the dead,' said a rosy-cheeked, bowler-hatted gentleman opposite.

Olivia nodded, numbly.

'I was wondering… my wife…'

Olivia closed her eyes, laying her hands flat on the table and waited. Nothing.

'I'm sorry,' she said. 'She is not coming through.'

'What about my sister?' someone called, hopefully.

Again, nothing.

People were starting to shift in their seats.

'Not even any knocking,' someone muttered.

'You can't just call spirits up like the maid,' snapped Mrs Hayes from the corner. 'They come to her.'

'Apparently not,' said a young man, to a round of giggles.

He was the one who had reached out to touch her as she went past.

'And just what do you know about it?' demanded Mrs Hayes.

'I know I should have spent my evening at Wilton's.'

'Is it any wonder Mistress Livia can't get anything through? This man's disbelief is blocking it,' Mrs Hayes said, raising her voice so the room could hear.

'Get away with you,' he scoffed. 'Haven't I paid my money to see something, like everyone else? Not my fault if nothing's forthcoming. I should have my money back.'

'No refunds,' announced Mrs Adworth, instantly.

The crowd grew restless. 'This is a sham,' someone said. 'I should call the police.'

'You'll do no such thing.' Mrs Adworth's voice rose. 'This is a respectable house.'

'Leave it, Alf.' A young woman, her hair adorned with roses, her corsets impossibly tight, stood and began gathering her things. 'Let's go.'

'Mistress Livia has not finished,' called Mrs Hayes, an edge of panic in her voice.

'Hasn't she? My apologies. Please continue, Mistress Livia, I am prepared to be amazed.' The young man resumed his seat and sat forward, chin resting on his fist in a show of avid attention.

Olivia stared at him, wanting to pluck something from him that would make him blanch but her head pounded and felt so thin, like an old, worn stocking, that she couldn't pick anything.

'Mistress Livia?' Mrs Hayes' voice came through gritted teeth.

'Mistress Livia indeed,' hissed a voice.

Across the room, the intense dark-haired man reached for his coat, an air of palpable disappointment about him.

There was a scrape of chairs. Olivia looked wildly about. Mrs Hayes' shape in the corner was rigid and furious.

'Hello?' It was all she could think of but it was enough to make everyone pause.

'So now she speaks,' said the young man and was hushed.

Olivia paused, letting the sudden silence deepen. 'He is faint,' she said. 'He is far away.' She paused. 'I am seeing… sand. He says there is sand.'

'Tommy?' A woman approached, her face pinched and eager. 'My boy was in the Boer back in '80. Sand, he said in his letters.'

'This is a young man. Very young. He's looking for his mother. He says…'

'What? What does he say?' demanded Mrs Hayes.

'He says that he's lost.'

The woman gave a small cry. 'They never found 'im. His mates, they looked but they never…'

Her voice trailed off into silence.

'I'm sorry,' said Olivia.

There was a pounding at the door.

'Police!' shouted a voice outside. 'Open up!'

Mrs Adworth turned to Mrs Hayes, her expression furious and furtive.

'Have you not paid them?' demanded Mrs Hayes.

'They tried to put the prices up.' Mrs Adworth shrugged. 'I wasn't having that.'

Mrs Hayes was across the room in two strides, her fingers closed around Olivia's wrist like a vice.

Everyone was moving at once. Chairs were shoved back, bodies rose. There was a jam in the hallway and Mrs Adworth had to climb the stairs to direct everyone.

'Please, ladies and gentlemen, there is a back door,' she said. 'I suggest you go that way.'

'What could they arrest us for?' Olivia asked, as the housekeeper dragged her bodily across the room.

'Whatever they like,' said Mrs Hayes. 'They're making a point.'

The dark-haired man walked past them, close enough now for Olivia to recognise him as the medium she had watched perform a few nights earlier. Their eyes met, and he gave her a nod, then she and Mrs Hayes slipped into the flow of bodies, letting it carry them to a dim kitchen where a rotting wooden door spat them out into a filthy back alley.

As the crowd disappeared into the night, Mrs Hayes gripped Olivia's arm and pushed her against the wall, made slimy with lichen and grime.

'What happened?' she demanded. Her face was tight with fury and her eyes gleamed manically in the moonlight.

Olivia didn't know what to say, but Mrs Hayes didn't wait for her response.

'Do you know what an opportunity that was?' she hissed. 'That was Charlie Frampton and Molly Adworth – from the Orpheus and the Alhambra. They discovered your precious Epidemius St. Joseph. Do you have any idea what it took to get them here tonight?'

'I didn't know,' wailed Olivia, but Mrs Hayes was already pulling her down the narrow, brick-walled street, slipping in mud and other effluence, her breath coming out in ragged gasps. Olivia stumbled along after her, pain and nausea vying with the sickening feeling of disappointment.

'I'm sorry I couldn't do more,' she tried. 'I just feel so sick.'

'We could have been *on stage*.' Mrs Hayes shook her head, barely acknowledging

Olivia's apology. 'You could have been a performer rather than just a spectacle.'

Olivia felt like she might vomit again.

'I – I am not well,' she said.

'No,' spat Mrs Hayes. 'You never were. I tried to help you. But it's over now.'

With brute force, she dragged Olivia down one side-street and they stumbled past a group of boys, who cackled and shouted, 'They're 'ere! They're 'ere!' to the distant policemen.

Somewhere, a constable's whistle blew and there was the sound of running feet.

'A cab, we need a cab,' said Mrs Hayes, her voice a panicked whisper.

'Oi! Stop there!'

Another whistle, closer now. More running footsteps.

In a panic, Olivia turned to see a cab waiting on a side street, the horse stamping its feet in the cold.

'Go,' said Mrs Hayes. 'I'll catch up.'

She shoved Olivia at the hansom cab. There was no time to argue. With icy fingers, she wrenched the door open and pulled herself in, just in time to turn and see a shadowy figure in a tall helmet knock Mrs Hayes to the ground and draw his foot back, as she lay prone in the mud.

The whip cracked, and the horse pulled the cab into the crowded streets.

THIRTY-TWO

The Hanged Man

The next few days passed quietly. Olivia was a subdued and frightened version of herself. She slept in my bed, lying so still beside me it scared me. For his part, Dr Richmond barely left his office.

The constable called to enquire about our 'excitement', as he put it. He had the grace to look sheepish, his helmet tucked under his arm, his moustache bristling.

'We'll keep a close watch,' he assured me. 'Things will be easier now that Dr Richmond has returned.'

I thought this a foolish assumption.

We had no word from Mrs Hayes and it seemed clear that Dr Richmond had made no enquiry about her. It was highly likely, Marian and I agreed, that the housekeeper was gone for good.

'Will he appoint someone new?' Marian asked one afternoon, as we made soup together.

'I don't know what he's doing.' I chopped vegetables at the counter. 'I should like to give him a piece of my mind.'

'Not too big a piece, miss,' Marian advised, eyes flicking to the doorway. 'If you leave, then I'm in a real bind.'

'I am going nowhere, Marian,' I promised stoutly, and drove my knife into the head of a carrot.

On the third day, I convinced Olivia to return to sleep in her own bed. Marian and I spent an industrious morning changing linens, moving the silk screen and trying to make the room as comforting and free of shadows as possible. We discovered the portrait of Miss Florence under the bed and, in an act of sheer defiance, I hung it back up on the first-floor landing.

I felt such recklessness, such light-headed contempt for Dr Richmond, it emboldened me. Olivia's father did not call her for further appointments. It was clear to me that she had never needed the appointments in the first place, and that his theory of hysteria was a mere phantasm, an act that had failed to impress the Royal College. This realisation filled me with a fury I could not express.

Olivia made no mention of her cards or Mrs Hayes, and when a new copy of *The Inner Eye* arrived, she left it untouched on the kitchen table until I used it to light the fire.

For our part, Marian and I tried to continue in our normal way but what had been a happy, productive routine was now tainted with fear and uncertainty. Even Captain Richmond seemed to feel it and, to our dismay, he rapidly regressed back to his old, bewildered state. This fresh loss was also something I blamed on Dr Richmond, although I could not say why.

By the third of January, I felt it was safe to walk to Fellwick. Ever since the attack on the house, we had stayed close to the grounds, but our supplies were increasingly meagre, and there'd been no word from Ed Byres about Alice's health.

'Are you sure it's wise, miss?' said Marian, chewing the kitchen pencil as she stood over an empty list. 'It's late in the day.'

'A walk will do me good and anyway, I refuse to hide.' My tone was defiant, although my nerves twitched at the idea of being alone in the forest.

I left Marian compiling a list and went to find Olivia.

She was sitting outside her grandfather's bedroom door, knees pulled up to her chest, head against the door frame. When I called her name, she shushed me.

'What are you doing?' I whispered, but stopped when I heard Dr Richmond's voice from inside. He was speaking to his father, and his tone was dark.

'These are opportunities that require me to take a more permanent residence in London,' he said.

'Well, I'm sure we will be fine without you,' said Captain Richmond. 'Miss Pearlie manages about the house well.'

He sounded as though he had just woken from a sleep. His voice was soft and muffled.

'It is the house that I wanted to speak to you about,' said Dr Richmond. 'I imagine, in time, it would pass down to me.'

'Naturally,' his father agreed.

'But if I am to be married, I must be ready to create a home for myself and Mina.'

'Mina?' Captain Richmond sounded puzzled.

'My fiancée.' Dr Richmond's voice sounded resigned. 'Mina Joyce.'

I turned to Olivia, startled by this new revelation. But Olivia glared at the door, her eyes glistening. It was impossible to read her expression.

'Oh yes? Good Lord. Well what about her?'

There was a pause.

'Father, we must sell Mistcoate.'

In the hall, Olivia made a small noise and clamped her hands to her mouth. I placed my hand on her shoulder.

'Must we?' said Captain Richmond. I could hear the shock in his voice.

'Father, we cannot keep it,' his son told him, briskly. 'The bills are sizable. I am afraid we could not support both Mistcoate and a London residence. We can barely support Mistcoate alone.'

'Where would we go?' asked Captain Richmond.

'Miss Joyce's father has been kind enough to begin a search for a new home.'

'Very presumptuous,' commented Captain Richmond. 'I have not even given my thoughts yet.'

'I simply must have the capital if I am to be married.' Despite his measured voice, Dr Richmond's words had a ring of desperation. 'Surely, you can see that?'

'What of your practice?' enquired Captain Richmond.

'It is not enough. The house must be sold.'

'I see. Well, there is still time,' murmured Captain Richmond, but his son cut him off.

'I need some assurances.'

There was a pause.

'About what?' Captain Richmond asked.

There was a thump, as if someone slammed their palm onto a table. Olivia flinched.

The following silence seemed to stretch on forever.

Then Captain Richmond said, 'I'm sorry, my boy. Must've drifted off there. You were saying?'

There was another long pause. When Dr Richmond spoke next, it was in a strange, almost tearful voice.

'I was just saying that you're right. The house is too much for us. We should sell it.'

Olivia moved, as if she wanted to race into the room, but I held her back. It would do no good, I knew that for certain. She opened her mouth to speak but I shook my head.

No, wait.

'Sell Mistcoate?' Captain Richmond sounded confused.

'It is a sensible decision, Father. We are right to make it.'

'I said this…?' There was another pause. 'Oh. Well then. That's good.'

'I will visit the solicitor when I am next in London. Dr Joyce knows a very reputable fellow. He will arrange for the sale of Mistcoate and we will see to it that you and Olivia are made comfortable in the best possible places.'

'Excellent. Solicitor, yes? Make sure it's someone reputable,' said Captain Richmond, trying to keep up.

'Absolutely, sir. I will keep you apprised every step of the way. But you look tired and I have much to do. I will let you rest.'

'Just as you say. Send up Florence if you can find her. Girl's never at home these days,' murmured Captain Richmond.

Olivia and I concealed ourselves in the shadows of an alcove as Dr Richmond stepped out of his father's room, easing the door closed behind him. He set off up the hall, his face set and his shoulders low.

Olivia spun to glare at me. 'How can he do this? I'm going to go and speak to Grandfather.'

'Don't.' I reached out.

She stopped at the touch of my hand, whirling like a cat before it bites.

'He tricked him, Julia. He lied.'

'And he will do so again,' I said, simply. 'You going in there will only confuse matters and make things more difficult. Believe me, if the decision has been made, there is little you will do to change it. Fighting will not help. I have tried.'

She stopped, her head on one side. 'You knew this was going to happen?'

'No.' I glanced away. 'When my father died there were… debts. My mother sold off everything to pay for them, including my belongings and the family home.'

Olivia's face was set in a mixture of horror and sympathy.

'Is that why you're in service?'

I nodded.

'She used the remainder of the money to send my brother to a prestigious school where he could meet the right people, get the right job, look after her,' I explained. 'There was nothing left after that.'

'I would never have let that happen,' Olivia said, passionately.

'What would you have done?' I said. 'Clung to the bedposts? Shouted in the street? Appeal to relatives? It stops nothing. Believe me. Nothing changes the fact that there is no money.'

Olivia looked bleak. 'I hate him.'

'I know.'

'What will I do?'

'We will make a plan,' I told her. 'I won't let you end up as I did.'

'He doesn't even want to marry her.' Olivia kicked at the rug, tears of frustration in her eyes. 'All this and he doesn't even want her.'

There was no point in arguing. She was right. Hadn't Dr Joyce said as much during that awful conversation weeks ago?

'I am going for a walk to Fellwick if you'd like to come?' I suggested. 'We can discuss the next steps.'

Olivia stared at the rug, tears dropping to the floor.

'I have to think,' she said, after a moment. 'You go.'

With one last look at Captain Richmond's room, she turned back up the passage, her shoulders set. I watched her go, a snake of anxiety slithering in my gut.

I was at the foot of the stairs when Dr Richmond strode into the hall, stopping short at the sight of me. It was the first time we had been in direct contact since he'd returned home. He looked undone; collar open, sleeves rolled up. His face had a blankness to it that made me want to slap some life into it.

You have destroyed that girl, I inwardly seethed. *You have upended her life. How will you answer for it?*

'Ah,' he said. 'Miss Pearlie. I require you in my office.'

I gripped the bannister so tightly the wood left red imprints on my fingers, and then followed him into the study.

A full ashtray on the desk indicated that Dr Richmond had taken on Dr Joyce's habit of cigars, and the pungent, spicy scent seemed to have seeped into the furnishings. The sideboard and drinks cabinet were dark, their compartments shut and fastened.

I did not expect an invitation to sit; would not have accepted one. The sight of him, moving around the room, collecting papers and sifting them into piles, acting as though everything was normal, enraged me.

'I have received your letter withdrawing your resignation,' he said. 'It is my intention to be in London more so your continued presence suits me for now. You may act as housekeeper in Mrs Hayes' absence. You will care for Olivia and Father in addition to your new duties, and you will help to pack away the house. I am to be married. We shall be leaving Mistcoate in February.'

'Congratulations, sir,' I said, coldly and Dr Richmond raised an eyebrow. 'I take it you are to settle in London? I am sure Olivia is excited at the prospect of a new home.'

At the mention of his daughter's name, Dr Richmond's jaw set and he looked away.

'Quite.' His tone was clipped and emotionless.

This is how they do it, I thought. *They call you to them and destroy everything with a word. It is hateful.*

'If you are to be moving to London, sir, are you sure you would not like me to continue some work with Olivia?' I said, not trying to hide how pointed my tone had become. 'Even if she is not to attend the season.'

'That will be unnecessary.' Dr Richmond's tone was curt.

'There are finishing schools...' I began.

He cut me off. 'Which cost money. Money that I can no longer afford to spend on Olivia. I have spoken to Dr Joyce. He has recommended some very reputable places which would create the right home for Olivia. Where she would receive the appropriate care.'

I took a step back.

'*Sanatoriums?*' I was horrified. 'Sir, such places are hardly right for Miss Olivia.'

'Have you suddenly acquired a medical degree, Miss Pearlie?' He gave me a fierce look. 'Or is it sheer arrogance that makes you believe your opinion is so worth sharing?'

I clamped my lips together, pressing them into a fine, white line.

'Let me make myself clear,' he continued. 'I am not paying you for your opinion or your superior manner, which you have used to great effect to mask a series of personal failings. I am paying you to follow instructions. Do you understand?'

I swallowed hard.

No sir.

'Yes sir.'

'As it stands, I cannot see how I can, in good conscience, write you a positive reference. I suppose I shall have to see how you conduct yourself in the coming time.' His tone was vindictive.

I met his gaze, holding it, despite how fearful I suddenly felt. I could not allow this. The man had lost all sense.

'I require you to tell Olivia none of this,' he continued, looking away first. 'Knowing her temperament, it would only distress her.'

'Sir, I cannot do that.'

His head snapped up.

'Excuse me?'

'It is highly likely that Olivia already knows,' I told him. 'She is an intelligent girl.'

But he was not listening. He had grown very still and his tongue worried at the corners of his mouth in a gesture I had never seen before.

'I see you are determined to undermine my role.' He looked furious.

'No, sir,' I said. 'It is just Olivia that I am thinking of.'

'It is not Olivia you should be worrying about, Miss Pearlie. Olivia does not pay your wages and, frankly, neither shall I.' A vein bulged in his throat. 'I like to think that I am an open-minded man but as head of this household I cannot allow this to continue. From this moment on you are dismissed from your role.'

I stared at him. It did not hurt the way I had thought it would.

'My reference?' I was surprised to find my voice calm and steady.

'Reference? You are lucky I do not write to every national paper denouncing you. As it is, I shall be writing to Mrs Spencer of your poor conduct and strongly suggesting she has nothing further to do with you.'

It was more than I could bear. Had I not defended his home? Fought Mrs Hayes and been brutalised, shamed and blackmailed for it? I had kept silent, kept the peace, kept secrets and was now to be dismissed with nothing. Again. No, I would not allow it to happen. I would not abandon Olivia to the madhouse. Not without a fight.

'On what grounds?' I said. 'You engaged me to educate Miss Olivia, to improve her manners and to be her champion. I have done all of those things.'

'You have been inconsistent at best,' he said, stiffly.

'And what of Mrs Hayes?' I asked, my voice rising. 'What about her treatment of Olivia?'

'Mrs Hayes' great failings do not excuse your own!' Dr Richmond was shouting now. 'And I will not be spoken to this way in my own house. You will receive no reference, you will receive no wages; it is enough that I have wasted money on dresses and nonsense that has all come to nothing. You will quit my sight and this household at the soonest opportunity, do you understand? I do not wish to hear from you again.'

The room seemed to shift under my feet. I could not feel my soles on the floor.

'And what about Olivia? Who will pack up the house?' My own voice sounded as though it were coming from far away. But Dr Richmond turned away.

'Good day, Miss Pearlie.'

He took a seat and turned his attention to the paperwork piled on his desk.

I felt myself turn and exit the room, not hearing or feeling my own movements, as if punch-drunk. Marian had left shopping bags hanging in the hallway. As I lifted them down, dazed and silent, I heard a rustle above me.

Olivia looked down at me through the bannisters, tears streaming down her cheeks.

'I will not abandon you,' I told her.

She made a sound of despair and disappeared into the shadows.

I stood for a moment, staring into space, then I climbed the stairs to my room, pulled out the medical notes from Mrs Hayes' desk and scribbled a quick note on a piece of paper.

This was in Mrs Hayes' room. She may have others. I wanted you to know. I am not her.

'Marian?' I said, when back down in the hall.

She appeared in the mouth of the kitchen corridor, holding a piece of paper. 'I have the list here, miss.'

She stopped short at the sight of me.

'Miss?'

It was then that I realised I was weeping. I sniffed, wiping my nose with the heel of my hand and held out the notes and my message.

'Would you please give this to Dr Richmond after I have gone?'

Marian gave me a confused look as we exchanged pieces of paper. 'Of course, miss. Was that him I heard shouting just now?'

I nodded, not trusting myself to speak. Already I could feel myself losing control, my throat burning with suppressed sobs.

I could not tell her. Not if there was still a chance of fixing it. It was bad enough that Olivia was in distress without also worrying Marian. When I spoke, my voice was unnaturally tight and high.

'Do not wait once you have given him it,' I said. 'Leave the room at once.'

I strode blindly down the hallway, grabbing my coat and hat, and fled into the cold afternoon.

THIRTY-THREE

Five of Pentacles

I was some distance from the house when my anger turned to fear. What had I done? Just as I had earned a place back at Mistcoate, I had thrown it away again. Now who would care for Olivia? Would packing up the entire house be left for Marian to do alone? I had been foolish. Foolish and rash.

It was afternoon, and darkness was already creeping through the trees.

Stifling a sob, I hurried my steps and did not pause until I stood outside Alice and Ed Byres' front door, knuckles stinging from knocking.

The sound of feet from within. The sound of Reverend Byres talking. 'You will, Alice. If I have then I don't see why you should not.'

The door creaked as it opened, emitting a wave of heat. Byres' smile froze at the sight of me, puffy-eyed and red-faced.

'Please. I need help.'

Without a word, Byres ushered me into the parlour, where Alice sat, bundled up in blankets. I stopped short at the sight of her. She was almost as pale as Olivia and had lost weight. The sight of me, dishevelled and tearful, made her sit up, a spool of thread dropping from her lap and rolling across the floor.

'Julia?' Her voice was weak.

'I thought you were in hospital.' I ran to her and took her warm hands in my ice-cold ones.

'Filthy place.' Alice shuddered. 'Hated it. Came home. What's wrong?'

She gasped between each word. My heart sank to hear it. She was worse.

My eyes welled.

'I have missed you, Alice. It's been so horrid…'

To my dismay, I began to weep.

'You're frozen. Sit down. Have tea. Ed?' Alice gestured to her brother, who was hovering in the doorway.

I sank down into a chair, allowing a warm cup to be pressed into my hands, and I told them what had happened.

Only when I'd finished did either of them speak.

'What now?' asked Alice, her thin face filled with sympathy.

I shook my head.

'I am so stupid,' I said, softly. 'I should not have argued with him.'

'You could not have stopped him from putting her into a hospital,' Byres' tone was rough. 'But he mustn't do it. I can certainly try to speak to him.'

'It's not him,' I said, wearily. 'It's those awful Joyce people. They will have put him up to it. Mina Joyce wants the money from Mistcoate, and Peter Joyce wants someone to bully. They hardly need someone like Olivia hanging about.'

Alice watched me steadily. 'But this does not answer what you will do.'

'Have you a workhouse here?' I asked, trying to smile.

She shivered. 'Never,' she said. 'Not for you.'

She gave Byres a brief, conspiratorial look, which he seemed to ignore.

'What is it?' I said. 'That look – what is happening?'

'There's news,' said Alice, suppressing a cough. 'Tell her.'

'It can wait,' Byres said.

'Please,' I said. 'What is it?'

'More tea.' Alice gestured at her brother. 'It is long.'

Byres complied, pouring fresh tea into her cup and talking as he did so.

'Well, after that night at Mistcoate, I contacted Sergeant Combs and our own Constable Denby. Of course, they could hardly miss this,' he waved a hand at his face, which was still bruised and healing. 'So they had to admit that the body they found could not be The Shambler.'

'But why did they ever think he was?' I frowned.

Byres grimaced. 'It seems that Sergeant Combs had some information he had not previously shared with us. This Shambler was not just active here, but in other areas from London to Ely and beyond. And for quite some time. He has only just reached us this past few months but he has been a regular sight in other towns. I also have a name.'

'Oh?'

'Archie Stern. An ex-military man and would-be sailor. Apparently he took shelter from one of the vicars in Peterborough last year and gave his whole story. The description and timeline fit so it seems he would be our man.'

'Stern?' I said, furrowing my brow. 'Where have I heard that name before?'

Byres gave me a curious look. 'I am told he was a soldier serving out in India who worked his way home the long way after being dismissed from the service, arriving in London with an opium habit and not very much money. His plan was to try and trace his wife.'

'Winnie?' I guessed.

Alice nodded, her face flushed with the heat of the fire. 'Exactly.'

'But when he reached her home, she was gone,' Byres continued. 'So he went searching for her.'

'Making a nuisance of himself wherever he goes,' Alice said.

'But why Mistcoate?' I asked.

'I would imagine that years of opium and alcohol have left him somewhat addled,' Byres said. 'The poor man is to be pitied really. Even if he did smash a pot over my head.'

'What of Winnie though? Is there no way to find or trace her?'

'We have no means of knowing where she is,' he said. 'Or if she would want such a man back as her husband.'

'Possibly this is why she disappeared in the first place,' Alice commented, sipping her tea.

We fell into silence, each lost in our own contemplation. In the quiet, we could hear the soft thud on the window, as a clump of snow fell from the roof.

It was growing dark, and Ed rose to light the lamps.

I looked at Alice. 'Do you think Sally Daly would give me a room at the Hive and Honey if I offered some work in payment?'

She made a tutting sound. 'Nonsense. You must stay here.'

Heat rose to my cheeks. 'I cannot impose on you.'

'I can go to the Hive and Honey if you prefer,' said Ed. 'But you could be of great use here.'

'Really,' Alice agreed, 'you'd be doing us a service if you came to stay.'

'I cannot pay anything.'

Alice dismissed this with a wave of her hand. 'We don't need money.'

My eyes brimmed with tears, both thankful and humiliated. 'I am so grateful.' And then I asked the one remaining question: 'What should I do about Olivia?'

Byres sighed. 'I think you may have done all you can for her right now.'

'You must help her,' Alice murmured, leaning back. She looked drawn, as though the conversation had exhausted her.

Ed draped another blanket across her lap, and she closed her eyes, leaning her head back.

He turned to me. 'Come,' he said, motioning for me to follow him into a hallway. He closed the door, leaving her to rest.

'She is worse,' I said, softly.

'The doctor is fairly certain now that she may never fully recover. The cold has not helped. The best we can do is slow the pace of it but…' He waved his hands, suggesting his own feeling of helplessness. His voice quivered as he said, 'I do not know what I shall do without her.'

'No.' I gripped his hands, clasping them in mine. 'We must not think of it. She is still here and winter will be over soon. She will be better in the spring. I will help.'

Wordlessly, he pressed my fingers. I wanted to lean forward and rest my head on his chest, to stay here in the warmth with him and Alice and forget Mistcoate ever existed. But I could not. Not yet.

'I promised to procure some things for Marian, and I should say goodbye,' I told him.

He reached for his coat. 'I will accompany you.'

'What do we do now that we know he is not dead?' I asked later, as we walked through the darkening woods.

'Continue the search, I suppose.' Byres adjusted his grip on the basket of supplies. 'I will be telling everyone to stay out of the woods, in case he is still about.'

As we rounded the corner out of the trees, Mistcoate blazed like a beacon, lights shining from windows where the curtains had not been drawn. That didn't seem right. Why hadn't Marian closed the curtains?

As we walked up the drive, heads down against the snow, I realised, with a jolt of fear, that the front door hung open.

'Ed,' I whispered, gripping his arm.

He saw what had shocked me and his jaw tightened.

We increased our speed, rushing across the icy garden to the house.

'Hello?' My voice echoed as we clattered into the hall. 'Marian? Olivia?'

No answer came.

'I will find Dr Richmond – you search the house,' I told Ed.

I raced down the corridor, my damp skirts tangling in my legs. There was a light under the office door.

'Dr Richmond? Doctor?'

It swung inward. Dr Richmond was splayed on his desk, one arm thrown out, the other cradling his head. A dark puddle had formed on the floor beneath him. I hurried over, shaking him on the shoulder.

'Dr Richmond?'

He gave a deep snore. His breath came in deep, whiskey-scented grunts, and I saw an overturned bottle next to his foot.

He was drunk.

Beneath his shoulder lay several journals, all like those I had found in Mrs Hayes' rooms. He had been going through them and either tearing pages out to feed them to the fire or scoring out lines in pen.

'Julia?' Ed called my name from down the hall.

I hurried to the kitchen to find it in chaos. Drawers had been emptied and the contents flung, there was flour all over the counter, and someone had knocked over the small collection of spices Marian had been accruing, sending multi-coloured patterns across the table.

Byres stood by the locked larder, the sound of sobbing coming from behind the door.

'It's Marian. Someone locked her in. She didn't call out at first because she didn't know who we were.'

'Miss Pearlie,' she called. 'Is that you?'

I gripped the handle of the cupboard. 'Marian, what is going on? Where is the key?'

'I think she took it with her,' called Marian tearfully from behind the door. 'You must find her.'

'Who?' I said, already dreading the answer.

'Miss Olivia. She locked me in here. She's gone.'

THIRTY-FOUR

The Struck Tower

Ed used the poker from the fireplace to force the lock, and Marian fell out of the larder, sobbing before I'd even caught her.

'What happened?' I asked, sitting her down at the table and hurrying to fetch her a cup of water.

'I c-c-came in to the larder to fetch dinner things. She must have crept up and locked me in. I'd left the keys on the kitchen table. I wouldn't normally, but Dr Richmond was so upset I forgot.'

Byres and I shared a look.

'Why was he upset?' I asked.

'I don't know, but he tore apart Mrs Hayes' room,' Marian said, tearfully. 'I did as you asked and gave him the notes you left. Next thing I know, he comes in demanding the keys and I tried to calm him, but the things he said, miss... he said Mrs Hayes had turned him into a monster. That she had made him do things – the experiments on Miss Olivia. He was crying. Miss, I barely recognised him.'

'Please don't upset yourself.' I patted her shoulder, feeling dizzy and deeply frightened. 'Did Olivia say anything to suggest where she was going?'

'No, but I heard her searching for something.' Marian gave a hiccup. 'She looked in Mrs Hayes' rooms but they were already in a state because of Dr Richmond.'

'Where is he now?' asked Byres.

'He's drunk.' I lowered my voice. 'No threat to us, but no help either. We must act quickly. Where is Captain Richmond?'

'I gave him a draft to help him sleep after Dr Richmond's rampage.' Marian blinked back her tears. 'It's for emergencies but if this isn't one, I don't know what is.'

'Sensible,' I said. 'Now, we need to find out where Olivia's gone. Marian, would you please search the usual places upstairs? If you haven't found anything in five minutes, meet us back here and we will decide what to do.'

Without a word, Marian hurried off. Ed and I stood amid the chaos.

He gave me a direct look. 'Where do you think she is?'

'I'm not certain, but she may have gone to the old cabin in the woods, near the river.' I was breathless with worry. 'We must find her. We will need blankets, brandy, a lantern, and anything else you think may be useful in a rescue.'

'If you think this is a rescue, I would much rather that I went out and you stayed here,' he said.

'You won't know where to look.' Something occurred to me, and I touched his arm. 'There's one place I must check first. Please wait here for Marian, I'll be back.'

With that, I rushed down the corridor to Mrs Hayes' rooms. Olivia could have left some sign of where she was going, I thought.

When I opened the door, my breath caught. Dr Richmond had moved through the housekeeper's sitting room like a whirlwind, tearing open drawers and scattering possessions. The desk had been torn into, with compartments forced open and paperwork thrown to the floor, boot prints livid against the white.

Something crumpled under my foot and I looked down to pick whatever it was off my shoe. It was the small lithograph of Mrs Hayes and, I could only assume, Mr Hayes. I should throw it away, I thought. I doubted she would be back for it. Still, I tucked it in my pocket as I continued searching about me for anything that could be useful.

In the bedroom, he'd ripped pillows open and torn the corner of the mattress off the bed so that it caught me in the shin as I went past, almost toppling me. I threw out my hands to steady myself and found myself leaning against the tattered remains of one of Mrs Hayes' posters. Even these had not escaped Dr Richmond's wrath. Singers and performers smiled at me from ripped faces; missing eyes, hair, bodies. Only the names remained intact. Iphegenia Miller, George Lassiter, Edwina Stern.

'Miss! There is something you must see.'

Marian appeared in the doorway, a note clutched in her hand. It was written on letter stationery in Olivia's large, shaky hand, neatly folded in half.

'It was in your room,' she explained, as I unfolded and read the brief message.

Goodbye. This is for the best. Don't try to stop me. Please.
Olivia

My stomach churned. How long ago had she left? It was already so cold and dark. 'I must go,' I said. 'I may already be too late.'

I ran back to the kitchen where Ed stood waiting, supplies hastily stuffed into a cloth bag. Marian fetched two thick cudgels from the coatroom, made of hard, polished wood that shone in the lamplight.

'Mrs Hayes kept these for protection,' Marian explained, seeing my puzzled expression. 'A quick swing to the temple sorts most things, miss.' She handed one to me and the second to Ed. 'If anything goes wrong, both of you sing out.'

She pulled a small bottle from a cabinet and shoved it into my other hand.

'Brandy. To warm you. And there are two lanterns near the door with oil.'

'The snow is coming down heavily now,' said Byres, helping me into a heavy tweed coat. 'Stay close by me. Marian, do you feel able to go to the constable?'

She was already pulling on a coat and scarf.

'I'll get help,' she promised.

Ed and I struck out into the night, the brandy bottle heavy in my pocket. The wind had picked up and it howled as it blew thick, white snowflakes across the trees. The cold bit into the flesh, chilling the bone. No matter how tightly I pulled my coat around me, I could not keep it out. We trudged towards the woods; Byres close behind me, a lantern clutched in one hand. It would be easy to lose each another, the sleet and snow made it so difficult to see and nothing could be heard but the wind and the crunching of snow.

I kept looking towards the trees, glancing left and right for signs of a dark, loping figure and searching for a slight, pale one.

Slowly the lights from the house faded as I plodded into the shadows of the forest. Time slowed. Sheltered by the trees, the wind was not so harsh, but woods are never quiet. I heard the rustle of bracken and the harsh *crack* of snapping branches from somewhere to my left and I raised my lantern.

'What was that?' I whispered.

Ed raised his lantern, peering into the shadows, his expression tense. 'I don't know. Stay here, I will check.'

Holding his cudgel in his other hand he moved carefully through the trees. His light grew smaller and smaller, until I could not see it at all.

'Do you see it?' I whispered. But he did not reply. 'Ed?'

I waited, as long minutes passed. I thought I could hear the sound of someone crashing through the undergrowth, but it seemed far away.

My blood turned to ice. Had he been attacked? He would not leave me here alone in the dark needlessly. Something was wrong. I had to find him.

'Ed!' I cried and charged into the dark after him.

Twigs, dried leaves, and snow crushed under my feet as I pushed my way through the unyielding forest. The cold made my jaw ache and my feet numb; the only heat came from the oil lantern clutched in my hand.

Every so often I stopped, listening until there would be a snap or a crunch and I would head off in that direction, calling for Olivia and Ed. Neither answered.

I had little sense of where I was now, the forest was even more disorientating in the snow. But I could hear the roar of the river above the rush of the wind, and I knew I must be heading in the right direction.

Suddenly, I emerged from the trees to find myself standing in front of the steep slope I remembered from that day with Olivia. The river was below me, high after all the snow, and heavy with ice.

I held my lantern up, squinting into the wind. Through the blowing snow, I could see the hut at the top of the ridge, dark and brooding. It looked empty. Abandoned.

I longed to turn and run, but something deep inside me knew Olivia was in there.

I tucked my skirt inside my boots and clambered up the icy hill, skidding and sliding, and clinging with my free hand to jutting stones, to ground me. The lantern swung and swayed, sending light spinning wildly across the grey stone.

'Olivia!' I called. But my voice was lost in the wind.

At last, I reached the top and faced the blackened shack. The roof was bowing under the weight of the snow, but the door was firmly shut. I raced to the porch and held up the lantern as I peered through the dirty window. Inside, shadows clung to the walls, obscuring much of the room from view, but I could see a small, huddled figure on the floor, one hand thrown out. A shock of pale hair contrasted sharply with the darkness. It was Olivia. She was not moving.

My breath caught.

I ran to the door and pushed hard, putting my shoulder to it. It opened with a screech of protest. The cold breath of winter swirled inside, carrying with it a pungent, yeasty, rotting smell as I dropped to the floor, inspecting her by the wavering light of the lamp.

Her skin was waxy. A greying bruise was blooming along her left cheek and under her eye, as though she had been beaten but as I stared, she took a deep, slow breath.

My heart leapt.

I took her frozen hand in my gloved fingers and pressed it. 'Livvy? Open your eyes for me. Olivia, please wake up.'

She did not stir.

Behind me, the bedstead clinked as something moved. The tendons in my neck tightened. Slowly, I turned to look. The bundle of rags I had mistaken for old blankets unfolded itself and sat up. Two gimlet eyes winked in the darkness. A voice, putrid with the smell of old meat and rancid alcohol, spoke from within the multiple layers of fabric.

'Two in one night,' said the Shambler. 'That's unexpected.'

As I stared, he swung his legs off the bed. In one hand he held a length of rope. The end was tied around Olivia's waist. I stared at the rope, rooted to the spot, my shaking hands still clinging to Olivia, my skin clammy.

'What have you done to her?' I tried to sound commanding but my voice trembled.

'Me?' He shook himself, and the smell of him filled the room. 'Nuthin'. Don't have to. Weather'll do it. Not everyone's cut out fer'it.'

He grinned, revealing empty spaces where the teeth had rotted out of his skull. His fingernails were long and yellowing; encrusted with dirt and the spongy mould I remembered from that night at Weatherall. When he rose from the bed, the chuckle he gave crackled in his chest. He still had the rope wrapped around his hand.

I tried to get to my feet but my legs felt weak, and I stayed in a kind of crouch beside Olivia.

'You leave us be. I am taking her home.' Remembering the cudgel, I pulled it from my pocket and brandished it wildly. It whistled through the air, connecting with nothing.

'Remove the rope,' I demanded.

The man's eyes gleamed. 'Think I'll keep her as a present for when Winnie gets here. Loves surprises, does my Winnie. Like when I came back and found it was all gone. The house. The neighbours. Her. Hell of a surprise, that was.'

'There is no Winnie here,' I said, my voice shaking. 'I'm sorry but you are looking in the wrong place.'

'Liar!' In an instant, he had my coat collar in his hand and he gripped me fiercely, pulling towards him. 'I've seen her. You're a liar. All you whores are liars.'

'There is no…' I began – and then froze.

The names on the posters in Mrs Hayes' room suddenly appeared, written as large and bright as if they were painted on a theatre safety curtain.

Edwina Stern. Ed Byres had said the Shambler was named Archie Stern.

Everyone at Mistcoate called her Eda. But her name was Edwina.

Winnie.

What was it Mrs Meadows had said?

She's a tough one, is Eda Hayes. Did you know she used to be in the Music Hall?

'You're Archie.' I breathed his name. 'You're supposed to be dead.'

He leaned forward, pressing his face into mine, a leering smile curling his lips. My stomach pitched at the smell of his breath as he spoke in a crooning whisper.

'Know me, do you, sweetheart? Was Winnie talking about me? That *bitch.*'

He yanked on my collar, tightening it into my windpipe.

'Let go!' I swung the cudgel, but a filthy hand shot out and caught it mid-swing. He pulled it from my cold fingers with frustrating ease.

'Reckon it's mine now.' He released my collar with a performative flourish, fingers spread wide, and I saw the end of the rope was held to his palm with only his thumb.

I lunged, pulling on the rope, trying to rip it from his hand, but he realised what I was doing and pulled it back towards him so suddenly and with such strength that I stumbled forward into him, the stench of befouled material and unwashed body making me gag.

I reached up, clawing at his hand, gasping in terror, trying to tear the rope from him. The struggle seemed to rouse Olivia, who groaned.

'Livvy!' I cried. 'Wake up.'

'She's for Winnie,' the man said. 'Winnie'll want her.'

I kicked out, hard, and heard a crack from his ankle. He gave a howl, wild and enraged. I dropped the rope and lunged for Olivia but he swung the cudgel, striking my jaw. The blow sent a hot wave of pain up my cheek to my eye.

I tasted blood in my mouth and spat it into his face, gasping in pain and terror.

I'm going to die, I thought.

'Julia?'

I glanced down to see Olivia blinking up at me, her brow creased and bewildered.

'Livvy…'

Before I could finish saying her name, the cudgel swung again, striking me in the ribs, driving the air out of me so that my scream was lost.

I staggered, air whistling through my lips, as I fought to breathe.

Olivia cried out, and scrabbled to press herself into the corner.

Before I could recover, a hand closed around my throat, shoving me into the rotten wall. My skull bounced off the side of the hut and I stood, pinned. My thoughts became liquid and incoherent as I struggled to think. There was something warm in my hair and soaking my collar. Everything began to go black.

The Shambler's breath scorched my cheek, flecks of spittle flying as he hissed, 'She's mine, you see. She don't like it but it's not her choice. It's *my* choice – it's always been mine. I choose, and you do what you're told.'

He dropped the cudgel. It hit the floor with a dull thud but it all seemed so far away. My hands fumbled uselessly at his arm but he barely paid attention. He was grappling with something – the fastening at the front of his trousers.

A strange calm came over me. I felt as if I could see everything with absolute clarity: Olivia, huddled in the corner; the cudgel, on the floor next to the rope.

'Pissed off on me, didn't she?' he wheezed, pressing the ruin of his face close to me, his left hand busy. The cold was making him clumsy. 'She took everything and what did I do to deserve it? Worked, gave her money. I was good, until she got her claws into me and pushed and pushed me. That's all you lot do – you push men until they give you a slap and then it's all crocodile tears.'

I reached into my pocket, my hands closing over the neck of the bottle of brandy Marian had given me.

'She's good at that... pretending,' he continued. 'But she can't run forever.'

I swung the bottle with all my strength. The glass shattered over his head, liquid spilling into his eyes and over the floor.

As if she'd been waiting for this moment, Olivia pulled a small kitchen paring knife out of her boot and drove it deep into the Shambler's leg, yanking downwards. He screamed and stumbled back.

The room swam around me and I fell to the floor, broken glass needling my palms, and I cried out.

But Olivia was suddenly next to me, her eyes trained on the Shambler, who swore and stamped, blinded by brandy and glass, trying to wrench the knife from his leg. The cudgel lay forgotten. She snatched it from the floor. I felt her squeeze my hand, her eyes darting to the door. I nodded.

Carefully, we eased ourselves upright and crept across the room.

But Olivia still had the rope tied around her waist tangling in her legs. Hearing it drag across the floor, the Shambler turned, his one piggy eye gleaming.

'*No*,' he growled, and leapt.

Olivia swung the bludgeon with surprising force. I heard a sickening crunch as the weapon connected.

The man staggered back, crashing into the wall. His body slid slowly to the floor. And then all was quiet.

'Hurry,' I urged, snatching the lantern from the floor where I'd left it. Olivia gathered up the rope, and we ran out into the cold.

The winds had died down, and the snow fell heavily. As we skidded across the icy ground, I heard Olivia murmur, 'I thought she would come. She said she would.'

But then she stopped, mid-stride, her gaze fixed on something behind me.

I turned, raising the lantern aloft.

Mrs Hayes stood under a tree, her face hidden in shadow. She had twisted her hair into a long, dark braid that fell over her shoulder. Despite the weather, she wore no coat; instead, layers of shawls and wraps were draped around her. She had tucked her skirts into the tops of a pair of tall boots and when she stepped forward, I saw a smear of mud across her jaw.

Her eyes glinted in the moonlight and when her hand shifted, something caught the light of the lantern. A knife. Not a pilfered kitchen knife like Olivia's. A long, sharp blade. She held it up, and snapped her fingers at Olivia.

'Come here, my dove. It's time to go.'

THIRTY-FIVE

Temperance

'Olivia, *no*,' I whispered.

I wanted to hold onto her, but I was so weak. Every part of me hurt. My head pounded viciously, and blood seeped from the corner of my mouth. I could taste it on my tongue. Any movement hurt. Little shards of glass were embedded in my palms. I seemed to be bleeding from so many places. My ribs burned with pain, and every breath took effort. All anyone would have to do was hit me again and I would lie down in the snow to freeze.

I watched helplessly as Olivia went to her, obedient as a dog.

I raised the lantern as if to hurl it, but the knife was pointed at my heart.

'Drop that,' Mrs Hayes snapped.

I bent, slowly, wincing at every moment, and set it down in the snow.

'We must go.' Mrs Hayes said.

'What about Julia?' Olivia looked to me.

'Don't you worry about Miss Pearlie.' Mrs Hayes kept the knife steady. 'We'll make sure she is dealt with.' She eyed my swelling jaw and bloodied face. 'Have you got the money?'

Olivia shook her head. 'It wasn't where you said. I checked everywhere.'

Mrs Hayes turned to me, glaring. The lantern on the ground lit her from below, giving her face a grotesque appearance.

'Where's my money?' Her voice was as tense as a garotte wire.

I spat blood, my thoughts thick and slow as I tried to form the words. 'So it was your money in the glasshouse? I left it where I found it. But…' I wavered, as the ground swam beneath me. When I spoke again my words slurred. 'Possibly your answer is in there.'

I gestured towards the hut behind us.

'Why would it be there?' Mrs Hayes asked.

In a last act of defiance, I squared my shoulders and met her gaze.

'Go and see,' I said.

Mrs Hayes gave a snarl of rage and swiped with the blade. I jumped back, the effort sending a shard of pain through my side.

I could hear pebbles falling off the precipice to the river far below, and I realised she was driving me towards the edge.

Below, the water was a raging torrent, swollen with snow and ice. Had it been like this on the night Florence Richmond died? Had she slipped on pebbles, blinded by sorrow and despair, and plunged forward into the dark water?

'Now, you listen, Pearlie,' Mrs Hayes hissed. 'I can either leave quickly with my money or leave slowly with no witnesses. You decide.'

'I haven't got your money,' I told her. 'Just go.'

'Eda?' Olivia sounded confused.

The lamp flame fluttered, and the light flickered across her face.

'Don't worry.' Mrs Hayes spoke without taking her eyes off me. 'It will look like an accident. After all,' her voice dropped, becoming almost conspiratorial, 'it's happened before. No one would question it if she were to slip.'

She thrust the blade forward and I flinched, edging closer to the icy bank behind me.

'You'd be just another stupid girl charging off into the woods at night.'

'Are you saying Florence Richmond was stupid?' I said.

'Now don't you try confusing her,' Mrs Hayes said and turned to Olivia. 'You know I didn't say that, my lamb.'

I clutched my burning ribs with my arm, forcing myself to stand tall.

'You never really liked Florence, did you?' I said. 'She questioned you. Wouldn't be manipulated. You were glad when she died, weren't you? How much would you like Olivia if she couldn't do what you wanted? But you saw that, Livvy, didn't you? In London.'

'Shut up,' Mrs Hayes snarled. 'You get out of her head. London was a mistake.

That's all.' The knife twitched.

A thought suddenly occurred to me. A painful laugh escaped me like a gasp.

'That was what the letters were about,' I said, marvelling at how I had missed it. 'Those weeks before Christmas. You were planning her séance. The letters were from your contacts.'

Mrs Hayes lifted her chin, eyes glittering with pride at her own cunning.

'A girl of her talent should be shown off, not locked away like that selfish, drunken fool Richmond wants to do. I wouldn't do to her what he's done.'

Olivia took a step back. Her face grew still and watchful.

'But you did. I saw the notes in your desk about his experiments with Olivia. You know what he did.' I raised my hand and pointed a bleeding finger at her. 'You *helped*.'

'He would've killed her with those drugs if I hadn't.'

'And what about when she wasn't there?' I said. 'All those nights in his office. Those strange noises in the dark.'

'That's none of your business.' Mrs Hayes snarled the words with such ferocity, I saw Olivia recoil.

'Did he end your affair?' I said. 'Is that why you decided to take this risk? Because he tired of you?'

'Eda?' Olivia's voice held a mix of anxiety and fury.

Mrs Hayes turned to look at her. 'She's lying.'

'Then why were his cufflinks in your room?' I asked, refusing to give up. 'I found them under the bed.' I took a step forward, shaking. 'You never cared for anyone. Not really. All you wanted was money and when you realised Dr Richmond had none, you turned to Olivia.'

'That's a lie.' Mrs Hayes' grip tightened on the knife. 'Don't waver now, my dove. I can give you a real life.'

'As a circus attraction?' I filled my voice with doubt.

'Maybe,' said Mrs Hayes. 'At first. Fame doesn't just happen.'

I turned my gaze to Olivia. 'Is that what you want?'

Olivia looked at me, tears streaming down her face. 'She said she would help me. She sent me letters. She said I needn't go to the hospital.'

'She lied.' I said it flatly.

'I meant every word of it,' insisted Mrs Hayes. 'She's told me things. Imagine knowing you didn't have to spend your life looking over your shoulder anymore. There's people who'll pay for that kind of peace and I intend to make our fortune.'

In the distance, I heard Ed Byres' voice, calling us.

'Olivia! Julia!'

It was closely followed by the constable's whistle.

'Who is that?' Mrs Hayes peered into the darkness.

'Please, let us go,' I pleaded. 'They never saw you, Eda. You can walk away.'

It was the wrong thing to say. She lunged at me, knife swiping through the air. It was a useless strike, meant to make me step off the edge and fall to my death. I might have done, had Olivia not let out a strangled cry, causing Mrs Hayes to pull back.

There was another blast of the whistle from the trees and a rustling and snapping of twigs. They were getting closer.

'Ed!' I shouted, but my voice was too cracked, I could not get enough breath. 'Over here!'

'Quiet!' Mrs Hayes swung the blade round to Olivia before she realised what she was doing, and hastily withdrew it. 'Forgive me, but we can't leave her here to tell everyone.' She began to advance on me. 'Close your eyes if you must but this has become tiresome.'

The blade glinted in the moonlight.

'What happened to Archie, Winnie?' I said.

The housekeeper stopped, her eyes glittering. There was another whistle, much closer.

'What did you call me?' she asked, but the knife point wavered.

I ignored the question. 'Did you tell Olivia your real name was Winnie Stern?'

Mrs Hayes gave a snarling sort of smile.

'Winnie Stern is dead,' she said. 'At least, as far as I'm concerned. Her husband beat her with a poker right on her own hearth. I was Hayes before I met him. And I was Hayes after I left him.' She gave a barking laugh. 'Men. They always take it too far. Archie was like that. Of course, it was all my fault. Or so he said. You can't argue with a drunk. Not while you're on the ground with your hands over your face.'

Her eyes glistened, tears catching the light of the lamp. Olivia stood stock-still, staring at the housekeeper as though she had never seen her before. Slowly, I slipped the lithograph from my pocket and held it up.

'Is that what happened to the baby?'

Mrs Hayes' expression froze. For a long moment she said nothing, and the roar of the river filled the air.

In the faint lamp light, I thought I saw a tear slide down her cheek, unheeded, as she stared at the image of her giggling, younger self. The knifepoint dropped.

'He used to make me laugh,' she said, addressing no one. 'There weren't many who could make me laugh. I don't think I'm the laughing kind.'

The whistle sounded again, but further away now. They had gone off the trail.

'You told me Archie was dead,' I said, flicking a glance at the hut behind Mrs Hayes. Was there movement there? The suggestion of rustling? A clinking from the bed? It was hard to tell, with the sound of the river so loud.

'He is. He died in a fire.' Her tone was flat. 'Now, enough of this.'

I glanced at Olivia, who was also looking back at the hut. Something shifted in the darkness, but before I could see it properly, Mrs Hayes was grabbing Olivia's wrist.

'What does it matter now?' she said, with a wild laugh. 'What does any of it matter now? Olivia, we have to go.'

'Winnie…' It was an animal growl.

I looked up to see Archie Stern, very much alive, framed in the doorway of the hut, his breath coming in laboured gasps.

At first, Mrs Hayes did not move and I thought she must not have heard. But, slowly, she turned, her shoulders rising defensively.

'*No*.' It sounded like a plea.

He leaned against the door. A long, dark thread of blood-mottled spittle ran down his chin, his mouth and remaining teeth were slicked black.

'My sweet girl,' he hissed, but his piggy eyes were cold.

She swung the knife towards him but her hands shook and she pulled Olivia in front of her.

'You aren't pleased to see me?' he said, shuffling towards us across the snow.

'You're dead,' she whispered, her voice trembling, one hand on Olivia's shoulder. '*She* told me. You're in the ground.'

'I think she lied,' said Archie with a blood-slick grin.

His speech was thick and slurred. The light of the lamp picked out the glass around his collar and in his hair and the beads of blood glistening on his skin like rubies. 'Come home to an empty house and no wife. What's a man to do?'

The knife trembled. 'You stay back!'

Seeing their fixed attention on each other, frozen in a tableau of horror, I reached down and took hold of the lantern.

'You never could outsmart me,' Archie Stern crooned. 'You're mine and you ain't going nowhere.' He reached out to her, and she swung the knife. It sliced his fingers.

He snatched his hand back, an oath hissing through his blackened lips.

'For better or worse, you said,' he spat, blood speckling the snow at his feet. 'You're mine. Whether you like it or not.'

He lunged forward, hands outstretched.

Mrs Hayes pushed Olivia hard to one side. I caught her before she could fall, and held her tight as I stepped away.

Mrs Hayes rounded on her husband, swinging the knife up as she turned, and driving it into his arm.

With a roar, he punched her hard in the mouth, crumpling her to the ground.

I pulled Olivia back, but I was too weak to move quickly. The stabbing pain in my side was worsening. My breath seemed to wheeze.

Suddenly, Stern was upon us, a fistful of Olivia's hair in his hand. Olivia made a terrified choking sound, too frightened to scream. Acting purely on instinct, I swung the lantern with full force. The glass shattered against his head, raining oil and flame down on Archie Stern.

For an instant, there was nothing but the sound of tinkling glass and my own harsh breaths. Then he ignited.

It happened with horrifying slowness. First there was smoke and then the flames caught, leaping into life on his sleeve, his shoulders, his hair.

He screamed and whirled, beating at the flames, but the oil had seeped into his brandy-soaked collar and the fire spread quickly. Head and shoulders aflame, he turned as if to run to the river but Mrs Hayes rose, the dropped cudgel gripped in one hand and advanced on him.

'Go!' I pushed Olivia towards the forest. 'Run!'

Mrs Hayes swung the knife, driving her husband back to the hut. He beat at her with flaming hands as he stumbled backwards, but she remained out of reach. I seized the cudgel Olivia had dropped, and joined her, forcing him towards the hut with its brandy-covered floor and old bedding. His foot caught on the porch and for a moment he paused, tilting in the doorway, then collapsed inside with a crash. I shoved the door to, ignoring the pain.

Mrs Hayes raised the blade above her head, as if to run in after him, but I held her back, gripping her arm.

'No. It's over.'

Even as I said the words, flames erupted inside, visible through the darkened windowpane. Archie screamed then, an inhuman sound I thought I would hear in my nightmares for the rest of my life. But the door remained closed.

Olivia stumbled back from the edge of the woods, and the three of us stood, watching as fire crept up the walls to the roof, until the darkness glowed from its light.

I wasn't cold anymore. In fact, we had all stopped shivering.

Finally, the screams stopped. I let out a long, shuddering breath.

Mrs Hayes turned to Olivia. Her face was curiously expressionless. 'Was this it?' she asked. 'Was this what you saw?'

Olivia nodded, tears rolling down her cheeks.

Mrs Hayes gave a low, shaky laugh and seized Olivia's hand.

'You had me worried there,' she said. 'Come, they'll be here any minute with all this to attract them.'

'No. Please.' I stretched my hand out to her. 'Come home. We'll tell George the truth. All of it.'

Olivia looked from the housekeeper to me. Her eyes were filled with tears, and there was blood on her face.

'I don't know who to believe anymore,' she whispered, misery hanging on every word. 'Everyone lies.'

She looked up at me and I realised there was something unspoken there.

Tell her, I thought. *If it's what I suspect, you need to tell her, Livvy...*

'Come now,' said Mrs Hayes, pulling at her hand. 'Next time she sees you, you'll be the toast of London. Mistress Livia the All-Knowing.'

Olivia pulled her hand free and looked at the housekeeper.

'I made it up,' she said.

Mrs Hayes blinked at her. 'You made up what?'

'I had no idea where your husband was,' said Olivia. 'I made it up.'

Mrs Hayes stared at her as though trying to make sense of what she was hearing.

'You were so desperate,' Olivia explained. 'I had to say something.'

'So you said *that*?'

Mrs Hayes' voice was low and threatening. Olivia took a step back and Mrs Hayes followed her, still gripping her hand.

They were too close to the river's edge but neither one of them seemed to notice.

'What about the rest?' demanded Mrs Hayes, her voice rising. 'Was it all a lie?'

Olivia hesitated. 'Not all of it.'

'But some? Some was still a lie. You let me do all this for lies?'

Olivia wept silently as she nodded.

Still Mrs Hayes advanced on her. 'You had me believing he could not find me so I stopped hiding and drew him straight to me. He would have killed me. Do you understand that?'

She grabbed Olivia by the collar and shook her, like a dog shaking a rag.

'You selfish little liar,' she hissed, her eyes wide with fury, her skin white and stretched with tension. 'You've made me look a fool. You've wasted years of my life on lies. I built everything on you – I gave up everything – Well, I'm not wasting one more second on you. I'm done with this. What good are you to me now? To hell with you!'

She shoved Olivia hard. Olivia's feet left the ground and she grabbed the housekeeper by the sleeve as she tumbled over the edge. The two of them plunged into the icy river.

I drew in a sharp breath.

The darkness of the river swallowed them both, pulling them along in a surge of white froth and green scum.

'Help!' I cried. 'Someone, please help!'

I knelt at the edge but could see nothing but the dark rushing of the river.

No, there was someone down there. A small, slick figure, staring up at me.

I was trembling but it was not due to the cold. The spectre of Christopher Kemp stepped into the river, malevolence radiating as he strode towards the spot where Olivia's pale head suddenly broke the surface of the water.

With a strangled cry, I leapt off the ledge.

The water was as dark as my nightmares and colder than anything I had ever known. My lungs froze and I gasped for breath. I tried to call out as the current carried me down towards Olivia, who I could see, her thin arms clinging to a rock, skirts dragging behind her.

A dark figure was moving through the water towards her. I struck out, breathless from the cold and the pain. My skirts seemed to weigh more with every second, pulling me down, but I would not give up. I did not stop until I reached her.

'I'm here,' I gasped, pulling her into my arms. Her eyes opened a little, her mouth trying to form words. I kicked against the current, trying to grab onto the icy rock beside her.

Something grasped my hair, pulling me under, my mouth and nose filling with water. I fought my way back up to the surface and looked behind me, expecting to see Christopher's menacing, dead face, pinched in rage and vengeance. Instead, it was Mrs Hayes, her eyes wide and mouth set in a grimace, clinging to my dress, dragging me down.

We fought in the water. I slapped at her hands, but I was too weak. My head went below the water, and I fought to the surface again. As soon as I drew in a breath, she grabbed me again. This time, though, I was ready. I jerked my head backwards.

There was a crack as my skull connected with Mrs Hayes' nose and forehead. I felt her grip loosen, and I kicked out again. I could feel the frantic scrabbling of fingertips trying to catch my clothing, but the river was running fast and her layers of scarves and wraps were now waterlogged.

Her face breached the dark water's surface once more, gasping. But she was soon caught in the current and dragged away. Or was there something else there? Something that wrapped its arms around her neck and seemed to pull her down? She gave one last watery cry before she was snatched down, under the water and out of sight.

THIRTY-SIX

Ace of Wands

Tuesday 24th January 1891
Inquest on Murderous Housekeeper in Fellwick
CORONER'S INQUEST THIS DAY

This morning the coroner ruled that the death of Mrs Edwina Stern, locally known as Mrs Eda Hayes, was accidental. The inquiry heard that Mrs Stern drowned in the act of abducting her mistress, Miss Olivia Richmond.

Thought locally to be a 'calculating woman', Mrs Stern had recently been dismissed from her position at Mistcoate House for dishonest conduct. It is believed her actions stemmed from a wish for revenge on her employers.

'They gave her everything, they did,' says Fellwick businesswoman Mrs Eugenia Meadows. 'But she pulled the wool over everyone's eyes. I hope the family can have some peace now.'

Miss Olivia Richmond was only saved due to the quick actions of the Richmonds' acting-Housekeeper, Miss Julia Pearlie, who arrived in time to pull Miss Richmond from the river. Both Miss Pearlie and Miss Richmond, known locally as 'The Mistcoate Witch', are said to be making a steady recovery.

'It was Eda Hayes who had us all calling her that,' Mrs Meadows states. 'Everyone I ever spoke to said they learned it from her. She had that poor girl convinced she could do all sorts. Really, it was all Eda Hayes feeding her information.'

Other witnesses have since confirmed that Mrs Stern was at the centre of an elaborate deception which saw Miss Richmond tricked into hosting séances, tarot readings and palmistry sessions for a price. These events included local gatherings at well-known houses, where everything was arranged by Mrs Stern.

Miss Richmond has stated that she was unaware anyone was charged for her 'services', stating, 'I believed I was helping people.'

Dr George Richmond of Mistcoate House has refused to comment except to express his gratitude to Miss Pearlie for her quick-thinking in saving his daughter's life, as well as to ask for privacy during this difficult time.

The coroner's inquiry was held at the Hive and Honey. Aside from being asked to verify facts of what happened in the river, my testimony was brief. My bruised, blackened throat and swollen, puffed face had caused a scandalised whisper as I had been helped to my feet to answer the coroner's questions. I waited, breath caught in my chest, for a reference to my own past shame but the snide accusations never came. I was excused after just fifteen minutes, with a look of sympathy from those in attendance.

I stepped out into the bright winter sunshine to find the square in uproar. A private coach had stopped nearby and boys from the livery stables opposite were poised to help unload bags. The coach door opened and a familiar figure got out. Dr Joyce turned and guided a woman, whom I could only guess was his sister Mina, down from the coach.

She stood, her nose wrinkled as though she smelt something unpleasant, looking at the hubbub around her. One of the boys approached to offer help, but she shooed him away.

Dr Joyce had spotted me and waved me over. 'Miss Pearlie!'

I was glad my injuries meant I did not have to smile as he strode towards me, his own grin faltering as the extent of my injuries became clearer with each step.

'Dr Joyce,' I said. 'You are here to visit the Richmonds?'

'Quite so.' His whiskers had grown since I last saw him, making him look even more like a weasel. 'I didn't have time to write, so no doubt we shall catch Georgie on the hop. We stopped in town to give him time to prepare. I wonder,' he paused, taking in my walking stick and battered face, 'if we took lunch here, would you inform him we've arrived, when you are back at Mistcoate?'

'I am afraid I am no longer employed by Dr Richmond,' I said, crisply. 'But I'm sure one of the boys will be happy to help you.'

I turned to go, but he held up a hand to stop me.

'Wait.'

I glanced up at him, surprised. 'Yes?'

Dr Joyce looked around, suddenly shifty. 'This business with Eda.'

I frowned. 'Yes?'

He looked uncomfortable. 'She didn't happen to mention… Not that anything she said could be trusted, the woman was clearly a lunatic. But did she…?'

'You have not been mentioned.' My tone was measured.

Dr Joyce sagged a little with relief.

'But you could be,' I said and raised my voice slightly. 'You were very close with Mrs Hayes, weren't you? During your stay before Christmas?'

The doctor took a step forward.

'What are you insinuating?' he asked, his voice harsh.

'Only that it looks odd, doesn't it?' I straightened my gloves. 'Your sister wants to marry Dr Richmond, but wanted Olivia out of the way. It's almost as if you paid Mrs Hayes to get rid of her.'

Dr Joyce went red. 'How dare you. That is not—'

'It's not beyond the realms of possibility,' I continued. 'After all, you're still planning on sending her to a sanatorium, aren't you? I can't see how that would look anything other than suspicious. Especially now that it's been declared that she is perfectly sane.'

Dr Joyce paused, uncertain.

'Good afternoon, Dr Joyce,' I said.

I let myself in through the back door to find Ed making Alice's tray. I never called him Reverend Byres now when we were at home. He chuckled as I told him about the Joyces.

'I am glad it is over,' he said, counting out two capsules from a bottle and placing them on a dish, along with a cylinder of tobacco rolled in thin paper. 'The pot is on the range. Will you take coffee with Alice?'

'She coughed less in the night, I thought,' I commented, setting aside my stick and selecting an extra cup.

'Yes,' said Ed.

We worked in companionable silence, arranging the medications and cures that the doctor had sworn would clear her lungs and help her breathing.

Neither of us liked to think of what life would be like without Alice, so we didn't discuss it. We rarely talked about the future at all. So I was surprised when he turned to me and said, 'What will you do now? I wonder, would you consider teaching at the school? Mr and Mrs Lewes have decided to make a new start and we are in want of a teacher. It comes with a small house.'

'Are you looking to get rid of me?' I smiled.

'Of course not. But you have no reason to stay in Fellwick now that the enquiry is finished.'

'Don't I?' I asked, softly.

Ed did not look at me as he stirred Alice's coffee. We made it as strong and black as she would take it, sweetened with sugar. The spoon clicked gently against the pottery mug.

'I think we both know how I feel about you,' he began.

'I would like to be certain,' I said.

The spoon's clicking stopped.

My heart fluttered, painfully. 'Ed?'

He reached out his hand and took mine. His skin was calloused from his work in the garden, warm from the coffee mug. My fingers, still healing from that hellish night, quivered a little at his gentle pressure. He ran his thumb over my skin.

'I cannot offer you what you want,' he said, softly. 'Not with Alice as she is. You cannot go on sleeping on a trundle bed in my sister's studio and having this unspoken feeling between us. I cannot have you waste your life, waiting for me.'

'Would it be such a waste?' I asked. 'What if Alice gets well again?'

'Maybe,' he said.

'Do you wish me to move out to the school house?' I asked.

He shook his head.

'No,' he said, his voice tortured and creaking. 'Because then what if some educated, handsome schoolmaster comes and I have to watch you slip away? But what's the alternative? Keep you here with a bachelor clergyman and his sickly sister to be a source of gossip?'

I cupped his hand in mine.

'None of those things have happened,' I said. 'Which leaves one question. What do you want, Ed?'

He lifted my hand and pressed it to his mouth, once again in a gesture that was not quite a kiss.

'I want so many things,' he whispered, his voice muffled against my skin. 'But I am so afraid to want them.'

I leaned my forehead against his temple.

'I love you,' I said. 'Let's leave it at that for now.'

We stayed as we were for a moment and then Ed drew in a breath, releasing my hands.

'I forgot to mention, there is post for you,' he said. 'Marian brought it down. I left it on the table.'

He lifted the tray. As I bent down to pick up the envelopes, I felt him lean in, and turned in time for his mouth to press against mine in a soft, honeyed crush.

'I love you too,' he said. 'Please don't leave.'

We embraced for a long moment. Then he went to see Alice, carrying the tray.

The first letter was encased in an expensive envelope with a London postmark. It read,

To Miss Julia Pearlie,
C/o Mistcoate House,
Fellwick

Dear Julia,

I am sorry for not having written sooner but really you should have left us with an address. Anthony has been quite frantic but I reassured him that you would be busy settling in.

I admit that, when Christmas came, we started to worry but then imagine my surprise when Mrs Huntingford from my bridge club told me that you were the talk of Norfolk. Mrs Huntingford is a close friend of the Rogers of Weatherall, who have painted you as quite the heroine. I'm given to understand that even the Joyces of Bayswater have been talking of you.

Well, this gave some indication as to why you've been so quiet, but how naughty, sister, to have kept all these wonderful contacts to yourself. Who would have thought Fellwick to be such a social hub?

You must write at once and let me know all about it and, of course, come to tea next time you are in town. I understand the Richmonds will be taking up residence in Kensington and I have been dying to make the acquaintance of Miss Joyce so you must invite her too.

Anthony feels very badly about your leaving and has asked me to enclose this envelope. I am quite certain it is none of my business but a thank you note to him would be appreciated. After all, it is a generous sum for a married father, even if he has just been made partner.

Please write soon,

Your loving sister-in-law,
Mrs Jocelyn Pearlie

P.S. Little Emmeline Pearlie was born at the end of November. She looks so like Anthony.

As I opened the paper she'd enclosed in her letter, a small note fell out. It was a cheque for thirty pounds, written in Anthony's hand. I turned it over and over in wonder.

I can go anywhere now, I realised.

I looked back to where Ed had stood moments ago.

Now my fate truly was in my own hands.

It turned out the Joyces had arrived with news of their own. Tired of waiting for Dr Richmond, they had sold their house in London and were in the process of finalising the sale of Mistcoate. They had arrived to ambush Dr Richmond with the news and start the process of relocating. It took less than thirty-six hours for them to strip Mistcoate of anything valuable.

Those present said that Dr Richmond stood back and watched, looking as dry and lifeless as the hessian wallpaper they attempted to take from the walls. Rumour had it that Peter Joyce was making it his personal mission to empty the drinks cabinets and what was left of the cellar himself, while Mina Joyce met with Captain Richmond once and then seemed to forget that he existed.

However, in an unusual turn of events, she had developed a greater liking for Olivia.

'They're forever in little huddles, miss,' said Marian, when she came to tea. 'I can't imagine what they talk about.'

'It doesn't matter,' I said. 'So long as there's no more talk of sanatoriums.'

'It is truly sad to see the house packed up.' Marian sighed. She said she'd surprised herself by weeping a little, hiding her face when Miss Joyce came near.

'She doesn't like to see it, miss.'

But the sadness was only for the loss of the house. Marian had been accepted as an apprentice cook at Weatherall and would be within half an hour's walk, on a good day.

'Miss Olivia would like you to come see them off at the station when they go to London,' she told me. 'She doesn't want to leave without saying goodbye.'

'Just you try keeping me away.' I smiled.

A few days later, I was reading in the sitting room when the doorbell rang. I hurried to answer it before Alice might be disturbed.

To my astonishment, I found Miss Joyce on the doorstep, two young women from the village standing behind her laden with luggage.

'Miss Pearlie,' she beamed. 'I hope you don't mind my intruding but I wanted to introduce myself and you know we're clearing the house for sale, so I brought some things for you. Goodness, this hall is so very small.'

She continued to chatter as I stepped back to let her in, also ushering in the women, who dumped the suitcases and bags before hurrying off. Soon, she was sitting in my seat, pouring herself a cup of tea from the pot on the table.

'I was looking through some of the old rooms and found these things that are, frankly, out of date and, therefore, no use to me. But, of course, I didn't want them to go to waste, and I immediately wondered if you might have some use of them.'

She took a sip of her tea before saying, 'And I thought you might be in need.'

I opened one of the bags and my eyes widened.

It was full of skirts, dresses, and blouses – even some stays and corsets. All must have once belonged, I imagined, to Florence. I stared at Miss Joyce, who wrinkled her nose at me in a mock display of affection.

'You're very welcome,' she said. 'I admit though, it's not just the little gift that brings me here. Now that we know more about darling Olivia, it is clear that we shall need someone to look after her wellbeing. Her Papa wishes for her to have the best of everything. Peter has sung your praises and convinced me that you are the best woman for the job. So I have been dispatched to ask if you would please come to London with us! It seems pretty clear that Olivia would be lost without you.'

You could name your price.

The thought trickled down the back of my neck, cold and oddly familiar. It was the witch-child's voice, but softer, more gentle. I did not see her now and had not seen Christopher since that night in the river. No sounds haunted me. No nightmares.

'Do not answer now,' Miss Joyce insisted, standing up and brushing her skirts. 'It is a lot to consider but if you would address your letters to me, I would be very grateful. George has so many other things to think about, with the wedding coming soon. We're leaving for London tomorrow so you can write to me there.'

So it was that less than twenty-four hours later, I found myself clasping Olivia to me as we stood on the platform at the train station.

'You will write?' she begged, her eyes filled with tears. She was once again in her fur travelling coat, a warm, felt hat pinned to her fine, pale hair. Her bruises, although still visible beneath her smoked glasses, were fading.

'Until you are thoroughly bored of me,' I promised.

'Mina told me she spoke to you.' She searched my face. 'You will consider the offer, won't you?'

I tucked a loose strand of hair behind her ear. 'I promise, I will consider it very deeply and let you know.'

It was another lie but one I did not feel guilty about. I knew I would not leave Ed and Alice, but I would not say that now.

A whistle blew.

'Come along, Olivia,' called Miss Joyce from the train carriage. 'We must go.'

'I'm glad you've found a way to get along,' I murmured in Olivia's ear.

She gave me an impish look. 'I gave her a palm reading I knew she would like. I think she will be useful.'

'What do you mean?'

'She understands my gift better than Mrs Hayes. You will come see us, even if you don't accept?' said Olivia, tightening the hug. 'She says she will take us to see Epidemius St. Joseph. I shall have new cards. Oh, and one more thing.'

From a bag at her side, she pulled out a small, velvet purse. It was the money from the glasshouse.

She raised a finger to her lips, smiling.

I was scandalised. 'Olivia! Please tell me you didn't.'

'I did what needed to be done,' she said, placing it back into the bag without a hint of apology.

'Come along, darling,' called Mina Joyce.

'I must go,' Olivia said.

As she reached up to kiss my cheek, I felt her push a piece of paper into my hand, and then she was gone and Captain Richmond was hobbling forward, supported by Dr Richmond and a cane.

'Goodbye, my dear,' said the captain, giving a deep bow.

'Thank you, sir. Goodbye.'

He reached out and gave my hand a squeeze.

'The sight of you does me good,' he said and then was gone, climbing into the carriage, assisted by Olivia.

Dr Richmond stepped to my side.

'I believe you have spoken to Mina,' he said. 'Please, do let us know what you decide. I know Olivia would be pleased. As would I.'

'Thank you,' I said. 'I shall send my answer.'

There was a moment of silence. Dr Richmond seemed to be preparing a speech. I resisted the urge to look about for an escape but then he spoke.

'I am ashamed of my conduct towards you and—'

He glanced over towards Olivia, who was being helped onto the train by Mina Joyce.

'I was not myself. I realise that now. It will not be repeated. I will spend the rest of my days trying to make up for it.'

He looked so dejected that, for a moment, my hardness towards him softened.

'I trust that you will, sir.'

Dr Richmond nodded, his eyes glistening and then he gave an uncomfortable cough and blinked away the burgeoning tears.

'In the meantime,' he continued, 'you will probably need this.'

He held out an envelope. I took it wonderingly.

'Your wages. And a reference letter.' His tone was stiff. 'I should never have refused to write it. Good luck, Miss Pearlie, with whatever comes next.'

Then he was up and into the carriage with the others. Another whistle gave a piercing cry.

Olivia hung out of the window, wisps of white-blonde hair escaping from her hat.

'Goodbye Julia! Goodbye!'

I waved back as the train began to pull away.

Only then did I think about the paper she'd given me. As the train rumbled into motion, I unfolded it. It held only a few lines in Olivia's distinctive scrawl.

I don't care what anyone says. I know what I see.

The train started to pick up speed.

I can still see him.

Was it colder? Despite the rushing of the train, everything seemed to have gone quiet. There was a strange clammy chill in the air.

He is still here. He will always be here.

Where had everyone gone? A moment ago, the place was full.

Let me know when you want to talk to him.

In the corner of my eye, a small figure stepped into my vision.
Love, Olivia

Plip...

TAROT GLOSSARY

Major Arcana

0. The Fool: New beginnings, optimism
1. The Magician: Action, making things happen
2. The High Priestess: the mystical, looking inwards
3. The Empress: Abundance, fertility
4. The Emperor: Stability, power
5. The Hierophant: Traditions, rules of society
6. The Lovers: Sexuality, passion
7. The Chariot: Progress, change
8. Strength: Courage, power
9. The Hermit: Solitude, self-reflection
10. Wheel of Fortune: Cycles, change
11. Justice: Balance, equality
12. The Hanged Man: Surrender, enlightenment
13. Death: Change, endings
14. Temperance: Moderation, good sense
15. The Devil: Destruction, losing power
16. The Tower: Collapse, release
17. The Star: Hope, positivity
18. The Moon: Mystery, the subconscious
19. The Sun: Success, all will be well
20. Judgment: Rebirth, new phases
21. The World: Wholeness, vitality

Minor Arcana

Suit of Swords
King: Serious, rational, masculine
Queen: Intelligent, communicative, regal
Knight: Determined, goal-oriented
Page: Immature, impulsive
Ace: New starts
2. Indecision
3. Betrayal
4. Rest
5. Conflict
6. Leaving for somewhere better
7. Secret plans
8. Powerlessness
9. Overactive mind
10. Self-sabotage

Suit of Cups
King: Deep feelings
Queen: Nurturing
Knight: Romantic adventure
Page: Creatively inspired
Ace: Emotional fulfilment
2. Compatibility
3. Sociability
4. Dissatisfaction
5. Self pity
6. Kindness
7. Indecision
8. Searching for something better
9. Self-satisfaction
10. Happiness

Suit of Wands
King: Career-focused
Queen: Zest for life
Knight: Risk taking
Page: Newly inspired
Ace: Creative spark
2. Contemplation
3. Rewarded effort
4. Safety
5. Disagreements
6. Achievement
7. Defensiveness
8. Speed
9. Pessimism
10. Exhaustion

Suit of Pentacles
King: Enjoying the good life
Queen: Healthy and calm
Knight: Cautious and sensible
Page: Student
Ace of Pentacles: Financial reward, clarity of life purpose, goals
2. Multitasking
3. Meaningful work
4. Fear, holding back
5. Money and health troubles
6. Charity
7. Patience
8. Hard work
9. Luxury
10. Financial success

ACKNOWLEDGEMENTS

A massive thank you to my amazing agent, Kate Nash and everyone at the Kate Nash Literary Agency for championing me and this book since 2020, when everything felt so strange. Thank you, Kate for your insight, wisdom and support. It is so appreciated.

I'd also like to thank my wonderful, funny and kind editor Christi, whose guidance I so appreciate, and everyone else at Moonflower Books – Jack, Emma – for their excitement about Olivia and love of what I do. Your enthusiasm is so uplifting, I'm so excited to be doing this with you.

Big thanks to the amazing designer, Jasmine Aurora whose gorgeous designs enthralled my students when they discovered I'd written a book and went googling my name. My year 9s were suitably impressed!

I'd also like to share my appreciation for Moonflower's incredible sales team, Martin Palmer and Katherine Rhodes, and amazing PR guru Tory-Lyne Pirkis for their hard work and dedication to getting Olivia out into the world. I am forever grateful.

Thank you to my department and my school, all of whom have been so supportive and kind. I'm so lucky to work with such incredible people who have so much creativity, drive and care within them. I so appreciate everything you guys have been and done – including being excited for me when I could only allow myself to be nervous.

I'd like to thank my parents, Sheila and David, for indulging this obsession with reading and writing from when I was young, and my wonderful stepson Jack who sat next to me every Saturday morning as I wrote while he watched TV. I'm hoping you won't get too old for that too quickly. Thank you to my wider family and support network who have been giving so much love to this book since it came into existence and, finally, especially thank you to Dean, for going on this journey with me, and to Andi, without whom none of this would have happened.

– Louise Davidson, October 2023

The Coming Storm by Greg Mosse

OUT 25 APRIL 2024

SCAN ME TO FIND OUT MORE

The hotly-anticipated sequel to 2022 Sunday Times Thriller of the Year The Coming Darkness sees the return of hero Alexandre Lamarque. He may have prevented the world from falling into ruin, but Alex knows his work is not done yet.

There's still a controlling intelligence out there, pulling together the strands of a new and even more destructive conspiracy. Battling with personal tragedy on one hand, and the intrusion of their new-found celebrity on the other, Alex and his allies must reunite for the fight of their lives. From the streets of Paris to the lithium mines of southern Mali, and to the mighty Aswan Dam, they come up against forces whose intentions are as devious as they are malign. Time is against them, and there's more at stake than ever.

About the author

Greg is a director, writer and writing teacher. He has lived and worked as a translator in Paris, New York, Los Angeles and Madrid. He now lives in Sussex with his wife, the novelist Kate Mosse.

MOONFLOWER

www.moonflowerbooks.co.uk

Piece Of My Heart by Penelope Tree

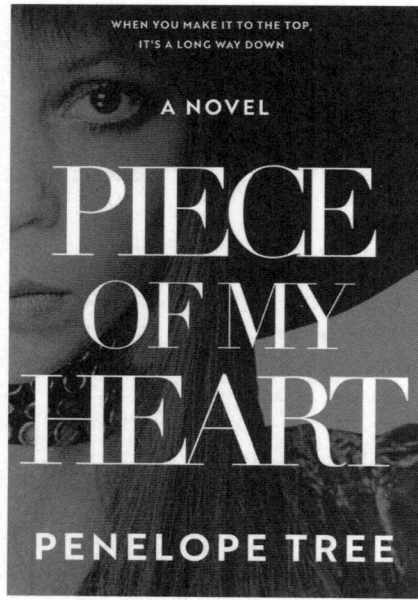

OUT 23 MAY 2024

SCAN ME TO FIND OUT MORE

MOONFLOWER

www.moonflowerbooks.co.uk

Fame. Money. Beauty. Sex. Love. Ari wants them all. And when she becomes the face of the 1960s, it seems like they're hers for the taking. Overnight, her life is transformed into a dizzying whirlwind of drugs, photoshoots, and parties, all with notorious bad boy photographer Bill Ramsey by her side.

But in the fickle world of fashion, nothing lasts forever – and addiction, Ari's eating disorder and increasingly dysfunctional relationship with Ramsey send her life spinning out of control.

How much more of herself must Ari lose to keep the things she always thought she wanted?

Based on a true story, *Piece of My Heart* is a stunning piece of autofiction in the vein of Esther Freud's *Hideous Kinky* and Chris Kraus' *I Love Dick*.

About the author

Model, writer and activist, Penelope Tree was the ultimate Sixties It girl. Born to a Conservative MP and an American socialite, she was discovered at the age of 13 by the photographer Diane Arbus and became an overnight sensation after an appearance at Truman Capote's Black and White Ball. A career in modelling followed – as David Bailey's muse, Penelope appeared on the cover of *Vogue* and travelled around the world. Now a practicing Buddhist and charitable ambassador, Penelope has two adult children and splits her time between Sussex and London.

Pagans by James Alistair Henry

OUT 24 OCTOBER 2024

SCAN ME TO FIND OUT MORE

Britain, 2023... only in this Britain, the Norman Conquest of 1066 never happened. An uneasy alliance of ancient tribes – the Celtic West, Saxon East and an independent Nordic Scotland – has formed, but the fragile peace is threatened by a series of brutal murders.

As the threat rises, Detectives Aedith and Drustan must put aside their personal differences to follow the trail, even when they uncover forces behind the killings that go deeper than they could ever have imagined.

Set in a world that's far from our own and yet captivatingly familiar, Pagans explores contemporary themes of religious conflict, nationalism and prejudice in a smart, witty and refreshingly different police procedural that keeps you guessing until the very end. Perfect for readers of Ben Aaronovitch, Neil Gaiman and Terry Prachett.

About the author

Screenwriter and editor James Alistair Henry first started writing while working as a bookseller. He joined the writing team for Channel 4's *Smack the Pony* and went on to write the BAFTA-award winning *Green Wing*, ITV comedy *Delivery Man* and cult hit *Campus* as well as episodes for smash-hit children's television shows *Bob The Builder* and *Hey Duggee*. James lives in Cornwall with his wife, a writer and Medieval Historian, and their two children.

MOONFLOWER

www.moonflowerbooks.co.uk

The Coming Darkness by Greg Mosse

Paris, 2037. With a double threat of rising temperatures and new diseases jeopardising public health, the world has never been more dangerous.

French special agent Alexandre Lamarque notices signs of a new terror group and connects it with an ominous sequence of events: a theft from a Norwegian genetics lab; a string of gory child murders; a chaotic coup in a breakaway North African republic, and the extraction under fire of its charismatic leader. And as the one man able to see through the web of lies, Alex may be the world's only hope.

About the author

Greg is a director, writer and writing teacher. He has lived and worked as a translator in Paris, New York, Los Angeles and Madrid. He now lives in Sussex with his wife, the novelist Kate Mosse.

Praise for The Coming Darkness

"Admirable audacity. One of the best thrillers of 2022."
THE SUNDAY TIMES

"A clever, fast-paced thriller."
THE INDEPENDENT

"Superb. Greg Mosse writes like John Le Carré's hip grandson."
LEE CHILD

SCAN ME TO FIND OUT MORE

MOONFLOWER

www.moonflowerbooks.co.uk

The Lost Diary of Samuel Pepys by Jack Jewers

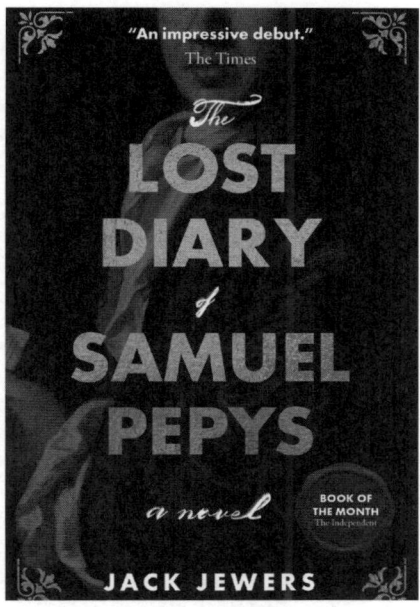

SCAN ME TO FIND OUT MORE

The diaries of Samuel Pepys have enthralled readers for centuries with their audacious wit, gripping detail, and racy assignations. Pepys stopped writing at the age of 36. Or did he?

This action-packed historical thriller picks up where Pepys left off as he is sent from the pleasures of his familiar London to the grimy taverns and shipyards of Portsmouth. An investigator sent by the King to look into corruption at the Royal Navy has been brutally murdered, and it's down to Pepys to find out why. But what awaits him is more dangerous than he could have imagined.

About the author

Jack Jewers is a filmmaker and writer, passionate about history. His films have been shown at dozens of international film festivals including Cannes, New York, Marseille and Dublin, and have received awards from the Royal Television Society and a BAFTA nomination for Best Short Film. The Lost Diary of Samuel Pepys is his first novel.

Praise for The Lost Diary of Samuel Pepys

"Book of the month... A zestful imagining."
THE INDEPENDENT

"One of the best historical fiction books of the year."
THE TIMES

"Swashbuckling action-packed drama."
WOMAN AND HOME

MOONFLOWER

www.moonflowerbooks.co.uk

Blue Running by Lori Ann Stephens

In the new Republic of Texas, guns are compulsory and nothing is forgiven.

Fourteen-year-old Bluebonnet Andrews is on the run across the Republic of Texas. An accident with a gun killed her best friend but everyone in the town of Blessing thinks it was murder. Even her father – the town's drunken deputy – believes she did it. Now, she has no choice but to run. Because in Texas, murder is punishable by death.

About the author

Lori Ann Stephens is an award-winning author whose novels for children and adults include Novalee and the Spider Secret, Some Act of Vision, and Song of the Orange Moons. She teaches creative writing and critical reasoning at Southern Methodist University in Dallas, Texas.

Praise for Blue Running

Book of the Month
THE INDEPENDENT & THE FT

"If there's one teen novel this year that readers will never forget, it's this one…"
BOOKS FOR KEEPS

"Brilliant."
HEAT MAGAZINE

"Gripping."
THE GUARDIAN

SCAN ME TO FIND
OUT MORE

MOONFLOWER

www.moonflowerbooks.co.uk

About Moonflower Books

The Independent Publishing Association's Newcomer of the Year 2023, Moonflower is a young, UK-based, independent publisher. And with books nominated for Daggers and Nibbies, we're already making waves. The books we hand-select are the ones that make us sit up in our seats. Books that break the mould. That are hard to categorise. The "it's like this, but only sort of" ones. In short, the kind of books that deserve your attention.

moonflowerbooks.co.uk

MOONFLOWER